# CHANGE HAPPENS

## Other Writings by Eugene A. Kelly

FOR WHAT IT'S WORTH:
A Guide for New Stockbrokers (1985)

FOR WHAT IT'S WORTH:
A Guide for New Financial Advisors (2001)

THE PENDULUM LETTER (1990–2019)

## Under the name E. Aly

107 SECRETS TO SUCCESS FOR THE GRADUATE

FOR WHAT IT'S WORTH essays (2019–   )

## Forthcoming

FOR WHAT IT'S WORTH:
Get Rich and Stay That Way Despite Wall Street (December 2021)

THREE QUESTION:
Short Story Collection (January 2022)

# CHANGE HAPPENS

## But Will They Understand?

E. Aly

Marshwinds
Press Company

ISBN  978-0-9614496-4-3 (Hardback)
ISBN 978-0-9614496-5-0 (Paperback)
ISBN 978-0-9614496-6-7 (epub)

**Library of Congress Control Number: 2021914933**

Subjects: FICTION/Literary; FICTION/Family Life; FICTION/Political; FICTION/Small Town & Rural; FICTION/Women

Book Club virtual readings and Q&A sessions are available by contacting:
Marshwinds Press Company
P. O. Box 21099
St. Simons Island, GA 31522
1-800-343-3751

OR go to **uniquereads.com**

Printed in the United States of America

Cover & Interior Design:  Creative Publishing Book Design

*For Judy,*
*who makes it all possible.*

# ORGANIZED CRIME CARTEL LEADERSHIP

1. Giuseppe "The Hammer" Strollo – boss
2. Aloysius "Ivy League" Carroll – counselor
3. Vincenzo "Big Vinney" Del Giorno – underboss and capo, west Massachusetts
4. Danny "Dapper Dan" Hogan – capo, Boston to New Hampshire line
5. Benedetto "Tico" Anselasi – capo, South of Boston to Rhode Island line
6. Rosario "Mad Dog" Giuliano – capo, middle Massachusetts, and personal enforcer for G. Strollo

# BERKSHIRE BOOK CLUB MEMBERS

1. Ernst "Cal" White-Callaway – judge
2. Maggie Latham – librarian, entrepreneur, mentor of abused and homeless girls
3. David Fogel – deputy sheriff
4. Harry Sheff – shoe repair store owner
5. Helen Inskeep – children's clothing store owner
6. Rick Branson – selectman, auto parts store and junkyard owner
7. Bell Edwards – hospital ER physician
8. Tony Ayala – plumbing business owner
9. Jerry Myrick – radio/IT/computer repair business owner, wheelchair-bound veteran

10. Javier "Junior" Soto Jr. – landscaping company and nursery owner, Hispanic community leader
11. Terry Rodriguez – homebuilder and contractor
12. Rosa Lee Dixon – restaurant owner in working-class neighborhood
13. C. C. Jefferies – owner of ten convenience stores around the county
14. Tomas Tommi – principal at elementary school
15. Geri Sparks – pest control business owner
16. Taylor Graham – president of Berkshire College
17. Jack Gianelli – outdoor equipment store owner
18. Eddie Keogh – barbershop owner
19. Wan Chu – grocery store owner

# CHANGE HAPPENS

## PART ONE

# CHAPTER 1

It started as an ordinary Tuesday in mid-June; later in the day, and forever after, Judge Ernst "Cal" White-Callaway would understand that this day marked the end of life as he knew it. The sky was the same icy blue as his eyes, not a cloud anywhere. The trees swayed gently in a steady westerly breeze. Cal knew rain was coming tonight as he gazed out his bedroom window while he tied his bowtie. At this moment, though, he marveled at the vista out to the river. He never tired of the estate's beauty. The wide expanse of green manicured lawn narrowed to an opening between the pine-and-cedar tree line. An abstract marble sculpture stood in the green space past the trees, just before the flowing river that marked the western boundary of the hundred-acre estate. Fleetingly, the Callaway estate lost in the 1930s Great Depression by his grandfather crossed his mind.

He quickly erased the negative thoughts, focusing on the view. He loved this house just as if it were his own instead of his wife's. If she's awake, he thought, I must tell her about this weekend. It could get messy if she had plans for the two of them to make an appearance at one of her charities.

Cal grabbed his jacket from the bed, slipped it on, looked at himself in the closet door full-length mirror, and adjusted his bowtie.

At forty-two, he stood erect, as slim as he had been in his twenties, with the rough-hewn look of a man who enjoyed nature and the outdoors. Silver streaks sprinkled his dark brown hair at the temples. His chiseled jaw framed the perpetual smile of his mouth. Leaving the room, he closed the door softly, not wanting to wake his wife if she was sleeping in her bedroom across the hall. He treaded lightly on the century-old oriental runner, passing the oil paintings of horses, dogs, and hunting scenes from the glory days of Berkshire County.

He crept down the back staff stairs to the massive kitchen, built originally for a cooking and serving contingent of five. His wife frowned on him using this staircase, but he didn't understand why one set of stairs, closer to where he was going, was not as good as the formal staircase leading to the front of the house. In the kitchen, their housekeeper was already hard at work.

"Good morning, Ella. Anything good for breakfast today?"

"Judge, you know I always got your favorite breakfast ready for you. Go on out to the patio. Your juice and paper are already there. The coffee's in the silver pot on the table, and so's the cream and sugar."

"There's a place in heaven for you, Ella, I just know it."

"Don't rush me there, Judge," Ella said with a broad smile.

Cal walked through the kitchen to the patio and sat at the table so he could admire the view across the gardens, which stretched from the patio to the sports complex. The kitchen garden, to the left of the patio, surrounded by a low hedge of boxwoods, was at its peak. Asparagus, broccoli, cabbage, and Swiss chard competed for attention with the multitude of herbs. The border beds lining the gravel path to the sports complex were a textured riot of white and lavender with various shades of red, yellow, and blue. Cal liked the wildness of the borders, more like two multi-colored ribbons of English garden than a manicured, homogenous display of monochromatic plant species.

After taking a sip of juice, Cal poured himself a cup of coffee and started reading the *Berkshire Times*, scanning each page for anything out of the ordinary. His attention focused on a story concerning a rash of drug overdoses at the hospital emergency room. He heard a chair scrape, looked up, and smiled. "Good morning, Catherine. Sleep well?"

"No, I didn't. This damn shoulder pain kept me awake."

"Didn't you take something to help you sleep?"

"I ran out of the damn pills and forgot to call for more."

"I'm sorry."

Ella pushed open the kitchen screen door with her back, carrying a silver tray holding Cal's breakfast. Without thinking, she said, "Here you are, Your Honor: two scrambled eggs, real crisp bacon, polenta, and a biscuit. Just the way you like it."

Catherine looked up from the section of the paper she was reading. "Ella, how many times do I have to tell you not to call Mr. White-Callaway 'Judge' or 'Your Honor'? In this house, he is Mr. White-Callaway. Is that clear? I'll take a cup of coffee, one sugar, and a teaspoon of cream." She nodded to her empty cup and the coffee pot.

"Yes, ma'am, I forgot. I'm sorry. Will you be having your usual breakfast?" Ella asked as she placed the tray in front of Cal, then reached for the coffee pot and poured a cup for Catherine.

"Yes, I will."

"Yes, ma'am." Ella turned and went back into the kitchen, her shoulders slumped but her demeanor steely.

"Was that really necessary?" Cal asked in a low voice.

"Yes, it was. She works for me. She will do what I want her to do and address us as I want her to. Otherwise, she can find another job."

"For Christ's sake, Catherine, she has worked for us for sixteen years—and for your parents for twenty-five years before that. She has been at Willview Manor as long as you have. I don't think she even called your mother and father Mr. and Mrs."

"It doesn't matter what she called my mother and father, nor how long she has worked at Willview Manor. She will do it my way, or she will leave. This is my estate, and my inheritance pays the bills. She certainly couldn't work here on a judge's salary," Catherine spat as she sipped coffee from her china cup. "By the way," she continued in a normal voice, "there is a marathon triple event for ladies this weekend at the club: bridge Friday night, mixed doubles tennis Saturday morning, mixed doubles golf Saturday afternoon, and a second round of bridge Sunday after brunch. The awards ceremony is at Sunday dinner. Since you've chosen not to play any of the games, the club pro suggested I partner with John Emerson. I didn't think you would mind."

"You didn't think I would mind, or you didn't care if I minded?" Cal asked, staring at Catherine until she averted her eyes.

"Don't give me that. Daddy urged you to take up all three games when we got married. You chose to hike your beloved Appalachian Trail instead. John is a superb athlete and master bridge player. I want to win and intend to win. If you want Ella to make your dinner Friday, Saturday, and Sunday, say so, and I'll arrange it."

"No, there are judges' meetings Friday through Sunday noon in Boston. I'll be listening to boring speeches and lectures, so you don't have to worry about me sitting home and moping."

"Well, I'd rather—" Catherine started when Ella appeared at the kitchen door with the house cordless phone.

"Judge—I'm sorry, Mr. White-Callaway, the deputy sheriff is on the phone. He says he must talk to you. I say to him you were having breakfast with Mrs. White-Callaway, but he says, 'Ella, take the phone to the judge.' Those are his words, ma'am. He says, 'The judge wants to take this call.' So I'm sorry the deputy sheriff is so insistent, Mrs. White-Callaway. I'll be right back with your breakfast tray."

"Oh, don't bother," Catherine said. "I'll eat later. I've got to go. There will be four of us from the Historical Society for lunch, and we'll eat here on the patio. I still want you to use the Limoges porcelain, cloth napkins, and dinner sterling silverware. I left the menu inside for you." She stood with a look that implied Cal never had time for her, dropped her cloth napkin on the glass tabletop, turned, and walked back into the sunroom without another word.

Cal lifted the phone to his ear. "What's up, David?" He sat, listening. After a few minutes, he asked, "We picked him up at 2:00 a.m., and this altercation happened at 6:30 a.m. breakfast? Was it the new inmate instigating the issue? Have you run his fingerprints? Okay, try every database, even DCF. Give me the results of the searches before court convenes. Have him at the courthouse holding cells this morning. Please call the DA's office and ask them to send over an ADA for our meeting this morning. I'll have Betsy try to squeeze him onto the calendar. Are you serious, it lasted for less than a minute? No one died, right? Okay, one last request: get me a list of all unsolved crimes, from the smallest to the most serious, including murder. Thanks, David. You were right to call. People will be glad it's over." Cal stood, pushed his chair in, and walked over to the kitchen screen door. "Ella, thank you for a wonderful breakfast. I may not be home for dinner. I'll let you know by two."

"Yes, Your Honor. Be kind to those poor souls you'll see today."

"You know I will," Cal said over his shoulder as he walked through the sunroom to retrieve his briefcase from his study.

§

"John, dear, the weekend is clear. We'll have a smashing good time and finish as club champions," Catherine said, speaking from her bedroom on her cell phone. "Yes, I do too. A light dinner at the club before bridge? Sure, sounds lovely. Friday at, say, four thirty? I'll see you then."

# CHAPTER 2

On the drive to the courthouse, Cal reached into his briefcase on the front seat of the Yukon Z71 and pulled out a go phone. Keeping his eyes on the road, he hit the speaker button, then speed dial number one, and listened as it rang twice.

"Good morning."

"Good morning, Maggie," Cal said. "Two things. Foremost, I'm set for a legal meeting in Boston this weekend. Second—"

"What time will you be leaving?"

"I have court in the morning, so I'm making sure I have a light calendar and expect to be on the road by one. I can hardly wait to see you. Second, did you see the article in the lower right-hand column of page five in today's BT? The article about the third college student to OD this week? I think a book club meeting is in order for next Tuesday. If you agree, will you call Taylor and see if we can meet at the college? Your call on where if not."

"No, I haven't read the paper. I'll look at it and send the emails after speaking with Dr. Graham."

"Three days till Friday. An eternity."

"You have a way with words."

"Bye," Cal responded before clicking off. He slid the phone back into its briefcase pocket without taking his eyes off the road.

His love of Berkshire County matched his delight with Willview. He loved the twisting narrow roads, which give no quarter to the ever-increasing traffic, forcing impatient humans to slow down and show respect. Berkshire County was unique. Though scarred in places by the encroachment of civilization, the natural beauty of the mountains, the lakes, and the waterways was untouched between the towns and homes. The community's character hadn't changed in over four hundred years, and he liked that.

Puritans from the Massachusetts Bay settlement had found their way westward to Berkshire County in the late 1600s, confronting the native tribes, whom they considered savages. The Puritans had held two staunch beliefs: the welfare of the community came before the welfare of the individual, and anyone who didn't subscribe to Puritan beliefs about God and the Bible had to convert or leave. There was no distinction between death and running off, and no doubt in the Puritan mind that God was on their side. God had given them the resources to eliminate the so-called savages and therefore do what was his will. After the safety of their settlement, the two Puritan priorities had been building churches and schools. Education was paramount for the settlers. Since the foundation of their community rested on the Bible, every citizen had to read.

Berkshire County citizens knew what they believed in and were resistant to edicts from the king or the colonial authorities he appointed. In August 1774, almost two years before the Declaration of Independence, fifteen hundred men in Berkshire County had assembled and kept the royal judges from taking their seats in Great Barrington. Tough, educated, opinionated, and determined ancestors set the tone for present-day residents. Mixing with later immigrants from the coast and New York did not change the character of the community. Even though Cal's family had been among the gentry immigrants from New York City, first to live as summer residents and later to enjoy the surrounding wilderness year-round, he considered himself part of this rugged, community-oriented heritage. It defined who he was and what he stood for.

§

Sitting like a bright beacon in an expansive green lawn, the Berkshire County Courthouse caps the top of a hill on Main Street, the road cutting Berkshire Township in half. Cal took Talcott Street, named after Major John Talcott, the leader of the colonial detachment in King Philip's War in 1676, around the hill to the back of the building, where the courthouse's four floors are visible.

The back has two entrances. On the right is a single door, always locked and accessed only by key card. This entrance is for court personnel and access is under a covered parking area. On the left is a vehicle courtyard secured by a mechanical steel door and surrounded by a twelve-foot stone wall topped with concertina wire. This entrance leads directly to five holding cells, where prisoners due in court stay until their appearance. The public courtroom, with the expected trappings of polished wood walls and pews, tile floor, past and present justices' portraits, and an elevated judge's dais, is on the third floor. After parking, Cal went straight up to his fourth-floor chambers.

"Good morning, Betsy," Cal said as he stepped off the elevator into his assistant's office.

"Good morning, Your Honor. Deputy Sheriff Fogel wanted me to alert him when you're ready for him. He's arriving now. His emails are in a folder on your desk."

"Tell him I'm ready."

Just after eight thirty, as Cal hung up his jacket and retrieved his judicial robe, Deputy Fogel's three-vehicle convoy eased through the courthouse yard's metal gate. Once the gate closed, Fogel and his driver exited the front car, the driver carrying a taser. Two deputies exited the third car and took up positions on either side of the prisoner van's doors. Both held batons and small nets.

§

Fogel flipped the holster safety strap securing his Glock 19, slid open the left middle door of the van, and stepped back, resting his hand on the grip of the pistol. Seated on either side of the young prisoner in the orange jumpsuit were two of the sheriff's biggest deputies.

"Okay, Officer Williams, you get out," Fogel said to the nearest one. "Mr. Paschal, Officer Williams is going to unlock your leg irons from the vehicle. Then he's going to unlock your manacles. It would not be good for you to make any sudden movements. Do you understand?"

"Yes, sir," the prisoner responded.

The prisoner transfer from van to holding cell went smoothly.

"Officer Morales, please see what the prisoner wants for lunch, and go over to Mary's Café and get it," Fogel said. Looking at the prisoner through the holding cell bars, he continued, "You can have anything you want. Just tell the officer. Later today, you'll appear in court to face charges. A court-appointed attorney will be in the courtroom. If you want to speak with an attorney before appearing in court, just say so, and one will visit you here. Do you prefer the attorney to come here?"

"Thanks for lunch, sir. No, sir, in the courtroom will be fine, I guess."

Deputy Fogel nodded and took the elevator up to the judge's chambers.

§

Entering Betsy's office, Fogel said, "Morning, Betsy. He ready for me?"

"Yep, go on in. ADA Carter is already in there."

Fogel knocked once and went in.

Cal looked up from chatting with the ADA. "Morning, David. I believe you know ADA Judy Carter. How are things at home?"

Fogel shook hands with them both. The muscular, ordinary-looking man in his late thirties had no fashionable facial hair to hide his baby-face features. If there was any unusual aspect of Deputy Sheriff David Fogel, it was the premature graying of his sandy hair and the scar on his face, running from the corner of his right eye down to his chin; these revealed that he had seen challenging times. "All's well. Donna is enjoying that school's out in one respect: She doesn't have to make a lesson plan each week. But having two boys, six and seven, makes her wish I had summers off as well. Thanks for asking."

"Well, I'll bet she's glad you're not Delta in Afghanistan anymore. How long did you serve?"

"I was an operator for ten years—did two tours in Iraq and two in Afghanistan. You're right; she's grateful I'm here instead of there. So am I. I miss the fellas, but not the unbelievable political mess Washington has got us in over there."

"Ms. Carter served in the navy." Cal looked over at Carter and asked, "Was your service on the line or in the Judge Advocate service?"

"Judge, I opted for sea duty, so I did both. Enjoyed every minute. Well, maybe not every minute," she said with a smile. The three of them laughed.

"Amen," said Fogel.

"David, how's Justin, by the way?"

"As good as he can be, under the circumstances. They won't operate. He's comfortable. Both he and Minnie understand the prognosis. He's told me he's not going to run for reelection. He and Minnie want to spend as much time together as they can."

"You're going to run, aren't you?"

"Yes, Donna and I have talked about it. She's on board. She understands I'll be out of a job if I lose. Her only comment was 'Okay, don't lose.' Worse than my sergeant major in Delta."

"David, I'm confident you'll make a great sheriff. It'll be important to announce early and get Justin's endorsement."

"Judge, the timing has to be his. I don't want to be seen as a guy walking on the body of a local legend."

"I'll talk to him. One press conference where he announces his retirement and endorses you will work. I'll discuss it with him."

"Thank you, sir. I appreciate it."

"Now, what's this problem you've got, David?"

"Problem *we've* got, Your Honor. I'd rather the two of you see it before hearing it. Betsy said she's set up a video system." Fogel looked around the room. The room looked more like a man cave for an outdoorsman than a judge's office. There was no ego wall, no law books on shelves wrapped around the room. In their stead, artifacts found in the wilderness, small stuffed animals, unusual stones, arrowheads, and black-and-white photographs were on most shelves, with oil paintings of nature scenes on two walls. A single computer sat on the credenza behind the judge's antique hand-carved partner's desk, handed down from his great-grandfather after being used by three generations before him.

"Over on the closet wall," Cal said, getting up from his desk. He opened an oil painting panel, exposing a computer monitor. Cal and Judy watched as Fogel navigated through the courthouse cloud to find the video clip he had prepared and saved. He found it and paused the video.

"Let me give the two of you the background before you see the action," Fogel said. "Late last night, one of my deputies, Officer Henderson, was doing his assigned cruising of the town, and at around two hundred hours he turned into the alley running behind Charlie Hanson's. He heard a noise coming from those dumpsters back there. He stopped, got out of his car, and started moving toward the dumpsters.

"A kid popped up, scaring the you-know-what out of Henderson, who pulled his service pistol and dropped his light. The kid was not threatening. Henderson said he was polite and docile. He arrested the boy, who was filthy and smelled like a dead deer after five days in the summer sun. He took him back to juvie. The CO made him take two showers and had enough sense to put the kid in solitary. Fast-forward to six hundred thirty hours. Here we go. Watch carefully—it happens fast."

Fogel hit play and the screen jumped to life, showing four young men in orange jumpsuits eating breakfast. Three of the inmates were at one rectangular table, while a fourth inmate was off by himself at another, hunched over his plate and eating with the vigor of someone who hadn't in a while. Fogel stopped the picture. "The new kid is the one off by himself. You know the other three, who are regular guests in our taxpayer resort. The big one across from the other two is the Hortense kid, who, this time next year, when we pick him up again, will be old enough to go to the adult jail. He's been a mean son of a witch—pardon my French, Ms. Carter and Judge—all his life. A real bully when he thinks he's top dog in the sandbox. The other two are the Walton brothers, giving real meaning to the phrase 'crime family,' since they're following their parents in that life."

"Hortense, former all-star defensive tackle for Berkshire High School," Cal said. "Likes to hurt people, male or female, just for the pleasure of watching them cry. He'll kill somebody one day."

"Well, not necessarily, Your Honor. Watch."

Cal couldn't get a good look at the new inmate's face, but noted his posture indicated he knew the camera was there and didn't want to be filmed. "David, did the boy give you a name when he came in?"

"Yeah, he said Paschal, but we don't know for sure. I'm going to slow this down some," Fogel said as he restarted the picture.

Hortense reached across the table and took the food from the smaller of the two Walton boys. There was no sound, but it was evident the boy protested and tried to drag his plate back across the table. Hortense half stood between the anchored table and bench and pushed the boy backward, causing him to fall across the bench he was sitting on. The second Walton boy jumped up and moved away from the table. Hortense grabbed his plate too and emptied the food onto the first plate, then sat back down and started eating.

"Okay, here it comes, guys," Fogel said.

Just as the Hortense boy started to take a bite, his head snapped around to the left. It appeared Paschal had said something. Hortense got up from his seat, walked over, and spoke to Paschal. Then he reached down and grabbed Paschal by his jumpsuit's shoulder. Even in slow motion, the three of them could barely see the action in the next few seconds. Paschal locked his hand onto Hortense's arm, pulled him forward and raked his extended fingers across Hortense's eyes. Hortense tried to pull back. Paschal kept a grip on his arm and twisted it over, then slammed his hand down on Hortense's elbow.

All three winced as the elbow gave way and Hortense sprawled over the table. Paschal calmly grabbed Hortense's good arm, twisted it, and slammed his hand against the second elbow, snapping it.

"Back it up, David, to the point when Hortense puts his hands on the new inmate," Cal said. Using the stopwatch on his Timex, he timed the entire incident from first bodily contact to finish.

"Less than one minute to disable someone of that size. That's impressive. Run it again, David, in slow motion. You know, I don't understand how this could happen. The Hortense boy looks bigger and stronger than the Paschal boy," ADA Carter said. "Deputy Fogel, please email me a copy of this clip."

"Yes, ma'am. The facts are the Paschal boy is about five foot ten, weighs about 170 pounds, but doesn't have an ounce of body fat on him. Like a wild animal, his strength is much greater than it looks like it should be. Frankly, besides the strength, his eyes are gray, and looking at him with his long straggly hair and facial fuzz is like looking at a wild animal. It took only five minutes for the COs to respond to the first hostile move by the Hortense boy toward the Walton brothers. I want you to see how Paschal acts when the COs get there."

Cal and Judy watched the video again in slow motion. When the COs rushed into the room, the young inmate dropped to his knees and clasped his hands behind his head. His demeanor was submissive. Cal watched intently. Something bothered him about the boy. He couldn't figure it out. "David, did you book him when you brought him in?"

"No, sir. We figured, before this altercation, we'd do the full process only if you decided to get the DA involved. Didn't figure we needed to give the kid a record for dumpster diving if there were extenuating circumstances, unless you thought we should."

"Okay, do this. Don't book him yet, but take a frontal mugshot. Only one, no copies. Didn't you tell me earlier you'd fingerprinted him?"

"Yes, sir." Fogel touched the button on the mike resting on his left shoulder and said, "Trish, call downstairs at the courthouse and have the CO take one frontal mugshot of the Paschal boy I brought in today. Send it to the judge's chambers ASAP. No copies kept."

Cal turned to the ADA and said, "What do you think, Ms. Carter?"

"Well, sir, the dumpster diving is up to you. My office will decline to get involved with that. In my professional opinion, this altercation is clearly self-defense. We would decline to prosecute based on this video. Deputy Fogel, have you interviewed the COs and the other two inmates that were being bullied?"

"Not yet. I wanted to show this to the two of you and get your direction."

"Go ahead with the interviews. Send a transcript for our files. What do you say, Your Honor?"

"I concur. If you agree, Ms. Carter, I'd like to charge Mr. Paschal with assault with intent to kill. Unless he asks for a jury trial, I can find him not guilty based upon the evidence. Agreeable?"

"Sounds good to me. I'll send our newest ADA over to be present in the courtroom, but he won't take part in the proceedings unless you request his services."

"What have you done with the fingerprints?" Cal asked Fogel.

"Sent them to every agency—Feds, state, and locals. How old do you figure the boy is?"

"My guess is fifteen to seventeen. No response on the prints? Did you send them to the Department of Children and Families?"

"Negative on responses. Sent to local DCF. Do you want me to send them to DCFHQ?"

"Yeah. You said this kid was filthy. We've had stories from residents and hikers about a wild child in the forests around here. Always figured it was one of those Yeti stories, you know, for the tourists. Maybe, just maybe, there's been some truth to it. Did you get me the unsolved crimes list?"

"Yep, emailed to Betsy thirty minutes ago."

Cal looked at the folder on his desk. "That must be what this folder is. I'm betting he's a runaway, probably from the foster system. Let me know right away if you get a hit from DCF, even if I'm in court." Cal leaned over his desk and pushed the intercom.

"Yes, sir?" Betsy responded.

"Betsy, Deputy Fogel has a new hearing to go on the docket. Pencil it in for first on the afternoon calendar. If the material I've asked him for comes in, let me know. I'll want to recess no matter what case I'm hearing. Please alert the clerk."

"Got it."

"David, get me that print info before lunch, whatever it takes. I want the photo in the next ten minutes. Excellent work, David. Ms. Carter, thank you for coming over on short notice. To recap, we all agree I'll handle the assault charge as self-defense, based on the video and testimony from the COs and other witnesses. I'll decide about the dumpster diving after I find out why the young man was doing it."

"No problem, Judge. Just doing my job." Fogel smiled. "Good to see you again, Ms. Carter." They both left the office.

Cal sat at his desk, thinking about the video. He couldn't figure out why he felt he'd seen the kid before. Looking at his watch, he started his daily pre-court ritual. He opened his center desk drawer and extracted a small money envelope containing a key, which he used to unlock a lower drawer and removed a Bible. Cal placed the cracked and brittle black leather book, with the gold page edging mostly worn off, in his lap. He pulled out an envelope resting inside the front cover and removed a photo of a young couple in hiking clothes next to a tent alongside a mountain lake. Also inside the envelope was a ring.

He turned the photo over and read the inscription: "To Cal, my future Supreme Court justice. Always use this Bible to remember Leviticus 19:15 and Deuteronomy 1:16–17. With everlasting love and faith, Josey."

Cal turned the first marker ribbon to read, "You shall do no injustice in judgment; you shall not be partial to the poor nor defer to the great, but you are to judge your neighbor fairly." He turned the second ribbon to read, "You shall not be partial in judgment; you shall hear the small and the great alike."

Shutting the Bible, he rested his head against the back of his chair and closed his eyes. He strove to be the judge Josey had wanted him to be. How he longed to see her again. He was so sorry. Cal breathed deeply, replaced the photo in the envelope with the ring, placed the envelope in the Bible, and put the Bible back in his desk. He locked the drawer and hid the key.

The door opened. Betsy stuck her head in and said, "I have an envelope for you from Deputy Fogel."

"Let me have it," Cal said.

She brought it over, then immediately turned and left the room, closing the door softly. Cal studied the photo. The eyes were the most intriguing. He had seen this kid before. He placed the photo in the file, put on his judicial robe, and walked out of his office.

# CHAPTER 3

At a quarter after eleven, the bailiff handed Cal a note from Betsy. He looked at his calendar and the assembled mix of defendants, attorneys, and law enforcement officers. "Court will recess until one thirty," he announced. Hammering the gavel, he rose, then turned to the judge's access door. He hurried up the stairs to his office.

"The file is on your desk. I merged the earlier file with it," Betsy said as he came through the door.

"Please alert Deputy Fogel to come up."

"I already did. He's on his way," Betsy said.

Cal smiled and shook his head as if to say, You're wonderful. In his office, he quickly shed his robe and hung it in the closet. He opened the file on his desk and began reading. No arrest record. No school record since halfway through the eighth grade. DCF had a fingerprint match for a foster child who disappeared three and a half years ago. The boy's name was Joseph H. Paschal. He was thirteen.

Cal looked up. That confirmed the age he had estimated. The kid had vanished. The foster family hadn't reported him gone; the school had notified DCF. Police had investigated but closed the file as a runaway. Cal sat back and thought about runaway children and their usual fate: the court system or a drug overdose. Not suitable alternatives. There was a knock at the door.

"Come in."

"Betsy said you wanted to see me, Your Honor?"

"Have a seat, David. How's your young prisoner? Did you verify his last name?"

"No, sir. He said it's Paschal."

"That fits. We received the file from DCF. The prints match a Joseph H. Paschal. He ran away three and a half years ago."

"I thought so. He's the politest prisoner we've ever had. Ate lunch, thanked the CO, cleaned up the crumbs, put them in the paper bag, and handed it back to the CO. Then he just went to his cot, lay down, and was asleep in a minute. No pacing, no arguing, no asking for a lawyer."

"Did you tell him one is available?"

"Yes, sir. He knows. Seems to not know what to do or how much trouble he may be in."

"I'll appoint one when he makes his appearance. I'll also make sure he doesn't accidentally get himself between a rock and a hard place. The file has nothing for the last three and a half years. What do you make of that, Dave?"

"Well, sir, he obviously hasn't been on the streets anywhere. Runaways clash with street patrols almost immediately. We want them in the system to fingerprint and get DNA since most runaways usually fall into a pattern of crime."

"Have your people taken his statement about this morning's incident?"

"No, sir. After our conversation and the video record, which clearly makes this self-defense, I didn't want to take a statement without a lawyer being there."

"Good thinking. What's the Hortense boy's condition?"

"He'll lose sight in his right eye. Paschal cut it like an olive, and the eye is not repairable. Hard to believe he didn't have a weapon. The left eye will have some partial sight. It's deeply scratched. Both his elbows are broke. They're fixable, but his range of motion will be less. His bullying days are over. Gives new meaning to that old saying 'Don't pick a fight with a stranger.'"

"What caused the eye injury, anyway?"

"Judge, Paschal's fingernails extend past his fingertips at least a quarter of an inch—on both hands. He uses them as weapons."

"Ever hear of that before?"

"Yeah. Centuries ago, warriors of an Indian tribe in the Southeast used fingernails as effective weapons."

"So be it. Justice served. Have your COs interviewed the two Walton boys?"

"Yes, sir. Both spoke separately, and their testimony was recorded and videotaped. They told the same story shown on the surveillance system. Hortense had been hammering them since they entered juvie yesterday morning. He took their dinner and pushed them around all evening. Said he was going to force them to give him a blowjob, but I personally think that was just talk to scare them. You know, that's the way people put the fear of God in children—all the homosexual stories about jail. Anyway, they said he ate his breakfast fast, then told them he was going to whip their asses unless they gave him theirs. They didn't want to stand up to him. They said the only thing the Paschal boy said to him was 'Leave 'em alone.' He said it two or three times, depending on which boy you ask. Both said Hortense turned to Paschal and said, 'I'm going to kick your ass, queer motherfucker,' then started over toward him. You know the rest."

"Sounds like Hortense has some obsession with homosexuality."

"Must have, but there isn't anything in his record. Probably just bravado."

"Have you sent the transcripts to the DA's office?"

"Yes, sir."

"Okay, in court, I'll handle the assault charge first. The dumpster charge second."

"Cal, uh, Your Honor . . ."

"Cal's fine in here, David."

"Cal, you know how sometimes you find a stray dog on the side of the road, and that dog is really skittish? But when you help it and treat it right, it turns out someone trained the dog right, just something awful happened in the dog's life to turn it wild? Well, sir, that's the gut feeling I get with this boy. He's got good breeding from somewhere. He was in foster care for a little over three years, and I don't know why he cut and run. I'm betting this boy needs help, not punishment."

"I concur. Can you get one of your people to call DCFHQ and get his entire file? Local may not have the full file. Use my name if it will speed the process."

"I'm on it. It'll be to you right away. When are you going to handle his case?"

"First case after lunch."

"Okay, I'll have the file here within the hour." Fogel rose, shook Cal's hand, and left.

§

Cal was eating a ham and cheese sandwich with chips and sipping a Coke when Betsy knocked once and came in, carrying an envelope.

"Deputy Fogel said you're waiting for this," she said, handing it to him.

"Thanks, Betsy. Give me a heads-up at one fifteen."

"Yes, sir."

Cal opened the envelope. The Paschal boy had entered DCF custody at age ten, when his grandmother died, leaving him an orphan. Cal looked and couldn't find anything in the papers about the boy's parents, not even the grandmother's name. There was no birth certificate. DCF had placed him in a foster home with a family named Stoner—Ralph and Gloria Stoner. Ralph cut timber, and Gloria worked as a clerk at Wilson's Five & Ten. No incident reports in the file until the boy ran away over three years later. What would make a thirteen-year-old boy run away? Too much discipline or abuse. Cal wondered which one in this case. He picked up the phone and buzzed Betsy.

"Yes, sir?"

"Betsy, call the head of DCF locally or, if necessary, at their HQ. These papers don't have a birth certificate, and I want one."

"Yes, sir."

# CHAPTER 4

"John, Aloysius calling. Do you have a moment?"

"Always for you, Aloysius." Emerson pushed his files to the edge of his desk and took a pen and tablet out of a drawer.

"Our little arrangement of sharing clients is going well, don't you think?" the voice on the phone commented.

"Yes. I just wish we got a bigger slice of the pie, so to speak."

"Patience, John. Our partnership will soon inundate you with lucrative work. I hope your firm can handle it all professionally. You handled that minor issue from Vermont smoothly, without repercussions. My client is happy with the way his entertainment business is developing out on Highway 20. He wants to reinvest the profits in other businesses in the Berkshires as well as build influence in the legal and political arenas."

"He always has our firm."

"We know that. You and your firm are going to be our quarterbacks in the Berkshires region. This effort we want to undertake will be a three-pronged approach. It's important to understand, John, this is a long-term project. We don't want to stumble by rushing or pushing too hard. Spread the word that you are the go-to law firm for selling businesses or raising capital for businesses that want to expand. Show me all the situations you notice; I'll decide if they're attractive. Got it?"

"Yes, that's exciting."

"Second, we want to make inroads in the banking community over there. We have several community banks that are interested in acquiring one of your local banks or taking a minority position if it comes with board representation. You and some of your partners can fill these board seats; I'll make that decision. Don't quote any numbers, but we will pay a nice premium for the right amount of stock in a viable bank.

"Third, next year is a gubernatorial election. That means the following year the governor reappoints sitting judges or replaces them with new judges. We want someone over there in that judgeship who understands how we think. It would also be helpful if the person had the potential to move up in the political arena. So, be thinking about a candidate."

"That's a good strategy. The problem is Judge White-Callaway. He's well liked, highly competent, and doesn't appear to be interested in going anywhere or playing ball with us."

"How well do you know him?"

"Not well at all. He and his wife are members of the country club. She's active in sports, golf and tennis, and is a master bridge player. As a matter of fact, I'm her partner in the club Ladies Mixed Doubles triple event marathon this weekend. She needed a partner, and the judge doesn't play any of the sports, so the club pro put us together because I'm as good as she is, and we're both better than the rest. It should be interesting. She's also the go-to charity event planner in the entire region. Knows everybody. She can raise money better than anyone. Her grandfather founded this firm, and her father was the managing partner until his death. She's let me know she has powerful feelings for the firm. That could be a plus in her opening doors for us."

"Well, that's interesting. Couldn't the judge go back to practicing law at your firm when we convince him to leave the bench?"

"Don't know. What I've heard from partners is that she pleaded with him to leave the bench and take over as managing partner when her father died suddenly. He refused to do so. The talk around the club is his refusal put their relationship in a deep freeze that won't thaw. Some say they now have a marriage of convenience. It's convenient to him for her to be super rich since he likes living that way, and it's convenient to her that he's in all the right legal and political circles around the state because she wants to be the most powerful woman in the Berkshires."

"Can you get close to him through her?"

"Don't know, but I can try. My first real interaction with her will be this weekend's tournament at the bridge table, golf course, and tennis court. We're having dinner early, before the first event. Let's see if we have any chemistry at the end of the weekend. From what the pro tells me, she's highly competitive. If we win, it should be good. If not, well, we'll deal with that another time."

"Win, then."

"Right."

"Any progress you make on these issues, I want you to detail the information and send to me on paper by courier. No big delivery firms—someone local or regional. Make sure there are no duplicates or trails on your computer systems. Don't address the memos to anyone. Have the envelopes delivered to Jason Owen, Bendix Hotel, 877 Boyle Street, Boston, Massachusetts. Do you understand what I'm saying?"

"Easy, Aloysius. We'll handle it just as professionally as we did the Vermont affair. By the way, I was out to dinner the other night and noticed all of the wineries on the menu were regional vineyards that are our clients. Their marketing plans must be outstanding since all their competitors left. Congratulations."

"Good marketing is always easy when the product is exceptional."

"Yeah, sure."

"Keep in mind, John, your firm is the attorney of record for those wineries. You're part of the marketing plan. Please make sure we serve them in all restaurants and private clubs in the Berkshires. That puts money in all our pockets. Let me know as any of these issues develop."

"I will. Thanks for the call."

Emerson sat back in his chair with his hands interlocked behind his head. He thought about how lucky he was to have stepped into this struggling law firm after Alexander White II died unexpectedly on the tennis court. It was easy to stabilize the downward spiral created by the firm's interim managing partner. It also allowed him to get out from under the cloud hanging over his departure from the firm in Nashua, New Hampshire. Sweat formed on his brow and upper lip as he thought back to that day four years ago. He'd been up for partner and expected it to happen soon. That Thursday morning, he had walked into his office and heard the security guard say the managing partner wanted to see him in the small conference room. He knew his hopes were going to be dashed when the managing partner and the head of IT were sitting on either side of the conference table, both with grave looks on their faces. Emerson hadn't a chance to sit down before the managing partner said, "Please explain these pictures to me," as he held out a folder for John to take.

Emerson had looked at the IT manager, who had looked down at the table. He knew what pictures they were talking about. He'd looked at the managing partner and said, "These are evidence I'm working with for a lawsuit."

"That's not my understanding. I've looked at the firm's case log and tried to find any identifying case number on these photo files. We have nothing like this on the books or in the potential client list."

The managing partner had looked over at the IT man and continued. "In analyzing the file containing this child pornography, it seems this garbage has been coming in steadily ever since you joined the firm. Please explain yourself, this time truthfully."

"I've told you the truth."

"That's a lie. I want you out of here now. I'm going to give you two choices: First, you can sign a statement saying you are personally responsible for these photos and you tried to hide them from the firm. Your second choice is for me to call the police, have you arrested for child pornography, and turn the photos over to them. We will then cooperate with the authorities and do what is necessary to have you convicted and disbarred. You have thirty seconds to decide what happens."

"This is not fair. If I sign the statement, what will you tell my potential employer who calls for a reference?"

"If you sign now, I'll tell them a partial truth. I'll tell them you're a talented attorney and did competent work. I won't go into any personal issues."

Emerson had pulled his Mont Blanc pen from his jacket pocket and said, "Where do I sign?"

He smiled, remembering it as another day when he'd made lemonade out of lemons. A few calls to former classmates, and he had found himself talking to the interim managing partner at White,

White, and Arnholt, a weakling more than happy to relinquish the role. Now it was White, White, Arnholt, and Emerson, where he garnered a full twenty-five percent of the profits. No one to challenge him. The whole of western Massachusetts was his to make his own fiefdom.

He looked down at the notepad. This could be—no, will be—the beginning of something great, he thought, and grinned.

# CHAPTER 5

At one thirty, Cal nodded to the bailiff, and the bailiff hollered for all to rise. Cal stepped out of his private entrance to the courtroom and climbed onto the dais. He took his seat and looked out over the packed courtroom—all seats were occupied and spectators were standing two deep in the back of the room. The courthouse grapevine had hummed all morning about the young prisoner. The bailiff had moved the police officers involved with the docket from the first row of the spectator section to the jury box since there weren't any jury cases today. Cal nodded at the ADA sitting with the police. Everyone took their seats and continued their murmuring once Cal sat. He banged the gavel once, and the room went silent.

A young man shuffled in from the prisoner entrance, his hands and feet manacled. Cal's breath caught in his throat, and he stared trancelike at the boy, realizing where he had seen those eyes before. Cal was staring at Josey's eyes. Cal barely heard the bailiff call out the case number: "Joseph H. Paschal, case number eight two six three five oh, charged by the state of Massachusetts with dumpster diving and assault with intent to kill."

"Bailiff, take those manacles off the prisoner."

"Your Honor, with all due respect, I'm not sure you want me to do that. The prisoner can become violent at a moment's notice."

Staring straight at the prisoner, Cal said, "Joseph, you're going to behave, aren't you?"

"Yes, sir."

"Take them off, please. What's your middle name, son?"

"Hinson, sir."

Cal froze. His heart skipped a beat. A momentary calm came over him before vanishing as quickly as it came, leaving him with deep feelings of dread and anxiety. "Your grandmother was Eloise Hinson. Lived on Sheridan Road, just out of town?"

"Yes, sir," Joseph answered. Panic rose inside of him. Joseph became visibly agitated, not looking at the judge. His eyes darted from one door to another.

Summoning all the professionalism he could muster, Cal asked, "Where are your parents, Joseph?" He kept his hands flat on the dais so they would stop shaking and never blinked or took his eyes off the boy, who was rubbing his wrists, wide-eyed with fear.

Joseph looked down and away from the judge. "My mother died when I was born, and my father died when I was six. He had an accident at work."

So that's why I could never find her, Cal thought. Oh, Josey, I'm so sorry. I've been looking for a ghost. He jerked his mind back to the present and the task of saving this young man from the situation he was in. He scanned the back of the courtroom, where legal aid public defenders and local attorneys congregated. "Mr. Clements, please approach the defendant. This is your lucky day to do pro bono work. You will represent Mr. Paschal in this hearing."

"Your Honor, I've got another case I'm involved with. I haven't even had a chance to speak with the accused. I've just heard the seriousness of the charges and need time to prepare a plea," said the young, energetic, and usually aggressive attorney. He came forward, standing just to the left and behind Paschal, pushing a half step into the first pew in order to put a barrier between himself and the boy, having heard about his lightning temper.

"Mr. Clements, I'm sure you do. Your opportunity to do this pro bono won't interfere with your making money. I'm sure Mr. Emerson will give you a gold star for your excellent lawyering in the next twenty minutes."

Clements's face turned crimson, embarrassed at having been spoken to in this way by the judge in front of a packed courtroom. His insecurity in court appearances reflected his lack of trial time. "Yes, Your Honor."

"Great, Counselor. If you feel the defendant is being railroaded or overly punished, you will have irrefutable grounds for an appeal."

"Yes, Your Honor," Clements said.

"Joseph Paschal, you have two charges against you, one felony and one misdemeanor. I'm going to take these charges individually and, depending on how you plead, pass sentence on each one. Do you understand?"

"Yes—yes, sir," Joseph answered, the severity of his situation sinking in. He looked around, trying to see a way to escape. He shoved his hands in his pockets, took them out, put them back in his pockets, took them out again, and finally folded his arms across his chest, rocking back and forth. He barely heard the judge ask his new attorney if he understood the charges and explain how this hearing would go.

"Yes, Your Honor, I understand. My prior comments still stand."

"Thank you again, Counselor. The first charge is assault with the intent to kill. Mr. Paschal, this morning, in the juvenile detention facility, you had a physical altercation with another prisoner. Is that correct?"

"Yes, sir."

"From what I understand, you plead not guilty by reason of self-defense. Counselor, please instruct your client to say those words, or you answer for him."

Clements stepped out of the pew and stood next to Joseph. He leaned over and spoke into Joey's ear before looking up at the dais. "Your Honor, my client pleads not guilty by reason of self-defense."

"Very good. Now, Mr. Paschal, give me your side of the story."

"The big guy was bullying all three of us. He grabbed my shoulder, and I got him to let go."

"What was your plan for stopping him from hurting you?" Cal asked.

"Your Honor, I didn't plan anything," Joey said, holding his hands out in front of him. "I just knew what it would take to make a bully leave me alone."

"Let's get the record straight, Mr. Paschal. As I understand your answer, you just did what it would take to make him stop trying to hurt you?"

"Yes, sir."

"Mr. Paschal, do you realize you could have killed him, over breakfast?"

Joey shook his head. "Oh, no, sir. If I wanted to kill him, he'd be dead right now."

A low murmur spread throughout the courtroom.

"Quiet," Cal ordered, banging his gavel once. "So, you just wanted to neutralize him?"

"Yes, sir."

Cal and everyone in the courtroom recognized the innocent truthfulness of the statement.

"I'd like the video from the detention center dining hall this morning and the statements from the two other inmates harassed by Mr. Hortense as part of the official record of this proceeding. Counselor, listen carefully. Joseph Hinson Paschal, from your statement and the statements of the two inmates the prisoner Ralph Hortense abused, as well as the statements of the deputies who witnessed the incident and the video recording of the incident, I find you not guilty of assault with intent to kill by reason of self-defense." Cal banged the gavel. "Now, to the second charge of dumpster diving—"

"If it pleases the court, my client pleads not guilty," Clements blurted out.

"Mr. Clements, two points of order. First, don't interrupt a judge when he is speaking. Second, don't press your luck. The dumpster in question was in an enclosed area and had a No Trespassing sign attached. The officer caught the defendant coming out of the dumpster, so it's going to be hard for your client to plead not guilty. Now, Mr. Paschal, seeing as how the police officer arrested you as you were climbing out of the dumpster, how do you plead?"

"Guilty, Your Honor," Joey said, looking down and then up at Cal.

For the second time in twenty minutes, Clements's face burned with embarrassment.

"Excellent choice, Joseph," Cal said. "I accept your plea of guilty and sentence you to four years of probation, under the auspices of the court. What that means, Joseph, is this court will supervise you, and you'll serve two hundred hours of community service each year, as selected by me. Do you understand?"

"Yes, sir."

"Bailiff, have an officer take the defendant back to a holding cell. Mr. Paschal, you will remain there for another two hours while I finish the docket. After that time, you will come to my office and be left in my custody." The bailiff began shackling Joey again. "That won't be necessary, Henry. Mr. Paschal is not stupid. He has no reason to strike out, do you, Mr. Paschal?"

"No, sir."

"By the way, Mr. Hin—Paschal, how old are you?"

"Seventeen, sir."

Cal wrote the age down while his mind raced. "Thank you," he said and nodded to the bailiff, who led Joey away.

§

Joey lay on the pull-down spring bed with its two-inch cotton pad. His senses were acute, the same level they reached when he had to deal with a rattlesnake or a hungry mother bear. He knew he was in trouble and, unlike the situations in the forest, his physical prowess and cunning couldn't save him.

When he was eight, he thought his Granny had died. The priest had told the children that if they prayed really hard, God would answer their prayers. That night Joey had prayed so hard he exhausted himself and fell asleep on his granny's bedroom floor. The next morning, his granny was alive. Ever since, prayer was what Joey turned to when life seemed to be turning against him. It had always worked. He prayed now, knowing God was the only power that could save him from a life in a cage.

Joey's mind returned to the present. Getting away dominated his thoughts. He assumed his wilderness demeanor, stretching out on the bunk and willing himself to reach a relaxed state of composure and stillness. His breathing slowed noticeably, his muscles relaxed, and his thoughts were of the cheerful scene he always imagined when disturbed. In it, his mother, who had died giving birth to him, was alive and holding him as a young boy, sitting on a hill under a lone tree with a gentle breeze blowing, while softly speaking in his ear: "I love you, my little Joey, and nothing can hurt you. Mommy is here to take care of you, my darling Joey. Mommy is here, and I will take care of you."

Joey jerked back to reality as he heard a shoe scrape the concrete floor. He didn't know where he was. Panic set in. Slowly, he remembered what had transpired. He breathed deeply, controlling the panic, and by the time the jailer got to the cell door, he was sitting up and smiling at the guard.

"Time to go, Mr. Paschal. You going to behave, or do I need to put these on?" the jailer said, holding up leg and wrist shackles.

"No, sir, I'm going to follow the judge's orders," Joey said, walking out of the cell and into an uncertain situation. He was confident he could deal with anything because God and his mother were nearby.

# CHAPTER 6

Cal sat at his desk with a yellow pad and a pencil. He had a list of calls he'd made. Starting at the top, the first call went to Jack Gianelli, the wilderness outfitter. Cal's barber was next. Dr. Taylor Graham, the president of Berkshire College, was third. The fourth call went to Ella, telling her he would not be home for dinner, and no, she did not need to fix a plate and leave it in the refrigerator. The last call was the most important. After the phone rang the fourth time, a breathless woman answered, "Cal?"

"I'm sorry to bother you, Maggie. She's dead," Cal blurted out, like a child telling an adult some important news.

"What, Catherine? How? When? Oh, my God."

"No, I'm sorry. Let me slow down." He took an audible deep breath. "Not Catherine. Josey. Josey is dead."

"What? How do you know? I'm sorry for you, Cal. How did you find out?" Maggie asked. A chill involuntarily ran through her as she realized the implication of this news for her relationship with Cal.

"That's the real reason I'm calling. Her son appeared in court this morning."

"Her son?" Maggie interrupted. "Did you know she had a son?"

"No, I had no idea. Yes, her son. He told me she died in childbirth seventeen years ago."

"I am truly sorry, Cal," Maggie said. "Is there anything I can do?"

"As a matter of fact, there is. I put the boy on probation for four years, under my judicial supervision. I need a place for him to stay until I can find a permanent home for him. I was hoping he could stay in your garage apartment until Monday. By then, I'll have a place picked out."

"Of course. No one is there right now. Does this mean you're not going to meet me in New York?" Maggie asked.

"Are you kidding? Of course not. Maggie, I thought you understood; nothing, nothing at all, has priority over my trip. I just need to stabilize Joseph before leaving Friday, that's all."

"Joseph? Is that his name?"

"Joseph Hinson Paschal."

"He doesn't have any family, friends, where he can stay?"

"Maggie, for the last three years, he's been living in the woods, without a home or interaction with humans, other than watching them and stealing what he needed." The reality of what he said hit home to Cal, and his voice broke. His eyes burned, and he breathed deeply twice. He was silent and shifted his mind to legal work, recovering his composure.

"Oh, Cal, of course, bring him here. I'll have dinner for the three of us ready by six. What time can you be here?"

"Close to then. We're going to Jack's store; Joseph doesn't have any clothes. They burned his, they were so dirty and smelly, so he's in orange—"

"Huh? Orange?"

"The orange jumpsuit inmates wear."

"Oh."

"Then we're going to Eddie Keogh's to get him a shave and a haircut. Well, sort of. He doesn't have much facial hair, but it looks scraggly. Then I'll take him to Nombergs, get a razor, that kind of stuff, and Chu's for some snacks to put in the kitchenette in the apartment."

"Okay, since he's been in the woods, I'll fix him a dinner to welcome him back. Cal, why the woods? What would make a—how old did you say he is, and how long was he in the woods?"

"He's seventeen, and he disappeared from a foster home when he was thirteen, so a little over three years."

"Bless his heart. He hasn't been to school all that time?"

"I don't know. He seems intelligent and aware of the world, if you know what I mean. He doesn't seem stunted in his knowledge. I called Taylor Graham, who is going to have him tested and interviewed by a psychologist at the college tomorrow. They'll figure out what high school grade is right for him. Getting either a GED or diploma is crucial for him to become self-sufficient. In the meantime, I'm going to find him a part-time job while he's in school. I'll supplement whatever else he needs."

"Sounds like a plan."

"It's the least I can do, Maggie."

"I understand. See you at six," Maggie said. Her mind raced. She realized her relationship with Cal would change now that he knew Josey was dead. The possibility of Cal finding Josey had always been a plausible alternative to Cal and Maggie's relationship, an under-standing that was never spoken. Maggie didn't mind. She welcomed the wedge since it saved her from having to build a barrier herself.

Maggie walked over to the kitchen island and pulled a pad and pencil from a drawer. She started developing a menu.

§

Cal hung up and sat back in his chair. That's why I love her, he thought. She's calm and willing to understand. He rested his head against the chair back, closed his eyes, and thought back to that fateful day. He and Josey had spent their "honeymoon" together the week prior, hiking and camping in the back country. They hadn't seen a soul. The irony was that they were both engaged to others. They had met at school. She was a sophomore, and he was about to graduate from law school. Her fiancé was a mechanic who had graduated from high school and gone to work for a big trucking firm, making good money, and he was anxious for Josey to marry him. She was determined to get a college education. They had agreed to get married after her second year of school since she could get a better position with an associate degree and continue college online at night.

Cal was engaged to Catherine White, the daughter of the most powerful lawyer in western Massachusetts. His mother, a friend of the lawyer's wife, had orchestrated his future. Cal's family had the pedigree but had lost the family money in the Great Depression—at least that's what the outside story was. His father and grandfather had enjoyed being Callaways more than they enjoyed working. Cal's mother had dominated the family, keeping up appearances even as the last of the family wealth leaked away steadily, funding his father's interest in the outdoors. Cal had adored his father and learned from him the infinite pleasures of the wilderness. By the time he'd gone to college, Cal's mother had let him know in no uncertain terms what his future held. He would go to law school, become a lawyer, marry Catherine White, and join her father's law firm. Step by step, the Callaway family was going to be restored to its rightful position based on the marriage and career of Ernst Harrison Callaway III.

Cal and Josey had first met by accident after sitting down at a communal table in the student cafeteria. The attraction was instan-taneous. They both knew it. Lunch became a regular ritual. They talked and debated nonstop until one or the other had to go to class. After several weeks, they occasionally skipped a class, went to the wilderness, and spent afternoons passionately having sex, talking, and enjoying newly discovered tidbits of lore or wondering about their surroundings. As the school year ended, they had planned a weeklong camping trip, careful not to let anyone know they were together. Her family and fiancé had been happy that she was going to Disney World with friends. His family and fiancée had thought he was on a solo hiking trip, the last before climbing the law firm's success ladder. The week had gone as they planned. By the end of the seven days, they both knew they were marrying each other. They agreed to tell their parents, break off their engagements, meet the next day, and get married. Before separating, he gave her a diamond ring he had bought from a pawnshop just before their camping trip. Josey cried. No man had ever given her a gift since she was a child, and, just as importantly, it represented their future together forever.

The next day, they had met at Cal's apartment. They tore into each other, ripping each other's clothes off in a passionate heat, fell onto the bed, and coupled until they both climaxed loudly. They held each other tightly, knowing their future together began this day. Slowly, their hands began exploring each other's bodies again. Josey, kissing Cal's ear, had said, "What did your parents and Catherine say when you told them?"

Cal turned his head away, looking at the wall. "I didn't tell Catherine," he said.

Josey had sat up, using one arm to cover her breasts and the other to pull the sheet up over her abdomen, staring at Cal quizzically. "Cal, what do you mean, you didn't tell Catherine? Look at me. What happened?"

Cal had sat up on the edge of the bed, looking at the wall, away from Josey. "I told my parents. My mother went ballistic. She said I would marry no one but Catherine. I owed it to her and the family to marry Catherine and join her father's law firm. She became hysterical. My father tried to calm her down, but she lashed out at him, and he just left the room. She told me that if I didn't marry Catherine, she'd never speak to me again. I just couldn't go through with it. It would hurt her too much for me to go against her wishes. She devoted her entire married life trying to build up the Callaway social position, back to where it was in the early years. It would hurt her too much. She ranted about my father and his lack of ambition. She said I was just like him and she wouldn't stand for another failure in the family. It was terrible. I just didn't understand what my marriage to Catherine meant to her. I'm sorry, Josey. I just can't go against my mother."

Josey had felt the bile climbing up her throat as her stomach constricted. In a daze, she had said, "No, you can't mean this. I told Howey last night. It devastated him. I could do it. Why, Cal? Why couldn't you? Don't you love me?"

Cal, still sitting naked on the bed, facing the wall away from Josey, hanging his head in his hands, had said, "I do love you. I just can't disappoint my mother."

"Son of a bitch!" Josey had screamed. "You didn't have the balls to tell your family and the little rich girl that you love someone from the other side of town. Goddamn shitty little sniveling boy. I thought you were a man, but you're just a little boy, hiding behind mama's skirt. You didn't even have the balls to tell me this before you had one last fuck, did you? You bastard."

She had pulled on her clothes while screaming at him. "You can't even look at me, asshole. Here, take your fucking ring and stick it up your ass." She pulled the ring off her finger and threw it at him, hitting him in the back. "Oh, my God. Oh, my God," she repeated over and over, sobbing and running from the apartment.

Cal had sat there, crying, for what seemed like an eternity. Finally, he'd reached down by the bed and picked up the ring, clutching it in his hand. It's going to be all right, he'd said to himself as he straightened up the bed and apartment.

§

Cal sat in his office chair with his eyes closed, tears streaming down his cheeks. He pulled out a tissue, wiped his eyes, and blew his nose. Josey, I'll take care of your boy. I'll see he has opportunities in his life. He unlocked his desk drawer, pulled out the Bible, and opened it, then looked at the inscription: May 21. He thought about Joseph's age. Could it possibly be? Cal buzzed Betsy.

"Betsy, send the Paschal boy in when he arrives."

"Yes, sir."

Cal opened the completed file, searched through it, and found the birth certificate validating Joseph's age and the names of his mother and father. He pulled two envelopes out of his desk and tucked them into the left breast pocket of his sports coat. He heard a soft knock on the door. "Come in," he said.

# CHAPTER 7

Joey opened the door and entered the office.

"Have a seat," Cal said, pointing to the two chairs in front of his desk. Cal cleared his desktop and looked at the young man across the desk from him.

Joey stared back while gripping the chair's arms, eager to do whatever was necessary to keep this judge happy until he got away.

"Joseph, you and I have a busy afternoon. First, we're going to get you some civilian clothes. I'm sure you aren't ecstatic about an orange jumpsuit."

"Uh, no, sir."

"Second, you're going to get a haircut and a shave. Third, we're going to buy you some toiletries and stuff. Finally, I've arranged for you to meet someone who will allow you to stay in her garage apartment until Monday, when you will move to a permanent place to stay. Any questions about this afternoon's tasks?"

"No, sir." Joey looked around the office, anywhere except at Cal. His spirits dwindled. The collections on display were evidence this judge spent a great deal of time in the wilderness. The implication was clear to Joey: he'd better move deeper in the wilderness and farther up the mountains.

"Joey," Cal said, trying to help the kid focus back on what he was saying, "tomorrow an officer will take you to Berkshire College for testing. Depending on how you do, you'll go back to school to get a high school diploma. During the next four years, while you're on probation, whatever school you go to, your grades will be part of the official court records. I'll arrange a part-time job for you, which will help with your expenses, and you'll do community service, selected by me, every weekend. Do you understand the importance of handling these tasks correctly?"

"Yes, sir."

"Finally, every Monday morning, you will report to me here at the court or wherever I assign you to go. I know this all sounds harsh, but it's so you build the right habits to succeed. Do you have any questions at this point?"

"No, sir."

"Okay, let's go. Maggie doesn't like people showing up late for dinner, and we have a lot to get done."

§

Cal turned into the alley behind Gianelli Outfitters and parked near the delivery door. The store is an old barn close to the highway that cuts through town. Its white paint is peeling in some places, and the rest is chalky from the sun. Everything a lover of the outdoors needs or wants is available there. Kayaks and canoes hang from the rafters. The saying is that if Gianelli doesn't have it, you don't need it in the outdoors.

Cal knocked on the door. It opened, and he saw the back room was empty except for Jack Gianelli. Cal waved for Joey to leave the car and come inside.

"Jack, this is Joey. Joey, this is Mr. Gianelli."

Jack held out his hand and said, "Joey, the name's Jack. Mr. Gianelli was my father. The judge said you needed new clothes. Let's see if we can fit you better than the local law enforcement tailor did." Looking Joey up and down, he said, "Large jackets and shirts, with a 32/31 pant size. Let's start there." He picked up a shirt and pair of jeans and handed them to Joey. "Go behind that curtain over there and change into these. Then go out front. Cal, what do you want him to have?"

Looking at Joey, Cal said, "Joey, pick out four sets of clothes for the summer and four for the winter, including shoes and boots. Got it?"

"Yes, sir!" Joey said grinning.

When Joey was in the storefront, Cal reached into his jacket pocket and pulled out his checkbook and pen. He wrote a check to Gianelli Outfitters, leaving the amount blank, and signed it. Handing it to Jack, he said, "Jack, this isn't something anyone needs to know about. Fill in the amount when we leave. If Joey ever shows up and needs or wants something, give it to him, and put it on my account, okay?"

"Sure, Cal. You going to explain it to me?"

"I will. The BBC meeting is Tuesday. You going to be there? I'll have the complete story by then. Right now, there's too many missing pieces."

"You bet. I got the email. I'll be there."

"Let's go see what Joey picked out."

Joey had the counter piled high with clothes. He turned to Jack and said, "Sir, is there any chance you have some all-wool winter clothes?"

"I think so, in the back. They'll be older styles. We switched to the new lightweight down-filled winter clothes that people like now. You don't want that?"

"No, sir. I prefer the heaviest-weight wool clothes for the winter."

"Yes, go back to the storeroom. Look on the shelves behind the curtain where you changed clothes. All my remaining wool is there."

Joey returned with a wool jacket, three pairs of wool pants, and four shirts and placed them on the counter.

"Joey, pick out a three- to seven-day backpack to put all of this in. Oh, yeah, and get a daily backpack to use for carrying your schoolbooks. By the way, I don't see any winter shoes," Cal said, looking from the clothes to Joey.

"No, sir. The boots I want are too expensive. I'll get those after I get a job."

Cal put his hand on Joey's shoulder and said gently, with a smile, "Go get the boots, Joey. It doesn't matter what price they are."

Joey took a pair of La Sportiva ankle-high waterproof leather and Gore-Tex mountain boots off the wall, bringing them to the counter. "If it's okay, I'll wear these today," he said, holding them.

"Joey, I'm curious. Those are heavy boots, and you want heavy winter clothes. Why? The deal with hikers today is the lightest of everything," Jack said as he ran the clothes through the barcode reader, folded them, and put them in the backpack.

"Sir, they've probably never been freezing, or been in a wind that never stops, or felt blowing sleet. Heavy wool is warm even when wet. Besides, if you wear heavy, you stay strong. At least that's what I've found. Same with the boots. These boots," Joey went on, holding up the boots, "are really stiff. Climbing rocks and stepping on roots will be much easier with these stiff boots than those lightweight hiking shoes."

"Interesting. If you ever need a job, let me know."

"Yes, sir. Thank you, sir," Joey said, grinning, as he sat in a chair and began changing from the prison slippers to the hiking boots.

§

Cal parked in front of the narrow glass-front store with its spinning red, white, and blue barber pole. They walked in and took seats in the row of chrome and cracked red leather chairs, facing the sole barber's chair occupied by a customer who talked constantly to the barber. Cal and Joey both picked up old issues of Outdoor Life and started flipping pages.

"Be right with you, Judge," Eddie said, not stopping his cutting but looking over at Cal and Joey.

"Eddie, this is Joey, a friend of mine. Joey, this is Mr. Keogh, the best barber in Berkshire County."

"Hello, Joey."

"How do you do, sir?"

Ten minutes later, Eddie was putting the cape around Joey's neck. "What'll it be, Joey?"

"A regular haircut, not a skin job, and a shave," Cal replied to Eddie.

"Yes, sir," Eddie said, wondering what was going on, but knowing better than to ask. Eddie finished the haircut and shave and looked at Joey. "I'll trim those fingernails for you. They're pretty long."

"No!" Joey snapped, clenching his fists. He realized he had spoken too harshly and blushed. "Uh, no, sir, they're fine."

Eddie looked over at Cal, who subtly shook his head. When Eddie started to unbutton the cape, Cal walked over to the chair, examining Joey's haircut. His right hand brushed the cape.

"Looks good, Eddie. By the way, did you get the email about the BBC meeting Tuesday?"

"Yeah, Cal. I'll be there."

Cal paid Eddie, turned to Joey, and said, "Now, one more stop and you go see Maggie. You won't ever be the same again."

§

Maggie stood at the kitchen sink, chopping potatoes and vegetables for the beef stew, when the first security light turned on. She put down the knife, rinsed her hands, and dried them on the apron as she took it off. She folded the apron neatly and placed it over the wire bar inside the cabinet door under the sink. A place for everything, and everything in its place. The second security light flicked on, and she looked through the glass panel in the kitchen door, which opened to the enclosed arbor extending from the garage to the kitchen. She watched Cal and Joey coming toward the house.

She quickly controlled her surprise at what she saw.

She pulled open the kitchen door just as Cal reached up and pulled on the outward-opening storm door.

"Joey, this is Maggie Latham, town librarian and all-around pleasant person," Cal said as he and Joey walked into the kitchen. "Maggie, this is Josey—God, I'm sorry, Joey Paschal."

Maggie smiled, held out her hand to Joey, and said, "Joey, welcome to my home. You two are just in time to set the table. Cal, we're going to be informal, so set the banquette, please. Use the blue and white casual pattern; it's in the butler's pantry. Joey, look in there as well, in the drawers under the cabinets, and take out the blue placemats and napkins. The glasses are opposite the dishes. We'll use the tall glasses on the second shelf in the center section. Please get three." Maggie, from her years as a librarian, knew the way to make a nervous young person relax was to give him tasks, the same way a parent does with her own child.

"Yes, ma'am," Joey said.

"Hold up, Joey," Maggie said, turning to look into his eyes. "You may as well learn right now. It's not good to make a woman feel she's old. Drop the 'ma'am' and call me Maggie," she said in a mock scolding voice, smiling.

Joey grinned sheepishly and replied, "Yes, Miss Maggie."

Maggie let the "miss" stay and returned to checking the pots on the stove. She took the sterling silverware from the kitchen island and completed the table setting.

She served family style. The boiled potatoes, kale, beef stew, and biscuits were in bowls so Joey and Cal wouldn't have to ask for more. Neither was shy about helping themselves to seconds and thirds. Maggie watched the two of them. She knew without a doubt.

"The two of you stay seated and pass me the bowls and dishes. Joey, I'm going to make you a plate for later, just in case you get hungry before bed. Now, for the good part: dessert. Joey, any chance you like chocolate cake with German chocolate icing like the judge does?"

"Yes, ma'am, I mean, Miss Maggie."

"Good. I thought you might," she said as she cut large pieces of cake for them and a small piece for herself. Handing Cal the dessert plates, she casually asked, "Cal, you say you want Joey to stay here through the weekend. Have you found another place yet?"

"Haven't had a chance to look, but I expect to have a place by this time Thursday," Cal responded as he passed one plate to Joey and kept the second for himself.

"Well, I was just thinking: My garage apartment is empty, and I haven't advertised it for rent. It's small, and Joey may not like it when he sees it, but if it works, he could stay there until he decides he needs a bigger place," she said, looking from Cal to Joey. "Besides, I need a handyperson to maintain my rental properties. We could work out something where the work covers the rent, and Joey gets cash to boot. How does that sound, Joey?"

"I—I don't know what to do. I've not worked on stuff like that," Joey said, eyes downcast.

"Joey, the tasks are simple. I'll show you what to do and make a schedule for you. You look like a guy who can get things done. What do you say? Is it worth a try?"

"I'm willing, I guess, Miss Maggie. If it's okay with the judge, I mean," Joey mumbled through a mouthful of cake, staring at Maggie like a puppy being trained by his master. All he could do was stare at this white-haired woman. She did not look old. Her face had no wrinkles at all and her green eyes sparkled. The white mane framed her face, and her lips were accented by pale red lipstick.

"There's only one problem," Cal said. Maggie and Joey, both crestfallen, turned to Cal, who stated, "Joey, unless I'm mistaken, you don't know how to drive."

"No, sir, I don't," Joey said, looking down at the table.

"That's no problem," Maggie said quickly. "I can teach him, and he could use the Wrangler since he'll have to pull the equipment trailer when he does the rental houses."

Cal laid down his fork with a serious look on his face and said, "There's no way you'll teach him to drive. If you do, he'll be in my court every week for speeding, running stop signs, and all sorts of violations."

Joey looked at the judge to see if he was serious, then looked at Maggie.

"Well, Your Honor," she said, "I expected you might make a false comment like that, so you'll have to teach him." She looked at Joey, smiled, and winked. Joey sat there, looking from one to the other, trying to determine if they were serious.

"Touché," Cal said.

"Why don't you take Joey over to the apartment and get him settled while I clean up? Stop by on your way out, and we'll iron out the details. By the way, I sent out the emails."

"Yeah, Jack and Eddie got theirs."

"Will this be a long or short meeting?"

"I don't know. That article on overdoses I mentioned? You know, the one in the BT this morning—God, that seems like an eternity ago—is the main topic. We'll see who knows what and take it from there." Cal turned to Joey and said, "Let's go get everything out of my car, Joey. Oh, yeah, tomorrow morning at nine, a deputy in an unmarked car will pick you up in front of the garage and take you to Berkshire College." Cal reached into his sports coat pocket and pulled out a folded paper. "Let's see. You're going to Gearson Hall to see Dr. Rebecca Lang. She's a psychologist and professor at the college. She's going to give you a bunch of tests. It's important you do the best you can, but it's also important for you not to worry about what you know or don't know. All we're trying to do is see where you are in your education so they can place you in the right grade for success. You okay with that?"

"Yes, sir," Joey said. Turning to Maggie, he said, "Thanks for dinner, Miss Maggie."

She handed him the food for later and the key to the apartment. "Good night, Joey. I'll be home at five fifteen tomorrow. I'll see you then," she said, smiling and looking directly into his eyes.

Cal saw the connection between the two of them and felt relief and a twinge of jealousy. His mind flashed back quickly to his own mother's demeanor with him. The comparison was stark. He reached into his pocket for his wallet, pulled out two tens and a five, and held them out to Joey. "Here's twenty-five dollars for lunch and snacks at the student cafeteria. It'll be a long day, but an important one. Now, let's get you settled." He put his hand on Joey's shoulder, looked back, and mouthed "Thank you" to Maggie.

# CHAPTER 8

Cal wrapped up the last of his cases Friday afternoon at twelve fifteen. His weekend bag was already in the car. He hurried from the courthouse, heading to Taconic Parkway. Everybody had their own way to the city. Cal preferred the Taconic–Sawmill–Henry Hudson route. With very few signal lights, traffic moved fast and was usually reasonably light. In the past, the only congestion came when he turned onto Seventy-Ninth, then Amsterdam and the dogleg through the park. As he began the three-hour drive, his mind was on Joey and his situation. Maggie was a godsend, the way she put Joey at ease, reading the situation and being willing to propose the option of Joey staying at her place, but Cal didn't know. He couldn't grasp what triggered Joey's violence, and he was afraid Maggie would press that trigger unintentionally.

The testing went well at BC, and they would receive the results Monday. That was the next hurdle: how to resume the education of a seventeen-year-old who had seen or, to some extent, not seen what was necessary to survive and grow in society. Merging from the Taconic to the Sawmill, Cal saw the traffic leaving the city building up. He would be at the apartment by four. His mind bounced back to the challenge of accepting responsibility for a seventeen-year-old boy, a boy who had spent the last three-plus years of his life, formative years, living alone in the woods. Why hadn't he gone someplace—a church, a school, even a hospital—seeking adult help? He didn't trust anyone? Why? God, how had he survived last winter? It was brutally cold and snowy. Would it ever be possible for him to acclimate to society? He was a bomb with a hair trigger. What set him off? He was too young to be unsupervised, but too old to go back to foster care. Cal's thoughts careened from one issue and its ramifications to another, giving proof to the complexity of the situation. Cal's judicial and legal training flooded his mind with questions, and he had no clue about the answers. He knew that the key to Joey was why he had run away and stayed in the wilderness. Cal felt the immediate pressure of finding a way to stabilize Joey's living situation. He knew Catherine wouldn't stand for Joey coming to Willview. A foster family, perhaps? No. Legally Cal couldn't keep Joey in the foster system once he turned eighteen. Besides, what if the foster parent tried to discipline Joey and a confrontation evolved? Foster care was out. Maggie had offered. There were risks, serious risks. Was this the best alternative for the short term? Maybe. What about school and work? Cal sighed, overwhelmed by the what-ifs.

Cal would ask the book club for help finding Joey a job, maybe something outside instead of inside, where he'd feel confined. Education was necessary first. The testing would help with that answer. Step one must be his getting a GED or high school diploma. Joey couldn't go to a regular high school. His temper's lightening trigger could cause unfixable problems. A tutor? Maybe.

Cal focused and tried to prioritize these jumbled alternatives. He needed answers soon. The Henry Hudson Parkway sign loomed ahead. Thirty minutes later he exited the HH at Seventy-Ninth and headed up the hill toward Amsterdam, where he turned left and then right two blocks later onto Eighty-First. Enormous crowds and the congested traffic around the American Natural History Museum showed the city was alive, and he loved it. The people, the languages, and their mannerisms were all exciting, as were the theater, the ballet, and the music. Mixing it all together, along with the natural and architectural beauty of the city, it was no wonder New York was the best city in the world.

Cal entered Central Park and came out on Seventy-Ninth street. In minutes he was at the garage entrance on Eighty-Second between Madison and Park Avenue. After giving his key to the attendant, Cal grabbed his weekend bag and entered the apartment building through the garage.

"Good afternoon, Jacob," he said to the back-gate custodian.

Stopping his work and walking ahead of Cal, Jacob responded, "Good afternoon, Mr. Latham. Good to see you again." He held the door to the front elevators open for Cal.

Cal opened the door to the eighteenth-floor apartment with his key. As he entered, he saw Maggie in the kitchen, pouring two glasses of red wine. She looked over her shoulder and said, "Your timing is always impeccable. Welcome to New York." She handed him one glass of wine. "To a marvelous weekend," she said, tilting her glass toward his. He put his bag on the floor and touched his wineglass to hers.

"There's no time like the present to make it marvelous. Do we have time before dinner?"

"I thought you'd never ask. We can enjoy these when we're finished—the first time. Dinner is here at six thirty, and the car will pick us up at seven fifteen for the eight o'clock curtain."

"Sounds like a plan," Cal said, wrapping his arm around Maggie's waist and kissing her as they walked toward the bedroom.

§

"Dinner's almost ready," Maggie called from the kitchen. "Will you set the table?"

Cal, in the living room, closed his book and walked into the kitchen. From the cabinets above the sink, he took out the hand-painted china and hand-blown crystal glasses; he arranged the seating so they were both on the side of the table that offered an eastern view of the city. The alcove dining area contained a custom-crafted mahogany table, a matching side table, and four chairs. The living room featured a sofa, two recliners, a television cabinet, an antique end table, and a glass coffee table. There were books, large paintings, and sculptures everywhere, making the room appear larger than it was. Two bathrooms and a bedroom rounded out their pied-à-terre in the sky.

Maggie had her plans for Joey. He could be the answer to her needs if—and it was a big if—Cal allowed it. She had to find the right time to discuss it with him. This weekend would be the right time. He couldn't have found another place for Joey so soon. The question was, would he agree?

§

"What a brilliant play. The Manhattan Theatre Club never disappoints. They seem to have a knack for finding the best new plays every season," Cal said as they emerged from New York City Center on Fifty-Fifth Street. "Are you up for walking home?"

"Oh, yes. Let's go to Fifth and switch to Madison at Fifty-Seventh. It'll be fun to see if there are any new shops," Maggie responded, taking Cal's arm and hugging it close to her. "I'm glad I'm here with you," she said in his ear.

"I'm glad I'm here with you," he responded, kissing her lightly on the cheek.

They turned left at Fifth Avenue. One block up, Cal steered them across to the east side so they would pass Tiffany's as they reached Fifty-Seventh. At the jeweler, he stopped, looking in the window at the diamond rings.

"You know, they make diamonds in factories now," he said. "Can't tell them from stones mined in Africa—at least that's what some people say. We'll have to make sure your ring is Tiffany GIA-certified as coming from a mine. They hold their value better."

Oh, no, Maggie groaned inwardly. He's starting early. Whenever he felt undue stress, he started. She needed to end it now, before it ruined the weekend. "I don't need a ring. I have you, and you have me. We have a good relationship without all that stuff. Besides, we have a more important issue to solve—Joey," she said, pressing his arm against her breast.

"I know, I know. Hope springs eternal. I figure one of these years you'll say yes. We'll probably be in our nineties, but who cares, just as long as you finally say yes."

"It seems to me I was saying yes, over and over, earlier," Maggie said, rubbing her breast on his arm, smiling, and pecking him on the cheek. "Besides, you're married, remember? Have you decided what Joey's future will be?"

"Assuming he can stay with you until Tuesday," Cal said.

"He can," Maggie replied.

"Great. Last Tuesday, when we had dinner the first time, I thought I'd have a solution for his living situation by Monday of this week. I don't feel good about my choices so far. I'll focus on it again on Monday. I'll find him a place where I can go by and take him to school. He'll have to walk home since he'll be out at 3:00 p.m., assuming he gets into high school. The challenge is his being willing to go. It'll be hard for a seventeen-year-old to sit in class with thirteen- or fourteen-year-old kids. He won't fit in. Joey's mercurial response to dominating people, essentially bullies, impacts where he lives and goes to school. If a kid or a foster parent tried to push him around, the results would be disastrous for everyone."

"Are you saying he might be living alone? How will that work? You won't place him with a family?" Maggie stopped walking and turned to look with concern at Cal.

"A family is best. However, the more I think about it, the more I realize acclimating to the social interactions of a family, much less the discipline of a surrogate dad and mom, could or would be too much at this stage." They resumed strolling.

"Cal, I was serious about what I proposed the other night." Maggie took Cal's hand as they walked along Madison, looking in the shop windows. "Last night, Joey and I had dinner. I didn't pry, but he told me that he read books most of the time over the past three years. It's surprising how many good things, like books, clothes, and utensils, people throw away. He's remarkably well read. Some of the books were old textbooks. My point is, Joey may be able to fit in as a junior or senior, with kids his age, instead of going back to the eighth or ninth grade. There's also the alternative that he's tutored for the GED. When will you hear back about the testing?"

"Dr. Lang is calling me Monday morning and emailing her assessment for Joey's court file." They stopped in front of Santoni to look at the shoes in the window.

"Aren't those beautiful? I wonder what they cost," Maggie said.

"Handmade Italian shoes in butter-soft leather? I'd guess about two months of a librarian's salary," Cal responded.

"Is that all? How about a judge's salary? I wonder how many colors they come in," Maggie retorted. They continued strolling. "Cal, I want to make a proposition."

"It's my job to make the propositions here, not yours," Cal said with a smile.

"Not that kind. The serious kind, about Joey. We had dinner last night. I have a deep feeling I can trust Joey. I told you, I need someone who is trustworthy to do some work for me at my rental houses. A person who can do it right and relieve me of those pesky calls about the yards, the plumbing, and such. A person who can keep them looking their best. I asked him last night—I hope you don't mind—if he would do some simple chores around my house this weekend. I told him I'd pay him. It's more like a test to see how much pride he will take in his work. I think he'll pass with flying colors, but I need to know for sure. If he passes, and I'll know as soon as I get home, I'd really like Joey to stay in the garage apartment. I don't expect I'll need it for at least a year. By then it'll be too small for him. He'll want more space. He can go to school, and after school and on weekends—"

"He has to do community service for four hours each weekend," Cal interrupted.

"I know, but that's four hours out of forty-eight. Anyway, I'll pay him a fair wage for his work, and he can pay rent. It'll teach him responsibility. The nights I'm home on time, he can have dinner with me. What do you think? Please say yes. I need someone like Joey—someone I can trust." Maggie stopped and looked up at Cal, trying to urge his acceptance.

"Maggie, I'll tell you what. Let's see how the psych tests come back. Joey is a good kid, but he can be highly dangerous if he loses control. Highly dangerous. I'm not sure I'm comfortable with you being alone with him. If he felt threatened, it could be a real disaster."

"Cal, I don't know what Joey has been through, but I do know abused young people. There's no doubt in my mind Joey is an abused person. I can tell. I know the signs. I also know how to reach young people who have felt the betrayal of adults, and I know how to help them channel their anger into something positive. One thing I know for sure: Joey won't hurt me. He has a crush on me. I'm sure it's a motherly crush, but he likes me."

"You think so, eh? And what makes you so sure, Miss Maggie?"

"Because I can wrap men like him around my little finger," Maggie said. What she didn't say was he was just like his father.

"Fair enough, but let's look at the psych tests Monday and hear what Dr. Lang says." Cal and Maggie stopped for the light at Seventy-Second Street. "Quadronno's in the next block. Think it's still open? I'd like some gelato."

Maggie looked at her watch. "Sorry, we just missed them."

She breathed a sigh of relief. Cal didn't say no. She knew she could mold Joey to fit into her organization. They continued to Eighty-Second and Park and entered their building.

# CHAPTER 9

It was 3:00 p.m., and Antonio's didn't open until five thirty. There was a table of six men eating in the middle of the main dining room. Giuseppe "The Hammer" Strollo, boss of the Massachusetts organized crime cartel, sat at the head. Outside, in both the rear and front of the restaurant, two of his associates loitered, ever vigilant for anyone paying attention to the restaurant. Back inside, a fifth individual supervised and watched the employees serving the meal. A sixth sat at the bar, off to the left, watching the five at the table with The Hammer.

On The Hammer's right sat Aloysius "Ivy League" Carroll, dressed in a navy-blue suit, white silk French-cuffed shirt, Hermès tie, and polished black boots. Carroll was the youngest partner in the history of the venerable Boston law firm Holliday, Edwards, and Carroll, whose offices in Chicago, Boston, New York, Philadelphia, Washington, Atlanta, Miami, Dublin, London, and Naples made it especially suited to represent the interests of its predominately East Coast clientele.

On The Hammer's left side, eating his second plate of short ribs and goat cheese ravioli, sat Vincenzo "Big Vinney" Del Giorno, cartel underboss and capo of western Massachusetts, including Berkshire

County. Seated next to Big Vinney was Danny "Dapper Dan" Hogan, capo of Boston and its surroundings up to the New Hampshire state line. Benedetto "Tico" Anselasi, capo of the area south of Boston to the Rhode Island state line, including Martha's Vineyard and Nantucket, sat next to Aloysius. At the foot of the table was Rosario "Mad Dog" Giuliano, capo for central Massachusetts and personal enforcer for The Hammer.

The Hammer raised his right hand. His associate signaled for the waitstaff to finish clearing the table. When it was done, the associate placed an instrument on the table and watched while the dials moved to show there were no wired or wireless eavesdroppers. He then left the restaurant, taking all the employees with him. The associate in the bar remained vigilant.

"Ivy League is here to give his quarterly update on your legitimate investments. Let's hear it, counselor," The Hammer said, looking at Carroll and nodding.

"Thank you. In the last ninety days, we have increased our control of forty small community banks in New England."

"How come we need banks? And when you say 'control,' do we own all of them?" Tico Anselasi asked.

"No, we don't own all of them. In every case, our nominees own at least fifty-one percent. In about half of the forty banks, our nominees own one hundred percent. We need to have so many because we want to stay below a certain bank size, the point where the regulators pay greater attention to money laundering and the composition of loans. We need the banks for two reasons. First, we move your street cash to the string of grocery stores, dry cleaners, food wholesalers, produce stands, gentlemen's clubs, ice cream shops, and flea market jewelry stands. These businesses deposit the cash into one or more of the banks we control. The banks turn around and lend money to the real estate and construction companies you own at multiple times your deposit amounts. You own one hundred percent of these real estate entities. Money is also invested in certain publicly traded companies. Any questions so far?"

"Yeah, Harvard—" Tico started.

"Dartmouth, actually," Ivy League said.

"Whatever. I understand the banks, the laundromats, and the real estate. I can ride by, see them, and know they will be there tomorrow. I can't see these stocks. Yesterday the stock market dropped over five hundred points. Poof! The money is gone. Why do we have to own stocks? It doesn't make sense to me."

"I'll explain. The small businesses you call the laundromats are great; however, they are small. The name of the power game in government, at all levels, is adding employees and spending money. This country continues to grow in the private sector as well. We don't just buy shares on a whim. We buy pieces of a few large companies standing in front of the flow of tax dollars being spent by governments at all levels. Governments now account for over twenty percent of all economic activities in this country. We want a piece of those dollars. These large companies sell governments, consumers, and businesses services and goods. These are very big companies, worth billions of dollars. Right now, our influence is through our friends on the boards of directors.

"The government wants to know whenever a stockholder owns more than five percent of a public company. To avoid their prying eyes, we've set up nominee owners in both this country and overseas to hold our shares. Presently, in three valuable companies, we and our friends overseas own more than twenty percent. Eventually, we'll own a majority. At that time, we'll be able to tighten control over the board and senior management. Frankly, Tico, these are your best investments. You don't pay rising taxes on them each year, like you do on real estate. The shares don't need roof repairs or costly insurance, and the annual cash flow from dividends is comparable to the net rent you get on real estate. Better than anything, the investment isn't in your name for nosy feds to identify. What if the stock market goes down? Frankly, we like it when those Wall Street thieves push the market down. They do it so they can buy cheap; we buy cheap as well. Understand? Relax. You're getting richer by the day."

"Relax is something I don't do. I'll take your big words for it. I just like being able to see my money."

"I understand. Questions?" Ivy League asked, looking around the table and waiting for a minute. "Very good. Here are your personal accountings for your percentage of the investment pie. You'll see an enormous increase from last quarter. Part of the increase is from your street activity, and part is from investment appreciation." He looked at The Hammer. "That's all I have, Mr. Strollo."

"Anybody else have anything to say?"

"Yeah, I keep hearing from Ivy League and other suits that the governor is a shoo-in for reelection. But when I go for my daily pint at one place in my area, my buddies are not happy with the governor. Ivy, are you sure this election is under control?" Dapper Dan Hogan asked, looking down at his manicured fingernails.

"Mr. Hogan, the only thing I can tell you for sure is this: we never lose an election. You and your access to the governor's office are safe."

"I wish I was as confident as you are," said Mad Dog Giuliano. "I'm hearing some of the same rumblings as Dapper Dan."

"Let me repeat: we never lose an election. You got nothing to worry about," Ivy League said.

The Hammer turned to Big Vinney Del Giorno and patted him on the arm. "Big Vinney, you want to discuss a problem in Berkshire County?"

"Yeah, Giuseppe. The local law stopped my best mule from Montreal and warned him not to stop in that county again or else he would go away for a long time."

"Is this mule part of your regular distribution organization over there?" The Hammer rested his hand on Big Vinney's arm.

"No. He freelances the goods he takes in payment for his services."

"So, he's outside your regular organization?"

"Well, yes and no."

"Vincenzo, it's either yes or no. Which is it?"

"I guess not, but he's really good at what he does, and I don't want to lose him."

"If it doesn't compromise your organization in Berkshire, then this matter has no business at this table. Right?" The Hammer said.

"Yeah, I guess so."

"While we're discussing Berkshire County, is your brother behaving himself?" The Hammer started patting Big Vinney on the arm again.

Big Vinney's eyes grew wide with fear at the mention of his brother. "Yeah, he's real appreciative of what you did for him in Vermont. He's promised no funny stuff with kids. He's learned his lesson; I swear on my mother's grave."

"I hope so, for everyone's sake. You contacted him?"

"No. You told me not to, and I haven't. No one can connect him to me or our organization." Big Vinney looked at Ivy League.

"Mr. Strollo, my firm has a strong connection with a local law firm in the Berkshires. The managing partner and I went to law school together and were roommates for a short period. I've arranged for

Vinney's brother to receive six thousand a month in cash. The local law firm sets up the physical transfer and bills my firm. We, in turn, allocate the expense to Big Vinney's personal legal fees," Ivy League explained.

"This legal guy in the Berkshires, is he good?"

"He's highly ambitious and vulnerable. There's another twist. Our strategy for western Massachusetts includes getting control of the district judgeship and other local political offices. He's going to be our point man in gathering up legitimate businesses that serve our purposes and putting our friends in public offices."

"What do you mean, your lawyer buddy is vulnerable?"

"He has some peculiar sex habits. The same as Big Vinney's brother. We have some pictures from his days in college, one situation where he caused a serious problem. I had to help him with an alibi. Nice guy, but kinky. He and I have worked out a strategy for making inroads in western Massachusetts. I'll know soon if he can deliver."

"None of my business at this point, counselor." The Hammer turned back to Big Vinney and said, "Keep your brother under control. It took a lot of juice to extract him from that mess in Vermont. Our friendship was the reason. Don't forget that, Vincenzo. I don't ever want any trace of a relationship between our organization and your pervert brother. Any other business we need to discuss?" He looked around the table. He stood up. No one else at the table moved. Seconds later, two of his associates appeared at his side. One picked up the surveillance equipment and stood at the table, watching the five seated men. The other walked out of the room, leading The Hammer through the kitchen and the rear door. The associate standing and the five men sitting around the table remained in place until the associate heard through his earpiece that The Hammer was in his armored Suburban.

# CHAPTER 10

oey looked up at the sun. Almost three. He'd be finished by four, time enough to go by Chu's and get some food that would last at least a week. He needed to get out of there before they found out. Thank you, God, for this opportunity, he thought. At least I'm not hungry anymore. His fullness wouldn't last, but his memories of Maggie and these past three days would linger for a long time. If he wasn't caught, he'd be the luckiest guy around.

Joey methodically moved from one task to the next. Finishing, he washed the tools and put them in their place. Maggie was clear: a finished job is when the tools are clean, put in their proper place, and ready for the next time. Maggie was something else. She was everything he imagined his mother would have been. Sitting for hours, looking over photos of his mom from when she was a baby until she was pregnant with him, and listening to Granny's stories about his mom had brought her to life. Hearing about what his mother was like had helped him imagine what they would've done together. They would have gone for walks since she loved to hike. She'd have taught him to understand everything around him, helped him avoid the bad people, and, most of all, loved him, held him, and kept him safe. She had been beautiful, just like Maggie was beautiful. That was fantasy, he realized. He knew what would happen if he stayed. No childish dreams could save him now, only escape.

Joey finished his chores the way Maggie wanted them done, went to his room above the garage, found a pencil, and checked off each task on the list. She even had pretty handwriting. He decided to keep his work clothes on since the jailer burned his—at least that's what the judge said. It won't be wrong for me to take these clothes, he convinced himself. I'll need the La Sportiva boots. The judge said I could get the mountain boots, and they'll make life easier. Hiking shoes won't be as good as the boots. The expensive pack would be nice, but the day pack will attract less attention, Joey rationalized. He'd need to look the part of a hiker and have a way to carry food. He still had fifteen dollars from what the judge had given him Tuesday evening.

Joey left the apartment and walked to the main house. Maggie had left the back door unlocked in case he wanted something to eat. Joey knew his mother would have done that, trusted him. On the counter was a note from her with twenty-five dollars. "Thank you for doing the chores. This is your payment. I'll see you Sunday evening, Maggie." She had signed the note the way his mother would have signed "Mom." She trusted him to do the work and do it right. He didn't want to disappoint her. Staying was out of the question, but he hesitated. If they found out, he'd die in prison, and he couldn't let that happen. He just couldn't. He had to leave before they found out what had happened before he went to the wilderness.

Joey took the note and the money and left the checked-off list in its place. He looked over and saw the glass cookie jar holding the cookies he and Maggie had made the night before. He took three cookies from the jar, leaving her four, wrapped them in a paper towel, and put them in his backpack. Not realizing it, he put the apartment key in his pocket with the money. He locked the house door, as instructed, and left.

He found it a simple walk to Chu's, the only grocery store in town. There was no choice but to risk being seen. Food for at least the next week, when they would be looking for him, was critical. Entering, Joey noticed the pretty young cashier. Other than Suzie, the daughter of his foster mother, he hadn't had much interaction with girls. Thinking of Suzie caused Joey to stop. He felt strange. Feelings of stress, loss, love, and thankfulness swirled inside him. He felt a chill, replaced by a feeling of dreadfulness, churning his insides. He realized he had been staring at the cashier, and she had been staring back at him.

In the first aisle, Joey grabbed a shopping basket. He picked his provisions carefully: the biggest plastic jar of peanut butter, a jar of honey, beef jerky, saltine crackers, four unripe apples and pears, a sturdy half-gallon jug of water he could refill over and over, a box of tea bags, and three butane lighters. Adding the prices up in his head, he figured it would cost twenty-eight dollars, and these items would fill his pack and last for over a week. He'd have to avoid the dumpsters for a long time. They now knew he was out there, and they'd be looking for him. Before, they hadn't known who he was or why he was there. The good thing was it was summer. The hikers on the Appalachian Trail, known locally as the AT, were increasing in numbers, and he could raid their food boxes at night. He could build up a store of food over the next two months to last into winter. It had worked for the past three years, and it would work again.

"Going hiking?" the cashier asked, jolting Joey from his thoughts. She looked at him, smiling. Her open, friendly, somewhat flirtatious attitude made Joey uncomfortable. He'd not experienced such a casual interaction like this in the past three years.

"Yeah," he said.

"How long are you going for?" she asked.

"Eh, just two nights," Joey replied, trying not to seem nasty, but not wanting her to remember him.

"Where are you going, Beartown Mountain?" she persisted. "I like to hike but don't go often because of work, and my husband doesn't like the woods. Says there are too many critters that bite or sting. What a dope."

"If he's a dope, why is he your husband?" Joey blurted out.

"Because we have a baby," she said, looking down at the counter. "That'll be $28.15," she continued in a professional tone, shoving the groceries into a plastic bag.

"Wait—let me just put those in my backpack. Thank you, and I hope you get to go hiking sometime," Joey said, handing her thirty dollars and smiling.

"Yeah, sure, sometime." The cashier gave him the change without looking at him again.

Leaving the store, Joey shouldered his backpack. Beartown Mountain would not be where he entered the woods. October Mountain was closer. He crossed Elmwood to walk on the sidewalk. Trying to look more at ease than he felt, he averted his eyes from the people sitting at outdoor tables, eating and drinking. He hurried down the hill, focusing on the curve in the road that would shield him from the busy commercial area. He knew there were about two miles to Woods Pond, October Mountain, and freedom. Three years in the wilderness made every house seem like a mansion to him. Three days at Maggie's made him realize there was a big difference in how people kept their homes and lives.

Scanning the houses as he passed, he was more aware of peeling paint; cars and trucks parked with uncut, dying grass around the flat tires; and tree stumps in front yards with flowerpots on them, trying to hide their ugliness. Garbage cans in the front yards competed for attention with other debris, obstructing the pleasantness of each house. Memories of the Stoner house came flooding back. That house of horrors had shared many of these unkempt characteristics. He shifted his thoughts to Maggie. She was as nice as he knew his mother would have been. She was as smart as he knew his mother would have been. She was as pretty as he knew his mother had been. She trusted him, just as he knew his mother would have. He shook his head, wondering why someone like that couldn't be in his life.

Joey looked up and saw Highway 7 looming in the distance. One mile after Highway 7 and he'd be free. They couldn't find him in the wilderness. No one could find him in the wilderness. Joey slowed his pace since the light was red and he didn't want to be standing on the side of the road, waiting for the light to change. He knew the highway had a lot of cops patrolling it. As soon as the light turned green, he quickened his pace and made it to the other side. Almost there. The sidewalk stopped; the path became grass and gravel. Almost safe.

Joey heard a car slowing down behind him. His heart raced. He kept a steady pace and didn't look back. What if it was a cop? He was just hiking. What if the cop wanted an ID? Left it at home. Where was home? Maggie Latham's. What was the address? Didn't know. Game over. He needed a plan: Just run into the woods on the right. October Mountain was close enough to reach before more cops could arrive.

The car pulled alongside Joey, and he heard the window go down. "Need a ride, young man?" an older male asked.

"No, sir. Just going a little further, but thank you for the offer."

"Okay, have a good hike," the driver said as he sped up.

Oh, Lord, just a half mile more. Suzie popped into his mind. What was she doing now? Where was she? Was she all right? He always daydreamed of what she'd be doing. In each dream, she was pretty like he remembered her. She was successful at whatever she was doing. Sometimes she was a student. Sometimes she worked in a business. Whatever she was doing, she missed him and thought about him as much as he thought about her. He liked to pretend he came into her life: they were together, happy, and doing things, like they were when he first arrived at the Stoner house.

Joey looked up and saw the road curve to the right, with the railroad tracks and the footbridge directly ahead. A few more yards, and then freedom. He crossed the railroad tracks and stepped onto the footbridge. The bridge over the Housatonic River is metal, but the parts over land on each side are wooden. Over the years, teenagers have carved their initials, hearts, and 4evers all over the railings. Dirt and mildew have blackened the wood. Joey thought about how his and Suzie's initials would be on here, except for Stoner. What if Stoner wasn't the only reason he had lost Suzie? What if he had never known Suzie? Would he still love her as much as he did? What if his mother, father, and granny hadn't died? Who would he love? Who would have helped Suzie when she needed it? Would he trade his love for Suzie to have his mother, father, and granny back? Did Suzie even think of him?

He ran his hand along the wood. If only he had a knife. Reaching into his pocket, he pulled out a quarter from the change he received at Chu's. Using the edge, he scraped the dirt and mildew until it read "JP + SS = 4ever." He stood back and looked at his handiwork. It wouldn't last long, just until the dirt and mildew came back. Maybe, just maybe, Suzie might come along, see it, and know it was from him. Satisfied, he headed across the bridge and into the forest, staying away from the power line right of way.

Once clear of open space and enveloped by the forest, Joey stopped and breathed deeply, feeling the comforting peace he always felt when alone there. The heightened sight and hearing he had developed over three years of living in the wilderness returned. The increased sensory perception told him he was home. He felt alive, attuned to nature, and at home among the forest's family of creatures: snakes, otters, raccoons, deer, bears, hawks, and other birds. It was as if they knew who he was, accepted him as one of their kind, and respected him, just as he respected them. Not killing a creature to eat was his creed. He'd eat freshly dead animals he came across, but primarily he existed on edible vegetation and berries as well as scavenged food from campers, houses, and dumpsters. It had not been a conscious decision to live as he did. Life had made him a part of the wilderness family. God didn't want him hurting members of his family. He knew that for a fact.

The wilderness gave Joey another joy: the free-flowing randomness of his thoughts. There were many discarded books in each of his hideaways. When in place, he read all the time. As he roamed the forest, he allowed his thoughts to bounce from one subject to another, forming opinions and then refuting those opinions with facts and feelings, then forming others. He liked to pretend he could change a situation he read about, that he was in the setting, saving the day for the characters or mastering a seemingly unsolvable problem. He enjoyed working through problems, sort of like untying the knotted fishing lines he regularly found alongside creeks or in trees overhanging a river, left by frustrated anglers lacking the patience to enjoy both the good times and the bad times in nature. The collection of colorful fishing flies he kept at his main hideaway wasn't for fishing. They were pretty. He liked them for just that reason.

Joey's excitement at being back in the forest, safe from arrest, relaxed him, but he felt different. Unleashing his thoughts usually led to a variety of subjects, but today, instead of bouncing around, analyzing the events of the last three days, marveling at the fact that he was back in the wilderness, safe, and not still in a jail cell, his thoughts riveted on Maggie and the way she was so much like he imagined his mother was. She was so pretty, so nice, so smart. Her smile was beautiful, and when she told the judge he could teach Joey how to drive, and then winked at Joey, it was exactly what his mom would have done. It was as if Maggie had raised him his whole life.

She always looked directly into his eyes when speaking to him. She knew what to do, what to say, and how to make him feel safe and cared for—no, that wasn't it. It was more than safe and cared for. He felt—loved. His granny had loved him and died. His mom and daddy had loved him and died. He tried not to use the word *love*, but there he did. Maggie seemed to love him. Joey's breath caught and he came back to reality. No, no, he didn't mean love.

No, please, God, I didn't mean it. Don't let anything happen to Maggie like what happened to everyone else who's loved me. Please, God, don't.

He kept walking, breathing faster from the rush of negative thinking. He reentered his mental playroom, pushing aside his fears. Again, his thoughts turned to Maggie. This time he wondered about Maggie and the judge. He was an okay guy, but not deserving of Maggie. She was better than anyone else. Joey could live with her. Maybe she would let him if he did the chores right.

*Stop!* he heard the voice of reality scream. You can't live with her, or anyone. If he went back there, they'd find out, and he'd spend the rest of his life in prison, in a small cell, with no trees, animals, or nature. Forget Maggie. Forget the judge. His escape was luck. The wilderness had kept him safe for three years and would do so for many more. Joey continued walking, his mind blank, afraid that reality was right. Luck was the only reason he was free.

He stepped over the fallen rotting trees, saw the blueberry bushes, felt the coolness as he passed under a denser canopy, all the while moving higher and higher. As he walked, his mind started sparking again, thinking of Maggie, the judge, Suzie, the forest, his life, and jail. He could take care of Maggie, do her chores, help fix dinner, talk about books and things happening, protect her. No one would know about the past. It had been three years, and they hadn't asked him anything while he was in jail. They knew who he was, and they knew about his time in foster care, but they had said nothing at all.

*Stop!* It's a trick! the voice shouted again. Do you want to live in a cage? That's where you'll live if they find out what you did. A cage.

He knew he had a good life here, where he was safe. It had worked for over three years. Don't make a mistake, reality's voice shouted, just because a pretty woman who you think is like your mother would have been, smiled at you, treated you like a real person, showed you she loved you, didn't pry into your past, trusted you—and loved you, and loved you, and loved you—Joey heard the forbidden word over and over, keeping cadence with his increasing heartbeat as he climbed October Mountain to one of his hiding places. He reached a wall of boulders. They were scattered and piled like a child's building blocks, pushed upward eons ago by receding ice, sitting helter-skelter on one another with their jagged edges reaching up the side of the mountain. Joey stopped his approach and sat still in a crevice of stones in sight of his hideaway, waiting for the light to fade. Since he had avoided trails and used his regular methods of evasion, he was confident no one had seen him since he entered the forest, but being sure was crucial since this was his most important hideaway in these woods.

At dusk, he left the camouflage and made his way to his hideaway. He marveled at how difficult the vertical climb of forty feet looked, yet how easy it was. His new boots made it even easier to use the jagged boulders as platforms to move higher. The tough part was squeezing into the hideaway and making sure there were no other visitors, particularly rattlesnakes. As soon as his eyes adjusted to the low light, Joey found everything as he had left it. Roaches and spiders scurried away from his presence. He placed his backpack against the outside boulder and took out one piece of beef jerky, a small scoop of peanut butter, and four saltines. He ate sparingly, still full from eating all he wanted for three days. By tomorrow, he'd be hungry. He decided to save the cookies till then and the following two days, one per day. He thought about the fun of baking with Maggie, the two of them taking turns running their fingers around the mixing bowl, and smiled. Then his mind jerked back to the dilemma of Maggie, the judge, the past, and the future. Like a major winter storm, his mind swirled through the facts, want-tos, what-ifs, and reality. He fell asleep, exhausted from the mental exercise of analyzing problems he could not resolve.

Joey's eyes opened when the first light penetrated the gaps between the boulders, just before dawn. This was his favorite time of day. He left his hiding place, foraged for berries, and relieved himself. Upon returning, he sat in the hideaway with his back to the outside boulder.

He reached for one of the books he kept there; looked at the title, *For Whom the Bell Tolls*, and opened it to the turned-down page. Reading usually caused time to speed up, so he concentrated on the story, letting the words transport him into the imaginary world of the writer. Today was different. Joey read a paragraph, and Maggie popped into his mind. Another paragraph, and Suzie popped into his mind. Another paragraph, the judge. Then the jail. Then his mother. The loop was circular, over and over. He couldn't concentrate on his reading. It was going to be a long day.

Hiking to his most important hideaway, deeper in the forest, would pass the time. Better, more interesting books were there. It was fourteen miles away, and the hike would feel good. Joey put his new provisions, except for one unopened pack of jerky, back into his backpack and slipped out of his safe spot. He avoided roads and trails except to cross them after careful observation, and his mind bounced like a ball from one thought to another. He felt content as the issues started clarifying themselves. The blue sky showed light clouds forming. A breeze from the west rustled the leaves. He sensed rain was coming. He heard hikers ahead or behind him.

Finally, he reached the AT and proceeded south, leaving the trail whenever it bent so that he was on and off, able to avoid surprise meetings with other hikers. Along the way, he picked berries for his food stash. Finally, he reached the Becket Mountain area. By the time he reached his hideaway, the tug-of-war among his experiences with Maggie, the judge, and reality had mentally exhausted him. The berries he'd gathered along the way, with some jerky, peanut butter, and saltines, comprised dinner. He looked at this meal, a banquet compared to the past three years, but a pittance compared to the past three days at Maggie's. The contrast was reality itself.

As darkness descended, Joey lay still and meditated into the alpha state. Leaving consciousness, he moved through the troubled area as he saw Ralph Stoner's face with its meanness and cruel laughter. Then he saw Suzie's face and the love, determination, and comfort she gave him. Finally, he reached a scene with a hill and a single tree, and his mother holding him, calmly saying to him, "I love you, dear Joey. I'll always love you and help you. Be strong, dear Joey." She held him in her arms. He looked up at her, and her face morphed into a face that looked like her and Maggie all at the same time. He drifted to sleep and slept all night.

He woke at first light, agitated, uneasy. The humidity was high. Rain during the night had been steady, but not a downpour. The clouds gave way to clear skies. Joey took two empty jars and his backpack, left the hideaway, and went to a lake a quarter mile away. He washed his face, rinsed out his mouth, relieved himself, and filled the jars with lake water through his Katadyn filter. His conflict with reality continued, with reality's voice aggressively announcing the consequences of capture again. The proposed reality, with Maggie at the center, fought back with an explosive reminder of the enjoyment he had felt during the three days earlier in the week. He wandered in a broad circle around the lake and surrounding forest, seeing and enjoying the movement of the birds and small animals as they went about surviving, ever vigilant to the dangers they faced. He moved higher and higher and farther from his hideaway. As storm clouds gathered, he reached his hiding place closest to the Ledges, his favorite site in the forest. The inner conflict continued, with the fear of prison slowly receding and the joy of life with Maggie taking on more concrete terms. He took the stories Granny had told about his mother, and what she would have done with him if she had lived, and inserted an image of Maggie and himself doing those things.

Heavy rain erupted midday Sunday. Joey looked out and knew it would stop by evening. He sat back and relaxed. He had to wait for the rain to stop. He dozed, jerked awake every so often, then settled back. He ate some peanut butter and crackers, built a small fire, and heated water for tea. When it was done, he placed the used tea bag on a rock so it would dry and be usable again, and he read. When the rain stopped, he gathered up his pack and headed out to the Ledges. He felt he was an observer of two gladiators fighting to the death in his mind. The pros and cons, once tilted clearly toward the wilderness, were now more evenly balanced, with the possibility of the horrendous outcome of prison shrinking and the possibility of happiness with Maggie growing.

Climbing by instinct rather than focus, he followed the AT upward, keenly alert to any noise—particularly sounds made by humans. Arriving at the Ledges, he moved off the trail so hikers couldn't see him, but he could see the entire valley with its roads and farms, as well as Livermore Peak across the valley and the Berkshire Hills in the distance. He sat and imagined he lived on one farm, taking care of the livestock, mowing the hay, and tending barnyard animals. Four times hikers, bent over with huge through-hiker packs, moved across the Ledges, barely stopping to enjoy the view. Two of the hikers were talking on cell phones. Joey wondered what the point was in completing a task when the enjoyment was missing.

He realized that this time of day at the Ledges raised the probability that these hikers would spend the night at the Mount Wilcox south shelter. He thought of the potential food supply for easy pickings. The raging gladiator battle between Maggie, the judge, and reality in his head subsided as he thought about the right way to raid the bear box at the shelter. As he worked through the process, his mind diverted to the last meal he had enjoyed with Maggie and her love and caring attitude for him. As the sun reached a point in the western sky where he knew he barely had time to reach his closest hideaway, Joey left the Ledges and turned right, away from the Mount Wilcox south shelter.

§

Cal arrived at Willview just before dark. Weekends with Maggie were always special and invigorating. Maggie's willingness to help with Joey's reentry to society lifted a weight from his shoulders. His only sadness was at the likelihood they wouldn't have a weekend like this past one for quite some time. At least he would see her at the BBC meetings. Catherine was not home. The awards ceremony and dinner would last until at least nine. Time alone was wonderful. He started unpacking his bag.

A cell phone started buzzing. He looked at the one on the table and saw that was not the one. It was the go phone, and a chill coursed through his body as he realized it was Maggie. He fished it from its concealed compartment. "What's the matter?"

"Cal, Joey's gone."

Cal's heart skipped a beat. He sat on the side of the bed. "Gone? Give me the details, please."

"All I know is he's not here. It looks like he left everything but the clothes he had on Friday when I left. He did every chore I had on the list, cleaned all the tools, put them where they belonged, came into the house, took the note and money I left for him, and left me the checklist of chores. Oh, Cal, why? Why did he leave? By the way, he took some of the cookies we baked Thursday night."

"You baked cookies with him Thursday evening?"

"We enjoyed a light dinner and talked. I didn't see any need to stop the conversation just because dinner was over, so I suggested we make cookies."

"What did he say about his situation?" Cal asked, his interest piqued.

"We didn't talk about anything in the past. We talked about his testing at the college. He said he was interested in going to school and graduating. I can't believe how long his fingernails are."

"Yeah, Tuesday Eddie Keogh asked him if he wanted them trimmed. His reply was a sharp no, and he clenched his fists. The hospital report on Hortense showed one eye sliced like a knife cut it. Joey didn't have a knife, just his hands. Those fingernails are a weapon—and a powerful one, at that."

"Cal, what are we going to do? That poor boy needs help. You've got to have David Fogel get his people to find him."

"Maggie, I can't do that. I've got to be careful here. I put him on probation so I could guide his reentry into a regular life. If the police look for an individual who failed probation, when they find him, he'll be a probation violator and will suffer the consequences. Violating probation is a serious issue, whereas the original crime was a misdemeanor. He's got to come back on his own, or I must find him unofficially and try to coax him back. The real question is this: is he back in the wilderness, or is he on the run? If he's in the wilderness, it'll be hard to find him unless he wants to be found. If he's on the run, he'll spiral down out there. He'll hurt somebody, and law enforcement will consider him a real danger. You know what that means. Oh, God, what a disappointment. Let me think it out. I'll come up with a plan in the morning."

"I'm so sorry, Cal. I know what he meant to you. Call me when you can tomorrow. I'll be at the library. Love you."

Maggie hung up, and Cal sat there. He didn't understand. The connection between Joey and him was real. He felt, no, he knew, there was trust between the two of them. His law training took over his mind and a gusher of questions came rapid-fire. Why did Joey bolt at the first opportunity? Why did he prefer the wilderness? Was it possible he was on the streets? No, Cal was confident Joey was back in the wilderness. His arrest took him involuntarily from his safe sanctuary, the wilderness, and that was where he would go back, where he felt safe.

Cal finished unpacking, went downstairs, and fixed a drink. He looked at the time; Catherine would be home in an hour. He sat in the conservatory, watching through the glass walls as the darkness slowly enveloped the landscape. Where could Joey be? Cal sat there quietly, focusing on what needed doing, but always coming back to the question: why does Joey prefer the wilderness to a civilized lifestyle? He knew the answer was the path to uncovering Joey's problems. Cal looked at the clock. He rose, fixed a stiff second drink, and took it up to his room.

# CHAPTER 11

At the courthouse, Cal shut his Bible and slipped it back into the desk drawer. As he stood, he realized he hadn't looked at Josey's photo. Why did he not look at her picture? Was it because she was dead, or because her son had left? Was that chapter of his life finally closed? Had she felt the same way he felt now when he rejected her? After putting on his robe, he took an envelope from his jacket pocket and went to Betsy's desk.

"Betsy, Deputy Fogel is going to come by and pick this up," Cal said, handing her the sealed envelope. "I'm expecting a call from Dr. Rebecca Lang at the college. If she calls, find out the best time during court recess to call her back."

"Yes, sir."

Cal took his seat on the dais and requested the bailiff begin calling the docket. He moved through the cases with speed and flat justice. Cal didn't search for the spirit or hidden extenuating circumstances as he normally did. With only four more cases until lunch, he looked up from the next case file. A chill moved through his body as the back door of the nearly empty courtroom opened slightly and a young man eased in. The boy slipped into the last pew.

Cal covered his microphone with his hand and said, "Bailiff, hold the next case. Call Joseph H. Paschal to the bar, please."

"Yes, sir. Joseph H. Paschal, approach the bench!" the bailiff shouted to the courtroom.

Joey rose from his seat and timidly approached the railing separating the spectators from the judge and court officials.

"Come inside the gate, Joseph," Cal said. "Glad to see you. What are you doing here?"

"Sir, uh, Your Honor, you told me I was to report to the court every Monday morning," Joey said.

"So, I did. Bailiff, please have a deputy escort Mr. Paschal to the probation office and get him scheduled to report to an officer on Mondays."

"Yes, sir," the bailiff said, motioning for a deputy to come forward. "Mr. Paschal, please accompany the deputy."

"Yes, sir," Joey said, moving toward the deputy.

"Mr. Paschal," Cal said.

Joey turned and walked back toward the dais.

"Does Ms. Latham know you're back?"

"No, sir. Miss Maggie—Ms. Latham wasn't home when I returned," Joey said, looking down.

"Well, young man, a word to the wise: as soon as you're set with the probation office, which shouldn't take more than ten minutes, I'd advise you to go directly to the library and brighten up the lead librarian's day."

Grinning, Joey said, "Yes, sir, Your Honor. I'll do that, sir."

"Then come back to my office upstairs by twelve thirty. Do you have any lunch money?"

"Yes, sir. I still have some of the money Maggie gave me for chores last Friday."

"Okay, get going. Bailiff, call the next case," Cal said, with more lilt in his voice.

Cal reached his office shortly before noon, and Betsy handed him his phone messages and the case files for the afternoon docket.

"Dr. Lang just hung up, Your Honor," she said.

"Try to get her on the line now. If so, put her through to me," Cal said before taking the materials from her and entering his office.

Not a minute later, Betsy buzzed. "Rebecca Lang, line two."

Cal picked up his phone and hit the blinking button. "Good morning, Dr. Lang. Thank you for calling me about Mr. Paschal's testing," he said, clearing the center of his desk. He pulled out a yellow legal pad and a pencil and wrote JOEY SCHOOL. "Please give me your assessment."

"Good morning, Your Honor. Mr. Paschal is an interesting case. He is a pleasant young man who lacks basic social skills. I don't know what environment he has lived in for the past several years, but he has above-average native intelligence. Besides the normal battery of psychological tests, I gave him the GED test just to see how much remedial work needed to be done."

"Really? How close did he come to passing?"

"He passed. He actually achieved a passing level."

Cal wrote GED—PASSED. "He passed. With what grade?"

"There's no grade, just pass or fail. In the soft subjects, such as reasoning and social studies, he did well. Actually, more than well. He told me he has read a lot during his last three years. His math and science are weak. He needs help with math; he only received the minimum score to pass. Science was a little better, so my suggestion is getting him help in the areas of algebra and data statistics. One tutor can cover both."

"What grade do you recommend for him in high school?"

"None. He won't do well in a high school environment. It's too structured. He passed the GED. My recommendation, and I told this to President Graham last Friday, is for him to be placed in summer school now, with a light course load of English 101 and remedial Math 99. In addition, I have a student, Issie, a junior math major, who's very good as a tutor. I believe she's the right tutor for Mr. Paschal. She can do it weekly through the summer. By the end of the summer session, I'm confident Mr. Paschal will be up to speed in math."

Cal wrote COLLEGE. "Slow down, Dr. Lang. Do you really believe Joey, Mr. Paschal, can handle college? That seems like a big step academically to me. He's not been in a classroom for three years."

"Where's he been, if not in class?" Rebecca asked, her interest piqued. She had been told to test him like any of the many "special" cases the college has in its Hand Up Program.

"You don't know?" Cal asked. "I thought President Graham filled you in on Joey."

"No, sir, he didn't."

"You should know, but it's confidential. Joey has been living in the wilderness for the last three and a half years, cut off from much human contact, surviving on his wits."

"Shit! Excuse me, Your Honor."

"No need to apologize. I had the same reaction. Now, you say you told President Graham that Joey should be admitted to college this summer. What did he say?"

"He said he'd need to talk to you," Rebecca said. Cal shuffled the phone message slips, and there it was, one from Taylor. "From what you just told me, I believe the summer session is best for Mr. Paschal, Joey, because the class sizes are smaller than in the fall, there's less structure, and a light schedule will allow him plenty of time for homework, getting familiar with the campus, and learning how to survive in the community of students and faculty. There is an alternative, of course. He can go directly into the workforce, but I believe that offers less opportunity for success than placing him in a loosely structured social environment such as college."

"Why is that?"

"You said he has been cut off from social development for at least three years. For an unskilled individual, a work environment can be brutal, particularly in the beginning. There is a greater risk he would fail and become discouraged while adjusting to his new environment and the need to learn a skill in a short time. In what I'm proposing, he would have a support group: me, the tutor, the professors, and, to a limited extent, the students he interacts with. It's your decision, but that's my opinion."

Cal wrote START NOW. "That makes sense. Okay, if you will, please line up the tutor. What is her name again?"

"Isabella Constanti. We call her Issie."

Cal wrote TUTOR—CONSTANTI. "Okay, you line up Issie to tutor Joey. If you don't mind, will you introduce the two of them? I suspect Joey will be shy about the arrangement. If you explain the need, he'll probably be fine. Call here to my assistant, Betsy Kimberly, and tell her how much the tutoring services will cost and where to send Ms. Constanti's check. Have classes already started?"

"Yes, sir, they started today."

"Okay, Joey won't be too far behind. We'll throw him into the situation and see if he sinks or swims."

"Judge, my guess is he'll swim in this academic environment. He's really a fine young man. He just needs guidance and the right amount of structure—but not too much."

Cal wrote JOEY SINK/SWIM and circled SWIM. "Thank you, Dr. Lang. I'll let you go to lunch now. Have a pleasant afternoon," he said, ending the conversation. He'd heard enough. He pushed the intercom button. "Betsy, first, Dr. Lang is going to call you and give you information about a tutor for Mr. Paschal. I believe the young lady's name is Constanti. By the way, this expense is personal, so take it from my personal checkbook. Second, get me President Graham over at the college.

"Yes, sir. Got it."

A few minutes later, Cal answered the buzz and said, "Hello, Taylor. Looking forward to seeing you at the BBC meeting tomorrow night."

"Yes. You calling about the Paschal boy? Becky said she was going to tell you she recommends he start on a trial basis in summer school. I've looked over the tests, including the GED. To be honest, Cal, his success is iffy. There's no question he's intelligent, but the molding of that intelligence has been spotty, which is understandable with what you told me about the last three-plus years."

"Taylor, will you let him try?"

"What if he fails, Cal? A failure could really do damage to him psychologically. Are you prepared for that?"

"Frankly, I don't know. There's a reason he lived in the wilderness for three years, and we don't know what it is. I'll tell you something else, just for your ears. He went back to the wilderness sometime last weekend. I think he went back to stay, but something, and I'm not sure what that something is, brought him back to the community. In my judgment, he needs a chance. As I told Dr. Lang, we just need to throw him in and see if he sinks or swims."

"Okay, he's in. Can you get him over here this afternoon? If so, have him report to Becky's office. I'll have an intern meet him there with the paperwork, help him get registered, show him around campus, and help him find the bookstore. It's an experiment. Let's hope for the best."

"Thanks, Taylor. By the way, Dr. Lang thinks he'll swim. Send the bill for fees and tuition to Betsy. She'll send a check."

"Not necessary, Cal. This fits our Hand Up Program. We'll cover the cost from the endowment."

"Thank you, Taylor, but no. This is my expense. The college is taking a chance, and I appreciate it. Joey will pay full freight, end of discussion."

"You're the judge. Try to have him here at two."

"He'll be there. See you tomorrow evening. It's in your personal conference room, isn't it?"

"Yup."

Cal sat back, retrieved the Bible, laid it on top of his desk, and reached into the back of the drawer to take out an envelope. He removed three hundred dollars, then replaced the envelope and the Bible and shut the drawer. Betsy buzzed and said Joey was outside. "Send him in," Cal said, then added, "Ask the sheriff to get a plain-clothes deputy in an unmarked car to take Mr. Paschal to the college at a quarter to two. Let me know when the deputy is ready, and I'll send Joey downstairs."

Joey walked into his future with a smile on his face, as well as lipstick on his forehead.

"Go into the bathroom and wipe that lipstick off your face, then come back here," Cal said, trying to keep a straight face. "You have a busy afternoon."

# CHAPTER 12

Driving, Maggie understood this was one day that made life worthwhile. Another successful shepherding of a heartbreaking victim. Four years ago, Rachael had been in a terrible place. Now, she was graduating with honors and a strong future. Maggie felt a parent's pride in watching a daughter go confidently into the world. This would be fourteen out of the nest, with five still being tenderly nurtured. They were all the daughters she couldn't have. Her eyes burned as she thought of what they had taken from her when she was young. She breathed deeply. Only happiness today, she told herself.

She turned the corner of Elm Street, reached up, and punched the garage door opener. The garage door rose and she eased into the space. She punched the button again and sat while the door descended. Only then did she unlock the Outback. She collected her handbag and the Dom Perignon, then headed to the trellis walkway.

Rachael was waiting in the kitchen with the storm door open and a big smile on her face.

"How's the soon-to-be honor graduate this evening?" Maggie asked as she stepped up on the porch and gave her a hug.

"Excited. I can't believe it's only a few weeks away." The two women moved into the kitchen.

"Something smells good," Maggie said.

"Nothing fancy, but I wanted to fix something special. I didn't get the honor of preparing a meal for the boss often."

"Oh, please. I'm not the boss. We're good friends."

"Our first course will be kale salad with bleu cheese, dried cranberries, chopped walnuts, and just a drizzle of lemon olive oil, paired with a Chablis."

"Good choice. Go on," Maggie said, leaning against the center island with her arms crossed and smiling.

"The main course will be rack of lamb, English mint jelly, white asparagus, and fingerling potatoes, paired with Ridge Monte Bello."

"Wonderful."

"Yeah, the Monte Bello is out of this world," Rachael said. "For dessert, we're going to have cheeses, fruit, almonds, walnuts, and cashews. We'll serve the champagne you brought."

"Outstanding."

"Everything is ready but the lamb. I'm slow-cooking it to medium, so we have fifteen minutes. Let's go to the living room and have a drink."

Maggie walked through the dining room and saw the table set with fine porcelain from Hungary, antique hand-blown stemware, and sterling silverware. A crystal bowl of freshly cut flowers rounded out the table setting. In the living room, she sat on the sofa and placed her handbag on the floor by her feet. A few peanuts and crisp crackers sat in a porcelain serving dish on the coffee table. Two embroidered linen napkins rested next to it.

"Wild Turkey Rare Breed on the rocks with a splash still the drink of choice?" Rachael asked.

"Wonderful. You are certainly an accomplished hostess."

"I've learned a lot about being a hostess in these past four years," Rachael said, handing Maggie her drink.

"Still graduating in the top five percent of your class?"

"Actually, it'll be the top three."

"Well, here's to the latest wonder woman, about to unleash herself on the world," Maggie said, holding up her glass to Rachael. Rachael crinkled her nose and touched glasses with Maggie. They both took a sip.

"It's hard to believe, isn't it?" Rachael said, her mood changing. She looked into Maggie's eyes, blinking rapidly as she started tearing up. "I can't ever thank you for what you've done."

"Easy, kiddo. You did it all yourself."

"I'd either be dead or still in the gutter if you hadn't picked me up and showed me it wasn't my fault, and I could be what I wanted to be. That you can't deny." Rachael leaned over and kissed Maggie on the cheek. "I won't ever forget. Remember what you used to drum into my head those early weeks when I was struggling?"

"I remember," Maggie said, reaching for her hand.

"'Successful people make a habit of doing the things failures don't want to do.' What are the things failures don't want to do? Just fill in the blanks with the hard things to do in any situation. Over and over, you showed me how easy it was to be successful if I remembered that fact. Now, I'm living proof. You helped me when I stumbled, never condemning, always understanding. Showing me God gave me two assets: my physical beauty and my brains. You showed me how to be a lady, how to turn my assets into strengths instead of weaknesses, how not to be crushed by the taboos men created to keep women down. You helped me understand I deserve all of this if I have self-respect and like myself." Rachael waved her arms around her and looked around the room. "You set up my tutoring clients and taught me how to have relationships with men without being dependent on or dominated by them."

"Thank you, Rachael, but that's the past. Let's talk about the future. What are your plans?"

"As I told you, a new tech start-up has offered me a job in Texas. Next week, on Tuesday evening, I'm leaving on the late direct flight from JFK to Austin. If everything is like they've said, I'm going to accept the job."

"Where are you staying in Austin?"

Rachael, grinning, said, "I've booked a junior suite at the Four Seasons. I've even scheduled a facial, massage, and a mani-pedi for the Fourth of July."

"Besides the job, will you have time for anything else?"

"Yeah, the firm's HR person is picking me up on Wednesday morning, and I expect I'll be finished by early afternoon. The hotel has arranged a rental car—Camaro convertible, no less—from then until Sunday, when I leave. I've looked online at apartments near work, and also in the part of Austin where all the art galleries and nightlife are. Wednesday afternoon I want to open a bank account. I'll spend Friday and Saturday apartment hunting and poking around."

"You'll need a brokerage account," Maggie said.

"Yeah. I can do both Wednesday afternoon."

"You might have to reverse those procedures. The bank and brokerage firm will require a street address before they open an account."

"Damn, I didn't realize that. No problem. I can search Wednesday afternoon and think about my choices Thursday while getting beautiful and pampered, then sign a lease Friday morning. I'll open the bank and brokerage accounts that afternoon. Yeah, that'll work. What would I do without you?" Rachael said.

"You'll be fine. Are you going to keep your present email account?"

"Should I?"

"Isn't it the UK account we set up in the beginning? It's your decision, but consider changing it and the provider. None of your tutoring clients have it, do they?"

"Oh, my God, no. They don't even know my cell number."

"Smart girl. When you open the bank and brokerage accounts, tell them you don't want paper confirmations or statements, that you want everything online, and give them a new email, one that won't connect you back here. You should get a new cell from another carrier and end the current number." Maggie reached down and took an envelope from her purse. "Here are two certified bank checks, made payable to you, to deposit in your new accounts. The one for five thousand is to go into your bank account, to help with some of the expenses of setting up your new home. The one for three thousand is to open the brokerage account. Make sure you go into the local office of a discount brokerage firm and sit down with someone to open the account. Tell them the truth, that you're just moving to Austin, starting a new job, and want to invest. Make sure you point out to both the bank and the broker that these are bank checks, and they shouldn't put a hold on the funds. Get a book of counter checks for the bank account. Oh, I almost forgot—the brokerage firm will offer you a debit card on the account. Tell them you don't want a debit card but will take checks. Do you still have the credit card?"

"Yes, but it has a low limit."

"That's fine. Are you going to keep banking with the bank you use now?"

"No, I don't want to do that."

"Smart girl. You may ask the HR people what bank your new firm uses and get a referral to the officer who handles the firm's business. That will smooth the way for you. After you deposit your first paycheck, request a higher card limit or switch to the card service used by the bank. If you do that, cancel the current card once you have the new one. A month later, apply for an American Express Platinum card. Then you'll be set. A month after moving, when the post office has your home address in their system, go open a post office box, not the smallest or the largest, but one where magazines can lie flat in case you travel with your job. A sure way to get broken into is to have mail stacking up at your apartment."

"Yes, good idea."

"One last thing. In late November, you'll receive a letter from a lawyer in New York, saying your mother's maiden cousin has died and left you some investments. Take the letter to the brokerage firm and ask the person who helped you open the account to tell you how to give wire instructions to the lawyer for sending your inheritance. Don't give him the letter. Ask for the instructions so you can tell the lawyer. I already know what to do. All I need is the brokerage DTC number, your account number, and the precise account title. You're helping the broker understand why this money is being transferred. Make sense?"

"Yes."

"When we began this journey together, I told you there would be a hundred thousand for you when you graduated. I was wrong. With your efforts and luck in the markets, you'll have a hundred and fifty thousand transferred to you in November."

"I—I can't believe it. My friends are graduating in debt and I've got this kind of money."

"Remember, from your mother's maiden cousin. The portfolio will be common stocks, preferred stocks, bonds, and money market funds. It's yours to do with what you want, but I urge you to leave it alone so it can continue to grow. Compounding of wealth is the key to independence."

"I don't know what to do with money. Will the broker help me?"

"Absolutely not. They're taught that investing is a buy and sell game. It's not, if you want to build wealth. With the letter from the lawyer—you understand, don't you, that there isn't really a lawyer?"

"Yes, it's from you, right?"

"Yes. Anyway, with the letter will be a small, easy-to-read, book entitled *FOR WHAT IT'S WORTH,* which is a set of rules for investing and your financial life in general. They're simple and will work at any time in the future, just as they have in the past. Follow them. It'll be easy to do if you don't get caught up in the garbage you see and hear from others who think they know."

"Fantastic, rules for success, just like what got me here." A beeping appliance sang in the kitchen. Rachael turned her glass up and finished her drink.

Maggie did the same. "Now, let's enjoy and celebrate your pending new life with a wonderful dinner," she said, taking Rachael by the hand.

# CHAPTER 13

"Your honor," Betsy said, coming into Cal's office after Joey left, "Mr. Soto Junior called. He wanted to know where the two of you are going to meet this afternoon."

"Thank God he called," Cal said. "It slipped my mind. Call him back and tell him to meet me at the AT parking lot where the trail crosses I-90. See if four thirty is still good for him. If not, find out when. After that would be good for me."

"Yes, sir."

Cal sat back in his chair. He realized the world's life cycle marched on. Josey gave way to Joey, and Javier Soto died and his son stepped into his shoes. He was confident the son was as true and strong as the father. He refocused and prepared for a light afternoon court calendar.

§

Cal, picking up the litter and rearranging the messages on the AT bulletin board, was waiting for Javier when he arrived in the parking area.

"Good afternoon, Javier," Cal said, extending his hand.

"Good afternoon, sir," Javier responded. He was in his early thirties, Hispanic, a big man, close to six feet, with a heavy, muscular build. The combination gave him a commanding appearance. Cal knew that Junior, as everyone who knew the family called him, was smart and had the same strong work ethic as his father and mother. Junior had played football in high school and received scholarships to several small colleges, but instead he worked with his father in their lawn and nursery business. Twenty years ago, Javier Sr. had bought fifteen acres of poor soil land just out of town and moved the family into a single-wide trailer on the land. After five years of struggling to succeed, he had come to Cal, who was practicing law, and asked for help. He had trusted a wealthy client, and the client had refused to pay for the services and materials after the job was complete. Javier was in a cash crunch, unable to meet the obligations he had incurred while doing the job.

Cal had called the bank and, unbeknownst to Javier Sr., arranged a loan with its president and secretly guaranteed repayment. Cal then went after the client in court, received a judgment against him, and forced the client to pay. Javier learned a valuable business lesson and made a lifelong friend.

Cal looked at Junior and saw the same determination, honesty, and fearlessness his father had shown. "Let's hike up to the spillway, and I'll fill you in on the BBC," Cal said, using the short name of the Berkshire Book Club.

When they arrived, Cal used the rushing water as background noise, drowning out their conversation from anyone listening. "Sit here next to the spillway," he instructed.

"Yes, sir," Junior said.

"Junior, how's your mom doing?"

"Staying busy, sir. That's always her way of handling difficult situations."

"How long were they married?"

"Fifty-three years. They were married when they were fourteen, back in Mexico, long before my dad made the trip across the border. Both used to say God made them for each other. She misses him, but when I ask her about it, she always says she doesn't regret that their time together is over; she just remembers and is thankful for the time they had together."

"Give her my regards. Your dad and mom were and are good friends of mine. Did your dad say much about the BBC?"

"He told me I was his successor in the group. After every meeting, he would give me an update about what was discussed, nothing specific."

"I'll fill you in. As you know, we've called a meeting tomorrow night. Will you be there?"

"Yes, sir. One thing my dad impressed on me was the importance of the BBC to the community, and his, now my, obligation to uphold the purposes of the organization."

"Your dad was one of the five original members. For you to under-stand your role, I need to give you some background on the origins of the BBC. Have you ever heard of a Bizango?"

"No, sir."

"A Bizango is a secret society in Haiti. There are several of them. They evolved from the maroons, runaway slaves in the 1700s living in the hills of Haiti, and they're the glue that holds the countryside together. Each has its own sphere of influence and territory. They are vodun societies with an emperor and queen. A fine man, a professor at BC by the name of Kawani Laigwenak intimately knew these societies. He was born in Haiti in the early 1900s. His mother was the daughter of a Bizango emperor and queen. Kawani said his mother was a twelve-year-old virgin when the queen selected a young French diplomat, serving in Port-au-Prince as an embassy attaché, to couple with her daughter until she conceived.

"The queen used her influence to have the diplomat returned to France, where he had a long and successful career in the foreign service, returning every so often to Haiti to see his son and lover. When Kawani was ten, they sent him to private school in France. Upon graduating from secondary school, he entered Oxford to study economics and literature. While there, he became interested in the study of African tribal economics. The simplicity and complexity of tribal society impressed him. He went to West Africa on a fellowship to see where his mother's family originated. He started along the Slave Coast, where the Efik of Old Calabar, a tribe along the Niger River, ruled. They gathered slaves from the interior on the coast of West Africa.

"It was here he first learned about the secret societies of the various African tribes. The Efik had chiefs, but the real power rested with the Egbo, or leopard society. This was his first encounter with male hierarchical societies where secret leadership decided important community issues. He ended up wandering for a year, traveling throughout sub-Saharan Africa, then across the middle of the continent, finding and learning about other tribal secret societies. When he got to the Maasai area, he stayed and absorbed much of their culture, including their twelve-man leadership group, and he adopted his name, Kawani Laigwenak. *Laigwenak* means "leadership" in Maasai. He left Africa, returned home to Haiti, and immersed himself in the rural secret societies dominating Haitian culture. His family's position in their Bizango gave him deeper access to the other Bizango structure and leadership. He left Haiti and came to the United States. He finished his education, receiving a PhD in African studies. Kawani came here to the college as a young professor and chose to stay even though he could have gone to Boston or some other large city to teach at a prestigious university when African studies became the rage.

"A little over fifteen years ago, our community, like so many across America, was fraying around the fringes. Crime was prevalent, drugs were rampant on campus and in town, and the public officials were incompetent or less than honest, losing citizens' respect. I was a young attorney, only a few years out of law school, working for my father-in-law's large law firm. Pro bono work was a portion of my practice, helping those who needed legal advice but couldn't afford it. Kawani came to me when a black boy, still in high school, stole two loaves of bread off a delivery truck. The boy was desperate. His mother was raising three children while his father was in and out of jail for drunkenness. Kawani didn't want the boy's life ruined because he helped feed his family. I had the charges dropped, and Kawani paid for the two loaves of bread. Using his contacts, he found a part-time job for the boy. That was the beginning of the BBC.

"Kawani looked around, using the eyes of an African and Bizango royalty, and saw the lack of true leadership in the community. The political and business establishment, built on European cultural values, focused on itself and its wants. He pulled together five original members, meeting every month, for a discussion focused on local issues. When a problem arose, the group requested help from others. That person became a member of the BBC, and today the members come from all walks of life in the community, able to observe all aspects and levels of society. The group does not seek publicity. As with the Bizango and African secret societies, we go to great lengths to remain hidden. By remaining private, we can use our resources to improve the community and stop harmful activities without the artificial restrictions that hamper society today, which distort the constitution, help criminals, and hinder law-abiding citizens.

"The number of members, nineteen, has been the same since the third year. Just as it is in the Maasai tribe, the first important duty of a new BBC member is to identify a successor when he or she can no longer serve. I expect you to give me a name tomorrow night in a sealed envelope. As time goes on, you may find you change your mind. That's fine. Just bring a name in another sealed envelope and ask for it to replace the first. We shred the first without opening it. Just as your father did, slowly nurture your successor in the obligation and responsibility of community citizenship. I've given you a lot of information so far. Questions?"

"Yes, sir. Dad never talked in detail; he just said the BBC was the genuine power in the community because they were outside the establishment. What did he mean, and what does the BBC do?"

"The BBC is not a nanny organization. It has no interest in trying to teach strict behavior or morals based on one religious belief or another. If domestic violence comes to our attention, there's a process we use to mitigate the problem. In addition, we scan the community and notice situations that are not examples of good citizenship. These may involve individuals or organizations hiding behind the law to take advantage of law-abiding citizens. Over the last two hundred and thirty plus years, the United States Constitution and Bill of Rights have morphed into a shield for evil and criminals rather than for the protection of law-abiding citizens. That's not right. The Constitution and Bill of Rights were written to protect citizens who respect the law and live within the law.

"Choosing to live in America under these two precious documents gives rights, yes, but also obligations. Some people ignore the obligation part of the equation. People preying on the community and others, committing crimes or acts leading to an unsafe community, should not have the Constitution to shield them from justice. A whole segment of society uses the Constitution unfairly. The BBC doesn't take the place of the police or the courts. We focus on situations we see that the police and courts can't address because of manipulation of the law by those who serve the criminal element. While we can't do anything about it in the country as a whole, we can in this community, and we do. The BBC members are the eyes and ears of the community. You'll see just how broad our reach is as you get to know the members."

"I see. Are there minutes I can read to catch up with what's going on?"

"No, Junior, there are no written records, just oral reporting and decision-making. There's no structure, either. There are nineteen equal citizens, both men and women, from all walks of life and levels of society, which is a change from the usual Haitian and African models, where the leadership is male dominated. There was another point Kawani was emphatic about. He felt the term *African American* was a backhanded insult toward every American of African heritage. He felt if a person was an American, the color of the person's skin made no difference. He felt that some well-meaning individuals and others segregating Americans of African heritage into a more specific group for any reason were really racists who, with smiles on their faces, wanted to make Americans of African heritage realize they were not the same as other Americans.

"The BBC meeting itself will be different from any other meeting you may have attended. There are nineteen chairs in a circle. At the foot of the circle is the speaker's chair. At every meeting, if a member has a subject to discuss, tell the group about, or ask for guidance or help on, the person sits in this chair or close to it. I sit in the last chair, immediately to the right of the speaker's chair. This was where Kawani sat before he died. It is the place unresolved issues come to rest, for either assignment or settlement. Any action taken or proposed by the BBC must be unanimous. Meetings rarely last more than ninety minutes. By the way, everyone is on a first-name basis only, no sir or madam. Do you want me to introduce you as Javier or Junior?"

"Junior, sir. I could never be Javier. He was bigger than life itself," Junior said, folding his arms across his chest.

"Yes, he was, but he was confident you were going to fulfill your dreams and, in doing so, bring even more respect and admiration to your family."

"Thank you, sir. He valued your friendship."

"Okay, that's it. Welcome to the BBC. Don't worry about your position. You'll be fine. Just absorb, and if you believe you can help in a situation, please do so." The light was fading as they made their way down to their cars. "Give your mother a hug for me," Cal said, shaking Junior's hand.

§

On the way home, Cal called Maggie. "How's your star boarder?"

"He's excited. He starts classes tomorrow. Dr. Lang and her tutor have convinced Joey he can fit in and do outstanding work. He's riding my bike to school, but he really needs to know how to drive. Neither of us can teach him tomorrow, but I'm available starting Wednesday, if you're going to shirk your duties as his probation counselor," she said with a mocking lilt.

"Sure. I assume we can use the Wrangler?"

"Yes, Joey can use it when working and going to school. Cal, do you think he'll do well tomorrow?" Maggie's tone changed to that of a worried parent.

"I hope so," Cal responded in the same tone. "My plan is to spend time on the weekends supervising his community service and trying to give him the moral support and guidance he needs to make the transition. We'll just have to see."

"We're having dinner in thirty minutes. Shall I set another place?"

"I'd like to say yes, but I can't. I just finished briefing Junior Soto on the BBC. You know he's taking his dad's seat in the circle."

"No, I didn't know who Javier selected, but it makes sense. Junior has really made a difference in their business and in the Hispanic community."

"I love you. Oh, by the way, try not to kiss Joey on the forehead every day, or else he'll get a reputation as a ladies' man."

"Sounds to me like the judge is jealous of his judicial charge. You, too. The meeting should be interesting. Bye."

# CHAPTER 14

Catherine White-Callaway, in her conservatory, sat at a table adorned with an Irish linen lace tablecloth, lace napkins, crystal stemware, and fine china bearing the White family crest, specially made for her grandfather over one hundred years ago. The heavy sterling silverware, also bearing the family crest, had been custom-made in Philadelphia in the late nineteenth century. The centerpiece came from her own garden and was arranged by her this morning. Catherine was pleased. Every aspect of the table was perfect, right down to the unique bird place-card holders.

The five guests and Catherine were comfortable in their Lilly Pulitzer dresses, with each woman wearing her best diamond tennis bracelet, engagement and wedding rings, and a choker length of pearls. The six tan bodies, coiffured salon-provided blond hair, and thin waists spoke volumes about belonging to this level of community engagement. Catherine, however, was the only one who had the latest Pulitzer design courier-delivered from New York's Madison Avenue for the occasion. The colors were rich and stressed her blue eyes. Catherine's menu of lobster salad on butter crunch lettuce paired with a chilled Chateau Rieussec "R" de Rieussec, followed by a frozen lemon bar, set the tone for lively conversation. As Ella cleared the table, Catherine smiled and silenced the group by tapping her wineglass with her fork.

"All right, ladies, let's discuss where we are in the preparations for the Mount Greylock Winter Drive. Mildred, why don't you start with a report on your venue search."

"Yes, Madam Chair—and, I will add, ladies' club champion in tennis, golf, and bridge. It was sneaky of you to partner with John Emerson rather than your gorgeous judicial boy toy. We want to know if the relationship with John is no-trump or love."

The ladies giggled.

"Well, I'm surprised you don't want to know if either of us had a hole in one," Catherine retorted. The room reverberated with peals of laughter. "Now, Mildred, if you're through collecting gossip, are we going to have a location for the Winter Drive?"

"Yes, Madam Chair, thanks to you, we are. I signed a lease on the Pittsfield Municipal Auditorium for the third Saturday in December. The space is larger than last year's ballroom, so we'll be able to have more silent auction items, a larger live auction event, and plenty of room for dancing."

"Wonderful. I knew you were the right person to handle that project. Well done. See me before leaving, and I'll give you a check for the deposit."

Mildred beamed. "No need for a deposit since I told Carl Simon you were the chair of the event."

"How kind of him. I'll drop him a note of thanks." Catherine made a note in her Moleskine. "Now, Earlene, how are the silent auction items coming along?"

"Wonderful, Madam Chair. We have contacted last year's donors, and they have recommitted for this year. We're now canvassing the other businesses and professionals who have not taken part in the past."

"Excellent. It warms my heart that we're this far along this early. Keep up the excellent work. With the larger space, we'll have room. Please get me the contact person, address, and item name for each of the donors. I'll write personal notes to each. If you run into any resistance from potential new donors, please don't hesitate to use my name or ask me to call them. Cal will call, if it comes to that."

"Will do."

"Kathy, fill us in on the live auction."

"Madam Chair, we have exceeded our live items quota. Publicity will be very important. I've been able to secure three nineteenth-century oil paintings depicting the Berkshires. While they don't have a signature, each has the date 1888 on the back stretcher. We believe the artist is local but don't know for sure. They're excellent oil-on-canvas scenes. Each could go for ten thousand dollars or more. In addition, we have the same super trips for skiing out west, sunning in Florida, and spending a week in New York City. I'm working on attaining the use of an apartment in the heart of London during the height of the theater season. I'll let you know if I'm successful."

"Exciting. Why don't you bring the oils by here and let me see them? I can always call my dealer in New York for him to research. I'm impressed. Margaret, fill us in on the entertainment."

"Madam Chair, my committee has narrowed the selection down to two choices. Last year the Eddie Bowen Dance Band played. We can get them again this year; however, it's the consensus of the committee that we need to find a band more attuned to the younger crowd. Last year, some guests left early, before the live auction. We think a livelier band will keep them on the dance floor. The committee is going next Friday evening to listen to Jose and the Chili Peppers."

"The Chili Peppers?"

"No, it's not a mariachi band, I promise. It's a mix of 1940s dance band music; line dancing, which is all the rage; and rock and roll dance tunes, both slow and fast. If they're reasonable and as good as billed, we'll go with them."

"Sounds good. A livelier band makes sense. See if you can get a CD of their music. Sarah may want to use it in her publicity for ticket sales. What do you think, Sarah?"

"Great idea, Madam Chair. Ticket sales start in one month. I've lined up promo spots on all the radio stations to run twice a week, starting in the fall during drive time. We'll be appearing on the regional television stations on their local-interest talk shows. The two weeks before the event, we'll be on the six o'clock local news programs as a news spot, highlighting the auction items. A new band will give us another publicity angle. We're on track with our preparations."

"What an outstanding group of committee heads! Let's meet in four weeks to have another update. Everyone comfortable meeting here for lunch again?"

They nodded their assent.

"Wonderful. Now that lunch and business are concluded, I'll have Ella bring out a rosé and some cheese and crackers. Who wants to start with the latest juicy news?"

"I will," said Earlene. "You won't believe what I heard about the couple who bought the Ledbetter Mansion."

# CHAPTER 15

The Berkshire Book Club members gathered in the Berkshire College president's private conference room. The chairs were arranged in a circle, with the speaker's chair at the bottom. As members arrived, they took seats in the circle according to their interest in being on the agenda. Cal motioned for Junior to sit by him. Without any fanfare, when the seats were full, Bell Edwards, the speaker's chair occupant, the physician in charge of the emergency room at the hospital, looked at Cal.

Cal nodded and said, "Good evening, everyone. Before we begin with the substance of our meeting, I want to introduce Javier Soto Junior. He's the designated second to his father, Javier Soto Senior. He prefers to go by Junior out of respect for his father. Now, this called meeting of the BBC is to put on the table knowledge of a rash of drug overdoses in the community. I'll turn the discussion over to Bell," he said, turning to him.

"Hello, everyone. About two thirds of the overdoses we're seeing in the ER are coming from the college, and the rest from young people in the service community who may be in contact with the college kids. Mostly, the drug problem is meth or ecstasy," Bell began.

"Sorry to interrupt," said Rick Branson, a selectman and owner of an auto parts store and junkyard. "What percentage?"

"That's okay, Rick," Bell said. "About ninety percent from these two drugs. We believe the drugs are coming from a single supplier."

"What makes you think that?" asked David Fogel, the deputy sheriff.

"Two different victims had a pill with them they were planning to take later or had just bought along with the one they took. We did a quick chemical analysis at the hospital to see what we were dealing with, and both chemical compositions matched exactly."

There was quiet in the room. Wan Chu, the grocery store owner, spoke up. "Do you have any idea where the students are getting this stuff?"

Bell said, "One of my weekend nurses is young and attended BC. I sent her in to talk with some of the female patients. All of them said they got the drug while partying with the soccer team. That doesn't mean it's a team member; it just means someone who hangs out with the team is dealing."

"What do you think we should do?" asked Geri Sparks, the owner of Berkshire Pest Control.

"That's above my pay grade. It's important we get it stopped because the incidents are happening with more frequency. We're lucky no one has died yet."

"Perhaps we can put the team members under surveillance to see what happens," David Fogel offered. "Bell, I'll need some names of victims. I could also insert an undercover officer in the college to see what she can find out."

"She," Geri interjected. "Isn't it dangerous? What if the girls are being tricked into taking the drug or don't even know they've taken it? Both drugs heighten sexual pleasure, right? Maybe their dates were trying to lower their resistance. Your officer could find herself in trouble."

"Geri, the officer I have in mind is street-wise, and this situation doesn't even come close to the danger she's faced in the past. I'd worry about some kid who tried to play her for a fool. I'll have a report back at our next meeting, as well as a suggested resolution. Bell, okay if I call you tomorrow?"

The meeting proceeded, with each member either giving an update on an issue raised in the past or bringing to light a new event in the community that warranted the BBC's attention. Finally, it was Cal's turn.

Cal explained the situation about Joey in detail. He then asked, "Questions?"

"Cal, we don't know why he went to the woods? Was he abused? Did he steal from the foster parents? Do we know who the foster parents were? Have we talked to them?" Helen Inskeep, a children's clothing store owner, asked in her usual rapid-fire manner.

"Let me take those in reverse order. We did find his DCF file. The foster parents were Ralph and Gloria Stoner, and they're dead. It seems the father died in a fall down some steps while he was drunk. The mother died from liver disease a little over two years later. Joseph ran away two months before the foster father's accidental death. There was never a DCF claim against the boy. We're not sure about the abuse. Before he went into the foster system, he went to parochial school. In the foster system, he switched to public school, so there's no documentation of a behavior change. His parochial school records show he was very polite and attentive to his studies. The public school records show he was shy and slightly withdrawn, which is characteristic of children who have experienced the trauma of losing parents at an early age. It's doubtful he committed a crime."

"Cal, was his grandmother Eloise Hinson?" Harry Sheff, shoe-repair store owner, asked.

"Yes, Harry, it was."

"Then I knew the boy's father, Howard Paschal, and his mother and grandmother. Both the grandmother and mother babysat for my kids when they were growing up. All three, Howie, Josey, and Eloise, were good people. Hard-working, minded their own business, and willing to help others. The boy comes from fine stock."

"That's good to know. All right, the next meeting is the second Tuesday of next month. We'll meet at the library next month in the second-floor conference room. Same time," Cal said as he stood. Everyone mingled, came over to Junior to welcome him, and left. Maggie stayed back until it was only she and Cal walking out together.

"My antique stores are running out of merchandise, so I'm going on a buying trip this weekend to replenish them," Maggie said. "We have a brisk business. This will be a fine weekend for you to teach Joey how to drive—unless, that is, you want me to teach him." She smiled, batting her eyelashes.

"When are you leaving?" Cal asked, obvious disappointment in his voice.

"Friday, right after I fix Joey's breakfast. He has an eight-thirty session with Issie, so I expect to be gone by then."

"Breakfast? You fix his breakfast as well as dinner?" Cal looked at Maggie in amazement.

"Not every day," she said defensively, and blushed. "Just those days I can."

"I believe you said he has a crush on you. Now I know it's a mutual admiration society."

"I'm helping him see that there are people who do care about him. Cal, he is so love starved, it's sad," Maggie said. "I'll tell Joey you'll see him Friday afternoon. He doesn't get home until late because he has to ride a bike, since he doesn't know how to drive."

"I get the message. Tell him I'll be there before dark. When will you be back?"

"Sunday afternoon."

"Good. We may have a surprise for you."

"Don't wreck the Wrangler. It's the only car I have to pull the maintenance trailer. Don't teach him any of your bad habits, either," Maggie lectured, then gave him a friendly hug and walked to her car.

# CHAPTER 16

Maggie finished the breakfast dishes while considering Joey's situation. She'd bet her life he was an abuse victim. When not on guard, his mannerisms were like those of a ten-year-old in his politeness and ways. She knew he was hiding something, something that happened to him. He wasn't a sociopath—she was sure of that. His insecurity was extreme. He needed love, lots of it. She knew he was also perfect for her needs.

Maggie went up to her bedroom and took off her housecoat, dress, bra, and panties. Walking to her closet, she put on a pair of cotton underpants and a workout bra that would flatten her breasts. A heavy white cotton blouse, a size too big, came next. The rest of the outfit was a plain, pleated, mid-calf full skirt; a one-inch stiff leather belt; flat shoes; and a loose, unstructured, lightweight jacket. A brown scarf to wear around her neck and drape down the front of her blouse, further obscuring her figure and posture, came next. At her makeup table, Maggie combed out her hair and pinned it up in an old lady's bun, then applied makeup to give herself an older appearance, creating circles under her eyes, the appearance of wrinkles on her forehead, and sunken cheeks. She took out a pair of glasses, put them on, and looked in the mirror. A woman of sixty-five or older, unattractive and sullen, stared back at her.

Satisfied she was ready, Maggie went into her closet, then reached back to close and lock the closet door. She walked over to the shoe rack hanging on the closet wall, stooped down, and felt for the soft spot under the lower shelf. She pressed it and pulled gently on the shelf, causing that part of the back wall to rotate on a hidden hinge, exposing a small room. When she bought the house, this had been an old-fashioned "trunk" room serving both the master and the adjoining room, typical of a time when a husband and wife slept in separate bedrooms. Maggie had turned half the trunk room into closets and the rest into this secret room.

There was no window, and Kevlar fabric lined the floor, walls, and ceiling. In the ceiling was a hatch leading to the attic space above the room, with access to an air vent in the side of the house above the trellised walkway connecting the garage and the kitchen. Next to the air vent was a rope ladder, coiled and ready for use. The air vent couldn't open or give way from the outside. Maggie didn't expect to need the escape route, but she didn't want to need it and not have it. To leave nothing to chance and to never suffer a negative surprise were two of Maggie's rules. On the wall of the secret room hung a Mossberg 590 twelve-gauge pump shotgun capable of holding nine buckshot rounds. The shotgun was always operational. On a shelf was a loaded Glock 26 nine-millimeter pistol, a suppressor, and a spare seventeen-round magazine containing soft-nosed rounds. Every room in the house had a concealed Glock 26 and multiple pepper spray tubes within easy reach. Leave nothing to chance.

Inside the room were a small desk and chair. She sat at the desk and pulled six prepaid cell phones from a drawer, each displaying a small piece of tape labeled with a single letter. From another drawer she extracted six Moleskine notebooks with matching letters inside their covers. She started with the book labeled A, picked up cellphone A, inserted its SIM card, and dialed the phone number listed in the notebook.

"Good morning," a voice answered.

"Good morning," Maggie said. "May I speak to Mike Todd, please?"

"May I tell him who's calling?"

"Evelyn Stodmeyer," Maggie said.

"Hold, please."

After a moment, a man said, "Good morning, Ms. Stodmeyer. How are you?"

"Fine, Mike. I'd like to stop by this afternoon and make a deposit. Will you be there at noon?"

"Yes. I look forward to seeing you."

"Fine. It will be a small deposit; however, I'd like to get information on IBM while I'm there. See you at noon."

Maggie repeated five more similar calls, setting appointments on the hour from one to six with five more brokerage firms, using different aliases for each. She took from a drawer five more envelopes labeled B to F, each containing cash and a deposit slip for a different bank. She placed the envelopes and cell phones in an oversized leather-and-canvas bag, then picked up the Glock and spare magazine. Upon leaving the room, she carefully closed the shoe rack until she felt the catch of the lock. She went to the bar holding her scarves, selected five different ones, and placed them in her bag. Maggie slipped the Glock and magazine into holsters and secured them on her belt, hidden under the jacket. Time to go, she decided.

# CHAPTER 17

The BBC meeting in the library's second-floor conference room started with David Fogel in the speaker's chair. He said, "Here's what my undercover officer found out. A student is dealing the meth and ecstasy. His name is Court George Henderson the Fourth, a rising senior taking summer courses to be able to graduate on time. He's street-smart—also evidently rich."

"David, if I may interrupt," Taylor Graham, the college president, interjected. "I know Court and his family. Both his mother and father went to BC, and they're big financial supporters as well. This will be a major disruption to the school and the community."

"Do they live here?" Rosa Lee Dixon, owner of Rosa's Real Country Buffet, asked.

"No," Taylor said. "They live in Cleveland, but they have ties all over the Northeast. Frankly, their money goes back to the early 1800s. I believe, but don't hold me to it, Court's great-grandfather was involved with the Rockefeller group, and his great-great-grandfather on his mother's side was a big real estate speculator and banker. I'm sorry, David, for interrupting, but I think this information is important to our discussion and solution to the issue."

"No problem, Taylor. It's good information. We monitored Mr. Henderson's cell and found out he gets a delivery every two weeks from a courier coming through from Montreal to Boston. We believe the courier serves some colleges and small communities on his own initiative, selling the drugs he gets in payment for the delivery of the real load to Boston. Henderson keeps the stash away from campus. Ingeniously, he buried a cooler in a wooded area about a half mile from the campus. He deposits everything there and then retrieves what he needs when he has orders, delivering to his clients at their dorm rooms, not his."

"Do you know where in the woods?" Eddie Keogh asked.

"Yes. We followed him one evening when he was selling to a student. Oh, yeah, by the way, he only makes a buy at night, on the interstate, at the intersection with Highway 20. It takes all of one minute. These guys are good. He takes the drugs to the cooler in the woods by a circuitous route. We didn't have to follow him. We already knew where he was going. Once we found the cooler, we installed motion-activated cameras in multiple locations, all trained to give various perspectives of the area. The cameras have recorded Mr. Henderson every time he's visited the cooler, as well as a few deer and raccoons strolling by."

"David, give us your assessment of what needs doing," requested Terry Rodriguez, a builder and contractor.

"Terry, there are many ways we can handle this, but based on what Taylor said, my suggestion is as follows. We needed to catch Henderson selling to a student. We've done that. He sold drugs to our undercover officer in her dorm room, but she didn't record the buy. She's setting up another buy, and it will be on film with sound. FYI, he offered the drugs to her for sex instead of money. She declined, but that gave us another crime, soliciting sex for drugs. Regardless, that's not the point. We have him receiving the drugs from the courier on video and audio, we have him placing the drugs in the cooler, and we have him taking the drugs out of the cooler, so he's going to prison as a drug dealer for at least fifteen years. The courier is another issue. My recommendation for the courier is to have a talk with him, convince him stopping in this county is not wise, and let him go. If he sells in this county again, we'll arrest him. I'm confident he'll stop coming here, though. Taylor can give us his suggestion for handling Henderson. Taylor, what do you think is best?"

"David, you have proof of Mr. Henderson selling drugs?" President Graham asked.

"Yes."

"I'm sorry, I should have asked regarding a legally binding criminal act."

"Oh, okay. The sale he made to my undercover officer, and his offering the drugs for sex, was not dependent on any extralegal activity we may have done in the beginning. This one isolated act is enough to put him away for fifteen years, without any legal hang-ups."

"If you can do that and have the evidence on film with sound, I'd like you to arrest Mr. Henderson as quietly as possible and hold him in jail overnight. The next morning, I'll call his father and ask him to come here. I'm sure he'll fly in on his own jet the same day. I'd like to meet with the father, son, you, and the prosecutor in my office. If everyone here agrees, I'll offer the elder Mr. Henderson a deal. His son withdraws from school and leaves the community, and all charges go away, but his son is never to set foot in this community or on campus again. They spare the Henderson name a scandal, the son isn't a convicted drug dealer serving at least fifteen years in prison, and this college and community removes at least one menace. Will that work for everyone?"

"What if he just starts dealing drugs elsewhere?" asked Helen Inskeep.

"We can't stop drugs from being sold on all college campuses in the country," David Fogel responded. "Hell, we can't stop it in this community, just suppress it and make it dangerous for those who try. Other communities have to take the steps they feel are right."

"What if the father tries to fight the charges? Gets a lawyer and has the evidence thrown out?" Tony Ayala, a plumbing contractor, asked.

David Fogel looked at Cal and responded, "Every step of the way, from taking statements from the girls in the emergency room to our surveillance of Mr. Henderson, we had warrants and court supervision and permission to do what we needed to do. He'll need a very good lawyer, no matter what, just to get a reduced sentence, and the family's name will be scandalized all over the country, particularly in the Midwest and Northeast."

"Mr. Henderson III will likely bring his attorney with him. He's most thorough in everything he does. I'll handle him," said Taylor.

The conversation passed around the circle until it came to Tomas Tommi, the elementary school principal. "This is probably nothing, but we have a situation developing at the school this week. Not everyone knows we have a summer school program for children of parents who work, as well as when a child needs some extra help preparing for the next grade. One of the third graders, I won't mention any names yet because I'm not sure there's anything to it, has had a complete behavior change. She's always been the teacher's helper and leader of the class. Suddenly, she's not herself anymore; she's angry and shows no interest in her schoolwork or playmates. Strange. Her teacher doesn't know how to handle this change."

"I assume she's called the parents?" Maggie asked, moving forward in her chair.

"She had them in yesterday without the little girl. They've noticed she doesn't want to go out and play with her friends. She tells them she's studying in her room, but if they go into the room, she's just lying on her bed, staring into space, holding on to her stuffed animals."

Maggie sat erect. "Tomas, someone has sexually abused this little girl. She needs help right away and must be removed from whatever situation has caused this abuse. Are you sure the parents aren't part of the problem?"

"No, I'm not sure of anything. Are you jumping to conclusions?"

"Tomas, I'm not—"

"I can't imagine anything like abuse happening in that household. There are three children, both parents are hardworking, and the family has always been tight knit, always doing things together, always showing up at PTA meetings, always at church."

"Tomas, I didn't say the abuse was coming from the family. It can come from anywhere. Can't the school nurse find a reason to speak to the little girl?" Maggie asked, a hardness in her voice.

"Sure, that's a good idea. I'll see about that tomorrow."

When all participants had been given an opportunity to speak, Cal said, "That's it for tonight. We'll meet at the regular time in this same room in two weeks."

The BBC meeting ended on that note.

# CHAPTER 18

"Joey, here's the key to the St. Clair house. The air filters need changing, as well as the smoke detector batteries. In my garage on the back wall, on the third shelf, are the A/C filters. Get two. Next to the filters is a box of nine-volt batteries. Get two, one for the alarm in the kitchen and one for the hall unit. Rearrange your work schedule so you do the St. Clair house between one and two. Go inside and get the filters and batteries changed first; then do the yard. The tenant will be gone. Oh, yes, get the eight-foot ladder off the garage wall and put it on the trailer. You'll need it. Go in through the garage and back kitchen door, not the front door. Any questions?"

"No, got it."

"Okay. Joey, if you think of any, use your new cell phone and call me at the library. Do you remember the speed dial number?"

"Three."

"Okay. Have you received your grades from school yet?"

"No, not yet. They should be coming any day now. I hope I passed," Joey said, showing the insecurity Maggie had worked hard to help him overcome.

She walked over to him, put her hand on his shoulder, lifted his chin with her other hand, and looked him in the eyes, smiling. "Joey, whatever your grades are will be fine. This is not a one-time test. This is a journey—your journey. The difference is you no longer make it alone. You have the judge, Becky Lang, Issie, and me to help you figure it out. Stay confident and calm and take one step at a time." She let go of his chin and tousled his hair. "Now get to work."

Joey loved driving the Wrangler. He took the doors and roof off, loving the wind blowing and enveloping him. The gears screeched when he failed to depress the clutch enough while shifting. He chuckled to himself, thinking about how the judge rolled his eyes whenever it happened. Winding roads up, down, and around the hills were like being on a roller coaster when driving the Wrangler. He knew it would be cold in the winter, but that was okay. It wouldn't be as cold as he'd been. His thoughts turned to his grades. He didn't know what he'd do if he let Maggie down—or even the judge. He was an okay guy. Working on the AT with him was fun. He was strong, and Joey realized the judge knew the woods almost as well as he did. Joey resisted Cal's requests to see Joey's hideaways. That wouldn't happen, at least not soon. If he had to run, he'd need every one of them. Please, God, don't let them find out, he prayed silently.

Joey turned onto St. Clair Street from Patriot Boulevard. At the end of the second block, he turned right onto a stub of a street that ended at a wooded area after a hundred feet. He reached for the garage door opener on the visor and pushed the button. The door opened on the left side of the two-car garage. Joey pulled the Wrangler in, leaving only the trailer with the lawn equipment exposed outside. Maggie was explicit; always pull the Wrangler into the garage all the way so the trailer is the only thing sticking out and different from the normal view of the home.

After one trip to each of the houses, Joey realized the six rental houses were alike except for the exterior color and material. Two were painted yellow and two tan, with the other two brick. They were not only alike but also identical in structure to Maggie's house, with two exceptions: there was no apartment over the garage and no second floor like in Maggie's house. In all six rental houses, the layout was the same. The houses sat on corner lots facing the main street. A two-car garage was separate from each main house and sat facing the side street, which ended in a wooded area just past the garage.

Connecting the garage to the house was a sixty-foot trellised walkway covered by Boston ivy, which grew up both sides and across the translucent cover. The walkway was brown concrete. It led from the garage side door to the kitchen door. There was a glass storm door, which opened out, requiring whoever was entering to back down a step for the door to swing. Inside, the house was identical to Maggie's, except there was a bedroom and bath where Maggie's house had a library and half bath on the first floor. There was only one bedroom in each of the rental houses.

Joey grabbed the ladder, batteries, and filters. He propped the storm door open with the ladder, then unlocked the kitchen door. He entered to find a house as neat and clean as Maggie's. In the three months he had worked for Maggie, he had learned her motto: a place for everything, and everything in its place.

The house was quiet. Joey retrieved the ladder and set it up close under the smoke detector above the kitchen island. He quickly changed the battery, folded the ladder, and moved to the dining room. The return vents were there and in the hall. He saw the first vent down near the floor, partially hidden by a plant. He changed the filter and moved through the living room to the front hall. There he found the second filter and the second smoke detector. He set up his ladder to do the filter first.

Joey had climbed up and was reaching to unlatch the filter when he heard the back door open and close. He couldn't let go of the old filter with the door resting against his head and the new filter held in place against his chest and under his chin. He didn't know what to do. Maggie had said no one would be home. Quickly, he took the old filter out and inserted the new one. As he was twisting the latches, he heard someone say, "Who are you?" He froze. He knew that voice.

Slowly, Joey turned and looked over his shoulder toward the sound of her voice. "Suzie, is that you?"

"Joey! Oh, my God, Joey, is that you? Jesus, Joey, I didn't know what happened to you. Oh, my God." Suzie reached for Joey as he climbed down the ladder. Tears flowed freely as they held each other.

"What are you doing here, Suzie?" Joey asked as he wiped the tears from his face onto his shirtsleeve.

"I live here, Joey. What are you doing here?" Suzie asked, leaving her cheeks wet. Joey reached over and wiped them with his hand, then wiped his hand on his shirt. Tears gave way to wide grins. "Let me put my books in my room, and let's talk," Suzie said, moving toward the bedroom door.

"I've got to change the smoke detector battery," Joey said, moving and ascending the ladder.

Suzie came out of her bedroom. "I'll be in the kitchen. Oh, Joey, where have you been? I want to hear everything." As she passed, she embraced his leg and rested her head against it. Joey finished changing the battery and eased down the ladder while reaching for Suzie's hand. Suzie took his hand in hers and kissed it. As he reached the floor, she laid her head against his chest. After a few seconds, she led the way to the kitchen, holding the glass storm door open for Joey to remove the ladder and old filters from the house.

When he came back inside, Suzie was sitting at the kitchen banquette, a plate of cookies and a cup of tea in front of her. "What do you want to drink, Joey?"

"Ice water, if you have it."

Suzie rose and went to the refrigerator. "I've got a Coke or orange juice, if you prefer."

"Nah, ice water will do. I still have to do the outside. Maggie said no one would be home, so to do the inside first. I hope she won't be mad at me."

"She won't. I had a class canceled, so I came home to study. How do you know Maggie?"

"I work for her and stay in her garage apartment."

"You work for Maggie? Since when?"

"Since June," Joey said defensively, looking down at the cookie he had placed on a napkin.

Suzie, standing at the sink, filling the glass of ice with water, sensed his discomfort. "Maggie is special, isn't she?" she said. "We need to tell each other about the last three years. Me first. A year after Ralph died, his insurance settlement ran out. Mama lost the house, and we moved to a single-wide out on Lenox Road." She walked back to the table and placed the water in front of Joey, then put her hand on his shoulder. "She never stopped drinking and finally drank herself to death. That happened the week before high school graduation."

Suzie sat down, not across the table from Joey but next to him. She took his hand in hers. Staring across the room at an oil painting of a kitchen scene in the nineteenth century, she continued in a monotone. "I got mixed up with the wrong crowd in high school. I knew, despite everything that had happened to me, I wanted to go to college and make a better life for myself and my children, if I ever have any. I wouldn't live the life I had been living. I would rather die than stay in that world. Two weeks after Mama died and one week after I graduated, the trailer rent was due. I didn't have it, so I had to move what clothes I had, and my books and stuff, into the old Ford. Remember the clunker?"

Joey nodded.

"I went around and got a job at the Wendy's on the late shift just in case I got into college. Well, that was bullshit. It didn't scare me to live in the car during the day, but it was spooky at night, so I figured I'd work then. It also gave me a place to wash up and eat. I was able to have one meal as part of my pay. I'd also clear the tables, so when someone didn't finish their fries or sandwich, I'd turn my back to the counter and stuff them in my mouth."

Tears rolled down Joey's cheeks. He didn't wipe them away.

Suzie continued. "I started going to the library, just to read and see how regular people act. People I would be like one day. Smart people, people who had time and money to read and learn. People who took pride in their lives. People who took charge of their lives. Know what I mean?"

Joey nodded, took a deep breath, and said, "Yeah."

"I met Maggie there. I'd go into the restroom on the second floor, figuring no one would see me, and I'd wash out a blouse or jeans, then take them out to the Ford, spread them out in the trunk, and they'd be dry the next day. Pretty smart, eh?" Suzie smiled and squeezed Joey's hand.

"Yeah," he said, sniffling.

"Here," Suzie said, picking up a paper napkin. "Blow your nose. The story has a happy ending."

Joey took the napkin and blew his nose.

"Maggie noticed, even though I didn't realize it. One day, she came to me and asked if I could do her a favor. I said sure. She said she needed someone to help her around her house. Said she would pay me. Would it be possible for me to come to her house that evening and have dinner with her? She said it wasn't much, just some meatloaf, mashed potatoes, green peas, and pie. I think it was an apple pie, but she makes all kinds of good pies. Have you had one of her homemade pies yet?"

Joey, still looking down and not trusting his voice, nodded.

"I was suspicious about her calling the law, but I was hungry and out of money. I had lost my job because the head of the night shift wanted to fuck me, but that wouldn't happen. Enough men and boys had their way with me anytime they wanted. Anyway, I walked into Maggie's house. It was all elegant. She had the dining room table set with silverware, good china, and crystal glasses. Just the way I dreamed my house would be when I grew up. She offered me the garage apartment to stay in and gave me some duties keeping the place the way she wanted it—a place for everything, and everything in its place." Suzie laughed.

Joey smiled and nodded.

"I didn't realize it then, but Maggie knew exactly what I had been through. She quietly and without fanfare moved me into a safe place in life. Within a week, she had registered me at BC for the next semester. She put me to work in her antique shops or ice cream shops, wherever she needed help. She paid me a fair wage, always more than I thought was justified. More than anything, she offered me her friendship without prying. She was the mother I had always wanted. A few weeks after arriving at Maggie's, I told her everything:

Ralph, Mama, the bad choices I had made, my anger, and what I wanted to do with my life. She just listened until I got it all out." Now Suzie was crying.

Joey looked up and wiped a tear from her face.

"When I finished with the past, Maggie explained how I could take charge of my life. How I could deal with men on my own terms, controlling the relationship. How I could use the assets God had given me to create a path toward a successful life. How I could be the person I wanted to be. She showed me what was truly right and wrong, how the most important aspect of life is belief in yourself and respect for yourself. Respect—that's an important word for Maggie, and I understand it. Not the respect defined by certain elements of society, who twist the word to suit their purposes. Respect by using the assets and tools God gave each of us to build ourselves into productive and intelligent human beings. She taught me that education was the most important way to develop God's second gift—my brain. That's what I'm doing and have done for the last two years. That's what my life's like, Joey. How about you? What have you been doing with yourself? Where did you go, Joey, when you ran away?"

Joey looked at the young woman he had known as a child. She had the same olive skin, the same brown eyes, and the same coal-black hair, but she wasn't a child anymore, even if to him she would always be the little girl he loved dearly. He hesitated. This was Suzie. Should he tell her what he was afraid of?

"When I ran away, I went into the forest. I figured I could find me a place to hide out until they stopped looking for me. Being returned to Ralph's was not a chance I wanted to take. I'd steal from campers, hikers, gardens, or dumpsters. Did pretty good, learned a lot about the wilderness, also found out I didn't want to be a forest ranger." Joey chuckled, and Suzie smiled. "Anyway, this past June, there weren't many campers or hikers, so I chanced going to town and raiding a dumpster, and got caught. The judge said he knew my mother and granny, so he put me on probation, got me a haircut and clothes, but more than anything, he took me to Maggie. You're right; she's just the way I always dreamed my mom would be. I stay in her garage apartment, take care of her house and her rental houses, and the judge got me a GED and put me into a remedial program at the college. I took two courses this past summer. Don't know how I did, but Maggie said I'll succeed. She really makes you feel good about yourself," Joey said, looking at Suzie.

"Joey, why'd you come back that night?" she asked quietly, squeezing his hand.

"What night?" Joey asked. His heart raced and his breath constricted in his chest.

"Joey, Mama saw you, and so did I. It's okay. The police asked Mama what happened. She said she didn't know, but you were there. I told the police, and her, that she was too drunk to know who was there, that you hadn't been there for almost two months, and that there was no one there but Mama, Ralph, and me. I hid the baseball bat between my mattress and box spring until the next day. Then I took it to the shed and cut it up in pieces with the electric saw and buried them. Why did you come back, Joey?"

Joey looked at Suzie with a mixture of childish fear and manly defiance. "Because of what you did for me. You didn't think I could hear you in your room. I heard you tell Ralph you'd willingly do the things he wanted you to do if he stopped beating me. That's why he stopped. I didn't understand at first. After spending time in the woods, I began to realize why your mama drank so much so fast some nights. She knew what he was going to do, and she didn't want to, so she'd get shitfaced in a hurry and leave us to that no-good bastard. I could take it. No matter what he did, I didn't cry. I'd die before that asshole ever had the pleasure of seeing me cry. Every time he hit me, I asked God to not let me cry, and God made sure I didn't.

"God's always been there when I needed him. I didn't realize what Stoner was doing to you. When I did, I came back. He came out of your room naked, and I was determined to give him what he deserved. When he reached the top of the stairs, I came up behind him, hit him with the bat, and pushed him down. I didn't care if I killed him or not. I wanted to, but I figured if he lived through that, he'd leave you alone, at least for a while, so I'd have time to figure out another way of killing him. So, to answer your question, Suzie, I came back for you that night. You had stopped Ralph from beating me, and I wanted to stop him from doing those things to you. I didn't know you saw me, but I thought I saw your mama looking out from her room. That's why I stayed in the woods. By then I knew no one could find me in the wilderness unless I wanted them to."

Joey fell silent. The two of them looked at each other. They didn't need to say love never goes far from the surface when it's real, built on genuine sacrifice for the beloved, even when it's buried for over three years. They just knew it.

"I guess I need to get the outside done," he said. "I've got to go to another rental house after yours." He stood and looked down at her.

"Joey, we need to talk some more. When will you be back here?"

"I come here on Mondays unless it's raining, then Tuesday."

"I'll be here next Monday. If you can, be here earlier."

"Okay."

Suzie watched Joey take the lawn mower off the trailer and start it. She went to her handbag, took the flip phone from its zipped pocket, and pushed speed dial number seven.

"Maggie, I need to speak with you immediately. Can I come to the library? Okay, second floor, writer's room two," Suzie said. "I'll be there in fifteen minutes."

# CHAPTER 19

Maggie was concerned. Suzie had sounded both scared and troubled on the phone. She positioned herself so she would see Suzie as she came up the steps and approached the writers' rooms, small soundproof boxes frequently used by local writers as well as young couples who found the spaces titillating. She started reshelving books outside room two, waiting for Suzie to appear. When she arrived, Maggie took a handful of books, intercepted her in front of the door, and followed her into the room.

§

"Judge, Dr. Becky Lang is on the phone. Do you want me to take a number or put her through?" Betsy asked.

"Put her through, please," Cal said, closing the file in front of him. He moved it to the completed pile and reached for a yellow tablet. "Hello, Becky. How are you?"

"Fine, Judge. I'm calling about Joey Paschal."

"Is everything all right?" Cal sat up in his chair, leaned over the desk, and wrote JOEY at the top of the yellow pad.

"Yes, sir. He's on his way over to see you. He got his grades today and came to me to talk about them."

"How'd he do?"

"All things considered, okay. He got C's. He's ashamed of the grades, though."

"Why is he ashamed? I don't understand," Cal said. He wrote the letter C twice on the first line of the yellow page.

"Joey is struggling with school. This type of institutional structure is new to him. In some respects, it's unbelievable, the way he built discipline into his unstructured life in the woods, but that was of his own making, not something imposed on him. That stress was challenging, but more challenging for him is his fear of disappointing you and Maggie Latham, whom he calls Miss Maggie and adores."

"Okay, forget the grades for a moment. How is he progressing on the integration into school life?" Cal drew a heart on the tablet page and put ML in the middle of it. On the next line, he wrote INTEGRATION.

"So-so. He doesn't mix well at school. I've spoken with his instructors, and they said he's quiet in class, doesn't interact much, but that's understandable. Issie said he's extremely polite, hardworking, and has a self-deprecating sense of humor. He needs time and self-confidence in the social world. He also needs your and Ms. Latham's support."

Cal wrote the words TIME and SUPPORT on the yellow page. "What do you recommend for the future, Becky?"

"No matter what, he needs to stay in school. I recommend Math 100, the follow-up basic math course, and that Issie continues tutoring him. I'm recommending he take Botany 101 and English Lit 101. This schedule should be relatively easy but still more challenging than this past summer. Joey told me he loves nature, and I think botany would be an easier science than biology, particularly for a young man familiar with the forest. The English Lit is because he said he read a lot, and he did well on the reading comprehension exams I gave him. If he passes all the courses this fall semester, at the end of spring semester, he'd be a sophomore. I'm confident Joey will be a fully engaged college student by then."

"What if he doesn't succeed in the fall and spring?"

"We'll know his path by the middle of the fall semester. If college is not working, we go to an alternative educational experience, perhaps an apprentice program. I don't know, but Joey and I will figure it out."

"Sounds like a plan. Please quarterback it as you see fit. I appreciate you. It's important to all of us in the community to help this young man. Please don't ever hesitate to call me about Joey on any matter at all. You have my complete support, and I'll tell you, Joey will not disappoint me or Miss Maggie, as he calls her. He adores her, eh? Well, I'll tell you a secret. The feeling is mutual. Thanks for the heads up, Becky. Let me know if I can assist you in any way. I owe you a lot. Have a good day."

"Yes, sir, Your Honor."

Cal sat back in his chair and reviewed his notes. He realized how tenuous Joey's place in society was. He had bolted once before. Cal wanted to make sure Joey didn't lose courage again. Maggie was the answer there. He reached into his briefcase and pulled out his go phone, then hit speed dial number one.

"I was just going to call you," Maggie said when she answered.

"Great minds that love each other think alike," Cal responded.

"Please. You've been reading too many romance novels."

"I wish. Joey got two C's in his coursework. Becky Lang said he's struggling with the school structure and needs reassurance he's not letting us—you and me, mostly you—down. He adores you. Those were her words, not mine. Can't say I blame him, but I'm still jealous."

"You should be. It's good for keeping your ego in check," Maggie responded. "Cal, what can we do?"

"He's on his way over here, according to Becky. I'm going to talk with him and urge him to tell you. Just be your usual self and help him understand you're proud of him."

"You know I will. Are you free Wednesday evening?"

"I think so. Why?"

"The three of us can have a celebratory dinner at my place. I'm off in the afternoon and can bake a cake, fix his favorite dinner, and surprise him with your being here. He might, as you say, adore me, but you're the father figure he looks up to. He'll enjoy it."

"I'll be there. I'll get there after court to help set the table."

"Good. We're going to eat in the dining room—fine china, sterling, and crystal. Show him one measure of what real success can bring. By the way, will you have a few moments after the BBC tomorrow night to talk?"

"Sure, anything in particular?"

"Yes, but not on the phone. Bye."

Cal hung up the phone at the same time Betsy buzzed him on his desk phone. "Judge, Deputy Fogel just delivered a manila envelope for you. Do you want it now?"

"Yes, please."

Betsy handed Cal an envelope inscribed with the words JUDGE WHITE-CALLAWAY'S EYES ONLY. Cal took his folding knife from his pocket and carefully slit open the clasp end. Looking inside, he saw another envelope. He looked at the return address: State Forensic Laboratory. He knew what was inside—the results from analyzing the two hair samples for a paternity test he had given David. The definitive answer about who Joey's biological father was. There was a physical resemblance, or at least Cal believed there was. He couldn't ask anyone else, even Maggie, whether they saw it. Maybe he just wanted

Joey to be his, something lasting between Josey and him, redemption for his moment of weakness. Assurance was in the envelope.

Cal ran the knife along the edge, slitting it about a quarter of the way. He stopped. Did he really want to know? If he wasn't Joey's biological father, would it change his attitude and sense of obligation to him? If he was his father, should he tell him? Would the news destroy the formative time of his life, when he had looked up to and loved the man he'd thought was his father? Would his last mooring to the social world break, sending him spinning out of control? What would he think of his mother if he learned he was Cal's son and not the son of her husband?

How could Cal tell Joey he had turned his back on Joey's mother? What would Joey think of him then? If he was angry with Cal, would he suspect Maggie wasn't being truthful with him, either? The knowledge could destroy Joey's relationship with Maggie. There was some magical connection between the two, like the love between a biological mother and son. It would devastate them. If Cal confused and hurt Joey, would it affect Cal's own relationship with Maggie? Cal withdrew the knife blade and placed the unopened envelope in the drawer with his Bible. He moved his case files for Tuesday's court to the credenza and waited for Joey.

# CHAPTER 20

Tomas Tommi sat in the speaker's chair, Cal to his right. "I'm afraid I don't have good news. The little girl I mentioned at our last meeting continues to have problems. The school nurse talked to her and felt something, or someone, was traumatizing her. That's only half of it, though. Two little boys, one in the second grade and one in the third, are displaying irregular behavior, acting out in class, and the second grader is regressing to toddler habits. He's wetting his pants, sucking his thumb, and occasionally using baby talk. Both teachers have called in the parents, who say they have also noticed a change in behavior. Both boys, by the way, also don't want to go out and play like they usually do. The third grader's parents said he never stayed in after school, but now he doesn't want to go out, just stay in his room, playing on the computer."

"Tomas, where do they live?" asked David Fogel.

"Over in the Quiet Glade neighborhood."

"Can you get me their addresses? If there isn't a problem at school, there has to be a problem somewhere, and if it's not the parents, which this outbreak of three implies, it's likely in the neighborhood."

"Couldn't it be somebody in a car or on the playground?" C. C. Jefferies, owner of ten convenience stores, asked.

"Possibly, but unlikely. God forbid, someone who takes a child in a car rarely brings them back. My bet is this predator is living around there somewhere," David said.

"I'll ask the clerks at my store in that neighborhood whether any new people have shown up," C. C. said.

"David, what do you recommend?" Cal asked.

"First, if Tomas could alert his teachers to watch for children displaying unusual behavior, perhaps we can get some information from a child. That'll be very difficult, because the predator usually scares them by threatening their family or pets, and the children think they've done something wrong. Second, have the school nurse check the kids as best she can without arousing suspicion or alarming the children that they're about to be abused again. Third, ask the parents to examine the kids when giving them a bath. Again, tell them not to alarm the child, because the child thinks something bad will happen if anyone knows what happened. I'll put officers who patrol that area on alert for strange behavior from any adults. I'll also check the sex crime registry to see if anybody registered lives in the area. Cal, I don't think we can wait two weeks for the next meeting."

"How about a meeting next Tuesday? Does everyone agree?" Cal asked. Agreement was unanimous. "Okay, David, if you need anything from me, call directly. This needs to stay within this room if an acceptable solution is to come of it. That's it. Be alert. See you next Tuesday, right here, same time."

Members filed out of the room, more quiet than usual, the somber discussion weighing on them. Maggie and Cal left, one before the other. Outside, she suggested they walk in the library garden. Once there, she guided Cal to a bench under a weeping yaupon tree. They sat, and she took his hand in hers.

"You're not telling me we're finished, are you?" Cal asked, trying to lighten the mood.

"No, but I do have something serious to tell you," she said, squeezing his hand tightly between hers.

"Oh, shit, what's the matter? Is it Joey?"

She shook her head, and Cal saw her chin quiver. Maggie breathed deeply. "I know why Joey lived in the wilderness for three years. Oh, Cal, it's hard for me to believe, but I heard it from someone who knows the complete story."

"Who?"

"You know most of the story. Gloria Stoner had a daughter during her first marriage. Gloria's daughter is two years older than Joey. Her name is Suzie. After Joey was there for a few months, the foster father, when he was drinking, began verbally abusing Joey, calling him a sissy, saying he was queer. He wanted to make Joey cry, but Joey wouldn't. Joey clammed up and ignored Stoner, which enraged the brute. He started getting physical, pushing Joey around. When Joey still didn't cry, Stoner started using a belt to beat him."

"How often did this happen?"

"Usually two or three nights a week, when Stoner came home from work after stopping to drink."

"Where was the wife? Why didn't she stop him?"

Maggie, still holding Cal's hand, laid her head on his shoulder, not stifling her tears anymore. "The mother had a drinking problem, or, God forbid, just didn't want to know what was going on. You see, Stoner had also been sexually abusing Suzie from the time she was eleven. Some nights Stoner brought home a fifth of Jim Beam, the mother's favorite whiskey. By eight, she had either passed out or started an argument, not about the kids but some stupid issue, and she would go into her downstairs bedroom and lock the door. This was the ritual—and her permission for Stoner to do as he pleased. Stoner would then turn on Joey. Over time, he progressed from a belt to a weighted rubber hose. Joey would never cry. He would sometimes whimper, asking God's help not to cry. Usually, the beatings didn't stop until Joey passed out."

"Why didn't someone at school recognize the signs?" Cal asked, trembling.

"Stoner hit him only where his clothes would hide the bruises."

"Joey could have said something to a teacher or counselor."

"Cal, my dear, you don't understand the thinking of a child being abused. They somehow believe they're at fault. In Joey's case, remember, he had lost his mother, his father, and his maternal grandmother. He had no one except the little girl. After Stoner beat Joey into unconsciousness, he would go to Suzie's room and rape her."

"Jesus Christ!" Cal exclaimed, hyperventilating and attempting to maintain his composure.

"This went on until Joey turned thirteen. Then, one night, after Stoner had beat him senseless, Suzie, who by then was fifteen, told Stoner she would become a willing sex partner if he would never beat Joey again. Stoner agreed, and she made him want to live up to the bargain. He never beat Joey again, but Joey ran away three weeks later. He went to the wilderness because he was afraid the DCF people, who never came to the house to check on him, would send him back there."

"So that's it," Cal said, now holding Maggie, with her head on his shoulder.

"Not exactly. Two months later, Stoner was drunk and having his way with Suzie. Around eleven, he left Suzie's bedroom on the second floor, and as he reached the top of the stairs, Joey stepped out of his old bedroom with a baseball bat. He hit Stoner on the back of the head and pushed him down the stairs. Joey didn't think anyone saw him, but Suzie did. Joey dropped the bat and went down to see if Stoner was dead. Gloria Stoner also looked out of her room and saw Joey, but she was still drunk. Suzie called 911, and they sent an ambulance and police car. She hid the bat between the mattress and box spring of her bed, told the police Stoner had fallen down the stairs drunk, and told her mother she had been too drunk to see anyone. That Stoner was naked and smelled of sex, and the mother was in a downstairs bedroom drunk, was clear to the police. They asked Suzie if she had any other statement. By that time, they had confirmed Stoner was dead, so Suzie said no. The cops didn't press the issue."

"Jesus Christ. Jesus Christ. No wonder Joey gave up on society. Why did he go back? What about Suzie?"

"Joey told her he had realized in those few weeks he was in the woods why Stoner had stopped beating him, why he would bypass Joey and go right to Suzie's room. After Stoner died, life spiraled down for Suzie and her mother. When her mother died too, Suzie ended up without a home, going to the library just to get out of the heat and wash up. Homeless people think no one notices when they hang around the library, but I do. I befriended Suzie, helped her make peace with herself and understand, as best she could, what her choices in life are. She made excellent decisions and now is starting her third year at the college."

"How did Joey find her?"

"She rents one of my places. I didn't know she and Joey knew each other. Her last name being Stoner didn't connect with me when you said who Joey's foster parents were. I sent him to do some inside work. Suzie came home unexpectedly."

"She's lucky she has a guardian angel named Maggie," Cal said, again trying to lighten the mood.

"I'm no angel, Cal, but she knows I'll give her guidance when she wants it, without the Pollyanna bullshit written by men to control women. Cal, if you let Joey know you and I are aware of his story, we'll lose him. Suzie said he's ashamed about what has happened to him and what he did, as well as deathly afraid he'll go to jail."

"You're right, as usual. I won't say anything, but I'm going to read the police file to make sure there's nothing in it that could cause Joey a problem."

"Good thinking. That's why I love you," Maggie said as she wiped her cheeks dry. She kissed Cal passionately. "Do you have time to come over?"

"Yes. For a short while."

"Come to the front door so Joey doesn't see your car."

# CHAPTER 21

"**W**ow, what do you have in this thing?" Joey asked as he picked up Suzie's backpack.

"Stuff we'll need, that's all." She smirked, her hands on her hips.

"Let's take a look." He set the pack on a dining room chair and opened it. "Binoculars, camera, first aid kit, compass, notebook, pen, raincoat—hey, it's sunny out there."

"It may cloud up," Suzie said defensively.

"Rain pants, cell phone, parachute cord, extra socks, flashlight, energy bars—two, no less."

"There's two of us," Suzie interjected, sticking out her bottom lip. "All of these things are in the Backpackers' Bible," she said, putting the items back in the pack.

Joey, smiling, reached out and touched her arm. He let his fingers slide down, amazed at the softness of her skin, until he held her hand. Their eyes met, and they stood gazing at each other, understanding what this second chance meant, not saying what they felt, not having to, but knowing being together again was wonderful. "Suzie, you're right," he said. "All of these items would be necessary if you were going alone or with someone else, but you don't need any of them with me. We're going to where I survived for three years. I want to show you the genuine beauty of the wilderness. All of these things, including the camera and binoculars, are just a distraction from nature and unnecessary."

Suzie looked at him, at the honesty in his eyes, and listened to his low, steady, confident voice. Thoughts of what he had gone through for her flashed in her mind. He was hardly old enough to fully understand what he had done. "I—I understand," she said. She wanted to hold him, but didn't want to scare him.

He took her hand and led her through the kitchen, then down the trellised walkway to the garage and the Wrangler.

"Won't we need some sandwiches for lunch?" she asked.

"I've made sandwiches and have water, and even four chocolate chip cookies. Not only that, but if you're not too tired, I'm going to take you to the Berkshire Café for dinner."

"Cool," Suzie said, squeezing Joey's hand and climbing into the Wrangler.

§

"You know, Joey, from a distance, these mountains look pretty easy to climb," Suzie said as she sat on a boulder, out of breath. "Don't look so smug, asshole," she snapped, looking up at him.

Joey said, "Don't worry, you're in great shape. You've just made the novice hiker's mistake. They think they can go up a mountain at the same speed they can walk on flat land. The proper way is to go slower, enjoy the surroundings, the altitude, and the perspective change. We're approaching the summit and have climbed, oh, I don't know, perhaps eight hundred feet. See how the ground has turned rocky? Look over there." Joey pointed to his left. "You can see how these mountains were born and how the glaciers carved out the valleys between them. We're coming to a place where eruptions cleaved a mountain into two peaks by the movement of the earth and glaciers thousands or millions of years ago. Look at the size of the boulders on that ledge and down between these two ridges. Think of the force of nature that pushed these boulders up and then carried some down into the valley."

Suzie, mesmerized by Joey and his wonder at the beauty and mystery of the mountain, saw not a little boy determined not to cry, but a strong young man who took pleasure in everything around him. She knew without doubt or hesitation that she loved this man and wanted to live her life with him. Just as quickly, reality intruded on her thoughts. She wondered if he would love her when he found out about her life. Could he understand? Could she show him how she truly felt? He understood what she had done for him in the past. Could he understand the present? Would he be willing to make a future for them if he knew everything?

"Are you paying attention to me?" he asked. "There's going to be a test, you know."

"Awesome. Yes, I'm kind of paying attention—to you, maybe not so much to the mountain." She stepped over to Joey and rested her head on his chest. "I'm the luckiest girl alive to be here with you."

Joey put his hand up to her hair and breathed in her scent, shutting his eyes so he could imprint this moment on his brain. "Come on, Suzie. We're almost where we're going to have our picnic."

He led her slowly up the winding path, showing her how to walk along the trail, avoiding loose gravel or rocks, using the roots to secure a good footing rather than tripping over them. As they climbed higher, the tree canopy shielded them from the sun even though the tree trunks were wider apart, giving them a view of the downward slope. Fallen and decaying trees, host to lichen, mushrooms, and fungi, evidenced the forest's life cycle.

"Look," he said. "We're going to have our picnic on this flat area." He pointed across the valley at the magical, craggy opposite wall of huge boulders.

"Do people who come here ever go to the other side?"

"Not usually," Joey said, staring at the jagged cliff edge. "It's difficult climbing up there, so most people don't."

"Have you done it?"

"Yeah. There are crevices in there where it's difficult to be seen from any direction, but we're not here to discuss that. We're here for our picnic," he said, standing on a ledge, looking at the valley leading off to the south.

Suzie hugged Joey's arm and rested her head on his shoulder.

He smiled down at her. "Hungry?"

"Sure."

He reached into the back of his vest and pulled out a poncho, spreading it on the smooth rock surface. Suzie stepped back, leaned against a boulder with her arms crossed, and watched him prepare the picnic. Joey took two bottles of water from the vest's side pockets.

"I've got a packet of flavored energy powder if you want some in your water," he said, looking up at her. "What? Why are you smiling like that?"

"No, I don't need any powder. I'm smiling at you and your domestication and knowledge of how to impress a girl with your take-charge attitude." She pushed away from the rock and sat facing him.

"Ham and cheese on rye, okay? There's also a mayo-and-mustard mix, plus provolone cheese. Some carrot sticks and those four chocolate chip cookies," he said, laying out the spread between them.

"Cool. There's only one problem," Suzie said, jumping up.

Joey's eyes went wide with confusion.

"I don't want to sit looking at you," she said. "I want to sit next to you and be able to snuggle with you." She plunked down next to him, wrapped her arm within his, and crinkled her nose at him.

The happiness he had felt all day resumed. "Suzie, you said you met Maggie at the library. She took you in, helped you get into school, and rents you your home. Do you work part-time anywhere besides Maggie's stores?"

She realized she had to be careful with her answer. Tell the truth, but not all the truth. Enough, but not too many details. "I told you Maggie sort of took me under her wing," she said. "She got me a scholarship for college, helped me get the right clothes, and taught me not to be ashamed to be seen in public. She helped me understand how looking at the facts correctly and using God's gifts are important. You know Maggie has some antique stores and ice cream stores around here. She's a real entrepreneur. I work in her stores. I rotate between them, depending on where she needs me. She pays me a salary and deducts my rent from that. I also tutor older students returning to college Monday through Friday evenings at home. I'm very lucky to have Maggie in my life."

"Me, too."

"Joey, I want to talk to you," Suzie said, putting down her sandwich and taking his hand in hers. She looked directly at him. Her eyes burned, and she blinked rapidly. Joey pulled her down so her head was in his lap, with her looking across the valley. He stroked her hair as she spoke. "You know what Stoner did to me. After Stoner got what he deserved, I felt dirty and like trash," she said.

"We don't need to go into all that. That's history. I've learned to live in the present," Joey said, still gently stroking her hair.

"I've got to say what I'm going to say so you'll be able to decide if you want to be my friend. When Mama and I lost the house and moved to the trailer outside of town, I was ashamed and started hanging with the wrong crowd. I did drugs, drank, and was sexually active just so I would be popular. Well, that didn't make me popular. It just gave me a bad reputation, making the kids I wanted to be my friends shun me. Mama was drinking almost every day. Drinking herself to death. One day she was dead. Didn't wake up one morning. I always got myself ready for school, taking a dollar or what change she had in her pocketbook so I could get a pack of crackers for lunch. That day, I came home from school and she was still in bed. It pissed me off, so I went in her room, shouting at her. I pushed her. That was when I realized she was dead. I ran to the next trailer, because we didn't have a phone, and had Mrs. Summers call the police and an ambulance. The next week I graduated, and a week later they evicted me from the trailer. I lived in our old car for a few months before I started hanging at the library and met Maggie. You're hearing this again because I don't want you to think I'm better than I am. Maggie showed me I can be the person I want to be. I want you to be my friend, but I don't want to deceive you." Suzie stopped talking while Joey continued stroking her hair.

"I understand," he said. "I remember the little girl who welcomed me into her home, before Ralph started being the monster he became. What got me through the last three years in the forest were my memories of your laughter, kindness, and sassy attitude. You were my only friend while I was in that hellhole. Let's do what we did in those days. Let's pretend the last five and a half years were a nightmare and we've awakened from that darkness. We're together; that's what counts. Even when you find the guy who will make you his princess, let's agree right now that we won't ever let each other out of our lives again."

Suzie hugged his legs tighter. She did what she wanted to do. "I'll never leave you, Joey Paschal, even if Prince Charming comes along on his white motorcycle," she said as she shifted her position to look up at him. Putting her hands around his neck, she pulled herself up and kissed him on the lips, her mouth slightly parted. She held the kiss for a while until he got over the shock of it and began responding. She fell back into his lap.

"I don't know what to do," Joey said, his face flushed with embarrassment. Suzie sat up from his lap, and he stood. Looking down at her, he said, "I've never kissed a girl before."

Suzie stood and put her arms around his neck. "Yes, you have. Don't you remember when you were ten, right after you came to live with us, you kissed me on the cheek when I shared my cookie with you?"

"That doesn't count," he retorted. When Suzie lifted her head from his chest, he quickly kissed her again, letting it linger.

"See, you do know what to do," she said.

"I—I just wanted to see if your lips were as soft as I thought they were the first time," Joey stammered, stepping back, picking up the vest, and putting it on. Suzie started helping gather the litter.

She said, "There is one thing I want to do for you when we get back to the house." She reached for his hands. "I want to give you a manicure—you know, trim these fingernails to just below the tips of your fingers."

"No," Joey responded, pulling his hands away.

Suzie pulled his body against hers, put her mouth close to his ear, and said, "At some point, I want you to put those fingers in special places, and you can't with long nails like those."

"Oh, I—I guess so. They'll grow back if I need them."

"You'll like what you do with your hands better without the long nails, I promise."

"We're not going back by the trail," he said. "I want you to see a part of the mountain that most people never see."

# CHAPTER 22

John handed Catherine an Aberfeldy scotch with a splash and one ice cube in a short crystal glass.

She looked up and said, "Thank you, John, darling." She took a sip. "Hmm, wonderful."

John sat on the sofa next to Catherine's chair. He reached over for a few peanuts. "Good scotch and pure water can't be beat. I'm delighted for this evening. It's kind of you to give me the time to discuss some ideas for the upcoming club golf championship. And please forgive me for being forward, but you look stunning. The way your hair frames your face brings out the sky blue of your eyes."

"John, darling, flattery will get you everywhere," Catherine said, taking a sip of her drink.

"By the way, I've made a reservation in Lenox at the Fitzgerald Inn for 8:00 p.m. Have you been there? They have a discreet booth in an alcove just off the bar area. Quite private and enjoyable."

"Wonderful. No, I haven't been there. Sounds very romantic. Do you take all your ladies there?"

"No, you're the only one. I wanted a special place for us to get to know each other."

Catherine sipped her drink, then put the glass on the coffee table.

"John, tell me about the law firm. How is it doing? Is the firm's relative position in the legal community improving or shrinking?"

"It's kind of you to ask. That is one subject, among others, I wanted to discuss with you this evening. Why are you curious?"

"The law firm was the fountain of my family's wealth. After Daddy died, the power and wealth from that source stopped. To me, it seems almost criminal to waste a potential money machine like that. I'm not an attorney, but I'd be interested in seeing if I could help revitalize the firm and restore its past glory."

John's hand trembled as he reached for his drink. He couldn't believe what he was hearing. This was the time to discuss his plan.

"Catherine, the firm is solid, but barely growing. You probably aren't aware, but I have associated the firm with Holliday, Edwards, and Carroll, an old and distinguished international law firm. We are independent; however, each firm assists the other with clients in its region. For instance, we introduced all our Boston clients to the Boston firm, and their clients in this part of the state and Vermont know they can receive advice and counsel from us when it's appropriate—a nice arrangement that should lead to more business in the future. There is something you could do that would be beneficial to both the firm and you, if you're interested."

"I'm interested."

"Your husband is wasting his talents on the bench. He should be in private practice. We have a place for him at the firm. I believe it would supercharge the firm's growth and, at the same time, put the two of you in front of a gusher of wealth, just as you had in the past."

"No!" Catherine shouted. "Cal had his chances and blew them! I don't give a damn what he does, but I'll tell you this, John Emerson: if you ever take him into the firm, I'll do whatever I can to see the firm, you, and that son of a bitch I'm married to fail miserably!" She picked up her drink, gulped it down, and slammed the glass on the table.

"Catherine, forgive me. I didn't know this proposal would offend you. I am so sorry. Please, let me make you another drink."

"Make it a double. I'm sorry, I shouldn't have had an emotional outburst like that."

"No need to apologize, my dear."

As John fixed her drink, Catherine shut her eyes, controlled her breathing, and decided she should explain since she had lost her temper. John was tan, thin, and virile. He was a master at all club activities. His hazel eyes captivated most women, including her. Importantly, he managed her family's law firm. He could be just what she wanted. The only question was, could she dominate him? She moved from her chair to the sofa.

"Here you are," John said, handing Catherine her drink. He sat next to her. "I had no idea you had those feelings about your husband. I don't know what led to them, but I do know he's a fool. Having a beautiful, skillful wife like you is every man's dream." He touched her hand and caressed the back of it. She pulled it away.

"John, neither of us is a child, so let's cut to the core. My first interest is the law firm. I want to take part in its growth and profits. I shouldn't have called Cal that, and I apologize for the outburst. Cal twice turned his back on the firm and the White family. I don't have a problem with his leaving the bench, but I don't want to give him a third chance to get rich off the White name."

"Forgive me for asking, Catherine, but with the severe feeling you seem to have toward Cal, why do you stay married to him?"

"John, you must not be as smart as I thought you were. His position on the bench allowed me to keep in touch with the legal community in the state. That's important to me. He isn't. If I'd met the right person, someone who could help me regain the prominence the family had when my father and grandfather were alive, I'd have dumped His Honor a long time ago." She looked at him and wet her lips.

"You've met him," he said, pulling her close and kissing her passionately. After a minute, she pulled away, downed her drink, and leaned over to kiss him while caressing his crotch.

An hour later they rested in his bed, her head on his chest and his hand stroking her hair. "John, you're a handsome, virile man with some interesting fantasies. I knew you were special when we won the triple-event marathon. We're not children. I can help you and the firm. I want you to do two things for me: First, I want to be part of the firm. I'm not a lawyer, so according to the law, I can't be a partner or a decision-maker. A non-lawyer employee compensated and taking part in a profit-sharing retirement account is permissible. I want you to arrange for me to have an advisory role at the firm. I don't want or need an office, but I want to be an observer at all partner meetings. My salary could start relatively low so the partners don't complain. When I've proven my worth, it could be increased to a level comparable to a partner. I'll be the firm's best rainmaker. Second, you want Cal off the bench, or else you wouldn't have suggested I help you place him at the firm. I want him off the bench too, and I want him disbarred if possible. You give me those two things, and I'll give you all the fantasies you can dream up. That's a fair trade, right?"

"Yes, it is. Getting Cal off the bench will take some capital the firm doesn't have, and it will take some lobbying of the governor to replace him. In addition, we'll have to unseat the Eighth District councillor."

"Is it true that the current governor is a shoo-in in next year's election?"

"Yes, and he's close to us."

"I don't want Cal reappointed. I want you to find someone the governor can appoint in his place and tell me how much it will cost to make sure Cal becomes unemployed."

"The senior partners at the firm have been discussing a way to get our fair-headed associate into the political game. We're confident he has the potential to make it to the governor's office and reestablish the statewide power the firm had under your father."

"Who is this golden boy?"

"Neil Clements, better known as Ace. Eleven years ago, he was all-state at Harrison High in football, basketball, and baseball. He left here and went to a small liberal arts college in Boston, didn't play any sports, graduated third in his class, and went on to Harvard Law. When he finished, graduating in the top five percent of his class, he clerked for the chief judge of the state supreme court, then returned home. We snared him from a Boston firm with a local office. He has the drive to be successful in politics, and we have the connections to help him."

"Ace?"

"That's a holdover from his athletic career. The public will love it."

"What will it cost to make sure he's appointed?"

"Probably a hundred thousand. Most of the money goes to the governor's campaign committee, and the rest to making sure our candidate is elected Eighth District councillor. As you probably know, Jess Simpson hasn't faced opposition for the last eight years. It'll take a greater effort to unseat him."

Catherine stood naked at the end of the bed and looked down at Emerson. "Take a good look at what's available, John, dear. You deliver, and I'll deliver. The two of us will rule western Massachusetts.

Now, I'm going to shower and get dressed. Call and change our dinner reservation to later."

§

She reached into her purse and took out her checkbook and a pen. "Please fix me a small drink while I take care of financial matters." She started writing out a check. "I'm making this check out to cash. Not only is it our secret, but we don't want to violate any state contribution laws. If it takes more, let me know. I want results, not excuses. Agreed?" She tore the check from the checkbook and handed it to John.

He sat looking at the check, not believing his good fortune. He took a sip of his drink and looked at Catherine. "No problem. I have the people this will be filtered through, so no one will know. Don't hold me to this, but what if we could get him disbarred?"

"John, really? You think that's a possibility? Really?"

"There's a possibility—a long shot, mind you. We'd have to dig up something from the past or fabricate some unethical or criminal behavior. Yes, we have friends who could make it happen."

"There's another two hundred thousand if you succeed in having him disbarred," Catherine said. She smiled, picked up her glass, and drained it. "I believe it's time to go. I'm famished."

§

"Aloysius," John said. "John Emerson. How have you been?"

"Fine. What can I do for you?" came back a curt reply.

"Gee, that's not a way to be with me. I thought we were closer than that."

"Sorry, I'm knee-deep in a merger transaction. Let me start over. Hello, John. Good to hear from you. Is that better?"

"All right, smart-ass. You gave me a job to do, and it's done, so to speak."

Aloysius sat up and turned on his phone recorder.

"Interesting. Tell me about it."

"I've become close to Judge White-Callaway's wife. She would like to see him leave the bench but was adamant he can't join my firm. She gave me a check for a hundred thousand to make sure the governor, when reelected, will not reappoint her husband as state court judge."

"Isn't that convenient? I don't see where that'd be a problem. Will you take care of the incumbent councillor?"

"Yes, but the money for that is in this hundred thousand."

"Go back and tell her you underestimated. Tell her it will take another fifty to take care of the Eighth District councillor."

"I'm not sure I want to do that. She's willing to pay two hundred thousand more if we can get Judge White-Callaway disbarred. It may require fabricating some issue. I'll have one of my associates research his past rulings to see if there's anything we can use. I don't want to overreach."

"Fine, let's see what we can do on the disbarment first. If you can't find something, we can come up with an issue. Get back to me soon so we have enough time to make everything foolproof. His wife, eh? This will be easier than I thought."

"Great. I'll get someone on it. In the meantime, please send me a hundred-thousand-dollar invoice for services rendered. I'll forward a check from our firm to yours when I receive it."

"It'll be there later today. Changing subjects, our mutual Boston client asked me the other day if the eight thousand monthly cash delivery was still going smoothly."

"Yes, it is. I assume our Boston client realizes you and I are each paid a thousand from that amount, and the net six thousand gets to the proper place."

"I've never given him details, and he doesn't have to know unless he asks for them."

"We appreciate being involved. It's nice to have a client of his stature see how discreet and professional our firm is. We're the right firm for all that client's western Massachusetts business."

"He does," Aloysius said. "I've got to go. Look in your email for the invoice."

# CHAPTER 23

The members of the Berkshire Book Club took their seats, with David Fogel in the speaker's chair. "Here's the situation. The individual was convicted of child molestation in Vermont. For some incredible reason, he was placed on probation rather than given jail time. As part of his sentence, he was to submit to electronic monitoring and not leave the immediate area. He removed the monitor four months ago and disappeared. Obviously, he showed up here. He's reclusive. If it weren't for C. C.'s clerks being alert, we probably couldn't have found him before he hurt other children. Best we can figure out, someone helped him get here. Someone set up a furnished house and signed a paid-in-advance twelve-month lease. They paid for cable internet a year in advance. He bought a computer and printer, and he's evidently hooked into the pedophile network, preying on children again. He set up one room of the house as what I'd call the abuse room. There's a bed, a lot of stuffed animals, superhero and princess posters on the walls, and a multi-camera video recording system. There's digital footage of the three children Tomas told us about." David stopped to let the information settle in. The mood was somber. No one spoke.

"How sure are you of what you're telling us, David?" Wan Chu asked.

"Confirmed on all accounts."

"You mean you've been in the house and seen this room, these tapes, and the computer?"

"Yes." Silence again as the members absorbed the implications of what had been said.

Finally, Helen Inskeep said, "How can we stop this and know it will be stopped forever?"

"That's the right question," Fogel said. "We can pick him up as a fugitive, ship him back to Vermont, and hope they lock him up, but there's no guarantee. The information I've given you now isn't even usable in court. He's been under surveillance ever since we identified him. If he tried to lure a child, we would intercede and arrest him. He stays at home most of the time, only going out at night, primarily to the convenience store, but twice a week he walks to Nancy's Tavern. We went in the house when he was at the bar and gathered the information we have, including fingerprints. If he tried to act out against a child, and we stopped him before he did, and then the matter went to court, there's no way we could be sure the results wouldn't be exactly what happened after his Vermont conviction."

Cal spoke up when David finished. "Does anyone here believe this problem in our community shouldn't be dealt with in a way that will make our community safe for our children again?" Most members shook their heads, with murmurs from some. "Let's go around the circle, and everyone ask questions or offer advice."

The right to speak passed around the circle until it reached Jerry Myrick, a wheelchair-bound veteran and owner of a radio, computer, and IT repair shop. "As I see it," he began, "we have an interesting situation here. David said we know for sure who's abusing our children. For want of a comparison, we know where there's a timber rattler in our midst. Somehow the law doesn't allow us, the community, to do anything about it. If we have him arrested, he may walk, just as he did in Vermont. Now, I've read both the Declaration of Independence and the Constitution. Matter of fact, I read both many times while bedridden in the VA hospital. When those gentlemen wrote those words, they were trying to protect the average citizen from the risk of a dictatorial government hell-bent on oppressing the people. They did not intend for their words to be used for protecting the criminal element that preys on citizens. I can't find a single word or passage that says a community of citizens, going about their lives and obeying the Constitution and society's laws, can't rid their community of a rattlesnake deliberately hurting the most vulnerable of us. It seems to me this differs from the student drug dealer. Hell, his customers knew what they were doing. They're just stupid. These second and third graders, according to what I've read in the Declaration and Constitution, have a right to be happy and safe children, and more than anything, they need protection from rattlesnakes by us adults. I say we rid this community, and communities everywhere, of this known rattlesnake and any other rattlesnakes associated with him. When he took the most vulnerable of us and injured them for life, he gave up his right to the constitutional protection our founders had in mind. That's all I have to say. Seems simple to me."

"Well put, Jerry. Anyone have any other thoughts?" Cal asked. No one responded. "Does anyone believe we should do nothing but call Vermont authorities?"

"If we call Vermont, what will they likely do? Somehow, some way, he had enough clout to avoid jail time," said Rick Branson, the junkyard owner.

"I agree with Rick," Jack Gianelli added. "Let's deal with the problem. He's injured three children in our community. Let's not stick our heads in the sand."

"Our babies are our most precious jewels," Rosa Lee Dixon said. "Shame on him. He made the decision to steal our jewels. My momma always said, 'I am responsible for my actions, and actions have consequences.' Simple to me, too."

"That's it, then. We'll see everyone at our next regular meeting. This issue will be dealt with." Cal touched David on the arm and said, "Let's talk for a minute when everyone leaves."

David remained seated, and Maggie moved over and took the seat to Cal's right.

He turned to her, leaned over, and softly said in her ear, "You don't want to stay here right now."

"Don't worry, I've got my big-girl panties on. If I can help eliminate this shit-ass from the face of the earth, I want to help," she responded.

Junior walked over to the three of them, turned a chair so he faced David, and said, "David, you know the dirt logging road that runs off 183 between the Stockbridge Bowl and the swamp?"

"I think so. About two miles along on the right?"

"Yeah, that's the one. I have a problem. That road is a boundary of our property, back where the property gives way to the swamp. Some kids must have borrowed my Bobcat backhoe, took it down there, dug a deep hole, and left everything right there, with the key in the Cat. Kids are something, aren't they? Can you get an officer to go down there, check for fingerprints or whatever you do, and see if anything can be done about these crazy kids?" With that, Junior stood, shook hands all around, and walked away.

"Well, that takes care of one big problem," David said in a low voice.

"Need help with everything?" Cal asked.

"No, it's under control. It'll be done soon. The house will stay as is, with a couple of exceptions. I'll wipe the house clean of fingerprints. We'll place miniature cameras at each entry and at the computer so that video will capture anyone who comes in. Replacing the current computer hard drive and destroying the pornographic videos is important. I'll do that. Cookies will document any computer trying to contact that one. It'll be interesting to see who shows up at the house looking for him."

"If you need anything, let me know."

"Yes, sir."

The three of them rose and left the room.

# CHAPTER 24

Joey sat in the dining hall, eating a sandwich Maggie had made for him. He looked at the two cookies she had baked lying on a napkin, savoring the idea of eating them soon. Eating is not the correct word; nibbling is more like it. Since leaving the wilderness, he took his time enjoying fresh food rather than raw or stale food scavenged from nature, campsites, or dumpsters. Maggie's food was too good to gulp down. Slowly allowing a cookie to melt in his mouth, then moving it around so all the taste buds had an equal opportunity to enjoy the goodness was more like it. He chewed the sandwich as he worked through the list of botanical facts he needed to know for the test.

"You look studious," Becky Lang said as she and Issie passed his table.

Taken by surprise, Joey looked up and said, "Oh, hi, Dr. Lang. Hi, Issie." He looked from one to the other. He then returned to his studies. "I've got a botany test at two. Just trying to review."

"We're having lunch, as well. Get back to work. You want an A, for sure," Becky said before the two of them moved off. Joey went back to eating and studying.

§

"Let go, you ass. You're hurting me!" someone yelled.

Joey's head snapped up. He knew it was Issie's voice. He looked around the dining hall and saw, across the large room, Issie bent to the left, with a large boy twisting her arm.

"Let go, goddammit! Let go of me!"

Becky Lang was trying to pull the boy away.

Joey shoved his botany notebook and two cookies in his backpack and began moving toward the scuffle. Becky was still pulling on the boy's free arm, trying to force him to let Issie go.

"Am I hurting you, cunt? Am I? Good, you deserve it. You owe me. I want my money, bitch."

Joey pushed through the gathering crowd of students. "Please let her go," he said calmly, naturally.

Becky Lang looked at Joey and recoiled at the look on his face. She sensed this situation was going to get out of hand if she didn't do something. She let go of the boy's arm, picked up her cell, and hit the campus security code for a faculty member requiring assistance.

"Please let her go now," Joey repeated. He dropped his backpack on the floor and kicked it under a nearby table.

"Who the fuck are you, asshole? Get out of here before you get hurt."

"If you hurt her any more, I'm going to stop you," Joey said, standing loosely, his arms by his side.

The boy looked at Joey, who was at least three inches shorter and forty pounds lighter than he was. He let go of Issie's arm, but not before giving it one more twist and shoving her into a table and chair.

"Thank you," Joey said, then turned to retrieve his backpack. As he did, the boy reached out and pushed him, spinning him back around. He drew back his left hand in a fist, preparing to hit Joey. Before he could swing, Joey grabbed his right forearm and pulled him forward while driving a foot into the boy's exposed right knee, forcing it inward. The popping of the knee breaking resonated through the room.

The boy cried out as he fell to the floor. Joey reached down, grabbed his right hand, and bent his little finger back until it broke. The boy screamed.

Becky Lang rushed over to Joey and tried to force him to let go. "Joey, stop! Stop! Issie is okay. Leave him alone," she said with her mouth up against his ear.

Three campus security guards pushed through the crowd and grabbed Joey.

"Let him go," Becky said. "I'm Dr. Lang. I sent the code. Take this young man to my office, Room 201, Gearson Hall. You," she said, pointing to the third officer, "call for an ambulance. Turning toward Issie, she said, "Issie, you okay? Do you want to call the police?"

"Yeah," she said, rubbing her arm. She wiped her tears on the sleeve of her shirt.

"Go back to the dorm. I'll tell the police to come see you there," Becky said.

Issie picked up her books from the table and started leaving, looking down at her antagonist writhing in pain on the floor. "Okay," she said.

Becky pulled out her phone.

§

"Your Honor, Becky Lang is on line one," Betsy said.

"Hello, Becky, everything good?"

"Not exactly, Your Honor."

Cal sat upright, reaching for a yellow pad and pencil. He wrote JOEY at the top. "Is Joey all right?"

"Yes and no. Let me explain. There was an altercation in the dining hall at school an hour ago. You know who Issie is, Joey's math tutor.

She and I were having lunch together. We had just spoken to Joey, who was in the dining hall studying. Issie is a wonderful person, but lousy at picking boyfriends. Her latest mistake came over to our table, saying Issie owed him money for a gift that he gave her right before she broke up with him. He got physical with her, twisting her arm and causing her to scream out. Joey heard her cries and came over, and the boy ended up attacking him. Joey broke the boy's knee and one of his fingers. He would have broken all of the fingers, but I stopped him. Otherwise, I'm not sure what else Joey would have done."

"Was Joey hurt?"

"Frankly, Your Honor, I'm not sure Joey even had an adrenaline rush. He never seemed excited. That's the good news. The bad news is what I saw in his face. I've never seen a look like that on a person's face before. I'm convinced he would have killed that kid if I hadn't stopped him. As is, the boy is probably never going to do much in his life that requires strong knees."

"Is Joey at fault? Was he arrested?"

"No, on both accounts. I'm the person who sent the emergency alert. I directed the campus security to take Joey to my office. I stayed and gave a statement explaining everything and corralled two students I know to give statements as well, telling the officers exactly what happened and who was at fault. Joey and I talked in my office. He wouldn't go into any reason why he did what he did, just said he was sorry. I made sure he was emotionally stable and let him go to his botany class, where he had a test."

"What's your professional assessment?"

"Joey is at risk. It's now clear that he was abused. I don't know when or for how long, but he's been brutalized at some point in his life. I suspect he has a deep, deep-seated anger inside him. He needs help. The problem is, Judge, if professional help guides Joey into facing his anger, it could destroy him. Believe me, Your Honor, when I tell you that the look on Joey's face, his calm demeanor, and his willingness to continue hurting someone who was incapacitated were bone-chilling, nothing like I've ever seen or studied."

"What happens to the other kid?"

"He'll go before the student disciplinary committee. I suspect he'll withdraw for a year. There's very little patience and understanding for students, particularly males, hurting another student, particularly females."

"Will Joey have to face the committee?"

"No, I've given a statement. If anything, Joey would be hailed a hero, but that's not good for him. I've asked that his name and identity be kept from the police record, as well."

"Thank you, Becky. I'd like to consider your thoughts on Joey receiving help with his anger. He has these outbursts only when someone is bullying another defenseless person. I can't say much, but you're right: when Joey was younger, someone severely abused him. The question is this: Joey has been back in civilization for what, four months? What if we give him more time? Time to realize how friendly people can be. Maybe, just maybe, he'll be able to lock that crippling anger deep inside himself and let the kindness he receives dissipate the anger."

"Your Honor, I understand what you're hoping for, but it's highly unlikely time will make a difference. Since he's a ward of the court, that's your decision."

"Thank you, Becky. Let's plan on discussing this in three weeks. Two weeks from now, Joey and I will be working on the AT all day. I'll make an opportunity to discuss this situation with him if he doesn't tell me about the incident before then. Is that agreeable?"

"Yes, sir. I will, however, put the incident in his file."

"Understood. Thanks for calling."

"Thank you. Bye."

Cal sat back, pulled out his Bible, and took out Josey's picture. He fingered the sealed envelope with the paternity information. Was Joey his son? Joey's courage in the face of everything was remarkable. Cal tapped the envelope on the Bible over and over. Maggie could dissipate Joey's anger better than anyone. He put the Bible, containing the photo, the envelope, and the ring, back in the drawer and returned to his brief.

# CHAPTER 25

Joey parked the Wrangler at the beach area of Benedict Pond. "Wait here till I go pay the attendant," he told Suzie as he headed for the front of the building, which housed the restrooms and store.

Suzie jumped out of the Wrangler and walked over to the pond. She knew the ducks were on their way south. Fall was fast becoming her favorite time of year, when the air was crisp and the leaves a palette of reds, yellows, rusty oranges, and some never-say-die greens.

"Want to go swimming?" Joey teased as he returned and reached into the Wrangler for his hiking vest. Both had layered up since the climb would start cool, but exertion would quickly elevate their metabolism.

Joey was ecstatic. This was the third time he was showing Suzie some of his life in the wilderness. This hike would show her the Ledges, a place he believed was the prettiest on earth. During the AT thru-hiker season, there was a steady flow of hikers heading to Mount Katahdin and the end of their journey of self-discovery, self-worth, or healing of their self-image. In late October, very few hikers made the climb to the Ledges. Joey was confident he could be alone with Suzie and share more of nature with her.

Suzie was giddy with happiness. She had dreamed about this day ever since finding Joey again. The sky was clear blue, the fall foliage past its prime but still beautiful. They walked hand in hand along the pond until they came to the pond head and crossed a wooden bridge. Suzie stopped, leaned over the rail, and watched the steady flow of water from up the mountain as it cascaded over the rocks and fallen branches and leaves washed down the gully. She turned to look at Joey and again knew she had made the right decision during the night. Hopefully he'd accept her point of view. She wanted to make him understand how she truly felt. She knew in her heart he loved her as much as she loved him.

Suzie reached over and hugged Joey. They resumed walking, holding hands, until they came to an old, paved road curving around the mountain. Suzie stopped and looked across the road. Facing her was a jagged boulder field covering the side of the mountain. There didn't appear to be any way over the boulders other than a slow climb on all fours, one outcropping to the next. "We're going to climb that?" she turned to look at Joey and asked.

He grinned and snorted. "It's worth the effort, but no, look again. You see the boulders, but look to the right. There's a narrow path, not free of rocks, but much easier to climb. C'mon," he said, taking her hand. "Follow me," he urged. He guided her up the mountainside, showing her the handholds, trees, and spots to place her feet so the climb was as easy as possible, which was still hard.

"I have a new respect for AT hikers. Even a day hiker must be in decent shape," Suzie said, bent over with her hands on her knees, panting.

"Stick with me and you'll get there, I promise," Joey said. After a moment, the two started again along a well-marked trail. "Remember the white blaze marks?" he asked over his shoulder.

"Yes, one blaze means the main trail. Two blazes, one above the other and just offset, right or left, means the trail is turning. The offset shows which way."

"Very good. You'll get an extra cookie at the top."

Three quarters of the way up, they came to another deep and wide gully with rushing water from a nearby high lake. The AT obviously went across the wooden bridge spanning the spillway and continued up the mountain, skirting the side of the ravine until the funnel changed direction and headed down the mountainside.

"The AT goes up that way," Joey said, pointing at the trail across the bridge. "I want to show you the lake before we go." He took her hand and walked to the left of the footbridge, along a faint trail leading through heavier brush. About thirty yards up the trail, he pointed out a tree trunk spanning the spillway. "That log was used to cross the gulley before the AT Conservancy built the bridge. A more challenging way, particularly with a fifty-pound pack on your back."

The trunk and its narrowness amazed Suzie.

"C'mon, there's something else," Joey said, taking her hand. Pushing through the chest-high bushes, Joey looked down and stepped from one rock to another until he was standing on a wide boulder next to a high mountain lake. He reached back and took Suzie's hand, leading her over the rocks. "This is marshy land, so step from one stone to the other. That's right."

She reached the last rock, saw the lake, and hugged Joey. "Oh, my God, this is awesome. Look at the colors still in the trees here. Oh, Joey, I've never seen anything like this." She looked at him.

Nervously, Joey gave her a quick kiss, hoping she didn't recoil. Instead, she kissed him back, let go of his waist, and put both hands on the sides of his face, pushing her tongue deep into his mouth. They stood there for a timeless period, kissing each other.

"We'd—we'd better go," Joey said, both nervous and delighted by their kiss. Suzie turned and stepped quickly across the rocks to the trail. She knew this day was the end of one life and the beginning of their future together.

They crossed the AT bridge and skirted the mountain. Suzie could see more of the mountainside as they climbed, but the trees blocked the vista after a few feet. Near the top, but two hundred feet from the crest, the trees gave way to an open view south and southwest across the valley to Livermore Peak. The Ledges' view stunned Suzie. She knew this was the perfect place for today. She looked down and saw rock ledges six feet below where they stood, and she looked up and saw stones stepping up the mountainside. The view down and across the valley was peaceful. The farms from this height looked like they were part of a fairytale of happiness and goodness.

"I'm speechless at the beauty," Suzie said. "The wilderness, the view, the sky, the coolness—it just can't be described. Thank you for bringing me here." She looked at Joey.

"Want to sit awhile, or are you hungry?" he asked.

Suzie knew this was the time. He'd know how much she loved him, and by his reaction, she'd know how much he really loved her. "Let's just sit and talk and watch the view. Do you think other people will come by today?"

"Don't know, but it's unlikely. Most hikers prefer easier stretches of the AT for day hikes, and serious hikers are long gone. C'mon, there's a good place just up above where we can sit, look out over the valley, and not be seen by hikers, since they'll all be looking at the valley as well."

Suzie followed Joey higher until he stopped at a flat space partly shielded from view below by boulders. Joey took off his vest and removed a poncho from its game pouch, spreading it on the ground. The two of them sat side by side. Suzie started kissing Joey's neck, face, and lips. He responded with delight. She then took Joey's hand in hers and kissed it, inserting two fingers in her mouth and caressing them with her tongue. Joey's eyes grew wide as a tingling sensation coursed through his body.

"Joey, I want to say something," she said. "Something that's real important to me. Will you listen and let me get it out before saying anything?" She was not looking at him, but staring down at the valley, not really seeing anything, concentrating on what she wanted to say and how she wanted it to come out.

"Sure, if that's what you want," Joey said, insecurity in his voice. He let Suzie continue to hold his hand, but he was as still as he had been whenever he saw a bear, a bobcat, or a human approaching when he lived in the woods. His insecurity was deep. He was happier than he had been at any time in his life, and he was afraid that happiness would be fleeting, replaced again by the loneliness and rootlessness he had experienced.

"Joey, you know what Stoner did to me. I told you I got in with the wrong crowd after he died. There's one thing I've never done, and that's made love to someone. To me, sex is biological, and answering that biological need is different from making love. Making love requires more emotions than physical effort. I always said I'd save making love for the man I wanted to marry. Most people think that's crazy. Sex and making love are the same, they think. They're wrong. When people have sex, they're looking to satisfy a biological need pleasantly. If the person they're with has pleasure, they think that's fine but mostly irrelevant. Making love is different. To me, making love to a man means seeking to pleasure the one I love as much or more than he pleases me. Giving him emotional pleasure is primary. If I pick him right, he'll be as interested in giving me emotional pleasure as I am in giving it to him. That's when I believe sparks will fly. Does this make sense to you?"

"I guess so," Joey said quietly. Joey didn't want to think of Suzie as a woman who had the right and ability to make these kinds of decisions. Joey felt he didn't even know how to act right around a woman. He had watched the judge and Maggie, and he was sure they liked each other, but he didn't know what to say or how to say it the way they did. He was fearful Suzie was trying to say they couldn't be together.

Suzie took Joey's hand and put it on her breast, over her clothes. "Joey, I can't have sex with you. You're the man I want to marry when we both get out of college. I want to make love to you. Right now, right here."

Joey felt her nipple harden, and he had difficulty processing what he had heard.

"I don't know. I mean, I don't know how, Suzie." His eyes were wide with fear. He hadn't expected this willingness of Suzie to give her body to him.

"It's all right. You don't have to know anything." She let go of his hand. Leaning over, she kissed him, her tongue pushing into his mouth until she met his tongue. Her hand reached his groin, felt his erection, and deftly unzipped his pants. She reached in and freed him, and he ejaculated.

"Oh, God. I'm so sorry, I didn't mean to," Joey moaned.

"Shh, that's normal. It happens all the time when a relationship is as new and loving as ours. Don't worry, there's more where that came from, and you'll have your erection back shortly. It gives us time to explore each other," she said as she wiped her hand on her jeans. "Help me get this blouse off."

Joey reached across and pulled it over her head, leaving her T-shirt and bra in place.

She pulled the shirt off her arms. "Reach around me and unhook my bra," she said in a husky voice.

Joey did so and kissed her.

"You're a fast learner," she teased.

The bra sprang loose, freeing her ample breasts. Joey sat back, just staring at her small, hard nipples. Suzie took her right breast, the most sensitive, in her right hand, and with her left, she guided Joey's head down and her nipple into his mouth. She laid back on the poncho, pulling him with her. Her suppressed emotions from Stoner's rapes, her memory of Joey saving her from them, and the years of not knowing where he was and whether he was safe, mixed with a confluence of love, hope for the future, spirit, and physical arousal were like a volcano erupting. The sensations washing over her consumed her. She arched her back and felt heat and sensitivity filling her groin.

"Oh, God, Joey—now, I'm coming. Oh, God, don't stop. Bite it gently, now harder. Oh, God. Oh, God. I love you, Joey!" She began furiously trying to take off his sweater. He sat up and pulled the clothes off his chest. She took his nipple in her mouth, kneaded it with her tongue against her teeth, knowing Joey would learn to do the same. She started unbuckling his belt and pants. Joey jumped up and pulled his pants off, almost tripping over them. "Now me, Joey, and hurry."

Joey knelt down between her legs and hooked his hands on either side of her waistband as she raised her hips off the ground. Her pants and panties came off as one. Joey's erection was full as he looked down at the glistening wetness she was offering him.

Suzie reached for his erection, pulling him on top of her. She guided him into her body, feeling the strength and hardness of him. She wrapped her legs around him, not willing to chance his slipping out. They kissed as she slowly started grinding her hips, prompting him to do the same. It didn't take long for both of them to rush into an orgasm. They lay still, panting. Joey moved.

"No, don't move. You still have an erection. That's one of the good things about being with the one you love the first time. You'll stay hard and come again."

"I don't think I can," Joey whispered.

"You wait and see. Slowly start swiveling your hips in a small circle. That's right. Now bend your head and gently bite my nipple again. Oh, God, that's it." She reached around his back and caressed his buttocks, pushing him deeper and deeper inside her, setting the rhythm she wanted. She started kissing his neck, and as the sensations rose, she began biting his shoulder to stifle her cries of joy. Joey was pounding her harder and harder.

Joey was the lover she had dreamed he would be. He did love her. All she wanted now was to make love for the rest of their lives. She didn't allow reality to intrude on this place and time.

The two of them climaxed together again. This time, their passion subsided. Suzie dropped her legs and hugged Joey to her. "I love making love to you," she said in his ear.

"I love you, too," Joey said hesitatingly. He rolled over to the side. He raised his head up on his hand and gazed at her naked body. "I don't know what to say," he stammered, caressing her breasts and running his fingers down her torso to her pubic mound.

"Just say you love me as much as I love you," Suzie said, snuggling against him.

"I love you more than life itself." They were both quiet, the realization of what this afternoon meant to them and their future sinking in. After a few moments, Suzie said, "I'm hungry," bringing them back to the present. She sat up, retrieved her panties and pants, and slipped them on. Joey found his pants and did the same. They quickly dressed, and Joey laid out lunch.

"Maybe we can do that again when we get to your house?" Joey asked, not looking at her.

"Awesome. You bet."

# CHAPTER 26

David Fogel, disguised as a shift worker, sat at the bar's end closest to the front door, nursing a Black Jack and water, looking into the narrow and deep Nancy's Tavern. He wore a Red Sox ballcap, big horn-rimmed glasses, two weeks' beard growth, a dirty T-shirt, a ripped and dirty short-sleeved blue denim work shirt, grimy jeans, and scuffed work boots. His hands and arms were soiled with permanent grease stains partially obscuring a multicolored ninja warrior tattoo on his left forearm. He smelled of sweat and grime.

The bar stretched two-thirds of the way down the left side of the restaurant. Five booths lined the wall on the right side. Nancy had spaced single tables between the bar and the booths. Four more tables filled the area past the bar. Nancy's was a simple place. A customer could get a hamburger, hotdog, BLT, eggs any way, fries, sausage, bacon, and polenta. Nancy knew her serious money came from the beer and whiskey she served, so she made sure the beer was cold, the drinks strong, and the food salty.

Even though she served a killer breakfast, she didn't open until three in the afternoon, and she stayed open until two thirty in the morning. Heavy drinkers and late-shift workers enjoyed a hearty breakfast before heading home. David Fogel chatted with the bartender while monitoring the booth where the target sat sipping a beer and eating a BLT. Already, this night was different. David had taken his bar seat at a quarter to ten, knowing the target would arrive promptly at ten, as he did every Tuesday and Friday. The pervert sat in the same booth on the same side of the table, his back to the door. Most men wanted to watch the door, sitting with their back to a wall to get an unobstructed view of the entrance. Doing that, however, meant anyone entering or sitting at the bar would see him. The target was less concerned about seeing others than making sure few people saw him. Tonight, he went directly to the booth.

David watched his left hand rub the underside of the table. The target found what appeared to be an envelope, evidently taped to the bottom of the table; he put it in the left pocket of his jacket. What was it—photos, money? David's heart beat rapidly until he combat-breathed, returning his heart rate to normal. Someone else knew the pervert came here regularly. David was confident the pervert's protector had left the envelope for him. Who was it? Were they local or not? Could they be the Vermont accomplice? Could it be the person who had arranged the target's house here? David searched the ceiling of the room. There they were. Two cameras. The potential double payoff of catching two pedophiles instead of one was exciting. He looked at his watch: a quarter to midnight.

"Herman, settle me up," he said.

The bartender came over and flipped a written tab in front of David, who pulled eight dollars from his wallet and handed them over.

"See you another time, Leroy," Herman said, separating the tip from the bill.

David walked at a fast clip, retracing the same path the target would take, zig-zagging the six blocks to his home. Three blocks away, he passed the front of a brown panel truck and quickly ducked alongside it. He slid the side door open, reached in, and extracted his vest. From the vest, he pulled a black ski mask and a stun gun. The fully charged and enhanced amperage gun would leave any target incapacitated for three minutes. David crouched beside the truck in the dark. Earlier in the day, wearing a Berkshire Electric uniform, he had disabled the streetlight. He checked his watch: five after midnight. Any time now, the target would be coming.

David heard a voice before he heard the footsteps. Oh, shit! He's talking on a phone. David calmly checked off his choices: abort or risk the person on the phone hearing the takedown and calling the police. The target reached the far side of the truck. David decided this was the time. He shifted the stun gun to his right hand, preparing to grab the phone with his left hand and stuff it in his vest to muffle any cries from the target.

The pervert cleared the front of the van, looking down as he stepped up on the curb. David came out of the shadows behind him and hit him in the back of the neck with the stun gun, grabbing the phone as the target crumpled to the ground. David ended the call and stuffed the phone in his vest.

He pulled out plastic zip ties and quickly secured the target's hands behind his back and his feet together, then put a hood over the perp's head. Three minutes were all the time he had. He ran around the front of the van and jumped in.

David drove up next to the target lying on the sidewalk, grabbed him by the belt and jacket collar, and lifted him into the van. He climbed in and slid the door closed. One minute to go. He hit the target with another charge from the stun gun, giving himself three more minutes, before he started the van and drove away. At the next corner, he turned left, went to a dark place halfway down the street, parked, and returned to the back.

He pulled a roll of duct tape from the vest, took the hood off, held up the target's head, and wrapped the duct tape around it, covering his mouth. The perp's head rested on David's knee while he started another strip, which he used to cover the pervert's eyes. Round and round, he wrapped the tape around the man's head, careful to cover his eyes totally but making sure he could breathe through his nose. He put the hood back on and extracted a soft black pouch from his kit. He took out a syringe, injected the body, and then relaxed.

David removed the cell phone from his pocket. Using his Gerber tool, he extracted the SIM card, then carefully placed both pieces in his kit. He returned to the front, lit a cigarette, and drove off. His watch read almost twenty after midnight. He headed to the house two blocks away, and later to the swamp road behind Junior's nursery.

§

Sitting in his family room, drinking a Black Jack and water, David twirled the iPhone between his thumb and forefinger. On his lap was the envelope, with the tape used to secure it under the table still sticky. It contained six thousand dollars in small denominations. It must be hush money or extortion money. How often did the transfer happen? If monthly, almost seventy-two thousand a year. If twice a month, twice that. Somebody didn't want a secret out. But who, and what secret?

David was calm after the adrenaline rush subsided. He twirled the iPhone again. The lack of a password on the phone implied the pervert was confident of his security. Even more stupid was not erasing past phone calls. The recent calls log showed them all, going back four months. Calls from multiple area codes, several from this county. Who? How to get the phone dumped, and the numbers crossed with names?

How to use the phone as evidence to round up a bunch of perverts?

He finished his drink and put the phone and the cash envelope in his vest. On the way to his bedroom, he stopped at the door to his boys' room. Slipping in, he checked the covers on both. The three of them had been to T-ball practice that afternoon. He thought about the three little children, the same ages as his boys, who now had nightmares, confusion, and fears they couldn't and wouldn't get rid of for a long time, if ever. Their worlds had shattered. Their parents' worlds had shattered. Why? Why and how had the system designed to protect the innocent turned into a shield to protect the guilty from punishment? He leaned over each boy and kissed him on the top of his head. Something had to be done. And, damn it, if he was the one to do it in this community, so be it.

§

"Your Honor, Deputy Fogel is here and requests a moment of your time," Betsy said over the intercom.

"Send him in," Cal said, getting up from his desk. He met David as the door opened. "Morning, David," he said, extending his hand.

"Morning, Cal," David said, shaking it.

"Have a seat. Want any coffee?"

"No, sir."

"Coke? Water?"

"Nah, I'm fine."

"Everything okay, David?" Cal asked, understanding why the visit was happening.

"Yes and no."

Cal sat up straight and reached for his pad and pencil.

"Yes, the community is safe again. No, in that it appears we may be playing that carnival game, Whack-a-Mole."

"Help me understand," Cal said, sitting back in his chair. David reached inside the side cargo pocket of his uniform pants and pulled out the cell phone and envelope. He placed both on Cal's desk. Cal looked at the items but did not move to touch them.

"Last night after ten, the person we discussed extracted that envelope from underneath the tabletop of the booth he was sitting in. Someone had put it there earlier in the day. It'd be a stretch of logic to think it had been there longer than a few hours, as the place didn't open until three. The phone isn't password protected, which is unbelievable, and the list of calls goes back four months, which is close to the time the individual walked away from his prior location and came here. He clearly felt secure here."

Cal sat and stared at the two items silently for a couple of minutes. "What did you tell me was happening with the computer?"

"I'll get to that. You'll be interested to know there are six long-range photos of first-, second-, and third-grade children in the photos on that iPhone. He was lining up future victims."

"Jesus, and someone in the community knew he was here and was giving him money, literally under the table," Cal said, shaking his head.

"After picking up the guy, I stopped by his house and switched his hard drive for an identical one, set up to place a cookie on any device contacting it. I have the original and all of the DVDs. Well, I don't actually have them. I smashed them and disposed of everything at the same time."

"No trace?"

"None. I'm careful when it comes to my work."

"Yes, you are."

"What about the phone? You want me to get the guys to dump it and check the numbers?"

"No. You're done. I'll take it from here. There is one thing, though. Can you find out if the tavern has security cameras? It sure would be nice to see who entered and sat in that booth yesterday afternoon."

"I checked last night. There are at least two. One is across from the booth. I'll need a warrant. We'll probably want to wait for a couple of weeks and ask for two months of video, just so there won't be any questions about why now. Betsy can download the phone records in the meantime."

"Heavens, no. You and I are the only two people on earth who can tie this phone and money to the missing person. When these are disposed of, there's nothing to tie you or anyone else to him. When you're ready for the warrant, call Betsy and give her the details. She'll write it up and I'll sign it. By the way, how are Donna and the boys?"

"She's great, the glue that holds my universe together. I'm coaching the boys' T-ball game this afternoon. I'm expecting one of these future Babe Ruths will turn out to be my retirement plan. By the way, what about the BBC?"

"It's over. That's all they need to understand, since that's the charge they gave us. If anyone asks at the next meeting, let me handle the response."

"For sure, Cal." David rose, shook Cal's hand, and left.

When the door closed, Cal picked up the envelope and iPhone and swiped the unlock button. He scrolled through the recent calls, amazed at how open this guy's communications were even though he was a fugitive from less than a hundred miles away. What or who gave him the confidence to take the risk?

He walked over to his closet and took out his boots, a pair of jeans, a shirt, a jacket, and his backpack, making sure he had some matches. He put the envelope inside the pack. After returning to the desk, he sat down, turned on the computer, and searched computer stores in Albany, New York. He wrote down the address of an independent store and buzzed Betsy on the intercom.

"Betsy, anything on my calendar after court?"

"No, sir."

"Okay, I'll sneak off and do some hiking."

Cal sat back and diagrammed a spreadsheet in his mind: phone numbers across, dates of calls underneath. This would let him know who had priority. He'd dummy up cases for phone companies to get records on names and addresses, then keep all the material for his court. He wouldn't want to explain how he knew what he knew to other jurisdictions' law enforcement.

# CHAPTER 27

oey and Cal walked on the wet wooden pathway through the floodplain, both cautious of the slippery footing. Earlier, Joey had followed Cal to the stretch of Jerusalem Road where they would finish for the day and left Cal's car there. They had returned to the AT parking lot at Main Street to begin their survey and hike. They both carried a bundle of cut lumber wrapped in a tarp, bound, and secured on top of their backpacks. Cal had picked this AT project because it would take most of the day, giving him an opportunity to talk with Joey about his grades and the incident at school. Thanks to Becky Lang, Joey had received no blame for the incident. In fact, he was a hero to the other students even though they didn't know who he was.

Cal walked behind Joey, in awe of the animal fluidity Joey showed as he walked and the constant movement of his head, swiveling from side to side and up and down, taking in his surroundings, sensitive to any danger that may be close by. The walkway was damp, and at low levels, water seeped through the spaces between boards. Only in two places did they find rotted wood that needed replacing. They stopped and efficiently replaced the soft wood with strong, fresh boards.

The ride over in the Wrangler was quiet. Cal, silently formulating his talk with Joey about his issues, did not notice the lack of conversation. Now, on the trail, Cal sensed Joey had something on his mind. Usually, Joey looked directly at him when they talked. On the trail, with Joey taking the lead, he was looking anywhere except at Cal. Cal felt his careful plan for Joey to move into productive adulthood was going to take a detour. At least carrying these bundles took away from the awkward silence.

Leaving the floodplain, they walked along the edge of some boggy woods paralleling a wire fence. At a utility right-of-way, they crossed over to natural forest, following the AT's white blaze through the trees as it curved up the mountain. They heard a stream rushing over rocks before they saw it.

"Let's stop at the stream and rest a minute," Cal said, his shoulders aching.

"Okay," Joey responded. They approached the old stone wall remnants on the creek bank, rested their packs against the wall, and sat on it. Cal retrieved two granola bars from his pack and handed one to Joey.

"Thanks," Joey said.

Cal knew Joey must have had a lot on his mind. He gave one-word answers and didn't look around or investigate the stream. Walking over to the edge of the stream, near the side of the ATC wooden bridge, Cal said, "Have you ever wondered why no one in the AT Conservancy removed this tire?" He was looking at a tire around an approximately thirteen-foot-high tree. Discarded years ago, the tire had become a part of the forest as the tree grew from a seed in the middle of it.

"Not really," Joey responded, getting up and walking over to Cal, looking at the tire.

"It's one of those things everybody figured someone else would do. Nobody in the Conservancy would want to cut down the tree. Cutting the tire and carrying it out would take too much effort. Then again, it might be here as an oddity for the thru-hikers to write about in their trail diaries," Cal said.

"Yeah, I've read some of those entries in the notebooks at the shelters. Some are good; others point to hikers who won't make the end of the trail," Joey commented.

"How do you figure that?"

"By the time the hikers get this far, their determination is as important as their physical strength. When you read the entries, their determination shows through in the words they use and the number of excuses they make."

"Hmm, I'll have to reread some entries. Good observation. Well, better minds than ours can figure it out. We have work to do," Cal said, walking over to his backpack and wood bundle.

They moved on, navigating an easy hike through open woods, the trail clearly worn until they came to a pasture's stone wall. No mortar, just flat stones piled one on the other, with two strands of barbed wire running along the top. Where the AT intercepted the wall, a two-step ladder with a wooden pole, about waist high, was snug alongside the wall. A similar ladder was on the other side, with a board laid from one side to the other so a hiker had only to step up on one side, using the pole for balance, and step over to the other, never having to engage the barbed wire or the carefully laid stones.

"This one doesn't need as much work as the one on the other side of the pasture," Cal said, "so why don't we tackle the other one first and save this side for last?" He put his bundle down alongside the fence.

"Cool."

As the two of them walked across the sloping pasture, Joey kept looking to his left at the house up the hill.

"You know that family?" Cal asked.

"No, sir."

"You seem uncomfortable, Joey."

"Well, sir, one winter, the first winter, it was cold. Freezing. My shoes fell apart. Out scavenging, I found the guy living there had left his muddy boots out on the porch. I took the boots. I'm not proud of it, but I did." Joey looked down at the ground.

"Joey, what you did was wrong. Do you remember the kind of boots and the size?"

"No, sir, I don't. They were big because I had to stuff leaves in them to make them fit. Then I guess I mostly grew into them. They were still too big, but I got by. Those were the only boots I had until you bought me these."

"I tell you what. This coming week, why don't we get a gift certificate for a pair of boots from Jack Gianelli's store? You write a letter of apology, and I'll see it gets to that family."

"Yes, sir. I'll save up the money from my work. I've already started saving for something."

"Here we are, so let's get the job done," Cal said as they reached the second of the two bridges, this one closer to the road where Cal parked his car.

Joey unbundled the wood in his tarp. Cal watched as he spread the tarp out on the ground and placed each board next to the other in the same sequence he would use them. Joey took the claw hammer and began dismantling the rotten parts. He worked efficiently and quickly, lost in the work itself. Cal sat down and watched. In an hour, Joey had completed the job. Cal stepped up on the pasture side, grabbed hold of the pole to make sure it was strong, and stepped over the fence to the other side. "Good job, Joey. Better than new," Cal said as he returned to Joey's side. For the first time that day, Joey was grinning, basking in the compliment. "How did you learn to work with wood like that?"

"I don't remember much, but my daddy, before he got killed, used to make things from wood and sell them. He taught me how to lay everything out in the shape of what you want. He said it made the job easier," Joey said with pride.

"He must have been quite a guy," Cal said, feeling a pang of jealousy. "Let's gather up this old wood, put it in the back of the car, and go back to the other bridge."

At the other wall, the repair work wasn't as extensive, and Joey finished in less than an hour.

"Another fine job, Joey. Let's have lunch," Cal said as he pulled the food pouch from his pack. The two sat on the ground, resting against the stone wall. "Joey, you seem to have something else on your mind. Want to talk about it?"

"Sir, I need some advice."

"Call me Cal, Joey, not sir."

"I really can't. I always called my daddy sir, and, well, you're the closest person to my daddy as anyone has been since he died."

"Okay, Joey, call me what you want. What's on your mind?"

"The most important thing is I need some way to make more money."

"Why?"

"Well, sir, I have a girl, and she's special. She's smarter than me and loves me as much as I love her. Guys give girls rings when they're going to get married, so I need to know what kind of ring, and then I need to figure out a way I can work more, maybe on the weekends, so I can buy her a ring. What kind should I get?" Joey blurted out, looking at Cal.

"Joey, how long have you known this girl?"

"Sir, that's hard to explain. I just found her a couple of months ago. She rents one of Maggie's houses. But I knew her a long time ago, before I went to the woods." He looked at Cal and said, "Sir, me and her are in love. I don't want to lose her to someone else, somebody smarter than me, or who has more money to give her things."

Cal understood Joey's insecurity was serious. "Joey, maybe I can help you. Let me ask you first, have you discussed this with Maggie? If this young lady rents from her, she probably knows her well and can help you understand she doesn't just care for your money. She must love you."

"Yes, sir—I mean, no, sir. I mean . . . I don't know what I mean." Joey looked down and took a deep breath. "No, sir, I haven't spoken to Maggie. I'm embarrassed to. That's why I hoped you could give me some advice. Yes, sir, I know she loves me, but she deserves someone who can take care of her. Right now, I can't do that, but I want her to know I'll be able to one day."

"Does she go to school?"

"Yes, sir. She's a junior at BC this year."

"Does she work?"

"Yes, sir, she works at one of Maggie's businesses, usually the ice cream shop in town. She also tutors each evening during the week, Monday to Friday. That's where she makes the most money."

"Joey, you're only seventeen and a freshman at college. That's a young age, and you'll have a difficult time trying to support a wife and maybe children."

"Sir, I know that. We wouldn't get married until she was out of college and I had a regular job."

"Joey, you can't work on the weekends because you have community service for the next four years," Cal reminded him in a soft voice. "The most important aspect of your life right now is to finish your education. That's why the only work you have is taking care of Maggie's properties."

Joey's face fell as he stared away.

"I know where I can get a ring, the kind a guy gives his girl when they're in love. I'll sell it to you, but you won't have to pay for it until you finish college. You'll sign an IOU to me for the value of the ring. Is that a deal?"

Joey quickly said, "Yes, sir." Then he frowned.

"What's the matter, Joey?

"Sir, I'm not really good at school. I know I should be, but sitting in a classroom, listening to a teacher, is not me. Trust me, I'm doing my best, I promise you that, but I want to be outside, doing something, sort of like what we're doing today. I know I can work hard and do my best, but I just can't seem to get my heart into school."

"Does this have anything to do with wanting more money so you can give your girl more things?"

"No, sir, I've known this since I started this fall semester. Dr. Lang and me have talked about it, and she said she understood. I'd like to work with my hands. I can read about things in the evening. But I want to see what I make for a living. Do I make any sense, sir?"

"Yeah, Joey, you make sense. Better sense than most guys your age. I'll tell you what: You have only six weeks remaining in this semester. You never want to quit in midstream anything you start and find hard. Finish out this semester, getting the best grades you can, and let's make a decision at Christmas about what you'll be doing next year."

Cal was impressed with Joey's maturity and attitude. He knew what he was good at and what he wasn't. Terry Rodriguez could give Cal advice. Getting him a job shouldn't be hard. Cal dismissed the thought of a potential bully causing a problem. "All right, let's pack up and take this old wood to my car. I'll drive you back to your Wrangler. I guess you're going to see your girl tonight?"

"Yes, sir."

"When will I get to meet this young lady?"

"Soon, I hope. You'll like her. Maggie does."

"Well, if Maggie likes her, she must be special."

For the second time, Cal was pleased to see Joey's spirits lift. Fatherly advice. He had never thought he would enjoy giving fatherly advice so much. For the first time in his life, Cal understood the satisfaction of being responsible for a young person. Helping mold a young man was love. He and Maggie could make a difference in Joey's life.

"Here, take this," Cal said, pulling fifty dollars from his pocket. "The two of you go to a show and get something to eat before or after."

"You don't have to, sir. I—"

"I know I don't have to, but I want to. Believe it or not, I had a girl when I was your age, too. I'll stop by Maggie's Monday evening with the ring."

"Yes, sir!"

# CHAPTER 28

"Why are you so nervous, Joey? School bothering you?" Suzie asked as they came out of the Massachusetts Museum of Contemporary Art in North Adams.

He steered them toward Main Street. "That place was huge," he said, trying to change the subject. "I'm not sure I liked all of that stuff, but the two enormous birds made from construction tools were awesome. So cool. Where'd they come from?" He kept his free hand in his pants pocket, tumbling the small ring box repeatedly.

"China. They were awesome. It's hard to imagine someone could think that up and have the patience to put them together. It took years. They're leaving here soon and going to New York, where they'll hang in the nave of St. John the Divine Cathedral. Now, that should be awesome. Maybe we can go to New York one Saturday or Sunday to see them there. It's only three hours away, so we can come back in a day. What do you think?"

"Okay by me. I'll see if the judge will give me the time away from community service, but I bet he will if Maggie says it would be good for me. They like each other." Joey's hand was continuously tumbling the small box in his pocket as they walked toward Main Street, where he had parked the Wrangler.

"Do we have time for lunch?" Suzie asked.

"Sure. Let's walk over and find a place with tables inside," Joey stammered.

"All restaurants have tables inside, silly. What's the matter with you?"

"Nothing. Come on, the light just changed." Joey half-pulled her into the intersection.

Main Street was different from what Joey expected. He expected it would be like Great Barrington or Lee, or other western Massachusetts towns with historic buildings on both sides of the street housing art galleries, restaurants, and clothing stores. Instead, one side was single-story new constructions, and one side left the way it had been over a hundred years ago.

Joey opened the door to the first restaurant they saw on the historic side. Suzie wanted to sit up front so she could watch the people go by, but Joey insisted on a table in the back, away from other occupied tables.

"Joey, what's up?" Suzie asked as they sat down. "You're acting like you have something on your mind, and you've been this way since you picked me up this morning. Now, what gives?" She looked at him, but he averted his gaze.

With his right hand still in his pocket, he was reaching with his left to hold hers when the server approached. He quickly drew back.

"Hi, I'm Abigail. I'm going to serve you today. May I get you something to drink?" She was older than Suzie and Joey, in her early twenties, and very confident in her abilities and looks. Her tight white blouse, showing full breasts nestled in a black bra, and tight blue jeans spoke volumes about her age and attitude. The dark eye shadow, light makeup, dangling earrings, and rhinestone belt said she was not going home after work. Her bottle-blond hair, pulled back in a ponytail and sticking out the back of a white cap with MoCA in big green lettering, completed the look. She appraised Suzie. Abigail did not feel Suzie stood a chance if she wanted this guy to pay attention to her.

"Just water for me," Suzie said, smiling, without intimidation from this walking sex goddess.

"I'll—I'll have a Coke," Joey mumbled, not even looking up to see the waitress.

"Great. Let me tell you the specials. We have a goat cheese, walnut, and arugula salad; a ham and Swiss cheese panini on a sourdough roll; and a brook trout plate with a medley of late summer vegetables. Each is eleven ninety-nine. I'll get your drinks while you decide what you want." She turned and left the table.

"Get anything you want, Suzie," Joey said, looking over the menu.

"What are you going to have?"

"I'm going to have the trout."

"I think I'm going to have the goat cheese salad," Suzie decided, putting down her menu. "Do you realize this is our third go-out-somewhere date, if you count the Berkshire Café and the movies?" she asked, smiling and squeezing Joey's hand.

"Yeah," Joey said, looking around the restaurant, which was starting to fill up. He'd better get this done. He turned his head back to look at her and started to say, "Suzie—"

The waitress approached and put their drinks on the table. "Well, have you decided, or do you need more time?" She stood over them with her pencil poised to take their orders, vying for Joey's attention.

"I'm having the goat cheese salad," Suzie said.

"Good choice," Abigail responded. "How about you, handsome?" she asked, looking at Joey and pressing herself against her bra.

Suzie noticed the maneuver and smiled slightly, interested in seeing what Joey would do if he even noticed the obvious signal.

"Huh?" Joey sputtered, turning red in the face at the compliment. Suzie giggled, and Abigail winked at Joey. "Uh, I'm having the trout, the brook trout," Joey said.

Abigail took the menus and turned to leave.

"Suzie, will you—" Joey began again. He started taking the box out of his pocket with his right hand. As he got it out and tried to maneuver his hand from under the table so the box would be in front of her by the time he finished the question, his hand caught the edge of the table, knocking the box away. It fell to the floor. "Oh, shit!" Joey said, too loud. Other diners turned to look. Joey pushed back in his chair in a panic, looking for the box on the floor.

"Joey Paschal, what is going on?" Suzie asked.

The box was lodged next to the table pedestal. Sitting on the edge of his chair, he bent below the tabletop to retrieve it. With the box in hand, as he sat up his head hit the table, spilling the Coke and water. "Oh, God, what a dunce," Joey moaned as Coke and water rolled off the edge of the table, onto the back of his neck.

Suzie jumped up, avoiding the liquids flowing into her seat. "Joey, what are you doing?" she asked. Then she saw the box in Joey's hand and grabbed it from him.

Joey grabbed the box back. Now he was kneeling on the floor, laughing, with Suzie and the rest of the lunch crowd joining in. "Suzie, will you—uh, will you marry me?" He opened the box to expose the ring Cal had sold him. The entire restaurant stopped laughing and went silent, waiting for Suzie's response.

Suzie stared at the ring, looked at Joey, and said softly, "You bet I will, my dear, dear Joey, you wonderful goofy guy."

She took the ring out of the box and put it on her finger, holding her hand out to see how it sparkled. Joey was sitting on the floor by now, arms on his knees, head hanging down, relieved the ordeal was over. The restaurant burst into cheers and applause. Suzie extended her hand to pull Joey up, but he sprang to his feet. She threw her arms around his neck and gave him a kiss designed to let Abigail know there was only one person making love to Joey, and it wouldn't be her.

"Well, you two lovebirds have certainly made a mess of this table, so I've moved you over here. Try not to destroy this one, you hear?" Abigail said, pointing to the table across from theirs. "The manager said lunch is on her, because she hadn't had such a pleasant laugh in years."

§

"I'll never take it off, Joey," Suzie said, looking at her ring hand as she lay naked against his body later that evening. She didn't know how her intense love of Joey would grow, but she didn't want reality to intrude on her happiness. She was the happiest she had ever been in her life.

# CHAPTER 29

Suzie stood naked in front of the full-length mirror, first looking at her hips, then her breasts. She turned sideways to the right and left. She felt alive, more alive than she had ever felt. Her breasts were firmer, and there was an ever-so-slight curve to her lower abdomen, the same way it protruded when her period was due. The only problem was she hadn't had a period in five weeks.

She knew, but she wanted to be sure. Not once had she used any standard multiple protections with Joey. She had deliberately left it up to fate. Ever since that day on the Ledges, she and Joey had loved each other, in a caring and passionate way, every weekend—sometimes three times, sometimes five. It was like they were thanking each other for past sacrifices and building dreams of the future.

Suzie smiled. She now knew she was right: there was a difference between sex and making love. The emotions between her and Joey were electric. He was a quick learner, knowing when to be rough, when to be gentle and sensitive, knowing when it took her longer, holding back until she was ready so they would reach the pinnacle of passion together. She decided to stop by the drugstore in the next town to buy a pregnancy test kit and use it at school.

She and Joey were going hiking tomorrow. She didn't know if she would tell him then or later, when they were in bed. If she was going to tell him while hiking, she wanted it to be at the Ledges. In the meantime, she needed to prepare for tonight and her visitor.

§

Joey made another pass with the lawnmower and, at the turn, glanced at the sky. Almost four. If he stepped up the pace, he'd finish by five and stop by Suzie's for just a minute. Pushing forward with the mower, he quickened his pace. There was good news: the judge had arranged for him to get a full-time job making and installing cabinets. Learning a trade. When she graduated, he'd be making good money. He might even have some money saved so they could get their own house. Things were good, really good. He finally understood what happiness was.

Joey emptied the mower into the black bag for the compost pile. He placed all the tools on the trailer and jumped into the front seat. Reaching down for his cell, he saw the time was almost five thirty. He started to call her. That was their agreement. Her tutoring client came at six. He wanted to surprise her with his news, so he didn't call. He had to hurry. Turning the key, he started toward Suzie's.

§

Suzie finished applying bright red lipstick and stood back from the mirror. Just the way Carl liked it. Her hair was teased out in a wild look. Her eye makeup was heavy. She had on false eyelashes even though her real ones were thick and long. He liked them this way, and he was the client. The rouge was heavy and exaggerated the hollows in her cheeks and her high cheekbones. The fire-engine red lipstick was what he really wanted. She applied more. He loved to see the ring of red around his boner when she finished the first round.

Suzie was satisfied with her hair and face. In her closet, she pulled out a red lace push-up bra that accentuated her nipples underneath her blouse. She slipped it on and positioned her breasts for full effect. Then she stepped into a red thong made of flimsy lace, making it as comfortable as possible. She needed to buy more since this was her next-to-last one. Carl was amusing when he ripped it off her. He could barely keep from climaxing by then. Carl was a nice man who had streetwise fantasies.

Suzie took her white blouse off the hanger and put it on, then knotted the tail just under her bra, leaving her smooth, brown belly and navel showing. She put on too-small black Capri pants and looked at herself in the mirror. Awesome. Any man would pay seven hundred and fifty dollars to spend an evening with a woman who looked like her. From her shoe rack, she took a pair of red, open-toed, four-inch-heeled pumps and slipped them on.

She glanced at the clock: five fifteen. He'd be here at six and gone by nine thirty. The table needed to be set and the rosé put on ice. At least Carl wasn't like Henry, who always wanted a big meal and whiskey before sex. Suzie walked out of the bedroom and headed to the kitchen.

§

Joey turned onto Suzie's street. He hit the garage opener button as he went around to the garage side. He decided not to pull the Wrangler into the garage. Since he was going to have only a few minutes before her tutoring client showed up, he circled at the dead end and pulled the Wrangler and trailer alongside the neighbor's house, across from Suzie's garage. He hopped out and walked into the garage and through the side door to the covered trellis walkway. He was as happy as a guy could be when going to see his girl.

Suzie saw the light indicating that the garage door was opening. She knew it wasn't six yet. Carl knew early was not acceptable. Her clients were never early. That was the rule. She walked to the kitchen door and panicked. Her heart skipped a beat when she saw it was Joey. She looked down at her appearance. When she looked up, they were staring at each other through the glass of the kitchen door. She pulled it open. "Joey, what are you doing here? You can't be here. You've got to leave, now!"

"I know I can't stay. I just want to see my girl and—" He looked her up and down. "Suzie, what do you have on? You're dressed like a, like a—"

"Street walker. I know. I—uh, I'm in a play at school. We had rehearsal. I'm late. My tutoring session is in fifteen minutes. Now go! Please, Joey!" She tried to turn him around and push him out the door.

"Can I at least have a kiss?" Joey pleaded.

"No, I've got to change. Go!"

Joey held still, grinning. "Aw, come on. You have twelve minutes."

Suzie looked at Joey, realizing the situation was deteriorating but knowing that if he was there when Carl arrived, it would be devastation. She slapped him across the face. "I said go, goddammit! I've got to change."

Joey stammered, "I—I—I—" Holding his hand where his face stung, he turned and fled out the door.

Suzie watched him as he ran down the walkway and saw him jump in the Wrangler and take off. She turned her eyes to the clock: five minutes to six. She closed her eyes, trying to will Carl to be late. Going to the front dining room window, she watched Joey's Wrangler turn the corner and head toward the highway. Halfway down the block, the Wrangler passed a red Mercedes C350. Suzie fought back tears, taking deep breaths and expelling them slowly as she walked to the kitchen.

She sent mental messages to Joey about how much she loved him. It was all she could do for now. She knew Joey wouldn't understand. She knew reality was intruding upon her happiness.

The light went on as the garage door went up. Suzie took the salad out of the refrigerator.

§

Joey woke, not knowing where he was. He slowly realized he was on the sofa in his apartment. After a minute, he remembered everything from the night before, when Suzie had slapped him and pushed him out the door. He was more confused than mad. After all, he was the one who broke the rule. After coming home, he wanted to talk with Maggie, but she wasn't home. He went upstairs and sat on the couch, trying to figure it out, and fell asleep.

Still, this morning, nothing made sense. Suzie was his girl and she loved him, but why had she slapped him? He realized it was his fault.

He looked outside through the window. Daylight and birds chirping greeted him. Getting up, he went over to the stove and saw it was seven thirty in the morning. He had to be at the ATC office in thirty minutes. He hurriedly jumped in the shower. After showering and skipping shaving, he went to the closet.

He and Suzie were going to the Ledges after he finished his community service, so he grabbed his wool pants and pulled on a cotton T-shirt and a wool shirt over that. Finally, he reached for his heavy wool outdoor coat and his wool skullcap. He hoped traffic was light, or he'd really be late. As he walked to the door, he picked up his backpack with the survival items he wanted and might need for a cold hike. He threw in a wool sweater and skullcap for Suzie. He would apologize to her for not calling. She loves me; she'll be okay, he thought. I should have called.

He took the steps down two at a time.

§

Suzie kept trying to call Joey every couple of minutes, in between sending him text messages. Her guilt and insecurity told her he was mad at her and wouldn't want to see her. She knew she shouldn't have slapped him. It probably reminded him of Stoner. She couldn't lose him again. He'd understand. He had to. He was her life.

She didn't understand why he wouldn't answer. Her anxiety gave her a queasy feeling in her stomach, along with the nausea she was experiencing from her pregnancy.

A wave of nausea hit her, and she stumbled into the bathroom and fell to her knees. Holding on to the toilet bowl, she threw up. When the nausea subsided, she pulled herself up to the sink and used a cold, wet washcloth to wipe the perspiration from her face. She made her way to the bedroom. She had time to lie down. He'd call—she knew he would. She'd rest and then go over to Maggie's and see if he'd said anything to her. He had to understand. She had saved him from a greater pain. She lay down so her stomach would settle.

§

Joey looked at the weather reports. A fast-moving winter storm was coming through. The National Weather Service had really screwed up. Joey understood there would be no hiking today. He didn't mind since the alternative might have been staying at Suzie's and watching a movie in bed.

"Milt, any groups out on the AT today?" Joey asked his fellow volunteer staffing the headquarters that Saturday morning.

"Nah. The hotels don't have outdoor activities now. At least, they haven't told us about any trips. You want me to go out and get us a sandwich?"

"I'm not hungry, but you go ahead. I'll watch this storm racing in from Canada. This is something to behold. I don't think I've ever seen one this big moving this fast. The temp started dropping an hour ago. We're about to get a taste of what winter is going to be like. Go on, just be back by twelve. I've got to pick my girl up by one."

"Sure, it won't take me that long. Thanks."

§

Suzie continued calling Joey's number repeatedly as she drove to Maggie's. She knew he must hate her. Maggie, though, would know what to do. She always knew what to do.

Thinking of everything she needed to tell Maggie calmed her down as she drove. Maggie never got excited or upset. She'd know what to do. Suzie pulled up to Maggie's garage and hit the opener button, then pulled in and lowered the door. She ran up the stairs to Joey's apartment, turned the doorknob, and rushed in to find the place empty. She raced down the stairs.

By then, Maggie was standing in the kitchen doorway. "Suzie, what are you doing here? You know the rules," she started, but then saw the shape Suzie was in. "What's the matter?" Maggie walked down to the bottom of the steps and held out her arms. Suzie rushed into them. "Come inside, dear."

At the kitchen table, Suzie, tears streaming down her cheeks, told Maggie of the confrontation with Joey.

"Dear, dear Suzie. I know how you feel, but you did the right thing. You took the least bad way out of a terrible situation. Joey is so head over heels in love with you, this won't be but a ripple on the pond of your life together."

"Are you sure, Maggie? Are you sure?"

"Yes, dear. When are you going to see Joey again?"

"We're going hiking this afternoon. He's picking me up at one. There's something else, Maggie," Suzie said, looking down at her lap.

Maggie froze. She knew what Suzie was going to say. She could see it in her body.

"I'm pregnant with Joey's baby."

"Are you sure?"

"Yes. I did a home test yesterday morning."

"I mean, are you sure it's Joey's baby?"

"Yes, I'm very careful. I do the whole regimen you taught me after every time, except when I've been with Joey. I wanted to feel him inside of me. It's Joey's. I'm sure of it."

"Well, that complicates things, to say the least. Okay, put that aside for now. Let's solve this lover's spat first. Joey's not answering his phone?"

"No, I've tried hundreds of times. He just doesn't answer." Suzie's chin quivered, and her eyes teared up.

"Calm down. That likely means he doesn't have his phone, or it's turned off." Maggie pulled her go phone from her bag on the kitchen counter. She called Joey's number and got voicemail. She disconnected and called Cal.

"Good morning," she said as soon as he answered. "I need your help. Joey and Suzie had a spat. Joey isn't answering his phone. Do you have the number where he's working this morning?" She listened. "Are you sure? I don't mind calling, but he'd probably feel better talking to you than me. Great. Call me back." Maggie hung up and turned to Suzie. "A friend is getting in touch with Joey and will have him call here. Do you want to wait?"

"Really? No, I want to surprise Joey with my news. If you talk to him, tell him I've gone ahead to the Ledges, and to hurry. That's where I want him to learn about the baby. Is that all right? Is that good?"

"It is if that's what you want, my dear. What time is it?"

Suzie looked at her phone. "Noon. Tell him I have everything for the picnic; just bring himself." Suzie smiled for the first time, hugged Maggie, and headed out the door.

§

Maggie sat at the kitchen table, her head in her hands. She realized that Suzie and Joey's youth, even after all the abuse they had endured, kept them from understanding how complicated this situation was. Reaching back into her past, she realized how important happiness was to someone who hadn't experienced it before. Could there be a stronger love than that between a young woman who had accepted repeated rape by a monster in order to shelter a young man from vicious beatings, and the young man who had killed the rapist to save her? Cal's role as father, and there was no doubt in her mind that he was Joey's biological father, would take Cal from his comfort zone. Joey was going to need him and his fatherly advice. Her go phone vibrated.

"Yes, Cal. Did you find him?"

"Sure, what's the problem? He's at the AT office, where he's doing his CS."

"Cal, are you sitting down? Joey and Suzie had a confrontation last evening, and she slapped him. He left without an explanation. She's been trying to reach him since last night, but he won't return her call. She's beside herself."

"I had to get him on the HQ phone. He didn't realize he left his phone at home. He said he's not sure where it is."

"Well, that explains that. Suzie will be relieved when she sees him. She has a surprise for him."

"Surprise? What kind of surprise."

"She'll have to tell him. She made me promise not to say anything."

"Joey said he gets off at a quarter after twelve. I suspect he'll come to your place to get his phone, if it's there, before picking Suzie up. He said they were going hiking, but they may not because of the weather."

"Oh, Lord. Suzie is on her way to the Ledges and will wait for Joey there."

"Okay, so tell him when he gets home."

"I will. I'll also call Suzie and tell her to come back here. Will I see you this weekend?" Maggie asked shyly.

"Yes, I'm free this evening. Does seven work for you? We can go to North Adams and have dinner at Angelo's."

"Sounds delicious. I'll be ready. See you then. Love you."

"Love you, too."

Maggie clicked off with Cal and hit the speed dial for Suzie. Instead of ringing, it went directly to voicemail, showing she was out of range.

Maggie closed the phone and sighed. She knew she'd tell Cal tonight about Suzie's pregnancy and Joey's future fatherhood. Plans needed to be made. She returned to making cookies for the weekend.

When the light came on in the kitchen, indicating the garage door was opening, Maggie knew it must be Joey. She rinsed the flour off her hands and dried them as she went to the door. Joey was about to go up the stairs to his apartment.

"Joey, you have a minute?"

He spun around quickly, startled, and said, "Yes, ma'am," then headed to the main house.

"What is that cracking noise?" Maggie asked, hearing for the first time the light rain starting to fall. She shivered.

"A fast-moving front is coming in, bringing sleet," Joey said.

"Joey, Suzie was here forty minutes ago, looking for you. She's upset you didn't return her calls. Everything okay?" Maggie knew it was best not to let Joey know she knew about the fight.

"Everything is fine. I don't know where my phone is; that's why I stopped by here before picking her up. We were going hiking, but this weather is killing that idea. It's gonna get bad before the afternoon is over." Joey stood on the bottom step, looking up at Maggie.

"Oh, no," Maggie said, her face contorting into a worried look. "Joey, she told me to tell you she went ahead to the Ledges and to come as soon as you can. She already has the picnic lunch."

Joey tensed and said, "Oh, shit! Oh, I'm sorry, Maggie. She can't be on the mountain. Nobody should be up there this afternoon. I've got to go get her." He spun around and ran to the garage. At the door, he stopped and looked back at Maggie. "Maggie, please call the judge. Tell him what you just told me. Tell him a bad winter storm is coming through fast. Let him know I'm going to get Suzie at the Ledges, and we'll make our way to the Mount Wilcox south shelter." He turned back to the garage and rushed through the door.

§

Maggie hit the speed dial on her go phone while pacing in the kitchen. Cal answered on the first ring. "Cal, Joey has come and gone. He's upset, but not because of his fight with Suzie. He said there's a fast-moving severe winter storm coming through here this afternoon. When I told him Suzie went to the Ledges to wait for him, he really got upset. He asked me to call you and tell you he's going to get Suzie and take her to the Mount Wilcox south shelter."

"I hadn't heard about the storm. Those kids shouldn't be up there if it's going to be bad."

"Joey knows that. Suzie didn't have any idea about the storm."

"I know, I know. Look, I'll go to ATCHQ and see what the weather report says conditions will be. Don't worry. I'll see you at seven."

"Okay."

At ATCHQ, Cal walked in and saw Christy, the afternoon volunteer on duty, and Junior Soto. "Hi, Christy. Junior, what are you doing here?" he asked, walking over and shaking both of their hands. "What's the story on the weather, Christy?"

"We have a whale of a winter storm coming in fast. The sleet is getting worse. It's going to get terrible around four and continue until morning. Then, bingo, it's over. Sort of like a polar vortex."

"Damn, damn, damn," Cal said, clenching and unclenching his fists.

"What's the matter, Cal?" Junior asked.

"Joey, the young man I told you about, is on his way up to the Ledges, where his girlfriend is waiting for him. He knew the weather was coming, but she didn't, so it's a safe bet she's not prepared for the severe drop in temperature. He left word with Maggie that he'd take Suzie, the girl, to the Mount Wilcox south shelter. That won't help them much, even if he can get her there, if the rain and sleet are as bad as you say they'll be."

"What do you suggest?"

"I'll call Clyde's and borrow an ATV to take more clothes and supplies so the three of us can make it through the night. This is going to be over in the morning, right, Christy?"

"Yes, sir."

"I've got a better idea, Cal, if you don't mind," Junior said as he took his cell from its belt holster and punched a button. Cal watched Junior but said nothing, waiting for Junior to finish his call.

"Trey, I need your help," Junior said. "Gas up and put two of the heavy-duty Gators on a trailer. Take them over to the Mount Wilcox dirt road off Beartown." Junior was silent for a moment. "No, the west road. There's an entrance to Beartown from Stony Brook. Enter there. Proceed to a sharp U-turn. Immediately after, on the right, is the dirt road leading to the Mount Wilcox south shelter. We'll meet you there. We'll be there in twenty minutes. Love you, son."

Junior hung up and turned to Cal and Christy. "Cal, we don't know what condition the young people will be in, so I figure if we could get them off the mountain, it would be better. You and I can operate the Gators. We can load up blankets, thermoses with hot soup, warm clothes, and whatever else you think we need."

"Junior, I don't know what to say."

"Don't say anything. Let's get what we need and meet Trey."

# CHAPTER 30

Joey sped through the center of town and started for the intersection with Highway 7. He blew through the red light at Main and Holly without stopping. Just ahead, on the right, he saw the drugstore. Slamming on the brakes, he turned the Wrangler onto the sidewalk. Leaving the Wrangler running, he jumped out and ran into the drugstore, banging the door hard against the wall. The clerk jumped at the noise. "Where are your back-pain things?" Joey asked, almost shouting at the girl.

"Aisle fourteen, or maybe fifteen," she stammered.

Joey looked up, scanning the overhead signs until he found the aisle, and searched the shelves. He grabbed three boxes of thermal pads and moved back to the counter.

The clerk picked up one box up and scanned the barcode. "Did you find everything you wanted?" she asked cheerfully.

"Yes, please hurry."

"Do you have a rewards card?" she asked, holding the scanner up so she could scan it.

"No!" Joey reached into his back pocket, pulled out his wallet, tossed it to the girl, scooped up the boxes, and rushed out the door.

The sleet was steady now. Joey felt it increasing in strength. He remembered other days in the last three years when weather like this had gotten ugly and cold in a hurry. Back in the Wrangler, he slammed it into gear and headed toward Highway 7. Mentally he told Suzie repeatedly he was on his way. As he drove, he opened the boxes and stuffed the contents into his coat pockets. He floored the Wrangler once he was on the highway, skidding on the icy road before the four-wheel drive caught. Please, God, no cops today.

He knew she had left Maggie's at noon and likely started climbing a little after twelve fifteen, so she'd be at the Ledges already. He pressed the accelerator harder.

At Blue Hill Road, Joey took the turn faster than he knew was safe. The Wrangler tipped slightly, then righted itself. Crossing Monument Valley Road, he barely slowed to see if anything was coming. He raced down the road as it merged with Stony Brook, then turned left onto Beartown Road just as a gust of wind slammed the Wrangler with more sleet. He saw Suzie's Outback in the Benedict Pond parking lot. Pulling next to her car, he grabbed his backpack with the clothes, energy bars, water, and survival items he carried to get safely off a mountain in cold weather. He knew they could get to the Mount Wilcox south shelter.

At an easy lope, Joey started toward the Ledges. He continued mentally telling Suzie he was on his way, convinced their love was so strong she could hear him. At the first bridge, the amount of water rushing off the mountain shocked Joey. It shouldn't have been that high yet. Suzie might not have made it to the Ledges. She might be on her way down or waiting for him at the stream above. He redoubled his climbing speed. Having been in this kind of weather before with fewer clothes than he had on now, Joey kept moving. His only thought was he'd have Suzie in his arms in a few minutes.

Joey hardly noticed the icy boulders on the cliff side. He knew not to even attempt the climb. He moved to his right and started advancing through the thick underbrush of the mountainside. His experience had taught him that when a lot of water is coming down, it's better to be in the underbrush than among the wet and thick roots, mud, and rocks of a trail. Reaching the level ridge halfway up the mountain, he picked up the AT's white trail blaze and started moving to the left, just off the trail, avoiding the muddy rivulet coursing down.

After a steady climb, Joey heard the roar of rushing water. The sound gave him a feeling of dread and a tightening in his stomach. The noise was louder than it should have been. A few yards further, he came around some trees and saw the angry stream that stood between him and Suzie. What he did not see was the footbridge. Moving closer, looking for the stone marker at the bridge edge on this lower side, he finally saw the posts under a few inches of water. "Oh, shit, the bridge is out," he muttered, amazed by the force the water was already exerting.

Instinct, built from three years in the wilderness, took over. The rain and sleet were steady. Joey pulled his hands into his wool jacket sleeves. Cold sleet still stung his face like a swarm of wasps. He moved to his left, looking for the old log bridge. It was higher up, closer to the lake, with the slope of the gully beneath it steeper. He felt the log might still be above the rushing water. His heart skipped a beat when he saw the log in place, with water rippling on its lower edge. He didn't hesitate. He started crawling across the log. Two-thirds across, the log tilted as his weight pushed it down, and the rushing water exerted itself. Joey went under the raging water. He felt himself rolling against the bottom debris and kicked, trying to get back to the surface.

His only thought was that Suzie needed him. He knew he had to get out of the water in the next few seconds, or he couldn't save her. Jerked violently to a stop, his backpack caught on debris, and his lungs burning, he willed himself not to take a breath. Pulling the quick-release shackles, he freed himself of the backpack. He shot forward in the grasp of the raging water. His left boot hit something solid, while his head broke the water's surface. Gulping air and freezing rain, he saw the outline of a tree on the bank only a foot in front of his face. He reached for the trunk and kicked hard.

He tumbled with the force of the water. Hooking his left arm around the tree trunk, he rolled his lower body up and out of the water. He heard more than felt his arm separate from his shoulder. Nausea washed over him as he felt the wet, muddy ground solidly under him rather than rushing water. He tried to raise himself on all fours. He collapsed to his left, close to going back into the raging stream. Rolling over on his back, he lifted himself, supporting his body with his right hand and arm. He was on the upside of the stream. "I'm coming, Suzie," he muttered. Staggering to his right, slipping on the muddy surface, steadying himself by moving from tree to bush to tree, he climbed the mountain.

Joey reached the Ledges and hollered for Suzie. No answer. He frantically looked over the edge to the ledge just below, where they had once climbed down and sat, holding hands and talking about the future. Suzie was not down there. He turned and looked upward, shouting her name again. No answer. Moving up and around a stone ledge, he spotted her. He rushed over and felt her. She was cold, too cold. Her lips were blue, and she did not respond to his voice or touch. Joey kissed her ear and whispered, "I love you, Suzie, and I'm here." He realized the two of them wouldn't get off the mountain until the storm was over. He couldn't carry her down from the Ledges to the shelter, which required climbing down five hundred feet and then back up another hundred.

He put his head between Suzie's breasts and heard the faintest of heartbeats. "Stay with me, Suzie," he said. Taking the thermal pads out of his coat pockets, he laid all six of them on the rock next to her. He took off his boots, wool socks, and wool pants. Lifting Suzie's lower torso with his right hand and leaning her against his body, he took her hiking shoes off, maneuvered her legs into the legs of his pants, and placed her feet in his hiking boots. "I've got great news, Suzie, I start a new job in January. Awesome, huh?" He pulled the pants up as far as he could and rolled Suzie closer to the stone next to her. "You know what that means? We can start saving for our own home. I need you, Suzie, just as I needed you those many years ago. Please stay with me, Suzie. You know you are my world, my everything."

He activated two of the heat pads and tied them with his socks onto her thighs inside his wool pants. "I'll be making cabinets in my new job. On the weekends, I can start making furniture for our new house. Stay with me, Suzie. I need you more than life itself. You are my love and my life." He took off his wool jacket and lifted Suzie's upper body. With his right arm and teeth, he wrapped the coat around her upper body. "Stay with me, Suzie. We have overcome so much, my love. We can get through this together." Turning her face toward the rock, he placed her on her side. He activated another pad and placed it between her breasts, on the outside of her own clothes but under the wool coat. "Hang in there, Suzie. These pads will get you warm. I'm so sorry about last night. I should have called. Please forgive me." He activated a fourth pad and slipped it under his wool coat, against her upper back. He took off his wool watch cap and pulled it over her head, stretching it down over her eyes and below the back of her neck. "Don't you look cute. If I had my phone, I'd take your picture to show all our future children." He activated the fifth thermal pad and placed it between the watch cap and the collar of his wool coat. "I love you. I need you. Please, Suzie, don't leave me alone. I want you to sing to me like you used to." He crossed her arms in front of her body, inside his coat, and activated the last pad and wrapped it around her arms where they crossed. "Please, Suzie, stay with me. I need you. I love you. You are my life, Suzie."

Joey lay down, spooning Suzie, holding the wool clothes tight against her body while trying to shelter her face against the sleet and the water coming down off the stones. "Dear God, please don't let her die. Please, God, please, please, please, don't let her die," he prayed.

# CHANGE HAPPENS

## PART TWO

# CHAPTER 31

Cal touched a tissue to the corners of his eyes. He sat in the dark conservatory, looking through the glass wall to the northeast corner of the estate. Snow patches remained from yesterday, but the sky was clear, with an explosion of stars and an eerie moonlight typical of a waxing crescent. His thoughts were of the two bodies at the Ledges, one wrapped in heavy woolen clothes and the other nearly naked, arms wrapped around her. He knew instinctively that Joey was dead. His Joey. His son, unknown for over sixteen years and loved dearly for almost six months.

Suzie was barely conscious, calling out to Joey, wanting to know if he was okay. Cal pried Joey's arms from around Suzie and lifted her up so Junior could wrap more blankets around her. He realized Joey had deliberately given his life for Suzie, using heating pads strategically placed under the wool clothing. Cal, holding Suzie, remembered what Joey had told Jack Gianelli: "Wool is warm, even when wet . . . They haven't been as cold as I have." Feeling the ice in parts of the frozen wool, he realized just how smart his son had been.

Had been . . . Christ, why? Why did Joey have to die now, just when he knew we loved him? Why? Cal had rescued hikers and canoeists many times and had kept his emotions in check, but that day he broke down in uncontrollable sobs while holding Joey's body. Without Junior's steady hand, none of them would have gotten off the mountain.

In the weeks since the tragedy, Cal had spiraled deeper into depression. The guilt permeated every aspect of his life. He faced and wrestled with the undeniable truth: if he hadn't turned his back on Josey, he would have raised his son with her, sparing Joey the unspeakable abuse and horrors he had faced in his first seventeen years. Not only did Cal's guilt overwhelm him, but he realized his own inadequacy. His son had given unconditional love to the woman in his life twice, while he, Cal, had turned his back on the first woman he'd loved and hadn't given his all to the second. Joey's love for Suzie was as high and as strong as the Berkshire mountains. He had killed to protect her and died to save her life. What an incredible human being.

How much he could learn from his son. Cal's breath caught in his chest. Layered on his guilt for abandoning his son and Josey was the guilt he felt for the act of rejecting her. In an epiphany since Joey's death, Cal had realized the enormity of the hurt he had inflicted on Josey. There had been days in these terrible weeks when he had hardly been able to breathe, getting through only by thinking of the courage Joey showed in his young life.

The lights flicked on in the conservatory.

"For God's sake, are you crying again? If it's not too much trouble to pull yourself out of that maudlin stupor, fix me a drink," Catherine said. Her voice jolted Cal back to the present. "We have thirty minutes. None of that cheap stuff you keep behind the bar. Use the Aberfeldy in the cabinet."

Cal looked at Catherine. Maggie's disappointment that he couldn't be at the library Christmas party tonight contrasted with Catherine's attitude. While Maggie and Cal kept their distance in public, they smiled and occasionally spoke and, after a function, found time to be alone. The biggest social event of the season, the Mount Greylock Winter Benefit, was tonight. Catherine, as chairperson, was the honoree. Catherine had let him know this was a command performance. He must be by her side.

"Ice?" he asked.

"One cube. I hope you're not a wet blanket tonight. I've worked hard for this evening to be a success and I don't want you spoiling it. Your little escapade with that juvenile delinquent was stupidity personified."

"Don't you call him that, dammit," Cal snarled. "He was a young man with serious challenges in his life, and he met those challenges heroically." Cal placed Catherine's drink on the table next to her and sat in his chair.

"He was a ward of the court. That means he was a delinquent, no matter how you try to sugarcoat it. I still find it appalling you buried that delinquent in the Callaway family section of the cemetery. I'm sure your parents are rolling over in their graves." Catherine took a sip of her drink. Smiling, she said, "I imagine you'll be lucky if there isn't a judicial investigation into the handling of his case."

Cal froze, his glass halfway to his lips. How would Catherine know anything about judicial inquiries? "What do you mean, investigation?"

"You're the one who failed to put the kid into the foster system. He was under eighteen, and that's where he belonged. What were you thinking? Did you want to play papa? The impeccable judge may have made the mistake of his career."

"Catherine, as usual, you don't know the facts and you've jumped to erroneous conclusions. Let's make a deal, right here, right now. I'll go tonight and to any other functions you require me to be at. I'll play the pleasant doting husband of the Mount Greylock Winter

Drive's madam chair if you agree to never, and I mean never, speak of Joey again. If you do, we'll—"

"We'll what, get a divorce? No, you won't do that, because it will be the end of your freeloading on the White name and fortune. So, let's not make empty promises, Your Honor."

Cal got up, placed his glass on the bar, and said, "Let me know when it's time to leave. I'll be in the study."

§

John Emerson was standing, talking to Ace Clements, when he saw Catherine and Cal enter the transformed auditorium. Metallic blue-and-white decorations made the cavernous space look elegant, along with the circular white tables with center greenery and blue-and-white flower arrangements. Catherine looked like the queen bee she was, he mused. He watched Cal take a step back as women of all ages moved in a wave engulfing Catherine with greetings and well wishes. What the ladies really wanted was to be recognized and smiled at by madam chair. After a few minutes, Cal placed his hand on her elbow and steered her toward the head table.

"Come on, Ace," John said. "Let's speak to His Honor and the queen of the evening." The two of them moved on a path to intercept Cal and Catherine.

Catherine saw them coming. "John, darling, so nice to see you. Who is this handsome young man with you?"

"Catherine, this is Neil 'Ace' Clements, an up-and-coming associate at the firm. Neil, this is Catherine White, the granddaughter and daughter of two of our venerable partners."

"White-Callaway," Catherine corrected.

"I'm so sorry, just a careless slip of the tongue. Neil, you of course know the distinguished Judge Ernst White-Callaway."

"Of course. Good to see you, Judge. That was very sad and unlucky, your ward of the court dying like he did. What was his name, again?"

"Mr. Clements, thank you for your concern. You know, one of the traits of a talented lawyer is remembering the names of clients. It was Joey Paschal, and you were his attorney when he appeared in court."

Clements's face turned red at the rebuke. He glared at Cal and said, "I'm sure I'll remember his name when I testify before the judicial inquiry panel."

Cal felt a chill of adrenaline. He smiled at the three of them. "We'd best make our way to the head table," he said to Catherine. "It appears the emcee is about to start the live auction."

Catherine ignored him and said, "John, darling, are you still going to wrap up the evening events? Please give a big thank-you to the sponsors, donors, and participants from me."

"Yes, I am. Anything special I should know?"

"No. I'm sure you'll represent the firm well. Thank you for helping." She and Cal continued to the head table.

"I look forward to seeing that son of a bitch on the other side of the bar next year," Ace said.

"Neil, you need to learn two things: First, keep your mouth shut about things you hear in private. Second, you can't do anything about what someone says to you, but you control one hundred percent of how you respond. Do you really believe Judge White-Callaway was cavalier about your retort to him? If so, you're not half as smart as I thought you were. You'd better hope the judge doesn't remember that little sparring next year, when the judicial investigation panel is announced. Let's get to our seats."

§

"Ladies and gentlemen, may I have your attention for just a few minutes? I'm John Emerson the Second, managing partner of White, White, Arnholt, and Emerson. In a moment, I'd like to thank our auction donors, sponsors, and you. But first, I'd like to recognize a unique and wonderful stalwart of our Berkshire communities, Mrs. Catherine White-Callaway, Madam Chair of this spectacular event, which raised a record amount for the Mount Greylock charities." John turned, clapping, to look at Catherine. Applause thundered through the hall as the entire audience rose to pay tribute to the best of the best charity socialites.

Catherine stood, held her hand over her heart, and gave small bows of her head to each section of the audience. She sat down, and so did the audience.

Emerson continued. "I'd be remiss if I didn't recognize madam chair's other half, the esteemed Judge Ernst White-Callaway. Judge White-Callaway, we appreciate you being here. With the death of the young ward of the court last month, we certainly would have understood if your attention were elsewhere. I'm quite confident inspection will exonerate your actions."

Cal smiled and realized Emerson was the one who had told Catherine of a judicial inquiry. Emerson's public slap in the face was intentional. Cal dismissed him as passive-aggressive, just like all the other chickenshits in the world. A voice inside him warned that he had better pay attention to what they said this evening. He must be careful and prepared. He pulled out his cell and sent an email to Betsy's office address.

His analytical side remembered Catherine and Emerson had teamed up for the country club's ladies' trifecta last June. Perhaps the two of them had a deeper relationship than he'd thought. He didn't care. They deserved each other. The governor was a shoo-in for reelection. If he initiated a judicial inquiry, that would be a problem. Would he move against a judge who was under judicial inquiry or had just been through one? Yes. Cal's judgeship was now iffy. Two words had been used tonight: inquiry and investigation. Their meanings were as far apart as night and day. Who was right?

Cal poured some sugar into his coffee and stirred it. An inquiry was usually over in a week. If it happened soon, it would be forgotten by November. If an investigation was warranted, that process could last for two years. Certainly, no governor in his right mind would endorse a judge under either event. Joey's death was a monumental tragedy; however, it was no different than if he had died in an auto or other accident. Cal's actions in handling the case were above reproach. Unless they knew Joey was his son. He had never tried to hide it, but he had also never disclosed the relationship. If Cal hadn't known who Joey was when he passed judgment, he would have made the same decisions. They could hold whatever hearings they wanted. Cal knew this inquiry or investigation, if it came about, had nothing to do with his actions and everything to do with removing him from the bench. He didn't think it would be so bad to leave the bench. No, not really. Goddammit, it wouldn't be bad at all, but it would be a disaster to be run off the bench under suspicion of negligence. He couldn't let that happen and expect to build a private practice. If Joey had been able to face his challenges, Cal could fight and surmount the challenges that faced him.

He looked over at Catherine. He saw the smirk on her face and smiled back.

# CHAPTER 32

Suzie's emotional collapse was more complete, more painful, and more debilitating than any she had experienced in her life. Worse than when Stoner was brutalizing and raping her. Worse than when she was living on the street in the old Ford. She still couldn't believe how quickly and irretrievably happiness, love, and her future had evaporated. Joey had given his life for her after she had slapped him and pushed him away. Why? How could he have been so loving? Sobs racked her body again when she realized he hadn't known about their baby. His love for her was so raw and complete and on display by his actions. Looping through her mind was the thought that if she and the baby had died as well, the three of them would be together for eternity. She felt she was falling into a bottomless, black abyss, tumbling out of control to she knew not where.

An anguished moan escaped from deep inside her. Suzie opened her eyes. Staring at the ceiling, she saw nothing but a baby growing into a child. She realized her life going forward had to be dedicated to making sure that child didn't experience the same type of childhood she and Joey had lived through. Joey had been her soul, and the baby growing inside of her was now her soul. Tension slowly ebbed from her body as the vision of the future in her mind's eye came into focus.

She curled up even tighter in the fetal position, one hand clutching the pillow and the other tightly held between her legs. Tears, once flowing freely, slowed to a trickle. She didn't know if she would ever smile again, but she knew she had to try for baby Joey's sake. She didn't know if she could see the beauty of the mountains again, but she knew she had to try so Joey's child would see the beauty he had seen.

Suzie remembered Maggie's admonition: "Tears are unhappiness leaving the body. Cry with abandon, and you will see the way forward." Joey hadn't let that monster Stoner see him cry. He had kept his unhappiness inside. Her life's love had told her over and over to see life as it was, not as she wanted it to be. Then, and only then, he'd say, can you overcome whatever obstacles life puts in your way. She clenched her fists as her tears stopped. She focused on Joey growing inside of her. This baby was her link to Joey. She saw the future as it was, accepted it, and thought about how to overcome the obstacles. This baby was Joey's flesh and blood. The baby's name would be Joey, no matter if a boy or girl. This baby would know real courage, the courage the baby's father had. She would take this baby to the Ledges and show the new Joey the beauty of the world her life's love had seen. She knew the infallible truth that this baby would know love from the moment of birth until Suzie's death. Suzie's plan for the future crystallized.

Suzie looked over at the clock on the nightstand. Maggie was waiting for her downstairs. Thank you, God, she prayed, for Maggie, who she knew was the savior of the hopeless. The plan was clear, if Maggie thought it was wise. She buried her face in the pillow and calmed herself. The garage apartment and everything in it still had the lingering aroma of Joey. She had begged Maggie not to change the sheets or clean the apartment. She allowed the scent of him to permeate every pore of her body. Maggie had to see the logic of what she proposed; otherwise, she may have to go on her own, but Maggie wouldn't let that happen. That wasn't Maggie.

Suzie turned on her back and rehearsed what she wanted to tell Maggie. She threw off the sheet and bedspread and lay still, trying to feel Joey's hands gently caressing her body.

§

Maggie sat at her kitchen banquette, drinking a glass of water. All of her adult life, she had focused on salvaging young girls whom society had failed to protect. The so-called system of protection—schools, courts, churches, and health care providers—allowed or overlooked monsters abusing, exploiting, and raping the most vulnerable. For twenty years she'd stood against the wave of abuse, snatching a pitifully small number of these girls away from the horrors and showing them how they, the young and innocent, could take the first of the two gifts God had given them all, their bodies, and use them to leverage the resources needed for nurturing and cultivating the second gift, the more important one: their minds. Time would fade the first gift, but only death could take away the second.

She taught these precious young girls that their plight was not their fault. It was society's distorted perspective that allowed men—no, not men, rather, perverts and pedophiles—to walk freely without blame or punishment. They were able to prey on young girls, children who didn't know how to protect themselves and who were afraid of being blamed by the system for the abuse. When the family abuser finally finished defiling the girl, or she ran away, there was nowhere for her to turn. The girls went from being dominated at home by perverts into the hands of pimps, who took the helpless and treated them just as bad or worse, pumping them full of drugs and alcohol, then selling them to anyone with a few dollars until their spirits and bodies broke.

Maggie had given fourteen girls the resources to escape that fate. She realized she had never thought about the boys. Tears flowed down her cheeks. She regretted not thinking about the boys. The abuse some of them suffered was as traumatic as what the girls went through. She realized the simplicity of the fact that all these children had ever wanted and needed was the love of an adult. Joey's parents had died when he was so young. His grandmother, as well. Why hadn't the social service system recognized what he and Suzie were going through? Her anger rose as she realized the system didn't see it because seeing it required doing something about it. For five months, Maggie had a son others denied her. Maybe she wasn't Joey's biological mother, but she loved him as if she had given birth to him. She had shown him the light of future happiness. Joey had loved her in return.

She closed her eyes and saw Joey's long fingers as he ran them around the batter bowl when they made cookies; his smile whenever she hugged him or gave him a compliment; the gleam in his eyes when she held him by the shoulders, looked him square in the face, and told him he could achieve anything he set his mind to. He had known she would be there to help him. She saw the times he had come in from school with his books and placed them on the kitchen island with a returned test paper sticking out so Maggie could see the grade, too shy to show her himself.

She choked on her breath. What could a young man with Joey's courage and belief in God have accomplished in this world, if given a chance? Her resolve and anger slowed her tears. She looked at her watch. Suzie would be down from the garage apartment in a few minutes. She needed a firm supporter, not one as devastated as Maggie was. Suzie's future would be difficult no matter what decisions she made. The decisions were profound for a caring person. Maggie would give guidance, but Suzie had to make the decisions on her own. Maggie remembered the Robert Frost poem "The Road Not Taken." Never had a poem spoken so clearly about a person's life decisions. She ran through the decision tree in her mind. What would Suzie do about her pregnancy? Would she need substantial time to overcome her grief? Should she move away with the money she had earned and drop out of school? So many crucial decisions, each hinged on the next. The only fact Maggie knew for sure was that the decisions needed to be Suzie's. The ramifications five, ten, and twenty years from now had to rest on her fragile shoulders.

Maggie believed the cruelest word in the English language was *if*. If Joey had called Suzie that Friday afternoon before going to her house, as they had agreed he would do, he would be alive today. If Suzie hadn't slapped Joey, he might not have misplaced his phone and would be alive today. If Suzie had waited for Joey at Maggie's, Joey would be alive today. If, if, if—always if. Hindsight was wonderful but worthless. Life unfolded only once, in the future, with all the unknowns and uncertainty clouding the vision. There was time pressure on Suzie. The window for making the most important decision was closing soon. All other decisions flowed from that crucial first one.

Maggie wiped away her tears, wet a dish towel with cold water, and held it to her eyes. She moved to the stove to prepare a healthy breakfast of eggs, bacon, polenta, and toast for the two of them. She saw the security light come on. Seconds later, the kitchen door opened and Suzie entered, dressed in Joey's shirt and pants.

"Hey," she said shyly.

"Good morning, sunshine. Please set the banquette. We're going to eat here in the kitchen."

Suzie ate half her breakfast and played with the rest, moving it around on her plate.

Maggie finished hers and pushed both plates away. "Feel like talking?" she asked, putting her hand over Suzie's.

"No, but I need to." Suzie looked at Maggie with sad, red-rimmed eyes.

Maggie squeezed her hand.

"I've been thinking about the future. I know I screwed up."

"You didn't screw up," Maggie interjected.

Suzie began to cry. "I did. It's my fault he's gone. I know that. I—"

Maggie pulled Suzie over to her and put her arms around her. In a low, calming voice, she said, "All the decisions you made were right at the time you made them. Don't play the if game. It will do you no good. It will cause you to make a mistake when deciding what the future, your future, will be. You and Joey had a love unmatched by any but a handful in this world. Take comfort in that. You do have serious decisions to make. They're your decisions, no one else's. There is money—your money—available to you if you want to start a new life. You have time to make that decision. The immediate decision is your pregnancy. If you think it's too much for you, you need to see Dr. Freedman soon. And if you want to keep the baby, you need to begin regular prenatal visits with him."

Suzie pulled away from Maggie and dried her eyes and cheeks. "Maggie, let me tell you what I think I want, and you tell me what you think of my plan."

"Sure, I'm listening."

"I want to have Joey's baby. This baby is the proof of our love, and it's the only way I can hold Joey in the future. If I have an abortion, I'm aborting Joey and everything we meant to each other. I won't—no,

I can't do that. When I hold this baby in my arms, it will be like holding Joey. When I kiss this baby, it will be like kissing Joey. When I talk to this baby, it will be like talking to Joey. This baby needs to know what an incredible and courageous person its father was. Does that make sense?"

"All the sense in the world," Maggie responded.

Suzie took a deep breath. "I want to go back to tutoring, as long as I don't show, and Dr. Freedman says it won't hurt the baby to have sex."

"Are you sure?"

"Maggie, sex is biological. Nature gives all of us that biological urge. To me, tutoring is strictly an unemotional event. I want to finish my degree and finish the program you outlined for me over two years ago. When I can't tutor during the pregnancy, I'll get a job somewhere to make ends meet. When little Joey is born, if you'll have me back, I'll finish the program. Does that make sense? Will you let me come back?"

"Suzie, I won't let you go away. Yes, my dear, it makes sense. We need to see Dr. Freedman together. Two sets of ears hear more and better than one set. If he clears you to resume tutoring, you'll go back to your place and resume. When you show, we can give a reason you're not available, and you'll move to a home in North Adams that recently became vacant. You'll stay there, go to school, see Dr. Freedman, and prepare for your baby. By the way, are you going to have Dr. Freedman tell you if it's a boy or a girl?"

"I've thought about that, too. No, I'm not. Frankly, it doesn't matter as long as it's healthy. This baby is Joey, and that's going to be its name, whether it's a boy or a girl. Joey will be with me always." Suzie's eyes filled with tears. She balled up her fists, took three deep breaths, and said, "Dammit! I won't cry anymore. Joey didn't cry when he faced challenges. I'm going to be like him. Crying is over. Doing my best is what Joey would want, and that's what I'm going to do, my best, with your help." She looked pleadingly at Maggie.

"Having Joey's baby is your decision. Now that you've made that decision, I've got to tell you, I'm happy. I'll give you all the support you want. I'm going to tell you something in confidence. Joey was more than a ward of the court. Judge White-Callaway thought of him as a son. So did I. Now you're my daughter, carrying my grandchild. I'll call Dr. Freedman's office and get an appointment for this afternoon. Tomorrow, we can get you settled back in your home."

"Does Judge White-Callaway still blame me for Joey dying? Does he know about the baby?"

"On the second question, no." Maggie squeezed Suzie's hand. "As to the first, Judge White-Callaway is processing very complex emotions about Joey's death. He needs time to understand all of them."

# CHAPTER 33

On a snowy Tuesday evening in January, the BBC gathered in the public library's second-floor conference room. Junior Soto sat in the speaker's chair and Geri Sparks in the chair to his left. With everyone seated, Cal said, "Good evening, and happy New Year. Junior will lead off." He nodded to Junior.

"Thanks, Cal. Happy New Year, everyone." Junior went on to explain how the influx of Hispanic immigrants had impacted the Hispanic community and the regional area. He had some suggestions for how the BBC members could assist and benefit from the integration process. When finished, he looked to his left at Geri.

Geri Sparks, owner of Berkshire Pest Control, alerted the group to an unfolding domestic violence situation. After some discussion, Helen Inskeep volunteered to take Geri and the woman to Safe Place, where the victim could receive help and counseling. Four of the men volunteered to have a talk with the man in the situation. The right to speak moved around the circle.

Halfway around, C. C. Jefferies said, "This is more of the nosy-story business that I thought each of you should know. An attorney from a local law firm approached me two weeks ago. He asked me if I was interested in selling one or more of my stores. When I told him no, he asked if I'd like to expand. It seems his firm has clients with capital they would like to invest in this area. He asked if I knew of any local business owners interested in selling or expanding. I asked him about the types of businesses his client or clients wanted, and he said they weren't picky at this point. That struck me as odd. Everybody here who runs his or her own small business knows that a complete novice to your business would likely fail before they learned the ropes. Anyway, be aware there are open checkbooks at White, White, Arnholt, and Emerson if anybody is interested."

"Did he mention a price to you, C. C.?" Rick Branson, a selectman and auto junkyard operator, asked.

"No. I got the sense I could name my price on a sale. Nothing was really said about how I would take on a partner. I really wasn't interested either way."

Harry Sheff, owner of a shoe repair shop, raised his hand and said, "One of my regular customers asked me if I was interested in selling my business. I've never thought anyone would want a business like mine. My wife has already gone out and bought some suntan oil in case we move to Florida." The group laughed.

"Harry, if you and C. C. don't want to sell, tell them to come see me," said Terry Rodriguez, a home builder and contractor.

Cal listened to the conversation with interest. The White law firm, as he called it, had lost its business law clients when his father-in-law died suddenly. He decided not to join the conversation. He looked over at Maggie to see if she had received any entreaties. She shook her head no. Cal decided a pair of his hiking boots needed new heels and soles.

The meeting broke up, with several of the BBC members stopping to speak to Junior and others conversing with Geri and C. C.

# CHAPTER 34

Deputy Sheriff David Fogel sat in his office, hunched over his desk, his right hand on the computer mouse. He looked at the Excel spreadsheet filled with phone numbers Cal had extracted from the pedophile's cell phone prior to destroying it. Fifteen separate numbers were on the screen, and three appeared to be robo-calls lasting three to five seconds, with the remaining twelve numbers having normal connection times. David identified the area codes of the numbers and attempted to reverse-engineer the out-of-state calls, with limited success. In the last five weeks of the pervert's life, four of the calls had gone to Orlando, Florida. Three had been to realtors' offices and one to an apartment complex. The asshole had been planning to move, David surmised.

Two of the other eight numbers had patterns. One number, with a Vermont area code, connected regularly. The last Vermont call had connected the day before the perp went to Nancy's to collect his money. David scanned the calls from this number and saw that the calls occurred on the same day each month. He decided this number could be the contact who managed the perp's life here. A monthly pattern. He was receiving six thousand dollars every thirty days. Who was it? A relative? An accomplice? More likely an accomplice. From

Vermont, how easy would it be to get the money to Nancy's? Why would someone in Vermont want to have constant contact with a fugitive hiding in another state? That would just invite in the FBI with all its resources. David's fingers drummed on his desk. What if the owner of the Vermont phone wasn't a Vermonter but from Massachusetts, with a Vermont cell? That made more sense and would make it harder to trace. He highlighted that number.

The second number was interesting. There were six calls from a Rhode Island number the first week the pedophile's phone was activated, and none after that. Why? Somebody masterminding the escape? Overseeing the safe house? Just unrelated solicitations? If the number was still active, was it an untraceable go phone or one registered to a specific owner?

Five numbers had connected with just one call each, all from the local area code.

The last number, from Boston, had connected five times. He figured that one should be easy to trace.

Three phone numbers: one from Vermont, one from Rhode Island, and one from Boston. David thought about how to get the owners' names and addresses without alerting them or the authorities in these other jurisdictions. Well, what the hell? He'd take a long shot. He pulled two latex gloves from his desk and moved to the file cabinet that stored inmates' personal property. He extracted a plastic bag of items, one of which was a cell phone.

He dialed the Rhode Island number. Within seconds, he heard a recording saying the number was no longer in use, with instructions to check the number and dial again. Next, he dialed the Vermont number. It rang several times before he heard the carrier's default robotic voicemail message. David hung up. That number was still active.

He looked down at the cell in his hands, erased both of the calls, and turned the phone off before placing the cell back in the bag and returning it to the file cabinet. He returned to his desk and picked up the phone, hoping Cal might still be in his office.

§

"The governor is on line one, Judge," Betsy said.

Catherine, Emerson, and Clements knew what they were talking about, crossed Cal's mind as he reached for a pad and pencil. "Good morning, Governor," he said in his best political voice, writing GOVERNOR on the first line.

"Judge White-Callaway, this isn't a social call. It's come to my attention that a young man, a ward of your court, died needlessly while performing court-ordered and unsupervised community service. I've appointed a judicial inquiry panel to ascertain the facts in the matter."

Cal wrote INQUIRY on the next line. "Your information is incorrect. Would you like me to send you the complete file on the matter?" he replied in an icy tone. He wrote LIES on the line next to INQUIRY, but controlled his anger. Gripping the phone tightly in one hand and clenching the pencil in the other, he understood his first opinion of this charade had been correct: It had nothing to do with Joey's death. It was all about removing him from the bench next January.

"Save the details for the inquiry. You'll be hearing from the panel in the coming weeks."

Cal wrote WEEKS. "Weeks?" he said. "This matter can be handled in a few hours. The file is complete. The facts are documented. Why not get it over with? I can be in Boston in three hours or tomorrow."

"Judge, don't try to tell me how to handle my duties. You'll hear from the investigators when they're ready."

Cal wrote INVESTIGATORS? The line went dead. Cal wrote OVER. He sat back and realized an inquiry usually comprised a couple of judges reviewing a file. The governor had used the word *panel,* inferring five judges and supporting staff, including investigators, and he'd said *investigators.* Cal's adrenaline rushed as he knew a judge found guilty in a judicial investigation was likely to be disbarred as well. He realized he was no longer in control of the situation and his judicial career was likely over. Laying his head against the headrest, he closed his eyes. He'd lost a son, and someone wanted to blame him for it just to take away this piddly job as local judge. Being a judge was rewarding in one sense, but it was just that: a job. One that barely paid a decent wage. The job was subject to certain level of insecurity every four years and ensured a financially tight retirement when the time came. His eyes popped open. This whole exercise made little sense. He wondered whom he'd made mad enough to go after his job. What politically connected person had he angered? One of the Boston-based law firms? Doubtful. In fact, they had always been professional in dealing with the court, and he had always returned the courtesy.

His thoughts switched to local firms. He quickly dismissed most of them. The fact that White, White, Arnholt, and Emerson was the only one capable of instigating this inquiry dawned on him. He remembered what C. C. had said at the last BBC meeting. WWA&E went on the next line. He knew they craved power, the power they'd lost when Catherine's father died and Emerson later became managing partner. After observing him for the past few years, Cal knew Emerson didn't have what it took to play in the big leagues. He must be hooked up with someone else. The question was who. Cal wrote CONNECTION.

WWA&E didn't have the financial base to push something like this inquiry. It had to cost serious money. Someone must have put up a large sum, probably six figures, to disgrace him. Catherine came to mind. He wrote CATHERINE. He quickly dismissed the idea as absurd. Still, she had the money, and they had an unhappy marriage arrangement. He crossed out her name and stopped. Knowing he was responsible for the unhappiness as much as she was, he felt guilty putting her name down. He had burst her dream of being the wife of the most powerful lawyer in western Massachusetts. She'd never forgiven him, but he didn't believe she was that mean and spiteful—or was she? It had to be someone who had faced the court and lost. A review of the last two years of cases a wealthy defendant had lost was in order. It was necessary to prepare for difficult surprises.

Cal tore the sheet of paper from the pad, crumpled it up, and threw it in the wastebasket. He started writing a headline on a new page. He stopped. Retrieving the crumpled page, he smoothed it out and fed the paper into the shredder. Easy with the emotions, he told himself. Stay focused. Get done what must be done. He went back to the new sheet and wrote PLAN B at the top.

He began writing one issue on each line: BBC, MAGGIE, OFFICE— PERSONAL ITEMS, HOME—PERSONAL ITEMS. He stopped and thought again—what if Catherine was involved? On the next two lines, he wrote NEW OFFICE and NEW HOME. Pausing, he felt the gravity of the situation and wrote NOW covering the next four lines. He hit the intercom. "Betsy, push the docket for tomorrow up to the morning. I want to be finished by one o'clock. Thank you."

"Yes, sir."

He dialed a second number. When a man answered, he said, "Billy, good morning. I need your help."

"Sure, Judge. What can I do for you?"

"I have two confidential rental opportunities for you. The—"

"Long-term or short-term?" Billy interrupted.

"Twelve months minimum. You have time for lunch today?"

"Sure, how about the diner?"

"Great. I'll see you there at noon."

Cal drew a line across the middle of the page. He divided the bottom of the page into columns, titling the left side OFFICE and the right side HOME. Looking around, he began listing items. Action gave him a feeling of being in control.

# CHAPTER 35

Big Vinney shifted his cell from his left ear to his right, saying, "Look, Harvard—"

"Ivy League, Vincenzo. Your crowd calls me Ivy League."

"Yeah, what I call you is bullshit. You ain't one of us. Your grandfather and father made their bones. You haven't."

"Vincenzo, we will not go over that again, will we? Let me make clear some facts: First, your brother didn't make his regular call to set up a money drop. Second, he isn't answering his phone. Third, our contact, who has access to the information, says his phone isn't pinging any cell towers. This information, taken together, means he has either gone to ground or skipped the area. Either way, he may be up to his old tricks, not wanting you or anyone else to find him."

"Maybe he's sick. Maybe he's on vacation. He swore on our mother's grave he wouldn't do any of that funny stuff with kids again."

"Let's hope he hasn't, Vincenzo. Mr. Strollo would be unhappy if your brother broke his word."

"I'll find out."

"Vincenzo, you gave your word to Mr. Strollo that you wouldn't contact your brother under any circumstances. Trust me, you don't want to go back on your word. You know Mr. Strollo takes a dim view of people who go back on their word."

"Listen, Harvard—"

"Dartmouth, actually."

"All right, Mr. Smart-Ass. He may be Mr. Strollo to you, but he's Giuseppe to me. We conquered the streets together. He spent as much time at my ma's table as I did at his. We were together when we made our bones. He's where he is because of me. Don't forget, Mr. Ivy League, if something happens to Giuseppe, you work for me."

"Are you finished, Vincenzo? When I speak to Mr. Strollo, shall I pass on to him your perspective?"

"You tell him whatever you want, Harvard," Big Vinney said, terminating the call.

He drummed his fingers on the table, mentally kicking himself for promising his ma on her deathbed he would look after the pervert. He wondered where the slimeball was. How to contact his brother without breaking his word to Giuseppe was the puzzle. He smiled and dialed a number. It rang only once.

"What number do you want? You must have the wrong one."

"No, I have the right number."

"Who is this?"

"Vincenzo. I'm calling for Mr. Strollo. There's a minor job only you can do discreetly. Meet me at five tonight at the pizza joint on Salvatore Street. Come in civilian clothes so you don't frighten the locals."

"I'll be there. Give Mr. Strollo my regards."

"Sure. Don't be late."

§

It was raining, increasing the darkness. Parking a block away from the house, Captain Charles Richards of the Massachusetts State Patrol put on his ball cap and pulled the hood of his black rain jacket over his head. He patted his left jacket pocket to make sure the Surefire light was ready. The Glock 26 Gen4 in his right jeans pocket was comfortable. He rubbed his hand along his left thigh to feel the seventeen-round spare magazine. Just like the old days in Iraq and Afghanistan. He missed the adrenaline rush of those missions. Even though he would kill no one tonight, the same rules applied: leave nothing to chance and expect the worst.

He opened the car door, slipped out into the rain, hunched his shoulders, and walked soundlessly toward the house. A dog barked. He stopped, located the sound, determined it was from a house in a different direction from the target, and resumed walking.

At the house, he searched for any light inside. Seeing none, he circled to the rear and moved to the back door. He picked the lock in seconds. Stepping inside, he shut the door softly. He stood motionless, listening. No sound at all. He went to the refrigerator and opened it. The light inside threw shadows across the room. There was plenty of food. Mold was on the fruit. He checked the milk—sour. Shutting the refrigerator, he walked to the hall.

Not a sound. The house was empty of life, he felt sure. Richards sniffed to see if there was any death odor. He drew his gun and held up his Surefire light. He started down the hall. Something was not right. He slowly opened the first door on the left. The room was empty. He entered the bathroom. Inside, he opened the medicine cabinet. Plenty of pills. Nobody who took that much medicine left town without it. Leaving the bathroom, he heard a noise and crouched down. The noise again. Squirrels or rats in the attic. He resumed walking down the hall. He turned the knob on a door and pushed it open.

"Jesus Christ," he muttered to himself. The room had posters of princesses, action figures, stuffed animals, and a bed. There were no windows. He stepped in and shut the door. Shining his light, he looked for the light switch. He flipped it. The red lights were indirect, coming from the tray ceiling. There had to be a camera in here somewhere. He examined each wall, looking for a line of sight to the bed. Cameras on all walls, hidden by a stuffed animal or peeking through a hole in a poster. He looked up and saw what looked like a lens in the light fixture. He backed out of the room and turned off the light.

He went to the room across the hall. No one was in the house. He flipped on the light and shut the door. A table across from the bed held a computer. He surveyed the room. The bed was rumpled but made up. Someone had taken a nap. He moved to the computer, pulled out the chair, and sat, looking around while the machine powered up. A bed, a chest, and this table with the computer. Spartan. When the icons were visible, he started clicking from one icon to the other, using the mouse. None had passwords and they were empty of material. The hair on the back of his neck rose. Oh, God damn, a trap. He turned off the computer, wiped off the mouse, and rapidly thought of everything he'd touched. Moving through the house, he wiped the surfaces. Expect the worst, he'd always been told. He hadn't done that because he hadn't expected a trap. He had to get out of there. The pervert was gone, someone knew he was gone, and they'd set a trap to see who would come looking.

That damn Big Vinney, he fumed silently. I'm gonna kill that son of a bitch. He would deal with that later. Getting out alive or unknown was the immediate task.

Captain Richards couldn't believe The Hammer had risked his cover for this operation. Back in his car, he sat for a few minutes and did an after-action analysis. He realized this was a Delta trap. His buddy in Afghanistan had used one. David, my friend, we need to talk, he thought. He started the car and left.

# CHAPTER 36

It was lightly snowing. The air was icy but not frigid. The sun was long gone. Maggie and Cal sat in her living room, the lights off, the curtains open. They were in separate chairs, each lost in thought. Cal's guilt over what had happened seventeen years ago continued to consume him. The thought that he was responsible for every horror Joey had endured in his life made him physically sick. He wore the knowledge like an Opus Dei metal thigh cilice. Rationalization had failed weeks ago. Drowning in an ocean of guilt, he could barely function. He slumped in the chair, his anesthesia of Wild Turkey Rare Breed on the rocks with a splash dangerously close to spilling on the carpet as he moved his hand in little circles.

Maggie looked at him. Make allowances, she thought. He just lost his son, a son whose life was mostly a horror story without guidance and protection from his biological father. Just as he can't do anything about that fateful decision to turn his back on Joey's mother, he can't do anything about the terrible past of a son he didn't know existed. He had strived to be a good man, but he hadn't worked on being a strong man. It took strength to think of others, and he didn't. He didn't know how Maggie was hurting, and she didn't choose to burden him with the knowledge. He didn't care to think about what Suzie was going through. She knew all of this, but she still loved him.

Well, she was going to make him uncomfortable. He'd said it only once, but she knew, on some level, he blamed Suzie for Joey's death. If only he knew the truth. He never would. His comfort zone was about to be shattered, and he would either sink deeper into depression or rise to the occasion.

Maggie took a sip of her bourbon. "Cal, Suzie came home from the hospital six weeks ago."

"Is she all right?" Cal asked. He took a sip of his drink. "The snow is beautiful," he commented.

"Yes, it is. Cal, Suzie is physically fine. No lasting effects from the cold."

"Thanks to Joey."

"Joey loved Suzie more than anything in this world, including life itself."

"I know. I just wish I understood."

"Understood what?" Maggie asked, trying but failing to keep the hurt from her voice.

"Understood that kind of love."

"You've never felt it?"

"I don't know. I love you; I know that."

"You loved Joey so much you're grieving for your mistake of seventeen years ago."

"*Grieving* is not the right word."

"Yes, it is. Your seventeen-year-old mistake has always been a factor in our relationship, and now your grief over Joey has taken center stage. You always held back."

"That's because I'm married, and you didn't want to commit."

"Okay, if that's your perspective, it's not mine. Marriage is a situation where two people choose to have a relationship. Many marriages become hollow because the spouses lose respect for each other. A person can be in a bad marriage but have a totally committed emotional and physical relationship with someone else. If both parties understand total commitment is more important than a piece of paper, the relationship can last and grow. Joey and Suzie had a relationship so rare, you and I can't understand it. What young woman, still a child, would accept repeated, violent rape to keep a loved one from being brutalized? What thirteen-year-old boy, barely in puberty, would murder to keep the girl he loved from being raped? You and I can't get our heads around those facts. When those two, thinking the other was dead, found each other again after three years, their love and happiness surpassed comprehension by us rational adults. Suzie was the most precious treasure in Joey's life. I know of your love for Joey. Nor do I have any doubt Joey was—no, is your biological son. Anyone with eyes can see it. Why, then, do you not have strong feelings for Suzie?"

"I don't dislike Suzie. We never got to know each other. I know Joey loved her. They hadn't reached an age when they really understood what love means."

"You are so wrong, Cal Callaway," Maggie snarled, shaking her head.

Cal looked up, shocked at her tone of voice.

She continued. "If you and I live to be a hundred, we won't have a clue about love like those two young people did."

"I know you're close to Suzie."

"Yes, Suzie is just like a daughter to me. Joey was, and is, the son I could never have." Her voice broke. She sipped her drink. Her anger at Cal's attitude grew. He knew nothing about genuine love. "Do you know why Suzie and Joey were scheduled to go to the Ledges that day?"

"No. I guess it was just another hike."

"Bad guess, Your Honor." Maggie took a long pull on her bourbon. "I was going to tell you at dinner that night. Remember we were going to a quiet dinner in North Adams?"

"Yes."

"The Ledges were where Suzie and Joey made love the first time. It was their special place. The past dissolved there, and the future began materializing for them there." Tears started flowing down her cheeks.

Cal looked at her, puzzled by her emotions.

"It was Suzie's idea to hike to the Ledges," she said. "Remember I said she wanted to surprise him?"

"No, I don't."

"Cal Callaway, congratulations. You're going to be a grandfather."

Cal dropped his half-full glass on the rug. "Are you serious?" he asked as he knelt, using his napkin to blot the spilled whiskey and putting the ice back in the glass.

Maggie watched with mixed feelings but made no effort to help. "Suzie is pregnant. That's what she was going to tell Joey at the Ledges. So, Merry Christmas, a few weeks later."

"Boy or girl?"

"She doesn't know and doesn't want to know until the baby is born. A healthy child is what she wants. She said the baby's name will be Joey, no matter the sex."

"Does she know about my relationship to Joey?"

"No. All she knows is you felt close to Joey and wanted to guide him to a successful life. That's all she should know, at least for the time being. To tell her more now will invite complicated questions with answers that provoke more complicated questions."

"How will she live?"

"Suzie works for me in my shops. She stayed with me from the day she got out of the hospital until two weeks ago. She's now gone back to the home she rents from me. She's a student at BC, as well. After the baby is born, she'll continue her studies. She'll learn the challenges of being a single mom, but I'll tell you, Cal Callaway, she's a resilient woman who will rise to the occasion. I'm confident of that."

Cal sat up in his chair. "I'd like to meet her and tell her how to get to Joey's grave. I'd like to get to know her, help her," he said. Cal felt his suffocating negativity lift slightly. "Maggie, there's something I need to tell you," he continued, and he explained his encounter with Catherine, Emerson, and Clements, as well as his phone call from the governor.

# CHAPTER 37

In early February, the weather wasn't as bad as it could have been. The sun was bright in a cloudless sky, with a projected high of thirty-two degrees. Even with the freezing temperature, half the customers wanted ice cream. The other half held their hot chocolate or coffee cups with both hands, looking upon the ice cream eaters with doubts about their sanity. Pouring a cup of hot chocolate for a customer, Maggie looked through the front window and saw a young girl sitting on a bench. She was huddled with hunched shoulders, her arms tightly crossed, her chin tucked into the top of her blouse. Her flaming red hair was stringy and unkempt. Her skirt was short, and her bare legs were squeezed together and shivering uncontrollably.

"Cary, take over the counter for me, please," Maggie said, picking up a large cup, filling it with hot chocolate, and wrapping a napkin around one of the four scones left in the case. She walked outside and crossed the street.

"Hi, I'm Maggie. I thought you might enjoy these." She held out the cocoa and scone. The girl looked up at her.

"No, thanks. I'm fine."

"I'm sure you are. That's my store over there." Maggie pointed across the street. "There's no charge for them; they're leftovers—at least the scone is. We'll have to throw it out if you don't take it. The cocoa is steaming. You'll need it while eating the scone. The baker made them drier than usual. He said it's the air density, but I think that's just a story." She put the scone on the girl's lap and the cocoa on the bench next to her. "There are plenty of seats inside, and a bathroom, if you want to come in. You're welcome inside." She turned and walked back to the store.

Inside, she went behind the counter but monitored the girl. Maggie knew it was up to the girl. She had seen this situation play out many times. Either she would eat the scone, drink the cocoa, and come in or she'd let her pride keep her from doing any of it. There was nothing more Maggie could do. She knew the girl was at a pivotal point in her life: crash and burn or hold onto her belief in herself by her fingertips. Pride was good in a person's life journey but sometimes deadly. It was hard to tell where the girl was on that journey.

The girl needed to care for her own survival and want more out of life. Maggie couldn't force her or do it for her. Come on, Red, Maggie silently urged. Use your self-pride to pick yourself up. Come on, girl. She watched as the girl looked at the store, picked up the scone and cocoa, and walked over to the trash can, throwing the pastry and drink in. She looked at the store, turned, and walked away, still hunched over.

Maggie shut her eyes. She reminded herself that she couldn't force a young girl to want a better life. What had brought her here? Maggie was sure of the reasons. Abuse? Maybe, but the anger was not there. Bad decisions? For sure. The girl's demeanor was one that came from finding herself in a place she'd never thought possible. She was pretty, so it may have been a case of growing up too fast and getting tangled up with bad boys. Maggie felt she'd been on the streets only a short time. At least she now knew there was a friendly face here. Maggie was confident she'd show up at the library soon. They all did when it got cold enough.

§

"Maggie, it's time," Suzie said. "I told my clients the story of studying abroad that you suggested. They all said they hope I'll return in the summer. Howie even gave me five hundred dollars for what he calls 'mad' money in Europe."

"That's his choice. He's a sweet man. Unfortunately, you won't be able to resume seeing him after your baby is born. You know there can't be any exchange of money or value between you and a tutoring client. Pack up your personal things. I'll be over in an hour to help. Rachael's home, now yours, is ready for you. It's closer to school and Dr. Freedman's office. We'll get you settled in. I want you to come here for dinner tonight. You can spend the night and drive back to your new home tomorrow. You met Judge White-Callaway only briefly, but you haven't really gotten to know him."

"Does he still blame me for Joey's death?"

"Suzie, he's struggling with it. I'm sure his striking out at you right after the rescue was from an emotional overload. It's very complicated, Suzie. He wants to get to know you. He wants to tell you how to find Joey's grave. You should know him. So, the three of us are going to have dinner tonight and several times in the future."

"Does he know I'm pregnant?"

"Yes, and he knows it's Joey's baby. Now, get packing. I'll see you in an hour."

Maggie replaced her cell in her bag. She unzipped another compartment and pulled out her go phone. She hit the speed dial button. It rang three times.

"Good afternoon," Cal said.

"Good afternoon, Cal. Dinner will be late, seven instead of six. Suzie is coming. It's time you start to know the mother of your grandchild. You'll like her. See you then. Bye." Maggie clicked off before Cal could respond.

Change. The more things changed, the more they stayed the same. Joey, my dear son, Maggie resolved, I'll find a way to put love and strength in your father's life. Oh, if only you were here, it would be easy. I love you, son. Maggie wiped a tear from the corner of her eye and took a deep breath.

§

"Do I look all right?" Suzie asked, looking pensively at Maggie.

"You look radiant, the way a beautiful, pregnant young lady should look," Maggie said, smiling at Suzie. She'd never thought she could love human beings as much as she loved Joey and Suzie. Even though she had shepherded fourteen other young ladies from the darkness of their childhoods into brilliant futures, with four others working their way to their futures, these two young people had touched her in a way she had thought no one could anymore. Both had the hard scars of abuse, but somehow there was an opening in their hearts and minds where the genuine beauty of their characters evidenced itself.

Maggie stood at the center island, placing the salads on their plates. "Suzie, please put these plates on the banquette. You can go ahead and pour the tea into the glasses. Judge White-Callaway will be here any minute." Maggie had decided they would eat in the kitchen instead of the dining room. The evening risked being stilted enough without the formal dining room setting. She thought back to the last time Cal and Suzie had seen each other and shuddered. It was in the ER right after Cal and Junior had rescued the young people from the Ledges.

Cal and Junior had felt Joey was dead, but hoped they could revive him. Thank God Bell Edwards, the chief ER physician, had been on duty. Seeing Bell, Cal had maintained his hopes for Joey. Bell put the young people in different ER rooms and assigned a team of doctors and nurses to each patient. He went calmly from one room to the other. It was Bell who had told Cal nothing could be done for Joey and caught Cal with Junior's assistance as he started crumbling to the floor. Before being given a sedative, Cal had lashed out at Suzie, shouting over and over that she was to blame for Joey's death.

Maggie, who had been in the room when Suzie revived but was not aware Joey had died, had watched Suzie burst into tears when she heard Cal. Every time he made an accusation, Maggie could see Suzie flinch like he had hit her with a rubber hose. Maggie had tried to talk to Suzie, to drown out Cal's shouts, but it was to no avail. Finally, the sedative took effect and Cal was placed on a gurney in another room. Maggie had sat on the edge of Suzie's bed and held her, telling her to think of her baby, who was all that mattered at that point.

Maggie had known she was the only person who then, and even now, understood the depth of the anguish and anger Cal felt toward himself. He had faced the fact last June that his biological son had suffered a horrendous childhood because he, Cal, had abandoned Joey's mother. His rationalization stifled the guilt since he could make it up to Joey. Now, he couldn't. Maggie had feared he would destroy himself before they could stabilize him emotionally and had even voiced her concerns to Bell without explaining why.

Maggie stood at the center island putting the salad together, breathed deeply and thought of Joey. She doubled her determination that this evening would be a success by bringing Joey's father and Suzie together, united with her in focusing on Suzie and Joey's unborn baby. At that moment, the first warning light went on. Suzie saw it and bit her lip.

Cal entered the kitchen, smiling what Maggie knew was his political smile. He came over and kissed Maggie on the cheek, then turned and offered his hand to Suzie. "Suzie, I'm glad we have this opportunity to get together. How are you?"

"I'm okay," she said with a smile.

"Dinner's ready, so why don't you two take a seat? I'll put the bowls on the table," Maggie said. She engineered nervous small talk. Neither Cal nor Suzie ate enough, and they avoided looking at each other.

Maggie finally put her fork down, looked from one to the other, and said, "Obviously no one is going to eat a healthy meal until the talking is over. Cal, say what's on your mind. We are all united in two facts. First, all three of us loved Joey with all our hearts and souls. Second, Suzie is carrying a part of Joey and will have his baby, which gives us the ability to continue loving Joey and showing him, through his child, what a loving family can be." She wiped her cheek and looked at Cal.

He reached over and squeezed her hand. "You have always been the strong one," he said to Maggie. Turning to Suzie, he said, "Suzie, I said some irresponsible things in the ER the night of your—our—tragedy. I'm sorry for those outbursts. We buried Joey in the Callaway family plot in the cemetery on Jackson Street. Do you know which one I'm speaking of?"

Suzie nodded her head.

"Good. What I'd like to know most is what Joey was like when the two of you were together as children. Not the negative situation Stoner caused, but the little things about him as a young boy. What did he like? What did he laugh at? What stories did he like? That sort of thing. Please, any little thing at all that brought him happiness."

Maggie could see the pain and the dark circles under those blue eyes that normally sparkled with a love of life. What bothered her as much as anything were the frown lines at his mouth that hadn't been there before the accident.

Suzie started talking with tears welling up in her eyes, and an hour later the three of them were laughing after she told them the story of Joey's proposal. While talking, she repeatedly twisted the ring Joey had given her. Nothing more needed to be said. The unspoken words said enough. A salve of love began reducing the pain of the last meeting. Progress, even a little, made Maggie happy. She could tell Cal was holding back, the way he did in their relationship. You'll come around, she thought. At least, you had better. Your pain, Cal, is your fault. Suzie's pain and mine are not our fault. Maggie gave him a hug as he prepared to leave.

He went over to Suzie, kissed the top of her head, and thanked her for sharing her memories.

# CHAPTER 38

Freezing rain beat against the windows as the BBC met in the second-floor conference room of the library.

Geri Sparks sat in the speaker's chair. She gave the members an upbeat report of the developments in the domestic violence situation. The right to speak passed around the circle.

Bell Edwards, the ER physician, spoke up. "Just wanted to let you know there are rumors swirling around in the banking community that offers are being made to every locally owned bank. At least one other regional bank wants to buy or partner with a local institution. As you know, I sit on the board of First National. No one made a definitive offer to us or our senior management, but my gut tells me someone is setting up a situation where the first bank to say 'Come get me' wins big, and the rest lose out. Like C. C. last meeting, I don't have concrete facts, but I'm confident times are changing around here. I think big money from the coast or New York has awakened to what a wonderful place this is. If anyone else hears anything, please pass it on."

Wan Chu spoke up. "FYI to all, I have received a written offer for my store. I'm considering it because it is just too good to dismiss out of hand. My wife and I have worked hard to get where we are, and we have always thought about going south when we retired. We just thought it would be years from now."

"Wan, that's good news for you and potentially bad news for us. Do what's best for you and your family and know we're happy for you. Anyone else? Thanks to all of you for doing what you can to defuse and improve the domestic violence situation. Now I have an issue I'd like to brief you on," Cal said. "As you all know, the young man I told you about last June lost his life in that freak winter storm in November. He was a ward of the court, as I helped him acclimate to society after living for three years on his own in the wilderness. There have been stories that he was on the mountain that day because of stringent community service requirements I imposed on him. That's not true. He had served his community service that day at ATCHQ and was finished. He went to the mountain because his girlfriend—no, that's the wrong word—his fiancée had gone there to wait for him. They had planned a hike to discuss their pending marriage.

"She was unaware of the developing storm. At ATCHQ he learned about the danger she was in. He saved her life and lost his. I made his entire court file available to the authorities. I received, however, a call from the governor over two weeks ago that he was impaneling a judicial inquiry to investigate the matter. Normally, these take two days. The judges on the panel read the file, call in witnesses if necessary, and then report to the governor. I don't know why there's this delay between the governor calling me and the impaneling of the committee. It should be routine. I've decided, though, to distance myself from the BBC when the inquiry is going on. Our work is critical to the community and best conducted in private. While there should be no connection between the inquiry and our work, I don't want a nosy inquiry member wondering about where I go if I may be attending a meeting. That's all I have."

"Cal, is a judicial inquiry standard procedure if someone dies while a ward of the court?" Taylor asked.

"Yes, and no. Yes, when something like this happens, questions arise, and the file is reviewed. I've been meticulous in documenting Joey's file. The file should have answered questions an interested party may have. So no, I don't know why it's being elevated to an inquiry level. Other than this is an election year, and, as you probably know, the governor reviews judges with the advice of the district councillor. This too shall pass, as the saying goes. Anyone else have anything we should know?" No one spoke. "Okay, have a good evening and stay warm."

As the members filed out of the room, Maggie asked, "Do you have time to come by?"

"Not tonight. I'll walk you to your car and explain. I wasn't exactly candid with the BBC. Something is not right with what's happening. This inquiry should be a routine matter. I told you the governor used the word *investigator*. There shouldn't be an investigator. My senses are on high alert. I've taken the precaution of quietly renting an office and a cabin on October Mountain under a corporate name. Certain files and personal items from my courthouse office and my study at Willview are there now. I don't know if this investigation includes Catherine, but I know she's aware of what's going on and has chosen not to share what she knows with me.

"I'll finish moving everything I want from my office at the courthouse tonight—everything, that is, except my great-grandfather's desk. By morning, I'll have any personal or confidential items from Catherine's home. With a little luck, I'll have to put everything back soon. I'd much rather spend the time with you. That raises another issue. If my fears are correct, this inquiry will get messy. We can't have any contact till it's over. Someone is trying to disgrace me or find me negligent; I don't want you or the BBC in the line of fire."

Maggie looked dismayed. "Do you really think it's that serious?"

"Maggie, I don't know. This could get out of hand. If I were found guilty of negligence, I could not only lose my judgeship but lose my law license as well. What I do know is, if I'm not prepared, a lot of good people could suffer needlessly, and I'm not willing to risk that. By the way, how is Suzie? I hope we can have another dinner when this is over. I've deliberately kept her name out of the file. We'll see if they try to call her as a witness."

"Do you think they will?'

"I don't know. If it appears likely, she may want to take a vacation in Florida or California for a while. I appreciate your putting us together. I can see why Joey loved her so much. Does she resent me?"

"Heavens, no. She knows what you did for Joey. Besides, as she says, 'Granddaddy Cal' is a nice guy."

"Granddaddy Cal, eh? Let's not get carried away, Granny Maggie." Cal smiled as she kissed him on the cheek.

# CHAPTER 39

aggie stood at the library's central desk, double-checking the friendly reminder email list to overdue book borrowers that a fine of ten cents per day was accruing. Out of the corner of her eye she saw a snow-encrusted, uncovered bright red head entering the library. Looking up, she saw the young girl she had tried to help last week. She returned to the email list while tracking Red's movements. She'll go to the bathroom first, Maggie knew, as Red looked around.

"Elaine," Maggie said to the young librarian at the desk, "please show the young lady who just came in where the bathroom is."

When Red came out of the bathroom, Maggie approached her with a cup of coffee. "Hi, I'm Maggie, the lead librarian. I thought you might like a cup of coffee. You must drink it with the lid on, and over in the café section." She tilted her head in the direction of the café, containing five high-top tables with two or four chairs at each. A big sign hung from the ceiling: NO BOOKS ALLOWED IN CAFÉ.

Red took the coffee from Maggie as they walked to the café, took a sip, and asked, "Do you have any sugar?"

"Right over here." Maggie diverted their direction to the counter with the cream powder, sugar, napkins, and stirrers.

"I'm sorry I was rude last week."

"I understand. You've been through a lot in your young life. You have a right to avoid strangers."

"How do you know what I've been through? You don't know me. I get along fine," Red retorted. Maggie smiled.

The two reached a table. Maggie turned to Red, holding out a chair for her. "I can see you're independent and on your own, likely homeless. A long time ago, I was on my own. I don't intend to pry into your life. Everyone has a right to decide for themselves how their life unfolds. Those who make good decisions survive and thrive. Those who make poor decisions die young. What path you take is up to you. If you want help and someone to talk to, I'm available. I can help you make good decisions. I can't and won't make them for you. Now, I must get back to work. Stay as long as you like. Anytime you need a bathroom and the library, or my ice cream shop, is open, you're welcome to use them. Enjoy the coffee. There's more in the pot."

Red sat, sipping her coffee and looking at Maggie. Kind strangers were new to her. She was sensitive to her body odor and filthy hair. Maggie didn't mention either or show revulsion. Red looked down at her clothes. The dirt was visible even though she tried to clean her skirt and blouse whenever she could. What she wanted was to get out of this mess she was in. She sensed someone standing in front of the table. She looked up and flinched.

"You didn't really think you could run away, did you, Audrey? Come on. You owe me for the opies you enjoyed last week. I've got some friends who want to party with you," said a middle-aged, squinty-eyed, potbellied guy. A muscular man in his twenties accompanying the older guy put his hand on her arm. Audrey tried to pull away and knocked the rest of her coffee off the table. The other people in the café looked at them.

"Get your hands off me," she said.

"Look, slut, you willingly came to work as a dancer, and you took the joyride. You owe me."

"Get your hands off her," Maggie said in a low voice. "Leave her alone and leave the library, or I'll call the police."

"Mind your own business, lady. She owes me. Go back to your desk. I'm leaving with her."

"No, you aren't," Maggie said, punching three numbers into her cell and hitting the speaker button.

"Nine one one, what is your emergency?"

"This is Maggie Latham, at the library. We have a situation. Please send an officer over as soon as possible."

"He's on his way, Ms. Latham."

"This isn't over, bitch," said the older man. "Come on, Arnie." The two turned and started out of the library. The potbelly turned to look back at Maggie, held his hand like a gun, and pointed at her.

"I take it they're not relatives," Maggie said. "Do you really owe him?"

"He goes by the name Slim. He runs the gentlemen's club out on Highway 20. Yeah, you could say I owe him." Red looked down at her hands, then away from Maggie. Her chin quivered. She shook her head and looked back at her. "I got into town last week from New Hampshire. I had a backpack with my money in it, but these two guys who gave me a ride stole it. They dumped me out on the side of the road in town. That's when you saw me sitting on the bench. After I left town, I saw the club and thought I could get a job serving. Fat chance. Slim is looking for girls to dance naked and party with customers and his friends. He gave me some opies, convinced me to dance, and then, well, I was the fresh meat. He kept me high—no, that's not true. I took the damn pills. Anyway, after two days, I knew

I either had to get out or accept what I was becoming. I figured I'd just as soon freeze to death. It was less painful."

"What's your name?"

"Audrey."

"Audrey what?"

"Audrey McKinney."

"Audrey McKinney, as I've said, I'm Maggie Latham. I'm the lead librarian. I also have ice cream shops, antique stores, and souvenir/jewelry stores in various towns in the Berkshires. My house has a small garage apartment. If you think you're interested, you're welcome to stay there until you get back on your feet. You'll have to pay rent, but you can work it off in one of my stores. Interested?"

Before Audrey could answer, two uniformed police enter the library.

"Hold on a minute, Audrey. Let me speak to the officers." Maggie walked over to them and said, "Thank you for coming, officers. The two men causing the disturbance left when they heard me call 911. I'd appreciate your noting in your report that one of them is Slim and the other is Arnie. I don't know their last names. I know they work at that strip club out on Highway 20."

"Do you want us to investigate further, Ms. Latham? We can go out there and bring them in."

"No, I don't believe they'll come back. I appreciate your quick response. It's nice to know we have you. Officers, remember, we have books for grown guys as well as students. Don't be strangers." Maggie smiled.

"Yes, ma'am. You have a nice day," one officer said.

Maggie walked back to Audrey. "Now, where were we?"

"What's the catch?"

"No catch except no drugs or alcohol. You can leave whenever you want. If you find you're being put upon, just walk out."

"Can I think about it?"

"Sure. The library closes at five today. You can either leave before then or leave with me at a quarter after, when I close up." Maggie smiled, turned, and went back to her work.

§

Red rode with Maggie. She lowered her car window enough to let some cold air in, hoping to dilute the odor coming from herself and her dirty clothes.

As she drove, Maggie said, "You'll find some clothes in the apartment. You're welcome to wear whatever fits. When we arrive, I'll give you a key and a garage door opener. That's the only way in or out. Why don't you shower, find something to wear, and bring your clothes over to the house? I'll wash them while we have dinner."

Neither woman noticed the F-150 pickup following them to the house.

# CHAPTER 40

"It was a setup," Charles Richards said.

"You don't know that for sure," Aloysius responded.

"You weren't there. I've arranged these setups in Iraq and Afghanistan. It's the perfect way to see who the enemy is. I'm just surprised Mr. Strollo put me in such a compromised position."

"Hold on, Captain. Don't go around shooting off your mouth. It's unhealthy."

"Yeah, well, losing everything we've worked for to get me in my position is beyond dumb."

"Why do you think Mr. Strollo asked you to do this?"

"Because Big Vinney said so."

Aloysius sat erect in his chair while pushing the recorder on his desk phone. "Captain, start at the beginning, and leave nothing out."

Richards recited his phone call, meeting with Big Vinney, and the trap he'd fallen into. Aloysius, listening intently, understood the gravity of the situation. Not only had Big Vinney disobeyed The Hammer's edict not to try to contact his brother, but he'd done it by utilizing and jeopardizing an asset that had taken eight years to put in place. It had taken time and patience to nurture the asset, and beyond that, Richards was extraordinarily valuable because of his record as a former Delta operator. He'd served in Iraq and Afghanistan. He'd won two Silver Stars, two Bronze Stars with Valor, and three Purple Hearts. In his early forties, he had the potential to move up to the highest levels of the Massachusetts State Patrol. If he believed it was a setup, it likely was one. But by whom, and where was Big Vinney's brother?

The Hammer was not going to like this turn of events. He was old-school—break heads and bones, rule the streets. But he knew those days were ending. Aloysius had put in a lot of work convincing Strollo and his capos that the serious money came in economic downturns, when legitimate businesses were cheap. He also knew The Hammer was not going to be happy, particularly if he heard it from the wrong messenger. Aloysius decided he'd better tell him before he heard it from one of his multitude of sources.

"Captain, thank you for calling. Forget this misadventure ever happened. If by some chance you're confronted, call me before speaking to anyone. If you're arrested, do not call from their offices. Have your regular contact reach us from a prepaid phone and then throw it away. Understand?"

"Yes, sir."

"Thanks for the information." Aloysius hung up and put the recorded tape in his pocket. He then reached for the phone again and dialed a number very few people knew.

§

"Cal, the trap worked. The problem is more complicated than we thought," David Fogel said, sitting in Cal's judicial chambers. He noticed fewer mementos on the shelves, and some of the artwork was missing. He didn't ask why.

"Explain, please, David."

"Three nights ago, the pedophile's computer turned on. I had placed a cookie on the new hard drive to alert me, and the cookie also turned on the webcam and sent the pictures it took to me. We have a clear photo of the person who entered the house. I took a fingerprint team out there the next day. The doorknobs were wiped clean and so was the computer mouse. Shortly after turning on the computer, the person realized the house was a setup and tried to cover his tracks. He missed one key on the keyboard, where we lifted a print, and we lifted three from the refrigerator door, not the handle."

"That's wonderful, or am I missing something?"

"The intruder was—no, that's incorrect, he is a dear friend of mine. He's the closest thing to a brother I have. His name is Charles Richards, and he's a captain in the Massachusetts State Patrol."

"Tell me you're joking. How is he a friend?"

"Charles—don't ever call him Charlie—and I were in Delta together. Matter of fact, we were in the same selection class. Served together in Iraq, where he won his first Silver Star and Bronze Star with Valor. In Afghanistan, we were on the same team. He's the reason I have my Silver Star. The Taliban ambushed our team as we withdrew from a messy operation. Charles went down early in an exposed position. I went back and pulled him to safety. Getting both of us behind cover, the Taliban shot both of us. It was no big deal. He would've done the same for me. But we sort of bonded, even more than the usual team comradeship. The rest of the tour, we were inseparable. We built a reputation as a two-man killing machine. Matter of fact, some clowns we served with made us T-shirts with TMKM stenciled on them. When my tour was over and I mustered out, he did too. I landed here, heard about an opening at MSP, and called him. He applied and got the position. His career advancement has been like a rocket. He's smart, both educated and streetwise. I can't imagine why he showed up in this mess."

"Do you believe he's involved with child pornography and abuse?"

"Hell, no. This guy is as straight as an arrow. I saw him cut an Afghani throat because the slimeball kept an eleven-year-old boy as his sex slave. He's not married because of who he is, an actual Rambo with a brain. I know this guy like I know myself. His showing up makes the situation more complicated than we thought. How and in what way, I'm not sure."

"Do you think he's working a covert op for MSP?"

"Maybe that's it. I sure hope so."

"Get me his details. If it is a covert op, a judge had to approve it. I'll make a discreet generic inquiry of his judicial circuit to see if there's an ongoing operation that may extend into the Berkshires."

"I'll have those to you today."

"Let's talk hypotheticals, David. Why do you suppose your friend was in that house?"

"I don't know."

"Do you think he was operating on his own?"

"No. Maybe. No, I don't. As I said, Charles is a straight arrow. I don't mean he believes in all of society's rules. He believes in the flag, the country, and the military. Charles is a first-class soldier, but he's no leader."

"Okay, therefore, we have two possibilities. First, the MSP has an active covert pedophilia op going. Second, your friend has two employers, the MSP and another. Who could that second employer be?"

"It doesn't take a mental giant to surmise the second employer is some sort of crime outfit."

"Do you believe organized crime has co-opted your friend?"

David thought for a minute and said, "Yeah, without a doubt. He has his own sense of right and wrong for the local level. He's seen—we both have—the hypocrisy embedded in our society, where the rulers make the rules to favor themselves. Yeah, he could do that."

"Let's keep Captain—what did you say his name is?"

"Charles Richards. Captain Charles Richards."

"Let's keep Captain Richards on the back burner for now. You mentioned before two numbers that intrigued you on that cell phone. Tell me why."

"The first number, with a Boston area code, appeared only right after the perp arrived in the Berkshires. After a couple of weeks, calls to and from that number ceased. The second number, with a Vermont area code, had regular contact with the perp. I suspect the cell is a prepaid phone, owned by a local who didn't want his calls traced back to him. I don't believe these are social calls. From the beginning, these contacts show a regular monthly interval and last for no more than one minute each. By the way, the perp called the Vermont number; the Vermont number never called the perp. The last of these contacts was made the day before the phone came into my possession."

"Have you called either number?"

"Yes and no. I called one number I didn't tell you about. It was a prepaid cell with a Rhode Island area code. That phone is no longer active. I called the Vermont number using an untraceable phone and got a carrier voicemail. I hung up. I haven't tried to call the Boston number. My gut tells me that number is the key to this issue, and I don't want to alert anyone."

"You're right. Can you make a records request?"

"Yes, but to request a record on a Boston area code, I must go to the MSP. There's a possibility Charles will find out. I could go directly to him, but what if he's tied into the number? After all, he's the one who showed up."

"Let me try a judicial approach. I can issue an eyes-only judicial request to the phone companies in the state, using seven different numbers rather than just those two. Can you get me the direct phone number for your MSP captain? I'll pull four other numbers from our files. It's a fishing expedition, but maybe we can get the info we want without showing our hand."

"I'll call back with his number. I've got it in the MSP organizational manual."

"Make it a priority, David. I don't know when this judicial inquiry will start. Once it does, I won't have normal access to the judicial system, and I'll focus on micromanaging the situation. For sure, we don't want any hint of this investigation."

"Cal, you seem extra worried about this inquiry. Any reason?"

"Something isn't right. I should have been instructed to send the Paschal boy's file to Boston. The governor didn't ask for the file. I sent it anyway, that same day, to the governor's office. They should have forwarded it to the panel. The panel should've finished within a week of the governor calling me. I've heard nothing from anyone. The governor mentioned an investigator. Inquiries don't have investigators; criminal investigations do. It fits with a judicial criminal investigation. Nothing in the file warrants that approach."

"Is there anything I can do?"

"Yeah, stay as far away as possible. If they're doing a criminal investigation, it's with trumped-up charges. If someone would lie to get to me, no telling what other lies they would tell to hurt anyone they think is a friend of mine. This too shall pass. Give Donna a hug for me."

# CHAPTER 41

"What do you mean, she wouldn't let you have the girl?"

Slim's eyes darted from Big Vinney's fat-encased, half-shut eyes to his expansive belly to the wall over his shoulder. "The cunt went into the library when she saw us. A woman who worked there called the cops. We got out before the cops showed up. The woman and the girl got in a car, and I had a guy follow them to the woman's house, so I know where she lives."

"Why did you want to know where she lives, for Christ's sake?"

"That piece of ass owes me," Slim said. "She can't just walk away. It sets a bad example for the others."

"Slim, stop thinking with your little head and start thinking with your big head," Big Vinney said. "This girl ain't worth it. You get rough with her and the library lady, and you put the entire gold mine under a bright, hot light. You want that, Slim? Forget this bitch. There are plenty more who want your opies and snort powder. Pay attention to your business. These other dancers don't know and won't know what happened to that one girl."

Big Vinney looked around the expansive room: three spotlighted pole stages, a long bar where two girls danced and teased the customers, circular sofas deep enough for lap dancing, and secluded areas behind curtains, where johns paid the big bucks. The Berkshire Gentlemen's

Club wasn't the Ritz, but it looked good. More importantly, it was Big Vinney's best money producer, money laundry, and drug distribution point. He patted himself on the back. His street people came in with the money and paid everything for a lap dance. The money went to the counting room, and if it was all there, new drugs were put into the dealer's car trunk miles away by people unconnected with the club. The street dealer left happy and reloaded with stuff, and the money was in the system. Nobody was delivering cash, just spending it on legitimate entertainment. No one inside was handling the illegal stuff. Smooth as silk.

"We have an understanding, Slim?" he said.

"Yeah."

"Say it, Slim: 'I'll forget about that girl and the library lady and pay attention to my gold mine.'"

"I'll forget about those two bitches and pay attention to my gold mine." Slim recited the line while looking at the floor.

"Look at me, Slim."

Slim looked up at Big Vinney.

"It's important nothing disturbs our business here. Got it?"

"Got it," Slim replied, looking away.

Big Vinney nodded to his driver and bodyguard. He stood and patted Slim on the cheek.

Slim sat still for ten minutes. He picked up a beer bottle from the table and hurtled it across the room. The employees ducked, waiting for more violence. Slim hollered out, "Arnie!" When Arnie didn't appear, he shouted, "Goddammit! Somebody find Arnie and bring him to me."

"Yeah, boss. I'm here." Arnie came around the sofa from the rear. "Calm down or you'll have a heart attack. What's up?"

"Me and you have a job to do, tonight. I want you to get two needles loaded with pure H, laced with fentanyl, enough to kill a horse. Meet me here at 1:00 a.m. Me and you are going to have some fun."

"Sure, boss, whatever you say."

§

Maggie and Red finished dinner and were sipping a glass of wine before clearing the table. "Red, around here, everything has a place, and everything is in its place. Most people don't realize their minds are constantly processing their surroundings. If the environment is messy, the mind is messy. Success at any task, particularly life itself, requires—no, that's not the right word, demands is the right word—a methodical mind focused on a simple goal. Success demands building attitudes and habits conducive to success. That's what I do around here. I'm going to show you, if you want me to, the right attitudes and habits."

"I want you to, but I'm not worth spending the time or effort on. When I look in the mirror, all I see is a loser, white trash, never able to do anything right. You know what? A part of me liked the drugs and sex. Whose fault was that? Mine."

"Red, you have a choice. Stay white trash, as you call yourself, which you are not, or become what you want to become. Where you have been and where you are now have absolutely no bearing on where you can be. You can succeed at any career you want. If you enter my program, you'll graduate from Berkshire College with the degree you want. You must do your best in your classes. That's the major requirement. This is your future if you want it, but it takes the right attitude, courage, and work ethic, as well as the ability to communicate in an elegant way. Look around you." Maggie waved her arm around the dining room. "Is this environment better than what you came from? It's your decision. By the way," Maggie continued, "I know adults have told you not to daydream. Be realistic, they said. That's bullshit. Pardon the expression, but that's the only one that fits. Tonight, and while you're here, I want you to daydream. I want you to dream big. I want you to dream in color and vivid details. Think of all the things you want to do and be in your life. Big dreams lead to enormous accomplishments. I'm off tomorrow. Why don't you let me show you what's possible? If you don't want to, I'll understand. Any time you want to leave, I'll give you some money and buy you a bus ticket to wherever you want to go. You can take two outfits from the apartment. Your choice, Red."

The two women cleared the table. Maggie gave Audrey two cookies on a plate and watched her climb the stairs to the garage apartment. She did the dishes, all the time thinking through Audrey's situation. Maggie didn't know if she'd hit rock bottom yet. Usually, that knocked sense into a young person. Right now, it was fifty-fifty that she'd stay. That was the way it worked. Maggie knew she'd done all she could do. She saw the apartment lights go out and the glow of the TV come on.

§

At 2:00 a.m., the first warning light came on in Maggie's bedroom. She threw off the covers and reached into the nightstand for the collapsible baton, flicking her wrist to expand it as she got out of bed. She went to the closet, reached under the shoe shelf, and swung the hidden door open. The camera display showed the intruders opening the garage door to the apartment as the second warning light came on. The two men climbed the stairs of the garage apartment. Maggie placed the baton on the desk and took the Glock 26 and suppressor from a shelf. She stepped out of the room, closed the door, and put on her bathrobe, slipping the Glock securely into the tightened robe sash. On the way out of the bedroom, she picked up her cell phone.

Slim and Arnie stood outside the garage apartment door. The only noise they heard was the TV. Arnie tried to turn the door handle. It wouldn't turn. He looked at Slim, who reached into his pocket and extracted two pieces of metal, inserted them in the lock, moved them around, and finally turned the handle. They crashed through the door. Audrey was sitting up in bed. Slim stifled her scream, putting his hand over her mouth and pushing her head into the pillows. He looked at her youthful body, undressed except for a T-shirt. "Shoot her with only half. We're going to have fun before giving her the rest."

Audrey's eyes were wide with fear as she struggled to free herself. Slim pinned her arms over her head with one hand, the other over her mouth, and had his knee between her breasts. Arnie opened a padded pouch with the two syringes. He leaned on her arm to hold it still, moving the needle close to stab the vein.

"Come on, give it to her," Slim demanded.

At that moment, the apartment burst into light. The TV sound muffled the suppressed Glock spit. Arnie cried out, dropped the needle, and grabbed his arm.

Slim's hand slipped from Audrey's mouth and she pleaded, "I can't breathe! I can't breathe!"

Slim saw Maggie standing there, holding the gun. He smiled.

"Get off of her," Maggie said calmly.

Slim didn't move. The Glock spit again, and Slim's right ear vaporized. "You shot me! You fucking bitch, you shot me!" he exclaimed as he rolled onto the floor, holding the side of his head.

Audrey scrambled out of the bed and over to Maggie. Arnie helped Slim up.

"Just the ear," Maggie said. "You're the two guys from the library. Red, reach into my robe pocket and get my phone. Take their pictures. You two, throw your wallets on the bed."

Slim and Arnie did so.

"Red, take their driver's licenses from the wallets."

With shaking hands, Audrey found the licenses.

"All right, the two of you pick up your wallets and lead the way to your car," Maggie said. At the car, she continued. "If I ever see either of you again, you will regret it. I don't know who you work for, and I don't want to know, but I now have your pictures and your driver's licenses if I ever need to find you. Get out of here." She stepped back as they got in the car.

Back up in the garage apartment, Maggie looked around. Very little blood. The soft-tipped bullets had fragmented and lodged in the back wall. She went over to the sink, looked underneath, and pulled out a bucket. She ran warm water into it along with a squirt of Dawn. Audrey was sitting on the bed, her knees pulled up to her chest, just staring. "Red, we need to get to work. Take this soapy water and sponge and start wiping anywhere there's blood." Maggie pulled the bloody sheets off the bed. "We'll get these in the washing machine now." She took two paper towels and carefully slipped them under the syringe, then wrapped it.

Red looked at Maggie. "They'll be back. You don't know them. That guy, the one who was kneeling on me, his name is Slim. He's the owner or manager or something at the club. I've seen him beat up girls because they weren't aggressive enough with getting money from customers. He's a sadist. The girls said the only thing he likes better than rough sex is beating a girl. They'd all leave except for the free opies and lack of money."

"Who's the other guy?"

"He called him Arnie. I've seen him around the club. I guess he's a bouncer or something. They'll be back. I know it. They said I'd never be able to leave."

"Audrey, look at me." Maggie put her hands on Red's shoulders and said, "They won't be back, I guarantee it. Look at that syringe. I'll bet it has enough of something to kill you. They were going to give you part, rape you, and give you the other part to shut you up permanently. I'll bet they had one for me too. Is that the life you want? Wouldn't you prefer a life where you're in charge? A life where men bend their will to you, not force you to do their bidding? You control whatever relationship you want to have with a man or men. You're financially independent of anyone, man or woman. When you were born, God gave you two gifts: a body and a brain. Your body developed naturally. You must develop your brain. Your body will lose its youthful splendor one day, but your mind will stay sharp until very old age or death. No matter what happened tonight, the choice is still yours. You must invent your own future. I can guide you. Now, I want you to spend the rest of the night in my house. I'll have this place put back together tomorrow. Let's finish wiping up the blood and go next door."

# CHAPTER 42

Cal listened intently to the testimony from both sides of a civil suit dealing with rights to place a commercial building partially on residentially zoned property. The only unusual aspect of this case was the large group of spectators. Cal knew this was a zoning issue; however, it wasn't a society-changing matter, so he didn't understand the large interest from the legal community. Maybe the rumors about the judicial inquiry that had been swirling all week were true. Friday afternoon court was almost over, and a nice weekend hiking and maybe seeing Maggie lay ahead of him. He sensed their relationship had changed since Joey's death and with Suzie being pregnant. Maggie wouldn't say anything, but Cal knew she was defensive about his opinion of Suzie. He blamed Suzie for Joey's death and couldn't let go of his feeling that Joey would be alive today if she hadn't gone to—

The double doors at the back of the courtroom burst open.

Cal sat up and reached for his gavel. Two individuals dressed in dark suits, white shirts, and striped ties were moving toward the dais. Behind them were several others, three of whom carried television cameras and two carried lights. Cal understood what was happening. The grapevine was right again. They had made their move.

"Judge Ernst White-Callaway, I'm Mark Wilson, representing the governor-appointed judicial criminal investigation panel. We suspend you from the bench pending resolution to the matter of Joseph Hinson Paschal's death while under court supervision."

Cal took a deep breath and said, "Will the opposing counselors approach the bench?" When the attorneys stood before Cal, he continued. "Counselors, you will have a new judge appointed on Monday. He or she will work with you to continue arguments."

With that said, Cal stood and left the courtroom. He climbed the stairs two at a time and opened the door to his chambers. Betsy was sitting at her desk, crying, watching a locksmith change the locks on his office door. Cal smiled and, leaning over her desk so as not to be heard, said, "Be calm. Everything will be all right. Protect yourself. If anyone tries to pressure you in any way to quit or do something you feel is unethical, you let me know. Don't worry about anything else. This will all work out."

"Jacket pocket," she said between sobs. She started crying even more as she handed Cal an envelope marked PERSONAL. Cal looked at the return address. It was from White, White, Arnholt, and Emerson. Is it court business or not? he wondered. It's marked personal, so I'll take it with me. By now, Mark Wilson and his associate had entered Betsy's office, followed closely by the horde of reporters and cameramen.

Cal looked at Wilson and said, "My jacket and briefcase are in there." He pointed to his office.

"You may get your jacket; however, I'll have to examine what's in the briefcase."

Cal smiled. "Certainly, Mr. Wilson. Check everything. Anything you feel should remain in the office, please remove, and Betsy will refile it."

The two went into the office. Cal took his briefcase from under the desk and opened it for Wilson to inspect, then moved to the closet to exchange his robe for his jacket. He felt an envelope in the breast pocket. Betsy must have felt the contents were important to keep confidential. He returned to the desk, looked at Wilson, and said, "I understand you're just doing what you're told. You stated in court there's a judicial criminal investigation into Joey's death. You didn't call it a judicial inquiry. Was that just a misuse of words, or is this a judicial criminal investigation?"

"I don't misuse words. Now, I'll ask you to leave these chambers. If you wish to remove anything further from the premises, you'll have to petition the judicial investigation offices."

Cal smiled, turned, and walked out. As he passed Betsy, he nodded. They had enjoined the battle for his career and future. He thought of Joey and took courage from how he had overcome so many obstacles. The unnecessary spectacle indicated the forces aligned against him were confident in what they had. Anger management was critical.

He rode the elevator to his SUV. Anger, relief, curiosity, and determination swirled in his mind. He couldn't think through a whole thought without another one interrupting. He looked down at the envelope in his hand. At his Tahoe, he put the briefcase on the front seat, opened it, and extracted his go phone from the pocket. Then he opened the envelope from WWA&E. He stared at two documents: The first was a petition for divorce from Catherine. The second was a restraining order demanding he not call her or come by Willview at any time, for any reason.

Cal shut his eyes and put his head back on the headrest. When it rained, it poured. At least the charade was over. He was sure the media had this divorce petition and the restraining order since the restraining order would put more doubt in people's minds about his character. Why a restraining order? There was no physical abuse in their marriage. He never got nasty when he drank. He'd never stolen from Willview. She would be cast as a victim, a role she loved. Catherine's gossip socialites would have a field day. The restraining order was proof of how lethal this assault on him and his future was.

He flipped the pages of the divorce decree, looking for the reasons. Irreconcilable differences. It did not mention Maggie. He put the papers in the briefcase, started the engine, and headed away from the courthouse. At the stop sign a half-block away, the jumbled emotions crystallized into relief and clarity as Cal realized he was freed from some of the shackles of guilt he'd lived with for years. He no longer accepted guilt for not being the husband Catherine wanted. He reached for his go phone and hit the speed dial.

"Good afternoon. You're finished early," Maggie said.

"You may want to watch the six o'clock news."

"Which channel?"

"It doesn't matter. They were all there."

"What are you talking about?"

"The judicial criminal investigation staff barged into my courtroom this afternoon, followed by TV cameras, guys with lights, and reporters. It was a real circus. They have suspended me pending their investigation. Notice I didn't say 'inquiry.' An inquiry is easy to settle. An investigation takes months and can lead to not only removal from the bench but also disbarment. It's not much consolation, but I was right: This is more than finding out about Joey's death. A full-blown effort is being made to destroy my reputation and chance of reappointment in January."

"Oh, Cal, I'm so sorry. How can the governor do this? Didn't he read the file you sent?"

"I don't think the governor intended to read it. Someone over here wants me off the bench. With this being a criminal investigation, it's possible it could also disbar me. The investigation can drag on past the election. That's not all the news I have for you."

"What else could possibly go wrong?"

"Well, wrong or right depends on the perspective. Catherine filed for divorce today. Not only that, but she took out a restraining order to keep me from contacting her or showing up at Willview."

"Are you serious? A restraining order? For God's sake."

"The timing is interesting. The restraining order was obviously to inflict the most public humiliation possible."

"What are you going to do?"

"There's only one downside to all of this. Maggie, we can't have any contact while this is going on. It's obvious whoever is behind this effort is playing with no holds barred. I can't allow you or the BBC to be collateral damage. I mentioned the leases I signed. If you need me, I'll be at one of the two places."

"Cal, you shouldn't have to go through this alone."

"I won't be alone. I know you'll be there when it's over."

"At least come by the library every so often so I can see you're taking care of yourself."

Changing the subject, Cal said, "By the way, how's your new tenant?"

"Struggling. It's difficult in the beginning when a girl's self-esteem is zero, and she believes she's as worthless as her tormentors said she was. In this case, it's doubly compounded because she realizes she's the one who made the poor decisions. Evidently, no one physically abused her, just told her she was worthless. Her family was indifferent and unloving, urging her to leave ever since she was sixteen. She had an encounter with drug and sex peddlers out on Highway

20. The best and most important factor is she consciously rejected that environment, so that was the first step in the right direction. Because of her circumstances, there's not an agency who can or will help her. She's smart, tough, and willing to talk and listen, though. I have faith I can help her. What she needs to do now is get angry, not at those who didn't give her love and parental care, but at those who took advantage of her, and at herself, because she's the one who's responsible for her actions. She needs to stop being a victim and take control. It'll happen. I'm confident."

"Know I'm thinking of you, even though I'm not around."

"You too." Maggie hung up.

She leaned against the book trolley. Maggie realized the divorce would complicate her relationship with Cal. Marriage would come up, she was sure of it. Their relationship had changed since Joey's death; even as they had both tried to reach out to the other, they were drifting apart. Maggie rested her head on the shelf where she was re-stacking books. She knew she had changed. Suzie and Red needed her, and their needs brought back painful memories. Those two came before Cal. She went back to shelving books.

§

Cal continued driving to his new place. At the intersection of Highways 20 and 7, he stopped for the red light. His fingers drummed the steering wheel. His analytical side caused him to pause. Other aggressive steps may follow a move like this. Someone may be following him right now. He didn't want to lead someone to his new home, where he had sensitive files. Cal turned left and then took the next left, headed to Vermont. After crossing the state line, he drove through the first town he came to and headed to the second, twenty-five miles up the road.

Approaching Woodsbury, he saw a strip shopping center with a Walmart. He pulled into the parking lot and began making a mental list. Leaving Walmart, he emptied his briefcase of papers and filled it with the items he had bought. He searched "Woodsbury" and "B&B" on his phone and found the number for the only bed and breakfast in town, where he reserved a room. He walked over to the liquor store next to the center to buy a pint of Wild Turkey Rare Breed.

He was out of his comfort zone but looked on his new adventure with trepidation and elation. He fully understood the collapse of his life as he knew it. Rather than being distraught, it relaxed him. The memory of what Joey had gone through and the courage he had shown gave Cal courage. His faith in his own courage drew from that fount. Before driving to the B&B, he pulled out his regular cell phone and extracted the SIM, then wrapped it carefully in a tissue and placed it in his briefcase. Now, except for Maggie, no one could trace him.

Fifteen minutes later, Cal was in the parlor of the Woodsbury B&B, sipping wine with four couples. One was from Virginia, one from New Jersey, one from New Hampshire, and one from Ontario, Canada. Interesting people leading interesting lives traveling. Cal realized that without his present circumstances, he could not and would not be there. He made a mental note to add time for short travel adventures in his new life. Reality set in. He was forty-two, about to be unemployed, and broke except for his judicial retirement. His salary would continue while suspended, so he could survive. His past life had benefited from his wife's, soon to be ex-wife's, fortune. He felt shame. How had he allowed himself to get into this predicament? Should she pay him alimony? The self-loathing that had become a part of him after Joey's death reared its ugly head. He couldn't believe he was even thinking about alimony. The man from

Virginia was asking him a question. "I'm sorry, I was lost in thought. What did you ask?"

"I asked if you were here on vacation."

"No, no. I'm a judge. I've got a complex case going on. I just came across the mountains to get away and have quiet time to think. It's lovely here, isn't it? What part of Virginia are you from?"

§

Monday morning Cal sat in a back booth of the Berkshire Luncheonette, an old-fashioned diner, like a time warp back to the fifties in the middle of town. It had been built in 1953, shortly after the father and grandfather of the current father and daughter co-owners had returned from Korea. Nothing had changed except for the red leather seat coverings, and those only when the customers complained enough about the duct tape or cracked leather. The individual juke boxes at each booth still worked, playing hits from the fifties, sixties, and seventies for the younger crowd who came in for milkshakes and what they called "cool" songs.

Cal's primary concern this beautiful March day was avoiding a subpoena. He returned from Vermont Sunday evening. The only time he put his SIM card in his phone was when he took a circular route, driving around parts of Berkshire County he usually avoided. He called David Fogel and asked him to meet for coffee at the diner.

The envelope Betsy put in his jacket Friday contained the results of tracking phone numbers. David Fogel had given him the MSP captain's direct number. Cal had sent the number, along with six others, to the phone company under a confidential judicial request. He looked at the resulting list over the weekend. He felt he'd seen two of them, but he'd looked at so many, his brain could have been playing tricks on him. Sitting on the table in front of Cal was the weekend *Berkshire Times*. His picture and story were above the fold, prime news. In contrast to the television, the reporting was factual and professional rather than sensational and inflammatory. He appreciated that.

It was David's day off, but he seemed anxious to meet. Cal looked up and saw a physically fit man wearing sunglasses, a Boston Red Sox cap, a Hawaiian shirt with the tail out, jeans, and work boots coming through the door.

"Sorry I'm late. I wanted to make sure 'they' didn't follow you," David said as he took off his sunglasses and slipped into the booth.

"Did they?"

"No, at least not right now. They may have a tracking device on your car. I'll check it for you if you want me to."

"Please. My car is in the lot on Janson Street, behind the brick office building. It's the white Z71. It's unlocked."

"I know. Cal, I don't know what's going on. I've been around long enough to know what's happening is a character assassination rather than a judicial inquiry. For what it's worth, I'd park my car at the courthouse, in your regular spot, and rent a car. As a matter of fact, I'd change rental agency and car once a week until this is over."

"Are you serious?"

"You bet I am. The word on the street is you've been thrown out of your house, and your wife has filed for divorce. Did you see that coming?"

"Yes and no."

"Which?"

"We've had a difficult marriage. Catherine expected me to run her family's law firm. But no, I didn't think she would use the inquiry as an excuse for divorce."

"Do you think she had anything to do with this witch hunt?"

"Frankly, I'm not sure. I do know someone told her about the inquiry long before it happened. That's why I wanted to meet." Cal took an envelope out of his jacket and slid it across the table. "The number search you wanted on your friend is in here. In addition, my soon to be ex-wife's cell and home numbers are in there. Can you run a search going back to December 1 on both her numbers?"

"Sure." Fogel took the envelope, folded it in half, and put it in his shirt pocket.

"I didn't recognize any of your friend's calls, although I think there are two numbers I've seen before on the spreadsheet we both have. Betsy gave me the list Friday as I was leaving, so I haven't had time to check."

"I'll check. How can I get in touch with you?"

"For the next couple of weeks, call my cell and leave a message. I don't keep my SIM card in when I'm at the office I've rented or the cabin I'm staying in. While driving in outlying areas of the county, I insert the SIM and retrieve messages. Receiving a subpoena for records I may have in my possession is my concern. I want to lie low until I see if there's going to be further aggressive tactics. On a more pleasant subject, when are you going to announce for sheriff? Is Justin going to endorse you?"

"The announcement is this Friday, and Justin is going to be with me and announce that I'm his choice, and he'll be actively campaigning for me. But, to tell you the truth, Cal, I'm not sure Justin will be around in November. He's fading fast."

"Give him my regards. I'd like to be there to show my support, but right now, that wouldn't be politically smart for you. It appears my judgeship days are over."

"Don't say that. This community needs people like you."

"Yeah, well, half my life is over. Perhaps this situation is a higher power directing me to do something else."

"We'll see. Don't forget to park your SUV and rent cars. Wait ten minutes so I can get in position, then take your car to the courthouse. If they follow you, I'll show up, and that will be your signal. If you don't see me, they didn't follow you."

"Thanks for your friendship, David."

"No problem." Fogel put on his sunglasses, pulled his cap lower, and slid out of the booth.

§

Back at his office, David compared the list of numbers to the spreadsheet from the pedophile's phone. There was one match, a Boston number. It was the number that had steady contact the first two weeks the perp was in Berkshire County. The same number appeared twice on the captain's phone. One call was over twenty minutes and the other twelve, clearly not misdials. David tried a reverse search. Nothing. Either the owner had requested an unlisted number, or it was a cell. He could call it, but what if someone picked up? Even saying nothing would alert the other party.

David tapped his pencil on the desk. After a minute, he picked up the phone and dialed. "Betsy, David Fogel. You doing all right?"

"Trying."

"Have the inquiry staff sealed Cal's office?"

"No, they changed the locks, but I have a key. A temporary judge is due in tomorrow."

"Good. Did they take his computer?"

"No."

"Did you say you wanted to take a twenty-minute break?"

"Yes. There's an envelope on my desk for you. Just came in."

"Super, I'll be right up."

David pulled a pair of latex gloves from his desk, then walked up the stairs to Cal's office, where he retrieved the envelope and saw a key and card with username and password. Once in, he used the online subpoena tab to request, in Cal's name, six months of past records of the Boston number and Catherine's two numbers. He backdated the request to last Friday morning. He hit send, returned the envelope to Betsy's desk, and walked back to his office.

After thirty minutes, he called Betsy. "Betsy, in the next few weeks, telephone records will arrive for Cal by email. Will you forward them to me when they arrive?"

"Yes. Then I'll delete them."

"Yes, good idea."

"Tell the judge he's missed."

"Yes, we all miss him, and it's been only one day."

David sat back, put his hands behind his head, and thought about the puzzles he and his team had worked on in Afghanistan, trying to separate the Taliban spies from the good guys. The satisfaction of solving the puzzles had been immense. David felt the same excitement with this latest puzzle.

# CHAPTER 43


Giuseppe "The Hammer" Strollo sat in his favorite stuffed chair in Antonio's bar. Across the small table sat Big Vinney. Sitting next to The Hammer was Aloysius "Ivy League" Carroll. On the table were three cups of coffee and an anti-surveillance device showing a green light.

"Vincenzo, thank you for taking the time to meet with me and sort out these issues," The Hammer said.

"No problem, Giuseppe. They're just misunderstandings."

"I'm sure they are. Let's start with two of your associates being shot. By a woman, no less. What's that all about?"

"Giuseppe, those two imbeciles went against my specific instructions to drop the issue. My club manager and his bouncer wanted to tie up a loose end, one of his girls who ran off. The woman she was living with, a librarian, interrupted them in the act and shot them. I found out the next day when they went to our doctor friend in the Berkshires. I confronted them, and they told me the story. Both are in no position to cause any more trouble—ever."

The Hammer kept his eyes on Big Vinney and said, "Aloysius, call our friends and see if a police report was filed. We can't have a mess like this traced back to the club." He then said, "Vincenzo, what kind of people do you associate with? Don't any of them understand the big picture? Can't you control your people? This isn't the movies; this is serious business. Our job is to extract dollars from the undisciplined and move the money into legitimate businesses. Are you sure these two idiots won't upset our businesses?"

"I swear, Giuseppe, they won't make a mistake like this again."

"That's what I thought. Now, tell me about your brother. Why did you try to contact him?"

"Giuseppe, you told me not to. I swear I didn't try to contact him."

"No, you used one of our most valuable assets to do it for you."

"You didn't say I couldn't use someone else to contact him and see if he was all right. I figured if a cop went over there, no one would be the wiser."

"You didn't think or see the big picture. It has taken us eight years to move this guy into a place where he can be of help. We expect him to be high in his organization in the future. You risked all of that to find out about your pervert brother? You don't understand the big picture, Vincenzo. We go back a long way, to the streets. I could always count on you to have my back. How did you convince him to take this stupid action?"

"I just did."

"How, Vincenzo? How?"

Big Vinney looked down at his hands. He looked at Ivy League, who stared back at him. "I told him you wanted it done."

"You told him I wanted it done. Now I understand why he took the risk. All right, Vincenzo. I have two understandings. First, the two imbeciles, as you call them, won't ever bring shame or a spotlight on our business again. Is that right?"

"Yes, Giuseppe."

"Second, you will never again use my name to get someone to do your dirty work for you. Is that correct?"

"Yes, Giuseppe."

"Go on, then. Keep out of the limelight. Forget about your brother."

"I will. I promise."

"I know you will, Vincenzo."

After Big Vinney left, The Hammer drank his coffee and turned to Ivy League. "I don't know why that librarian didn't call the cops and have those two morons arrested, and I don't care. Our guardian angel intervened. Otherwise, our whole operation in the Berkshires would be at risk. I also don't believe Vincenzo has snuffed out those two. He's too evasive. Call our sources about that police report. If they didn't file one, drop it. Then call Mad Dog and tell him I want to see him after nine tonight. He can meet me at my house. Tell him to come alone, no driver or associate."

"Do you want me there?"

"No. Just Mad Dog."

"Yes, sir."

# CHAPTER 44

Cal enjoyed having a window in his new office. His rented desk was situated so he could see outside. No subpoenas had arrived since his suspension. He gradually returned to a normal routine, allowing people to know where his temporary office was. This day in late March was what he called a Chamber of Commerce day: a chilly breeze, fast-moving cotton-ball clouds, and bright sunshine. It flattered Cal as every day brought at least one person looking for legal advice. He gave referrals to practicing attorneys, explaining he couldn't practice law until the resolution of his status as a judge. The unexpected potential legal activity reassured his flagging confidence in his future. As long as they didn't disbar him, his ability to earn a living buoyed his spirits. While he was visible to the public at the office, he still guarded where he lived and kept his most sensitive files.

No one knew where he lived, not even Maggie. Maggie . . . God, he realized it had been four weeks since he'd spoken to her. I've got to go by the library and see her, he decided, or at least call her. As this thought crossed his mind, there was a knock at the office door.

"Come in. It's open," Cal said.

A man in his mid-fifties, dressed in a pinstriped suit, white shirt with French cuffs, regimental striped tie, and gleaming black dress shoes entered with two young associates, both in navy-blue blazers, light-blue shirts, red ties, khaki pants, and loafers. The gentleman crossed over to Cal's desk with his right hand extended. "Judge, I'm Josh Trimble, and I'm running for governor."

"Have we met before, Mr. Trimble?" Cal asked, rising and extending his hand.

"No, sir. I'm from the Boston area—Newton, to be precise. I'm not a lawyer, just an entrepreneur. Your reputation led me to read some of your rulings and comments on the law. Excuse me a moment, Your Honor." He turned to his associates and said, "Why don't the two of you go outside and gather up a crowd and local media for a press conference? Tell everyone I'll be speaking in fifteen minutes, say, at eleven thirty. Okay? Go to it."

The staffers left.

Trimble followed them to make sure the door was closed. He returned to Cal, who pointed out a chair across the desk. "Now, where was I? Oh, yeah, the pundits say I don't have a snowball's chance in hell. We'll see. I know where the sitting governor is vulnerable, and I need your help in Berkshire County. You're well respected and looked up to, even with this character assassination going on. You'll receive an email to your official address this afternoon. Do you still have access to it?"

"Yes, if the email is addressed to me and doesn't pertain to court business. My secretary forwards them to me."

"In that email will be my official positions on the issues I feel are important to the people of Massachusetts. I don't expect you to agree with all of them. You're welcome to show me the error of my thinking on any issue. I welcome multiple viewpoints. I ask only for you to read them carefully. If you feel you can support me, I'd be pleased to have your support, either privately or publicly. The word in Boston is you've pissed off someone with a lot of money. This person is footing a six-figure bill to discredit you in the eyes of the governor and the public. Do you know an attorney by the name of Emerson? He's aggressively campaigning against the sitting councillor in the Eighth District in favor of a candidate who will lobby for his protégé, a young lawyer by the name of Clements, to be appointed to your judgeship."

"Ace Clements," Cal says. "That makes sense. Now I'm beginning to understand. I might also know who the money source is."

"Good for you, Judge. If you feel you can support and vote for me, I'd appreciate it." Trimble rose from his seat.

"You won't ask for a contribution?"

"Success has blessed me, Your Honor. I'm self-funding my campaign. Rightly or wrongly, I don't believe in just throwing money at a campaign. I've set a goal of meeting and asking for support from at least thirty percent of the voters in this state. If that's not good enough, so be it. I believe in the people. Please read my thoughts on governing. Support me if you can." Trimble held out his hand and Cal rose to shake it.

"I'll read the email. I promise you that."

Trimble looked at his watch. "Time to go." He turned and walked out of Cal's office.

Cal went over to the window and saw a group of about thirty, with one TV camera crew. He couldn't hear what Trimble was saying.

Later that evening, while having dinner at the diner, he heard: "I've just met with one of the most honest and respected men in Massachusetts, Judge Ernst White-Callaway, and I hope to get his support."

This guy has balls, Cal thought.

§

After five, Cal crossed over to Vermont. He put the SIM card in his regular phone and retrieved his texts and voice messages. He removed the card and put the other SIM in his go phone. Maggie's number rang twice.

"Are you all right?" Maggie asked.

"Yes. I'm keeping my SIM cards out of my phones except for early in the morning and evening, while driving, just in case someone is still snooping. I'll probably go back to using my regular cell at the office."

"That guy running for governor didn't have any trouble finding you. That was some announcement he made to the media. Talk about an obvious choice between two candidates."

"My office is no longer a secret; it's in the redbrick building on Janson Street. He also gave me information as to what's going on. I told you about what happened before and during the Mount Greylock Winter Benefit. Trimble confirmed everything I suspected, maybe even Catherine's potential role in this situation. He said I pissed off someone with a lot of money and clout in Boston. I'm not sure it's her, but I can't find a case when I ruled against someone with a lot of money who might hold a grudge."

"Cal, that's so hard to believe. She's hurting her own social standing. Why would she do that? It makes no sense."

"I don't know. Catherine is used to getting her own way. I disappointed her when I gave up her father's law firm. Catherine never felt elevated by my judgeship. If anything, she felt I settled below her station in life."

"How sad. Are you taking care of yourself? Why don't I fix you a late dinner?"

"That's not a good idea. I don't want any of the mudslinging to hit you. With this divorce thing, I don't want Catherine or anyone else making up stories, even if they are true. No one aside from Suzie knows how close we are. It needs to stay that way for a while. How are things going with you?"

Maggie hesitated, wanting to choose her words carefully, not lying but also not telling the whole truth. "Fine, mostly."

"That's vague enough to cause me some concern."

"No, no concerns. The young girl I mentioned, the one staying with me, has finally decided her future. We've talked through the issues. A couple of weeks ago, she saw the downside of the life she'd experienced lately. I'm hoping she made the right decision. I'll know in the next few weeks. She has made so many bad decisions, she's hesitant and could change her mind. It takes time to build her confidence back."

"What has tipped her into rethinking her future?"

"Bad men who abuse women for a profit."

"What happened?"

"Oh, nothing much. Just an eye opener for her."

"Well, I hope it turns out the way you want."

"I do too. It's her decision. I've done all I can."

"I miss you. How are things with the book club?"

"The book club misses you. We have a meeting tonight. Not much on the agenda. Should be a short meeting. I miss you, Cal. Be strong. I'm here if you want to talk. I haven't asked—where are you staying?"

"I have a cabin in the woods. Homey. When I can, I'll build us a fire. We can roast marshmallows and make love on the bearskin rug."

"Bearskin rug? How about an air mattress? I look forward to it."

"Good night."

"Good night."

§

The BBC met in the second-floor conference room at the library. The chair immediately to the right of the speaker's chair sat empty. Rosa Lee fidgeted in the speaker's chair. When everybody took their seats, she said, "I'm real nervous, so cut me some slack. Sitting over there"—she pointed to the seat she customarily sat in— "I didn't realize this was like the electric chair."

Everybody laughed.

She continued. "Our community has a problem. One of our finest is under attack. By whom, we don't know. They say he wasn't caring or responsible in handling that Paschal boy. As my mama would've said, that's a bald-faced lie. If you remember, when that boy surfaced last summer, Cal said he'd bring him around to meet us. I remember the first time, I would've sworn they were father and son—not because they looked alike, which they did to some extent, but because of the love Cal showed for him. He was gentle but firm, guiding him to good manners, showing him how to respect people through example, laughing with him, smiling proudly, like a daddy.

"Cal ate regularly at my kitchen, and he brought the Paschal boy several times, particularly on the weekends. I know we're not a political organization, and usually I don't care who's governor. Don't get me wrong; I vote every election. That's my responsibility—not a privilege, a responsibility. I take it seriously, just like going to church. This time, however, I'm going to actively work for and vote for that Trimble guy. I don't know who's pulling the strings on the current governor, but if they're against Cal, I'm against them. I don't know much, but I do know right from wrong. That's all I got to say. Now, will someone please switch seats with me?"

"I will, Rosa Lee," Jack Gianelli said, getting up from his chair. He hugged Rosa Lee as they passed each other. After taking his seat, he said, "Rosa Lee has said all that needs to be said about Cal's situation. No one could say it better. I just want to report: The young man we discussed earlier this year in the domestic situation is working. He's seeing a counselor and is improving. The four of us who spoke to him rotate keeping in touch, letting him know we care about him. Geri tells me the young lady is getting help with her issues. Isn't that right, Geri?"

"Yeah, Jack."

"Two attorneys, working pro bono, are putting together a child support and visitation program. That's all I want to report. Anyone else?"

No one responded. The meeting ended.

# CHAPTER 45

"**I** want to thank the West Massachusetts Foundation Board for your confidence in me," Catherine said. "It will be my privilege to chair the fiftieth-anniversary West Massachusetts Charity Ball. I promise you it will be a night to remember." She smiled, looking around the board table and pausing to make eye contact with each member. "We have seven months, during which my committee will be busy beavers. On behalf of the auxiliary, please know we will make you proud—and call on you for your help."

The board clapped as Catherine took her seat.

John Emerson said, "Having no further business, this meeting is adjourned." He walked over to Catherine and kissed her on the cheek. "Madam Chairwoman, will you do me the honor of having lunch in the partners' dining room?"

"John, darling, that would be lovely."

They left the paneled boardroom. In the hall, Catherine stopped to look at the oil portraits of her father and grandfather. She then studied John Emerson's portrait. "Three powerful leaders. That's why this law firm will resume its place in the state's power structure."

"With your help, my dear, with your help." Emerson took her by the elbow and opened the door to the partners' dining room.

They went to a table for two in front of the window overlooking the mountains. A server in a white jacket, white shirt, black bowtie, and black pants held the chair out for Catherine. The oriental rugs spread around the room complemented the polished pine flooring, paneled walls displaying individually lit oil paintings, white tablecloths, sterling silverware, and crystal stemware. Catherine took the most pride in the fine china emblazoned with the law firm's WWA&E logo. There would always be two Whites at the head of the firm, and a third White would ensure the firm's prominence grew.

"I set the menu; however, the card in front of you lists the courses in case there's an allergy issue," Emerson explained. "Pairings will be from the firm's private cellar. We source our wines from the northeast. The vineyards are owned by our clients."

"Really? How impressive. Tell me, John, any progress on merging the two North Adams businesses I referred to the firm?"

"Yes, we have structured a tax-free exchange of stock. Both parties are happy, and our fee is handsome."

"I'm delighted our arrangement is working."

"I knew it would, my dear. Here's to a brilliant future for us and the firm." He held up his wineglass. They winked at each other while toasting.

The server served the first course, a tomato basil soup drizzled with extra-virgin olive oil. He poured a light Chablis. His station was immediately behind John. His only responsibility was to the table of the managing partner and his guest. Standing stone-faced, he observed carefully as the couple finished one course after another. He heard everything and retained what he heard. He was a student at BC, on the Hand Up Program. His mother had raised him and his four siblings as a single mom operating a restaurant in a working-class neighborhood. She'd taught him everything he knew about professionally serving customers. His training helped him become the star server in the partners' dining room, always available to the managing partner and his guests.

"Catherine, remember when I told you it may take more than the original hundred thousand to guarantee Cal would lose his position?"

"Yes, John. How much more?"

"The original amount moved through our associated law firm in Boston to the governor's reelection committee. I can safely say you should enjoy what your money has bought so far. Cal's character is now highly questionable, and by November he will be a pariah. Cal's disbarment probabilities have risen. The governor appointed a friend of ours to run the criminal investigation."

"Really, criminal investigation? Disbarred? That's more than I ever hoped for. How did you arrange that possibility?"

"We were able to insert some damaging speculative information in the file once it got to the governor's office. There are three issues, any of which could be used as an excuse for removal from the bench and disbarment."

"Wonderful. When will my divorce be final? It would be awesome if the divorce were finalized around the time they disbar him. You're right; I'm getting my money's worth. How much more do you need?"

"It will take another one hundred thousand to make sure we replace the incumbent district councillor with our friend, and in January, another one hundred thousand when the judicial panel finds Cal guilty of criminal negligence. Call it icing on the cake, my dear."

"After we finish this delicious lunch, we'll go back to your office and I'll give you another check—made out to cash, of course. You're making sure my name is not associated with this . . . this . . . what do the spy novels call it? Oh, yes, a covert operation. How exciting." Catherine held up her main-course wineglass, tilted it to John, and drank the wine in one gulp.

The server was standing at his station, looking directly into the dining room; however, his attention was riveted on the conversation at the table.

The partners who had known Catherine's father paraded over to the managing partner's table to pay their respects. The younger partners, after finding out who Catherine was, made the same pilgrimage, more to impress the senior managing partner than to speak to the beautiful woman with him. Catherine's father's memory flooded her mind and, as usual, ended with her hatred of Cal. When her father had died suddenly, Cal had refused to leave the judgeship and return to the law firm. Some imbecile had taken over, and the firm had slowly died until John appeared on the scene. She looked across the table at John and smiled.

You don't know it yet, John, but we're going to be married, she mused. Together, we'll make western Massachusetts mine. You realize your fantasy every time the little girl clothes come out of the closet. My fantasy is the price John will pay. She continued to smile, basking in her thoughts of power and riches. When they got back to his office, she'd give him a check and the little-girl sex he craved. She knew the frilly little-girl panties she had on would do the trick.

A quickie in the managing partner's office. How exciting. She felt the heat rising in her groin.

# CHAPTER 46

Cal sat at his desk with a yellow pad in front of him. Looking at it, he saw his two-line handiwork of the last thirty minutes: (1) Judicial investigation? (2) Money? Tension and stress had become his closest associates. He turned on his computer and went to his official judgeship site. After eight weeks, he was amazed no one had changed the username and password. He logged in and looked at the incoming messages. Among the non-court emails was an encrypted one from the phone company security office. Cal rifled through his desk, looking for his notebook of passwords. He entered the correct one and saw a six-month printout of phone calls pertaining to a small group of numbers.

What was this for? Why had these been sent to him? He closed the file and went to his sent box. Scrolling backward, he searched for when he may have requested these numbers, and saw a request from the fateful morning before the judicial investigation staff had appeared in the afternoon. He read the email sent that day. That wasn't his wording. It was dated at 10:00 a.m., when he'd been in the middle of a court—

Cal stopped. David. He was going to run a search on Catherine's two numbers. Perhaps he did that and more. He wouldn't have had to go through the official judicial subpoena channel unless he had a highly confidential number to trace.

Cal picked up the phone and dialed David. Not getting an answer, he left a brief message of his name and the words *Call me*.

His life's fragility came back to the forefront. Not knowing what was going on was the worst part. No word from Boston in almost two months. That was a sign his adversaries were organizing a surefire assassination. He sensed the game plan was to drip on his reputation until late summer or the fall; then they'd hit the media with the full investigation, giving the governor plenty of reason to remove him from the bench, not just fail to reappoint. They could disbar him. He would then have an uphill battle. Cal felt a queasiness at the thought the governor may move to disbar him. He was ambivalent about being a judge, but not about his reputation and ability to practice law. He loved being a judge, yes, but he'd have a difficult financial life if he continued. As it was, he was short on money and would need to tap into his judicial retirement account to make ends meet if he lost his salary. Disbarment would mean bankruptcy in a relatively short period of time.

What Cal loved about being a judge was taking the time to distinguish the bad people from the ones who were good but had made a poor decision and must pay the consequences. In his mind, paying society for the mistake while still leaving a future for the defendant was the purpose of a proper judge. In civil matters, determining who was right in a dispute was satisfying. Were these feelings of service and accomplishment worth giving up financial security?

Joey entered his mind. Cal wondered if he could have given Joey a legacy of security if he had lived. Suzie and his future grandchild popped into his stressed thoughts. He wondered if he had any obligation to them. He immediately shook his head. Of course he did. His thoughts turned to Maggie. When they married, would he have the right to ask her to 'get by' on a judge's salary? He stared out the window as reality painted a grim picture of his future. He was not happy.

Living off Catherine's inheritance allowed him the luxury of having status in the community while enjoying the trappings of wealth. That dreamland was over. The balloon had popped. Reality was here. He felt shame. He had to face the choice of futures, but first, he had to survive this onslaught of character assassination. His phone rang.

"Morning, Cal. David. I got your message."

"Thanks for returning my call. I got the most interesting email today from the phone company. They said it was in response to a confidential judicial subpoena. The problem is I didn't send one."

"Yeah, I know. I sent it for you. I knew you were busy. Betsy forwarded it to me, as I requested. Do you have time for me to come over?"

"Yes, I'll make time in my busy schedule."

Fifteen minutes later, David Fogel, in full uniform, walked in carrying a whiteboard. "Afternoon, Cal. A visual will be easier to understand than my trying to tie everything together orally." He looked around, took a chair, and moved it to the side of Cal's desk, placing the whiteboard on it, and slid the other chair where he could reach and point to the board. On the board were names, with lines connecting some to others.

"Complicated," Cal said, studying the board.

"Complicated and uncomfortable. We'll start with Catherine." He pointed to the board. "I combined her two phones." David flicked out his baton to use as a pointer. "These are multiple phone calls she made to John Emerson on his private unlisted line, the Vermont cell. The same one the pedophile called monthly. The pedophile is here." David pointed at another box on the diagram. "Remember, we believe these calls were made the day before he received his monthly payment. We now know who was supporting him."

"We can't prove that, can we?"

"Legally, no. Follow this line from Emerson over to here." Fogel moved the pointer across the board. "This is the number for the Berkshire Gentlemen's Club, out on the highway. I'm betting Emerson arranged for someone connected with the club to make the drop."

"Damn. Outstanding work, David."

"Hold on, Cal. Here's what's going to blow your mind. Remember there were a series of calls to the pervert the first two weeks he was in our community?"

"Yes, from a Boston number."

"That's right. That line is an unlisted number for an attorney at an old and prestigious law firm, Holliday, Edwards, and Carroll. The partner in question is Aloysius Carroll, better known on the dark side of society as Ivy League."

"What are you saying, David?"

"Look at this line from Emerson to Carroll." David moved his baton. "The two talk regularly. They were classmates at Dartmouth Law School."

"Emerson was funneling money to the pedophile?" Cal asked. "Carroll knew the pervert, communicated with him until he was settled, and engaged Emerson? Damn, damn, damn."

"There's more."

Cal looked at David and then at the board, where even more lines led to Carroll.

"That email you sent on your last day as judge was because I couldn't get past the block the phone company had on Carroll's number," David said. "He's big stuff, Cal. A confidential judicial subpoena was the only way around his protection. He's strictly corporate law."

"Now, come back over here." David pointed to another box. "This is my friend on the MSP. He talks to Carroll from time to time." He traced the line to Carroll. "Now for the bombshell. See these lines leading from Carroll? These are the private phones of the leadership of organized crime in Massachusetts. One of them is Big Vinney Del Giorno, the Massachusetts underboss and western Massachusetts capo, who also runs the Berkshire Gentlemen's Club."

Cal sat back in his chair. Both were silent for a couple of minutes, looking at the web of conspiracy. Finally, Cal asked, "David, do we know the name of the pedophile?"

"You're good. In Vermont his name was Caperson. I took a chance and ran his prints through the MSP organized crime database. I got a hit for a Salvatore Del Giorno. See Big Vinney? Well, his full name is Vincenzo Del Giorno. The pervert is—was—his brother."

"No wonder they're looking for him," Cal said. "There's another facet to all of this. Remember the last two BBC meetings, when the talk was about WWA&E spreading around the word that they had buyers for local businesses?"

"Yeah," said David.

"I'd bet the farm that money is coming from Carroll's clients through Emerson."

# CHAPTER 47

"Deputy Fogel, there's an MSP captain here to see you."

David looked up from working on the budget papers scattered from one end of the desk to the other, on the credenza, and on the floor alongside his chair. "Who did you say?"

"It's—" the officer started.

David's office door banged open. A short, muscular state trooper, distinguished by the captain's bars on his shoulders, the Sam Browne across his breast, and a waistline much smaller than his chest, rushed in. "The hottest guy she's ever seen in an MSP uniform, and definitely better looking than her boss, you no-good local wimp," the man said.

David Fogel jumped up from his desk, stepping on the budget papers on the floor, and gave Captain Charles Richards a bear hug. "I'm so proud of you," David said. "To be able to make captain in the Massachusetts Student Patrol is a remarkable feat. How many twelve-year-olds did you have to arm wrestle for the promotions?"

"At least I'm not sitting around playing Wyatt Earp in some godforsaken mountain valley."

The two-man killing machine held each other at arm's length and then kissed and hugged again.

"Good to see you, Charles," David said. "It's been too long."

"Good to see you, David. How is Saint Donna?"

"She's fine. We now have two boys, second and third grade."

"She's now a triple saint, if they take after you."

"How about coming for dinner tonight? I know she'd love to see you."

"Love to, but I have to get back. I'm here on business and finished early. Thought I'd take my old buddy to lunch."

"Great idea, my treat. I'll take you to a place where you'll get the best meal of your life. Course, when we walk in with these uniforms, half the people will leave, and the other half will shut up. I'll call Rosa Lee and give her a heads-up, just in case. This is a working person's restaurant. Many of the patrons speak Spanish, if you get my drift."

"I do. That's not my beat, so it doesn't concern me."

David grabbed his hat, and while the two of them walked to Captain Richards's unmarked car, he called Rosa Lee. Riding over, David told Charles all about married life with children. Charles reminded David about the single life with female variety and cold food at night. The banter was light and focused on their shared past and separate futures.

After parking at the restaurant, Charles picked up a newspaper resting beneath the front seat and took it in with him.

Rosa Lee greeted them at the door. "Afternoon, Sheriff. Who's this hunk acting as your bodyguard, and you not even elected yet?" She gave David a hug, pulling his head down to her shoulder. Softly, she said, "Tell Cal I need to see him. It's important."

He straightened and smiled at her. "Rosa Lee, this is Captain Charles Richards of the MSP. Charles and I shared all-expenses-paid vacations in Iraq and Afghanistan."

"You two, come with me. I've got you a corner table where you can swap war-story lies without scaring the rest of the customers." Seating them, she said, "Tea for both of you? It's buffet style around here, so fix your plate when you're ready. Pile it on. Both of you are too skinny." She smiled and left. They fixed their plates and returned to the table. Both men dove into their lunch, eating silently.

Finally, David looked at Charles and said, "What can I do for you, Charles?"

"Just listen carefully," he replied. The two men looked directly at each other. "Remember that traitor who led us into an ambush in Afghanistan? While I was in the hospital, the traitor disappeared. Never heard from or seen ever again. The neatest thing was you didn't say anything to anybody. It was like it didn't happen. You set up the traitor's house as a trap. A lot of bad actors were uncovered and dispatched with a minimum of fanfare. Really awesome.

"In the last twelve months, a convicted child abuser and molester dirtbag in Vermont skipped town. He used an alias, but his actual name was Salvatore Del Giorno. Ever heard the name Del Giorno?"

David nodded.

"Through his brother's contacts, the pervert got probation instead of jail time. One family doing a favor for a long-time neighbor. After five months, the ingrate skipped town and came to western Massachusetts. His brother promised his patron never to contact the pervert again. Being stupid, he broke his promise and sent a third party to check on him. You know what I mean?"

"Yeah, I do."

"The pervert's brother did another really stupid thing."

The hair on David's neck stood up. His senses moved to high alert. He remained quiet.

"The brother has businesses and employs people. In his line of work, the employees know not to take any initiative. Here, one business manager took exception to something a librarian said and did."

David thought of Maggie's safety. Before he could say anything, Charles continued.

"To make a long story short, the manager and one of his workers decided to teach the librarian a lesson."

David's stomach turned. If they had hurt Maggie, Charles didn't know what hell would be unleashed onto his associates.

Charles continued. "The librarian taught those two bozos a lesson instead. Their boss found out because the two of them needed medical attention for superficial gunshot wounds. The boss told his friend he took care of them so they wouldn't present a problem again. In his line of work, that has a specific meaning. You understand?"

"Yeah," David answered.

"It became known that they were still at work and more determined to have another meeting with the librarian. Do you read the *Boston Times* every day?"

"Not every day, just when I have the chance."

"I didn't think so. That's why I brought last Friday's." Charles unfolded the newspaper and pushed it toward David.

David looked down and saw a headline: "Reputed Mob Boss Dies in Fiery Collision." He read the first paragraph, detailing the untimely death of Big Vinney Del Giorno. When he looked up, Charles looked bored.

"The bottom line is this," Charles said. "No one cares about a missing pervert. The two employees are probably visiting the pervert in hell. Who knows? They just won't be renewing their library card."

"Okay, how can I help?"

"A judge over here issued a subpoena for a phone number in Boston. It's probably in everybody's best interest for that investigation to end, since there's no real reason anymore for it to proceed."

"Understood. There's another piece to the puzzle. There's a certain phone number over here calling that Boston number regularly. The party over here has a vendetta against that judge. Someone with a lot of money is paying the holder of this local number a large sum to inflame the governor against reappointing the judge in January."

"Two points, David. First, the judge should look at those closest to him. Second, this issue will likely take care of itself in November. The process is too far along to change the current governor's stance, but who's to say he'll be the governor in January?"

"I see. So, there's no reason to waste tax dollars and time on these issues, is there?"

"You were always the brightest of the two of us. Now, how about you let me have that piece of pecan pie, and you get another?" Charles reached over and slid David's dessert toward his side of the table.

§

Maggie was sorting books on a cart at the library's front desk when David Fogel walked in. She smiled. "Sheriff, I didn't file an arrest warrant for delinquent book fines on those two handsome young sons of yours, so to what do I owe the pleasure of this visit?"

"Hello, Maggie. Is there somewhere we can talk privately?"

"There are some rooms on the second floor." She turned to the assistant at the desk and asked, "Courtney, any of the writing rooms vacant?"

"Yes, ma'am, both are."

Maggie got the key to room one. "Follow me, David. Donna enjoying her time when the boys are in school?"

"I'm sure she is. She's not teaching this year, so I gave her some watercolors and a sketch pad for her birthday. She's getting back into what she loves."

Maggie let the two of them into the room and shut the door. The room was small. David sat on the edge of the desk, while Maggie leaned against the door. She folded her arms and squinted her eyes. "What's wrong, David?"

"Nothing's wrong. At least I don't think so. Maybe you should tell me. I hear you had a couple of intruders in the last two months." He looked intently at her.

"I don't know how you would've heard that," she said, looking away.

"A reliable source, Maggie. One who knows both needed medical help from gunshots, in such a way there was much persuasion and little blood. I checked with the police department. The parties involved did not file a report, nor any of the neighbors."

"See? Your source must be wrong," Maggie retorted.

"No, my source isn't wrong. They never filed a report. That's not why I'm here. If there was an altercation, those two men will not—no, cannot ever, under any circumstances, do it again or talk about it. That's what I wanted to tell you."

"That's good to know, if there was any invasion like you describe."

"Fine. Now I must return to my taxpayer-funded vacation resort to see to it my guests enjoy their evening meal on time. Good to see you, Maggie."

"Good to see you, David," she said. "David, with everything Cal has going on, his plate is full right now. Don't you think there's no reason to give him more to worry about?"

David was silent as he looked at her.

"Please," she said.

"You're right. His plate is full."

# CHAPTER 48

"It's about time you showed your face here, Your Honor. Look at you!" Rosa Lee stepped back and surveyed Cal from head to foot. "Skin and bones! You need two platefuls of Rosa Lee's fine cuisine. I'll set up a table around the corner. There's someone I want you to see."

Cal followed Rosa Lee to the assigned table.

"What are you drinking, Judge?"

"Iced tea, please, Rosa Lee."

"Go fix your plate, Your Honor."

Cal went to the buffet and surveyed the fried chicken, pork chops, chicken-fried steak, mashed potatoes, cooked cabbage, macaroni and cheese, fried okra, greens, field peas, and squash casserole. Apple pie, peach pie, and chocolate cake sat on the dessert table. A working person's selection of food, matching the clientele. A bountiful home-cooked buffet for a fair price, served family style at long tables.

The clientele was mostly in dirty boots, old jeans, and sweaty T-shirts, though they had vigorously scrubbed hands and arms. Most took a moment to give thanks for what was on their plates. Scattered among these pillars of the economy were a few professionals. Everybody was equal at Rosa Lee's. Cal returned to his table and pushed his food around, not hungry.

"Here's your tea, Your Honor," said Lorenzo, Rosa Lee's son.

"Lorenzo, have you grown! Sit for a minute, if your mother will let you," Cal said, pointing to the chair across from his. "Catch me up on what you're doing. Still at BC?"

"Yes, sir. I'm a junior."

"How are your grades?"

"So far, three-point-nine out of four cumulative," Lorenzo said with a big smile.

"Outstanding!" Cal said, holding out his clenched hand for a fist bump. "Have you thought about what you're going to do when you graduate?"

"Yes, sir. I'm sitting for the LSAT in May. That will give me an idea of what it's like, then I'll sit for it again in October. I'll be applying to law schools then."

"Have you any particular school in mind?"

"Yes, sir, whichever one gives me the best scholarship. I'll apply only to established law schools. That way, any school I choose will give me the opportunity for a good legal foundation. If I study hard and pay attention, the school doesn't matter as much. Success is up to me. With the biggest scholarship, and maybe grants, plus a part-time job, I'll graduate without all that killer debt so many people have."

"Smart young man. When you decide where you're going to apply, please let me know. I'd like to tell them about you, your mama, and how I've watched you grow up."

"Thank you, Judge. Mama wanted me to tell you something she said was important. While I was serving at White, White, Arnholt, and Emerson a few days ago, Mr. Emerson was having lunch with this lady. The other staff said she was Mrs. White-Callaway."

Cal smiled.

"That sounds like my wife. Mr. Emerson is her divorce attorney. You may not know, but her grandfather and father were managing partners of the firm. Maybe they were finalizing my divorce," Cal said. He thought of their proposal. They had demanded she keep her assets and he keep his, and they would split the joint account, in which there was nothing. Obviously, her concern was having to pay alimony or she was just anxious to get rid of him. He had signed the papers the day he got them, agreeing to all terms.

Lorenzo brought Cal back to the present. "I don't want you to think harsh of me, Judge, for what I'm about to say. I told Mama, and she said I needed to tell you so the record could be set straight. Mama said I'm doing right by telling you because they're doing wrong by you."

Cal looked at Lorenzo. "It's okay, Lorenzo. I have a feeling I already know what you're about to tell me, so don't feel bad."

"Mr. Emerson asked your wife for another two hundred thousand dollars to stop your reappointment and get you disbarred."

"That's a lot of money. What did she say?"

"She said, 'Whatever it takes.' But that's not all he said to her. He said he has a friend in Boston who placed some papers in the official judicial inquiry folder you sent to the governor. Mr. Emerson said the papers will turn the inquiry into a criminal investigation, which will stop your reappointment and cause your disbarment."

"Damn. Excuse me for that, Lorenzo. Are you sure?"

"Yes, sir. Real sure. I was standing right behind him."

"Well, that explains why a one-week inquiry has turned into a months-long investigation. It also explains why they haven't interviewed me or others about Joey's death. Lorenzo, thank you for being alert and attentive to this issue. I promise you no one will ever know about this conversation. You aren't aware yet, but you've fulfilled one of the basic tenets of the legal code of conduct. In law school, you'll learn that it's the obligation of every attorney who discovers a crime is being committed to tell the authorities the known facts. That's what you've done. Your mama is rightly proud of you."

"Yes, sir." Lorenzo got up, gave Cal a fist bump, and returned to the kitchen.

Cal started eating and thinking. He still felt sorry for Catherine. He loved Josey, and even though Catherine didn't know about her, he was sure she knew his heart wasn't in their marriage. That gulf between them had only widened when he accepted the judicial position. Later, when her father had died suddenly, his refusal to leave the bench had caused the chasm between them to become as wide as an ocean. That was when they'd started sleeping in separate bedrooms.

Obviously, she hated him. What to do about it was the question. He decided that could wait. Cal knew exactly who to call in Boston to find out what the file said. Whatever was incriminating must have been a lie, so he could refute it. That was always the Achilles' heel of a liar. Cal ate his lunch with gusto, looked at his empty plate, and got two desserts.

# CHAPTER 49

udrey sipped the Monte Bello. She had never thought wine could
be this good. Her first reaction was to gulp it down, let it start
the buzz. Maggie had shown her how to take a small amount, move
it gently around her palate, recognize the many flavors, and slowly
let it wash down her throat. Like everything else Maggie had taught
her, this experience was from a life she had never known outside of
books and magazines. She placed her wineglass on the table next to
the smaller white wineglass. It looked perfect with the crisp white lace
tablecloth, the heavy sterling silverware, two different-sized forks to
the left, a knife and spoon to the right, a butter knife on the small
bread plate, and a dessert spoon just above the Rothschild Birds fine
china dinner plate.

Audrey liked having one size glass for the first-course white wine,
and a larger glass for the main-course red wine. People who lived this
way were genteel. She wanted to be genteel. Maggie was that way.
Audrey wanted this program to work. Maggie was true to her word.
She did not rush her or put pressure on her. Maggie only gave advice
when asked. She showed what life could be like. Maggie was a role
model. Audrey's eyes started burning. She touched the corners with
her napkin.

"You okay, Red?"

"Yes, perfect. Maggie, you're right. This is what I want to be and do. You're also right that where I came from and where I was three months ago are irrelevant to where I want to be and go in the future. I trust your belief I can do this."

"Red—and I call you that because it will be the name your clientele will call you—always remember the most important part of the next four years is your education. You'll start college in June for the summer session. Your studies will go year-round so you can take more courses in four years than the minimum necessary to graduate. You're in my program to get an education, not just a degree. You will want to broaden and deepen your knowledge in your chosen field. I'll pay all your educational expenses. Part-time work at one of my stores, rotating to whichever one needs help, will give you spending money. You'll live in a home just like this one, except it won't have a second floor and will have only one bedroom. You will have one tutoring client per night, Monday through Friday. The client will arrive at six and leave by nine thirty. If he wants to leave early, so be it, but under no circumstances is he to stay late."

"What if he doesn't want to leave?"

"He knows and accepts the rules. That has never been a problem because each client wants to return the next week. It's important that you are Red, and he is the name in the file. There's no need for last names. You must understand, any tutoring client you have has more to risk from being exposed than you do. That's important. The file will list the three most important interests of each client. You'll become well versed in these interests, conversing with the client about his favorite topics. From six to seven, the two of you will sit in the living room and have no more than two drinks, which you'll fix with just one ounce of liquor in each. On the coffee table, you'll have a few nuts and trail mix. If he sits in the middle of the couch, you sit in a chair. If he sits at the end of the couch, you sit at the other end. Keeping separation between the two of you will build tension and anticipation. It puts you in command."

"That makes sense. What if I see him another time, somewhere out in the community? Do I say hi?"

"It's highly unlikely you will ever run into a client. If you do, turn and walk away. Do not recognize him. These are good questions, Red. Now, as I was saying, at seven, you will take the tray with the glasses and snacks into the kitchen. The meal will be prepared beforehand, just warmed while the two of you have drinks. You will sit at the head of the table and your client to your left. Pace dinner so that dessert is being served no later than ten to eight. When dinner is finished, send your client to the living room and clear the table. Never leave dishes or any remnants of dinner out. The elegance of the setting comes crashing down if you do. Elegance is the most important aspect of what takes place. It keeps your client in check. After ten minutes, excuse yourself provocatively, and go to the bedroom to prepare yourself and the bedside. Return to the living room appropriately dressed for what is to come. Nothing sleazy. You must look like the gift of a lifetime, which is what you are. End up in bed and finished by nine. This leaves you an appropriate amount of time to disengage in an elegant way, reminding him how virile he is and how you are looking forward to next week."

"What if he wants more?"

"Good point. Passion is not perpetual. All men are different. Some finish with one orgasm, while others need two in an hour. You work that out. Red, I can't emphasize enough the importance of elegance in every part of your life going forward. You can't just play-act it. You need to absorb and show it in everything you do, from attending classes to doing your laundry to handling your clients. Here's why. God gives every newborn two gifts: a body and a brain. The body develops naturally as the baby matures through the years. The brain develops according to its environment, but a person can nurture, expand, and develop it to excel in their interests. That's the educational factor that is so important to a successful life.

"Whenever you have sex with a man, you are giving him a gift, one that meets his biological requirements. You are in control unless you fail to exercise that control. You can do whatever you want sexually with your clients, but always make sure what you do does not demean you and cause him to lose respect for you. They will always ask. You should always divert the request to some action which is acceptable to you as an elegant person. If you control the situation, the conflict will rarely come up. When the client leaves at nine thirty, you will first go through the ritual I have explained. This is critical in making sure you avoid STDs and do not get pregnant. Only then do you clean up the kitchen, putting everything in its proper place. Once a month, you will see Dr. Freedman, an OB-GYN. He's elderly, but you'll love him. You can discuss any sexual questions with him and receive frank and honest answers."

"Every month?"

"Every month and anytime you want or need to between the scheduled appointments. Your weekends, other than working in my stores, are your own. If you choose to date someone, that's your business. There are two rules you cannot break: First, you cannot see one of your tutoring clients outside your weekly scheduled visits. Second, under no circumstances can you bring someone to your home, male or female. Your home has aspects set up for your safety, either when you are with a client or home alone. You should never answer the front door. The door has a steel casing and three bolts, making it nearly impossible for anyone to break in. The windows are shatterproof and designed to withstand objects blown into them by one-hundred-forty-mile-an-hour winds. When the garage door goes up, a warning light comes on in every room. This alerts you that someone is entering the house. If you're not expecting a client or me, you'll know to take steps to protect yourself. When the garage door leading to the breezeway is opened, a second warning light comes on.

"You'll notice there's a glass storm door at the kitchen entrance. It's shatterproof. It opens outward, so anyone approaching must step back, giving you more time to deal with the situation. When a warning light comes on, don't hesitate. Call 911 and me. If someone is determined to climb the ten-foot fence around the rear garden, all the outside lights and both warning lights will come on. In the unlikely event that an unruly client or an intruder is inside the home, in every quarter of every room is a hidden pepper spray tube. Use it on the attacker. Also, in each room is a nine-millimeter Glock pistol with laser sights. Get the nearest gun and shoot the individual. Shoot until the magazine is empty."

"What if the police find out I'm a whore?"

"Whore, prostitute, tramp, floozy—these are all words from a male-dominated society designed to suppress the ability of women to control their gift from God. The Ten Commandments don't say 'Thou shall not have sex for money or pleasure.' The commandments say a person shouldn't commit adultery, which is defined as sex with someone other than the person's spouse. You are single. You don't know your tutoring clients' marital status. That's none of your business. There are at least forty-nine references in the Bible about prostitution. Interestingly, one of the most insightful is Joshua 2:1–10, where two spies for Joshua stayed with a prostitute when spying on Jericho. In Joshua 6:17–25, Joshua's army spared the prostitute Rahab, who secreted the spies, and all who were with her in her house, when they destroyed Jericho.

"Now, if prostitution is evil, why did they spare the woman? I'll tell you why: If male authorities don't control women's sexuality, women will have the upper hand if they use their sexuality properly. Society's corrupt and spiteful attitude toward women's sexual gift is what propagates trafficking of children and women. Have you ever wondered why police arrest women and their clients, but rarely the pimps? Think about the Berkshire Gentlemen's Club. Why does it exist? For two reasons: first, because the lawyers twist the law to protect it, and second, just as importantly, because the owner is paying someone. Because of the injustices in the laws, you need to make sure your clients don't give you gifts or money. If they don't pay you, you're not a prostitute. When they try, you must elegantly and firmly decline. If they persist, clearly explain you won't take it and they won't be back to see you ever again. When they leave, call me and let me know. Now, let's talk about money.

"You'll have the house and a car for your use. I'll deduct the rent from your earnings. You will have a clothing allowance. If you choose, we can have fun, girly shopping outings together. Your decision. As I've mentioned, you will not have school expenses. There won't be any medical bills. When you graduate from BC, you'll select a part of the country where you want to live. You'll have money to smooth the transition to your new life. Once you're settled, you'll receive from a deceased maiden aunt an investment portfolio valued at a minimum of one hundred thousand dollars. You will have your whole life ahead of you; you will know how to control your relationships with others; you will have a career of your choice, not one foisted on you by necessity; you will have no debt; and you will have a net worth able to grow and make you wealthy as you pursue your career and life."

"I don't know what to say. I promise you I'll make you proud and study hard. You'll have to help me with the rest."

"I will. We're in this together."

# CHAPTER 50

Cal had requested to see the judicial inquiry file on May 5. Under inquiry rules, he had to be given the file within twenty-four hours, but they hadn't delivered it. He sat in his office and reviewed the law. The Massachusetts attorney general and state bar's unwillingness to share the file confirmed what Lorenzo had said: the action was a criminal investigation, not an inquiry. Cal knew all the bar officials and considered them friends. For them not to alert him to the situation meant the evidence in the file was so damaging it could lead to criminal charges and disbarment.

Cal loosened his tie, unbuttoned his shirt collar, and lowered the air conditioner thermostat to below seventy degrees. He mentally urged himself to calm down. Success in winning this epic battle for his career and future rested on his being cunning and clearheaded, not panicky. Sitting in the overstuffed green velvet reading chair, worn with age, that he had found in one of Maggie's antique stores three weeks ago, he stared at the desk, his fist pounding the arm of the chair over and over as he thought about the situation. He shut his eyes. Something in that file was false. Lorenzo had heard that from the man who put it there. If he could see the file, he'd recognize it immediately.

There was only one true issue that could bring Cal's world crashing down: if someone had found out that Joey was his son and that he hadn't disclosed it in the court documents. When he'd passed judgment on Joey, he'd had no idea the boy was his son. Could that possibly be what was in the file? Could that be why Catherine was so hell-bent on destroying him? She had thought she was getting a hard charging, money-focused guy and ended up with a totally different situation. There must have been more to her actions than just hating him. John Emerson was obviously ruthless, just like her. They had the same interests in playing country club royalty. Perhaps they had a deeper relationship than he realized. She'd always wanted to be powerful. He knew the hatred for him may have started the ball rolling, but an addiction to power was the genuine force behind what was going on, and John Emerson was the facilitator.

What was Emerson's actual relationship with the pedophile? Could he be a pedophile, too? Did Cal want to know? Catherine and John were trying to destroy him. Should Cal try to destroy Emerson or both? Reality set in. He needed to forget the revenge and just focus on the goal: survive their attack, and then make sure he could survive financially. Clearing his name and being reinstated to the bench were paramount. After survival, the future looked cloudy. Should he stay a judge? Could he build a financially successful law practice? Did he want to join a firm and be a partner? No. He knew law firm politics were not for him. What a mess. Calm down, he told himself. One obstacle at a time.

He felt calmer prioritizing his actions. He buttoned his collar, straightened his tie, and pushed the thermostat back above seventy. Moving to the computer, he sat with his hands behind his head. If they knew Joey was his son, the lynching would have already taken place. They would have steamrolled him. They don't know that truth, so what they had was a lie. He realized he needed to go to the state supreme court under the rules of an investigation rather than an inquiry. He finished typing his request, read it over, and hit send.

They, whoever they were, suggested an email should be put in the draft folder for ten minutes before sending. If Cal had followed that advice, he would never have sent it. It was gone now. He wondered when Catherine was going to finalize the divorce. He hoped soon. He thought of Maggie. Perhaps she could meet him for dinner in North Adams—but he realized that was stupid. At that moment, his computer dinged, indicating a new email. He looked, and it was a reply from his friend at the state supreme court. He opened it and saw an attachment. One hundred and twenty pages. What he had sent the governor wasn't that large. He checked the printer for paper and started printing it out. A chill came over him as he felt his blood pressure recede.

§

Cal rubbed his eyes and saw it was almost midnight. He had no idea that much time had flown by. At least he'd finally separated the doctored pages from the real file. Whoever had inserted the new pages was good, good at making them blend in. They might have retyped the entire file. Scary how devious people would go to such a length to destroy him.

There were three damaging reports in the file. The first said Cal had used Joey inappropriately by having his community service focused on the AT instead of multiple agencies. It accused Cal of using Joey to do the hard physical labor required by Cal's position in ATC leadership. Joey's body showed multiple past fractures plus a separated left shoulder. Cal could refute some of those accusations through testimony from his fellow ATC leaders. Second, Joey's lack of survival gear was totally false, yet hard to refute. The fact was Cal didn't have any idea why Joey hadn't taken basic survival gear when he went to the Ledges that day. The report inferred Cal did not give him time to get equipped. Cal knew he had gone to get Suzie, but Joey had known what to expect on the mountain. It finally dawned on Cal. Yes, Joey had known the wilderness better than anyone. He would have taken clothes to protect Suzie, but by the time he was found, he had taken off his clothes to save her. Joey was always aware of his situation, particularly in the wilderness. Hell, he'd lived there for three years. He had to have clothes for Suzie. He knew she didn't know about the polar vortex coming through. Where were the clothes? He would have had a backpack. Cal had bought him two at Gianelli's.

Cal pulled out a yellow pad. At the top, he wrote DAY OF DEATH. On the next line he wrote:

1. I SPOKE TO JOEY ON THE PHONE WHEN HE WAS AT ATCHQ.

Could he prove what they'd discussed? No. On the next line, he wrote:

2. JOEY LEFT ATCHQ BEFORE I ARRIVED. WITNESSES.

The report said Cal had ordered him as a judge to go to the mountain that day. Since he'd left before Cal had arrived, it was up to Cal to prove that he hadn't demanded Joey go to the mountain. He wrote VOLUNTEERS AT ATCHQ CAN REFUTE????

Cal drummed his pencil point on the yellow pad. He knew why Joey had gone to the mountain. Very little had ever been said about the rescue of Suzie. It had never made any TV broadcast, just the local *Berkshire Times*. Suzie could establish why Joey had gone to the mountain that day. Did he want to get her involved? Did he want reporters interviewing Suzie? If she was interviewed, the accusers would know she was pregnant, and she'd have to admit under oath that Joey was the father, and that would mean people poking around in her life and Joey's life. They'd be sure to find out about the Stoner years. That couldn't happen, no matter what happened to Cal. There had to be another way.

Cal wrote:

3. JOEY UNPREPARED FOR STORM.

The third accusation was that Joey had a separated shoulder and previous fractures that had healed without medical attention when he died. Cal didn't know anything about them. He reflected on the aftermath of the tragedy. The shoulder injury was recent and unknown to Cal. He had been inconsolable about Joey's death. He hadn't taken time to read the autopsy. How foolish. The report also stated Joey had old bone fractures in the ribs, arms, and legs. Stoner had created pain. Inferred in the report was that the injuries happened while he was a ward of the court. The shoulder separation must have happened on the mountain. Maybe he'd slipped. Back up, Cal thought. He knew Joey had stopped at the drugstore to get the heating pads. The clerk had called the police, but since Joey had given her his wallet and it contained more money than necessary for the pads, Cal had gotten the police report squashed. He ran through it: Okay, so Joey was in the car, rushing as fast as he could. He didn't take time to put the pads in his backpack; he stuffed them in his coat pockets. At the mountain, he would have taken his backpack with him if he had one. Cal reached into his briefcase, pulled out his go phone, and hit the speed dial for Maggie.

After four rings, Maggie answered. "Everything all right? What time is it? God, it's near midnight."

"Sorry to wake you, but it's important. It's about the day Joey died. You said he came to the house to get his phone, and you spoke with him, right?"

"Yes. Why?"

"Did Joey favor his left arm in any way?"

"What do you mean, 'favor his left arm'?"

"Let it hang down. Appear in pain. Only use his right arm. Act like he had a separated shoulder."

Maggie hesitated. "No, not at all. He was Joey, very demonstrative when excited. Once I told him Suzie was on her way to the mountain, he became agitated. There was no indication of an injury. Why do you ask?"

"I missed the coroner's report section that said Joey had a separated shoulder when he died. If he didn't have the injury before, it had to have happened on the mountain. That meant he slipped and fell. I finally received the file the governor has, and it has three false reports, one of which is that I demanded he go to the mountain without basic survival gear. He had none when we found the two of them, so it must be somewhere on the mountain. He may have lost it when he separated his shoulder. At least, that's my speculation. The separated shoulder also explains why he didn't get to the south shelter with Suzie. She was unconscious, and he couldn't carry her." Cal's voice broke as he realized what Joey's last minutes had been like. There was silence.

Finally, Maggie said, "Why are you asking about this now?"

"I requested the judicial file on Joey's death because I surmised something wasn't right. As I said, someone placed documents and accusations in the file, one of which states I sent Joey to the mountain without proper survival gear."

"Suzie could straighten out the record, couldn't she?"

"She could, but not without having to testify under oath. She likely would be asked who the father of her child is, and every other aspect of her life would be combed through, including her and Joey's time in the Stoner household. I'm not going to allow her to be subjected to that questioning."

"Thank you for protecting her. What are you going to do?"

"I've got to find a way to prove Joey had survival gear, even if I can't prove I didn't send him to the mountain that day. I'm hoping I can find witnesses who will testify Joey went to the mountain voluntarily." Cal paused. "How are things with you?"

"Good. I miss you."

"Sorry to wake you. Go back to sleep. Miss you too."

Cal picked up his pencil, skipped two lines on the yellow pad, and wrote HURTS SHOULDER—HOW? On the next line, he wrote:

1. PARKS AT BENEDICT'S POND.

Joey's shoulder had to have been all right there. Cal closed his eyes and mentally walked from the parking lot through the low areas on the boards, which were slippery. If Joey fell there, he couldn't have climbed the mountain, no matter how strong his will to rescue Suzie. Cal wrote:

2. BRIDGE COVERING RAVINE AT LOWER LEVEL.

Unlikely, as he would still have had a hard climb from there.

3. BOULDER FIELD ABOVE ROAD.

Possible. Cal put a star by this line. He thought about the trail above the boulder field. It sloped upward, but wasn't steep or difficult. He felt a sensation come over his body as he wrote the next line:

4. HIGH LAKE SPILLWAY.

This was the most likely place. Cal remembered a need for a new bridge in December. When had it failed? Was it before or after the storm that day? What if it was out, or collapsed, when Joey was trying to cross? Joey had gotten across because he made it to Suzie.

Cal put two stars on this line. He realized he may have had the answer. If Joey had taken his backpack to the mountain, it wasn't with him when Cal and Junior arrived. It must have been somewhere between the Ledges and the Benedict Pond parking lot. Another hiker may have found it, or it was still there in the brush, or . . . Cal realized the most probable answer: underwater. He looked at his watch. It was 1:00 a.m. Nothing could be done now. He slept at the office in the overstuffed chair rather than driving to his cabin. Turning out the lights, he saw a streetlight through the window. Maybe that was the light at the end of the tunnel. Hopefully, it wasn't a train roaring toward him.

§

Cal believed the hours waiting for the ATCHQ to open were the longest of his life. Life was interesting: time flew by so quickly sometimes and crawled at a snail's pace at others. Finally, staff members should be there. He opened his cell and hit speed dial seven.

"ATCHQ, this is Brian."

"Brian, Cal. I need some help."

"Sure, Cal, what's up?"

"I need some volunteers to go up to the high lake spillway on the AT leading to the Ledges, the spillway where the bridge was washed out last fall. By the way, do we know when it washed out?"

"No, it was discovered the first week of December, so sometime in late November, since it routinely checked out in mid-November."

"If you remember, Joey Paschal died at the Ledges in late November. It's possible his injury happened crossing that crevasse, and he lost his backpack. It's important we find the backpack, if it's there. Could you email the volunteers and see if a small contingent is willing to search for it?"

"Unnecessary. Me, Phil, and Steve are hiking this afternoon. We'll go look for it. Joey was an all right guy. It'd be cool if we could find it for the family. Want me to call you, if we do?"

"Please call either way. No, I'll tell you what. Why don't the three of you meet me at Little Italy Pizza Place at, say, seven tonight, regardless of whether you find the pack? My treat."

"You're on. We'll see you then."

§

Cal looked at Joey's backpack. His mind shifted to legal work so he could keep his composure. "Fellas, awesome job. Where was it?"

"Not two feet down the gulley from the old log bridge. It was underwater and hard to see. It would have been there forever if Phil hadn't noticed the red strip and gone in to cut it loose."

"Great job, Phil," Cal said, looking at the beaming young man stuffing pizza in his mouth. "Fellas, this is really important. I want the three of you to document that you went to the mountain and searched for and found the backpack. Explain where it was and how you got it loose. Then I want—"

"Sorry to interrupt, Cal. Stevie shot video of our search on his phone. He wanted to impress all the girls on Facebook with his Daniel Boone wilderness skills." Brian poked Steve in the shoulder.

"Seriously, you have film of the search? Unbelievable. Yes, Steve, if you could email it to the ATC, the film can be archived in the official search records. You guys are the best. The last thing I need you to do is inventory the backpack, date and sign the inventory, and then put the backpack in the lost and found bins until it's claimed."

§

Examining the file going to the state supreme court one last time, Cal was content. The original was on white paper. The fake pages were now on buff paper. Attached testimony and evidence refuting the fake allegations were on buff pages. Best of all was the video, on CD, of the three hikers finding Joey's backpack. Cal closed the file and put it in a FedEx overnight box. He was satisfied he'd done all he could do, and it should be enough.

It took only four days for the state supreme court to notify the governor's office they were closing the file on Judge Callaway and turning the false evidence over to the state's attorney for opening a fraud investigation. The governor's chief of staff called Cal and notified him he must be back on the bench the next day. Cal was sensitive to the fact that the governor didn't call. The chief of staff said press releases would be forthcoming the next day. Cal was sure the TV stations and regional media would ignore the reinstatement if they received the press releases.

He picked up the phone and called the *Berkshire Times* reporter who had written the original story of his suspension.

"Newsroom, Carolyn Sieber speaking. How can I help you?"

"Ms. Sieber, this is Cal—Judge Callaway. You earned a scoop. You're welcome," he said without waiting for a reply. "It's payback for the professionalism you showed when reporting my suspension. Do you have a pencil? Good. You want to call Mitchell Steppins, the chief of staff to the governor. He just called to lift my suspension from the bench. The state supreme court found false documents in the Joey Paschal file once it arrived in Boston. The judiciary has forwarded the fake charges to the state's attorney for a fraud investigation. If you start with the chief of staff and then speak to the state's attorney's office, you may scoop everyone else. By the way, here is the chief of staff's direct confidential phone number." He rattled it off. "Have a pleasant and busy afternoon. Bye."

Nothing was on the evening TV news, just as Cal expected.

The next morning, the bold *Berkshire Times* headline read, JUDGE ERNST "CAL" CALLAWAY CLEARED OF ALL CHARGES. In a sidebar above the fold was an explanation: "Fraudulent charges against Judge Callaway referred to state's attorney for investigation."

By the evening news, there wasn't anything the TV stations could do but report on the new developments. By then, Cal had finished his first day back on the bench. One obstacle hurdled, he thought.

# CHAPTER 51

Packing up his temporary office, Cal felt relieved to be going back on the bench, even if he knew it was just long enough to let the public know about his exoneration. The phone rang.

"May I help you?" he answered.

"No, but I'm going to help you, Judge White-Callaway. This is John Emerson. I represent Catherine White-Callaway in your divorce proceedings."

"John, stop the formal crap. Shouldn't you be talking to my attorney?" Cal was wary of the call. Emerson knew the proper protocol. Cal knew Emerson was behind the effort to remove him from the bench but couldn't, as of now, prove it.

"I'm calling to inform you your divorce from your wife is final. You no longer have the right to use the White name."

"Thank you for your call," Cal said and hung up. He placed his elbows on his desk, rested his chin on his clenched fists, and sighed. His sham marriage was over. Elation and despair were his two emotions. He felt a weight had been lifted from his shoulders, but he couldn't clearly see the future. Now he could take Maggie to any restaurant he wanted. They could walk down the street holding hands, like they did in New York. He was Ernst "Cal" Callaway III again. He liked the sound of it. One obstacle down, but more to go.

It had been two and a half weeks since he'd received the falsified file on Joey's death from the state supreme court and solved the riddle of what was happening to him. His phone rang again.

"May I help you?" he asked.

"Cal, it's Billy Hart, your faithful real estate wizard. Enjoying the cabin in the woods?"

"Morning, Billy. What's up?"

"Scuttlebutt has it you're getting a divorce. If that's the case, and I'm not saying it is, something is coming up you need to know about."

"Well, it's not true. I am divorced, as of thirty minutes ago. You're the first I've told. I'm no longer White-Callaway, just plain old Callaway."

"Cal, you don't sound too broken up about it, so if you're happy, I'm happy. Now I know I need to see you. Do you know the old Ledbetter mansion on Key Street in Lenox?"

"Oh, yeah. When I was little, I used to run around in that place when my mother went for tea with Heloise Ledbetter. What about it?"

"At five o'clock today, I'm listing it at a steal. You can't build that house for three times the price they're asking."

"Billy, I'm a judge. If I've learned anything, it's the truth in the old saying that if it's too good to be true, it probably is."

"Now, now, Judge. Good things happen to good people. Here's the story. Some southerners from Georgia came up in the summer and fell in love with the area. They bought the home and retired here. They were so mesmerized by the culture in the summer they didn't even notice the sticks attached to the fire hydrants so firefighters could find where to attach their hoses when the snow was five feet deep. Lonnie Albertson, over at First Berkshire Bank and Trust, said the husband came in one day in late February, after a snowy and frigid couple of weeks, and said he and his wife were leaving and the bank could have the place. He stopped paying the mortgage and the taxes.

"Lonnie had made a ninety-five percent loan to value since the couple was rich. He's in an awful place. By the way, the couple left it partially furnished. They had renovated it extensively as well. New roof, new HVAC, fresh paint. Best of all, they took that enormous kitchen, built for a staff of seven, and turned it into a nice regular kitchen and a master suite of two rooms and a bath. You could live in that suite, cook in the kitchen, and use the double parlors—remember the ten-foot pocket doors?—as your offices. The dining room could be a conference room. You could close off the upstairs if you wanted."

"Billy, I'm a judge, at least for the time being. I don't have that kind of money."

"You don't need money. Lonnie will give the place to anyone who'll catch the back payments up and take over the mortgage. Shoot, he'll be flexible, just to keep this white elephant—excuse me, house—off his ORE rolls."

"What's ORE, Billy?"

"Our rotten experience. Just kidding. Other real estate, aka bad loans. Your PITI on the house will be only sixty percent greater than what you're paying me in rent for that office and cabin in the woods."

"I like this office and cabin in the woods."

"Cal, that's not you. Whether you know it or not, you're a pillar of this community. You have a position here. Hiding in the woods and working out of a dumpy office is not you. You should be in a place where the community knows Cal Callaway is always available. That's reality. Don't shoot the messenger for saying it."

"Billy, you're not worth the bullets. How long do I have to decide?"

"Until a minute before five this afternoon."

"I'll get back to you by then. By the way, Billy, thanks for thinking about me. It's nice to know I have a friend."

"You have more than you think. Don't forget to call."

Cal thought about the house and about what Billy had said about hiding out. Billy was right. He had been hiding. He didn't like that about his existence. Now that the divorce was final, he could ask Maggie to marry him. If he had this house, she could take her rightful place in the community. When this travesty was over, it would be perfect. Why wait till the future was crystal clear? Fear?

A timid knock on the door interrupted his thoughts.

"Come in. It's open," he called out as he stood and started toward the door.

Ella, his old housekeeper from Willview, opened it and stepped in.

"Ella, come in! This is a pleasant surprise." Cal saw the tears on her cheeks. "What's wrong, Ella? Do you want some water?" He went back to his desk and pulled out some tissues, handing them to her.

"No, Your Honor, I don't need any water."

Cal directed Ella gently to a chair in front of his desk. He placed his hand on her shoulder. "Tell me how I can help you, Ella."

"Judge, Mrs. White-Callaway gave me two weeks' pay and told me not to come back to Willview anymore." She broke down crying.

"Take a deep breath, Ella."

"I've worked nowhere else in my life. She told me not to use her as a reference. How am I going to get another job? I've got Mama to take care of." She started crying again. Then she said, "Mama is getting where I can't leave her alone too long. She's forgetful and sometimes wanders off." She let out a woeful wail. "What am I going to do, Judge?"

"You said Mrs. White-Callaway gave you two weeks' severance pay?"

"I guess. She paid me for two weeks and said not to come back."

"That's what's called severance pay, Ella. Here's what you're going to do. Go home and fix you and your mama a wonderful dinner. Look at me, Ella." He held her hand. "I promise you, you will have a job within two weeks, making at least what you were making at Willview."

"Really, you promise? Thank you, Your Honor. Thank you, thank you. Oh, I just knew you'd have an answer. Thank you, thank you, Judge." Ella stood.

Cal wrote his cell number on his business card and gave it to her. "Call me on Monday and I'll have it all worked out for you." Cal hugged her and walked her to the door.

He returned to his desk and stared out the window. What a bitch. Why did Catherine do that to Ella? He took out his yellow pad and wrote ELLA at the top of the page. Four potential employers went on the list, and then he stopped and put his own name down. He drew a circle over and over around his name. He pulled his judicial retirement account statement from his desk. The balance was just over $435,000. If he liquidated the funds and used the money to get established, he might be able to build a practice before going broke—or maybe not. Did he have the courage to try?

Joey came to mind. He would have the courage. Cal was Joey's father. Perhaps Joey's courage came from him.

Cal picked up the phone. It rang only once before being answered. He said, "Billy, what's the chance to see the Ledbetter house now?"

"I'll pick you up in fifteen. Smart move, Cal."

"Just looking, Billy."

"Yeah, sure. You can buy lunch afterward."

# CHAPTER 52

Cal waited at the Fitzgerald Inn for Maggie, who was driving back from Suzie's in North Adams. Suzie was in the last weeks of her pregnancy, both scared and uncomfortable. Cal reflected on the fact that it was mid-June, a year almost to the day since David Fogel had called and said he'd arrested a boy living in the wilderness. Who could have imagined the turmoil of the past year?

Cal looked around at the elegant setting. This was perfect for what he wanted to do tonight. He fingered the ring box in his jacket pocket. If she didn't like it, she could exchange it. This place was only slightly larger than his new home. Cal felt humbled by the fact this restaurant and his home and others like it were second and third homes to the New York and Boston rich. He thought about his plan. As soon as Ella came into his office, he knew he couldn't stay a judge. Here he was, two weeks later, with a huge mortgage and responsibility for Ella and her mother, and about to propose to the woman he loved. Life in the fast lane. He liked the feeling.

Maggie walked into the restaurant, saw Cal, and accompanied the maître d' to the table. Cal stood and kissed her lightly on the cheek.

"What a lovely place," Maggie said, looking around the candlelit dining room. The glow refracted off the crystal glasses like stars in the night sky. A harp player strummed soft music in the corner. "I've never been here. Its reputation is correct. This is a real treat." She smiled at Cal while the server came over and stood off to the side.

Cal, looking at Maggie, said, "Wild Turkey Rare Breed, short glass, one cube, a splash of water?"

"Yes, thank you."

He looked at the server. "Two of the same, please." When the server withdrew, he continued. "I always longed for the day we could sit in a restaurant like this and not worry about who saw us."

Maggie reached over and squeezed his hand. "You've certainly been the talk of the town these last few months. It's hard to believe someone in the governor's office falsified documents in Joey's file. Do they know who did it?"

"No. Evidently they didn't handle the file properly, so several people in and out of the governor's office could have been the culprit. They're working on it. How hard, is the question. The important point is the episode is over, and now everyone in this community knows the truth. We'll see in November how important that is."

"Are you enjoying being back on the bench?"

"I'm enjoying proving they railroaded me. My perspective of the judgeship has changed."

"How so?"

"Maggie, you above all others should know life is complex. In the last year, two facts became evident: first, life is precious and easily snuffed out, and second, being too dependent on others for your livelihood is a sure road to poverty."

"That second lesson is quite cynical, isn't it?"

"Really? During the last fourteen years serving this community as a judge, with my position totally dependent upon the good graces of the governor, it was satisfying but built financially on a foundation of sand. If anyone was closer to the governor and wanted the position, he could find a reason to replace me, no matter what. The governor announced my suspension, and his chief of staff announced the reinstatement. What does that tell you?"

"That the governor won't endorse you in January."

"Maggie, I'm going to resign my judgeship effective August 1 and go into private practice."

"Are you serious? What firm are you joining?"

The server returned with their drinks.

Cal waited for the server to leave and said, "I've ordered dinner and wine pairings for both of us. What's interesting is they only serve wines from New England wineries. It seems most of the local restaurants are now serving the same wines. I hope that's acceptable?"

"It sounds wonderful."

"Here's to the future," Cal said, holding his glass up for Maggie to clink. "I'm not joining a law firm. I'm going to hang out my shingle as a sole practitioner. That brings me to other news. Are you familiar with the Ledbetter mansion?"

"Is that the huge house on Key Street?"

"Yes. I've bought it. I'm doing the bank a favor. They hold the loan on the house, and the owners defaulted. Putting the house in the bad loan account would impair their capital too much. I'll live there and have my office there. By the way, Catherine, bless her devious heart, was foolish enough to fire Ella from Willview. She's coming to work for me. I'm paying her what she made before, but there's a difference. First, she and her elderly mother will live in the master suite off the kitchen. Second, the three of us will share our meals from the same pot, so to speak. Ella won't have to pay rent, buy food, or pay for her mother's medicine. I'll cover whatever Medicare and insurance don't. It's a fabulous deal for me. I'll take a bedroom upstairs, and the rest of downstairs will be my office."

"You've been busy, to say the least. Catherine certainly isn't making intelligent decisions." Maggie wanted to tell Cal about Suzie, but she didn't know how to bring up the subject. He was like a little boy, spewing news out rapidly. Maybe after dinner, she hoped.

"Yes, thank goodness. Perhaps I should send her a thank-you note."

The server brought their soup. Conversation turned to local news, the library, and Maggie's stores. Suddenly, Cal couldn't think of anything to talk about except his proposal at the end of the meal. He was confident their future together would be exciting. Finally, he said, "How is Suzie doing?"

"She's scared. Her OB said she could deliver in the next two weeks. She's determined to be strong after Joey is born, but the realities of being a single mom, going to school, and working are setting in."

"Joey? It's going to be a boy?"

"We don't know. Remember, I told you, she said she'd call the child Joey whether it's a boy or a girl."

"I remember now. I forgot."

"Do you want to resume having dinner with Suzie and me, now your ordeal is over?"

"Sure."

Maggie sensed the half-heartedness of his response.

They enjoyed the three courses, while small talk was stilted, and the silence grew awkward. Cal thought about his proposal, and Maggie focused on Suzie. The server cleared the table and asked, "Do you wish to see the dessert cart?"

Cal looked at Maggie, who shook her head. "Just coffee, please," he said. Now was the time. "Maggie, let's talk about us. That's not right. God, I can't believe I'm nervous." He reached into his pocket and pulled out the ring box. He opened it and set it on the table in front of her. "I'm not the Hallmark type to go down on one knee, but will you marry me?"

Maggie looked from Cal to the diamond ring and back to Cal. "Oh, Cal. You know how much I love you, but I can't marry you or any other man. I just can't." She reached for his hand.

Cal coughed as his heart skipped a beat. How and why had she just said no? He didn't move his hand as she tried to hold it.

"Cal, I want to be in your life, and I want you in my life," she said. "However, you can't be my life, and I can't be yours. My life is like yours. It's complex and requires my undivided attention. There is no man but you, and there won't ever be another man as long as you'll have me. Marriage, however, is out of the question. There are others who need me desperately, and I will always be there to help them. While you are Joey's biological father," Maggie's voice faltered, and she used her napkin to stem the tears falling from her eyes, "for the first time in my life, I realized what it was like to have a son. I learned how vulnerable these abused young boys are. I learned that young boys need people, both male and female, to show them love as much as young girls do. Somehow, I'm going to try to help young boys and girls. Oh, Cal, please understand."

"I understand," Cal said. He reached for the ring box, snapped it closed, and returned it to his pocket. He signaled he was ready for the check. After signing, the two of them rose. "I'll walk you to your car."

At Maggie's Outback, she turned to him and said, "Please understand. I love you."

"I understand," he said, but when Maggie hugged him, he was unresponsive.

Driving away, she allowed the tears to flow, washing away the unhappiness she felt. He didn't understand, but there was nothing she could do. No man was going to dominate her life.

# CHAPTER 53

"**Y**our Honor, Maggie Latham is on line two," Betsy said, coming to Cal's door.

Cal covered the handset at his mouth. "Ask her to hold for a second." He returned to his current call and said, "Junior, Betsy's calling me. I've got to run. May I call you later about the renovations? Thanks." Cal hit line two and said, "Everything okay, Maggie?"

"Suzie is in labor. She's at Berkshire General. I thought you might want to know."

"Yes, thank you. Berkshire General. Got it."

"I'll let you know when the baby is born. I've got to run. They won't let me back there, but I'm hoping to see the doctor."

"Okay. I'll get some flowers over there." Cal hung up and sat back in his chair. She had to call; he should have called her. He shook his head. It was good to hear her voice. He'd missed talking with her even though he was the one refusing to communicate. Since that night at the Fitzgerald Inn two weeks ago, all he'd done was pout like a little child. The pain of her rejection had collapsed his optimism and enthusiasm for the future. Being rejected by both the woman he didn't love and the woman he felt he did love hurt more than he'd realized. He had turned off his go phone, which was cruel and childish, but at least hiking each day helped him get over the hurt. This realization hit him like an avalanche as he sat at the Ledges and talked to his son. On one level, he felt he understood Maggie's reasoning. On another level, he felt being financially successful would have made her accept.

While hiking to the Ledges that day, he remembered what he'd told Joey: the future has nothing to do with the past unless you let it. Cal's future was in his hands, not the governor's or anyone else's now. There was no sense in pouting over Maggie's rejection. He loved her, but he felt a distance that was never there before they fell out of touch during the divorce and judicial crisis. Did that mean he didn't love her? He now had responsibilities to Ella and her mother. He wondered if he had a responsibility to Suzie and baby Joey? Maggie had accepted a part of him all the years he had to sneak around. He didn't know why he couldn't accept a part of her. Wasn't that genuine love, when one person accepted being in another's life to a limited extent but loving them wholly?

Cal hit the intercom button. "Betsy, please come in here."

She took the seat in front of Cal's desk.

"Betsy, I wanted to let you know confidentially that I'll be resigning from this judgeship effective August 1. I'll be sending a letter to the governor tomorrow. I was going to do it today, giving a full thirty-day notice, but Ms. Latham just informed me I'm going to be a grandfather later today."

"Cal—I'm sorry, Your Honor, a grandfather? Don't you have to be a father first?"

"It's complicated, Betsy. Yes, a grandfather. I'll explain tomorrow. I need to get to the hospital. Call my cell if you need me." Cal stood to leave.

Betsy stood and said, "What are you going to do, Cal, after you resign?"

"Hang out my shingle and beat the bushes for business."

"I'd like to apply for your paralegal position."

Cal, putting on his jacket, stopped and looked at her. "I don't know what to say."

"Please say yes."

"Betsy, you have a good, secure position here. You can't give that up to take a risk like this. You have a husband and children to consider."

"Cal, you're no risk. I'll take a cut in pay. I've stayed in this job only because of you. If you go, I go. I'd like to go with you, please."

"Of course, you're hired. You've made my day. Now, I'm going to have a second good thing happen to me. I'll let you know if it's a girl or a boy. See you tomorrow." He stopped and said, "Damn. I forgot to tell you to reschedule everyone from today to tomorrow. On second thought, leave tomorrow open. Schedule three days of hearings spread over the third and the fifth. Stack them sunup to sundown. Thank you, Betsy." He rushed out the door.

§

Maggie was sitting in the visitors' lounge, flipping the pages of a financial magazine. What propaganda bullshit, she thought. Maggie knew the world was in the last phase of the fourth great secular economic cycle. Radical change was evolving, and the elites didn't even see it.

She threw the magazine on the table. The gift store might have an interesting book to pass the time with, Maggie mused. Poor Suzie, back there by herself. She's got to believe she's not alone.

She looked up and saw Cal leaving the elevators, looking right and left. She waved. He came over. She rose and hugged him. "I've missed you," she said, leaning up to kiss him.

"I've missed you and love you dearly. We can talk about all of that after the baby is born. What's the situation?"

"She's fully dilated and has had an epidural. She wants a normal delivery even though the doctor gave her a choice of a C-section."

"Anybody with her?"

"No, they won't let me back there because I'm not a blood relative, and I forgot to get a medical power of attorney. I can't believe I forgot to get it."

"I'm the baby's grandfather. Doesn't that make me a blood relative? She shouldn't have to go through this alone. Who's her OB?"

"Dr. Freedman."

"Dr. Martin Freedman? Is he here?"

"Yes, on both counts."

"Get the nurse to page him and tell him Judge Callaway is here and needs thirty seconds of his time."

Maggie went to the nurses' station and requested the page. A coded request went over the PA system for Dr. Freedman, and a few minutes later an elderly doctor in scrubs walked into the visitors' lounge. Cal rose and shook his hand. He said, "Marty, I hope all is well. How's Mary doing?"

"She's good, Cal."

"Marty, you have a patient back there by the name of Suzie Stoner. She's having my son's baby. You may have heard about my son's death last November at the Ledges, saving her and their unborn baby's lives. Ms. Latham, who is like a mother to Suzie, and I, the grandfather of the baby, should be with her. Does that make sense?"

"For sure, Cal. I didn't know you were the grandfather. Follow me."

The three left the waiting room. Dr. Freedman said to the nurse behind the desk, "Please outfit these proud grandparents with gowns, masks, and caps and take them to Suzie Stoner's room."

Suzie lay in bed, her feet in stirrups, eyes wide with fear, tears running down the sides of her face, and fists clenching folds of the sheets, when Maggie and Cal entered the room. Maggie raced over to Suzie, pulled down her mask so Suzie knew who she was, and then fetched a washcloth and wet it from the ice water pitcher beside the bed. She gently wiped Suzie's face while talking softly and telling her she would be there until Joey was born. Suzie tried to smile. She looked over and saw a man standing by the door, and she didn't recognize him behind the mask and cap. She looked at Maggie.

Maggie smiled and said, "It's Judge Callaway. He knows many people. He didn't want you going through this birth alone. He's a proud grandfather who wanted to be with his daughter."

Suzie looked back at Cal and again at Maggie. She started to speak when a contraction convulsed her. When it subsided, she looked at Maggie and stuttered, "What?"

"I'll explain everything when Joey is born. Just know that Cal is Joey's biological father and your baby's grandfather. That's how we can be here in the room with you. We'll both be by your side until you deliver." Maggie motioned for Cal to come to the other side of the bed.

Cal walked over and took Suzie's hand. She looked up at him and held on tight. Maggie slid a chair behind Cal so he could sit, then went back to the other side and continued to wipe Suzie's face with cool water.

Five hours later, Suzie delivered a healthy baby boy.

§

Maggie and Cal left the hospital an hour later as Suzie slept, and he walked her to her car.

"You're a natural as a delivery support granddaddy, Judge," she said.

"You're not so bad yourself, Granny."

"Let's make a deal. You don't call me Granny, and I won't call you Granddaddy."

"Done. You want some company?"

"I thought you'd never ask. Park in the garage. You'll be awhile," she said before passionately kissing him, her tongue searching deep into his mouth, her hands on both sides of his head, pulling him to her.

# CHAPTER 54

"John, Darling, these are the people I want at our wedding," Catherine whispered as she looked around the elegantly dressed crowd at the oceanfront estate. Red, white, and blue bunting was everywhere. Small American flags and greenery were the centerpieces of the white tables scattered across the immense lawn. Servers in white jackets and black pants, carrying silver trays of food, beer, and wine, moved through the crowd of people enjoying the perfect late afternoon on the manicured lawn. An easterly breeze cooled the temperature and kept the bugs at bay.

John Emerson smiled at Catherine. He was pleased as he realized he was about to hit the trifecta of good luck: within the next year he would marry Catherine White in the decade's social wedding in the Berkshires, he was the managing partner of a growing law firm thanks to his future bride and Aloysius, and he was an associate of Aloysius Carroll and his select clientele. Looking past Catherine, he saw Aloysius approaching.

"Good afternoon, John. Who is this lovely lady you are speaking with?"

"Aloysius, may I present my fiancée, Catherine White. Catherine, this is Aloysius Carroll, our host for this festive Fourth of July outing."

"My pleasure to meet you, Mr. Carroll," Catherine said, extending her hand. "John and I look forward to returning the hospitality the next time you are in the Berkshires."

"It's a pleasure having the two of you here. I look forward to seeing the both of you on my next trip to your delightful part of the state, Ms. White."

"Tell me, Mr. Carroll—"

"Please call me Aloysius."

"Yes, Aloysius, if you'll call me Catherine. If you don't have your own cottage in the Berkshires, I'd love to have you stay at Willview. You would have your own suite of rooms, and the staff will make sure you're comfortable."

"Thank you, Catherine. I'll consider that offer on my next trip. Now, if the two of you will excuse me, I've got an impromptu meeting with Josh Trimble to finalize a small matter in the Eighth District," Aloysius said.

§

"Mr. Trimble, thank you for attending our Fourth of July picnic. We appreciate your taking time from your busy schedule. Have you met everyone?"

"Thank you for inviting me, Mr. Carroll. Yes, I have. An impressive array of business leaders. Some I knew, but a lot I didn't, and now I have a pocket full of business cards. I also appreciate the campaign contribution and help from the volunteers. How can I help you, Mr. Carroll?"

"Please, call me Aloysius." Ivy League reached into the side pocket of his navy-blue double-breasted blazer, pulled out a card, and gave it to Trimble. "My private number is on the card. It's for your use only. I trust you to respect that request. If you need anything, anything at all, please call."

"Thank you. Obviously you don't need my card since you already knew how to reach me. As I said, how can I repay you for your help?"

"There is a small matter in the Eighth District. You previously came out in vigorous support of Judge Callaway, and you were smart to do so. As you know, he was reinstated to the bench after the accusations against him were found fraudulent. Your support has given you a substantial lead in that district."

"Yes, and what about Judge Callaway?"

"It would be helpful if he weren't reappointed to the Eighth District state court in January. If you're governor, would you have a problem with that?"

"Not at all, because I intend to appoint him to the state supreme court. He's one of the brightest legal minds in New England." Trimble fixed a steady gaze at Ivy League, searching for his reaction. "Besides, there's an ongoing investigation to find the person or persons who doctored the file on that boy who died. When the culprit is uncovered and behind bars, Judge Callaway will be an even bigger hero."

"Nothing will come of that investigation."

"No? You seem sure of your knowledge."

"Mr. Trimble, I'm paid to be sure of my knowledge. What you do about Judge Callaway is up to you, as long as he's not reappointed in the Eighth District."

"Do you have a replacement in mind?"

"Yes, an outstanding young attorney, Neil Clements."

"No problems I can see, Aloysius."

# READING GROUP GUIDE

1. Judge Cal White-Callaway made a difficult and irreversible decision seventeen years ago. He has regretted that decision ever since. Have you ever had a friend who made a serious mistake when young and had to deal with the consequences for years? Have you ever made a serious mistake that affected your life? How have you compensated for it?

2. Catherine White-Callaway is in an unhappy marriage. Is her disappointment in Cal for turning his back on her family's tradition of power and wealth justified? Should Cal have told Catherine about his desire to serve as a judge before they were married? How do you think their marriage could have found a mutually beneficial accord?

3. Maggie keeps her background private, but her intense focus on saving young abused or homeless girls comes from her background. Do you think Maggie is a savior to these young women or just using them for her own profit? What would you have done different from Maggie, if anything?

4. The Berkshire Book Club (BBC) is an organization established to protect the community. Do you believe they serve that purpose? If you were a member of the BBC, would you have handled the situations in the story differently?

5. Joey was removed involuntarily from his "safe" places in the wilderness by being arrested. At the first opportunity, he went back, but he didn't stay. What do you think is the primary reason he left the safety of the forest for the risks of society? Do you think Joey made the right decision? Have you ever been in a situation when you had to make a choice when the risks were high and unknown?

6. Catherine and her circle of friends commit a great deal of time to charitable events in their community. What do you believe are the motivating factors for this effort? Are there situations in your circle of friends when it is important socially to appear involved in charity work?

7. Both Catherine and Maggie are strong, determined women. While they have opposite opinions about Cal, do you think they could be friends if he were not in the middle? Why? Which of these two women do you identify with?

8. Cal appears to have grown and left behind the idealized life as a judge he would have had with Josey. What are some of the reasons you believe are really behind this decision? Cal is middle-aged at forty-two; do you think that chronological point in his life has anything to do with his decision? Could or should he have had children with Catherine? Do you know individuals who reached Cal's age and completely changed the course of their life? Have you thought about making a major life change?

9. In the story, organized crime is infiltrating the Berkshire communities' legitimate businesses, judicial system, and political structure. Can and should anything be done to stop them? In real life, many

activities considered criminal in the past, such as drinking alcohol, gambling, and using marijuana, are now either legal or becoming legal. What do you think will be the ultimate effect on communities?

10. When the story ends, Cal is leaving his judgeship, Catherine is going to marry John, and Maggie is searching for ways to help young boys as well as young girls. Suzie is facing the situation of being a single mom in a challenging position. Organized crime is achieving all of its goals for the Berkshire communities. What do you think the future holds for each of these characters? If you were one of these characters, which one would it be? What would you do in their place?

# ACKNOWLEDGMENTS

Several people helped make this book a reality. Angela Wade was the first non-family person to read the original draft. Her insightful and skillful analysis of that flawed document gave me the direction to move forward. Her support of my other writings was equally important.

Luke Palder and his team at ProofreadingServices.com did an outstanding job in developmental editing, copyediting, and proof-reading. Any residual mistakes are mine.

Thanks go to Dr. Murray Freedman, who helped me with thoughts on female health.

Thanks also to my fellow writers and our tutor, Gareth Dickson, in the Oxford University Writing Fiction II online course. Their comments on sections were helpful in sharpening the manuscript's focus.

I would like to thank my fellow writers and our tutor, Samina Ali, in the Stanford University online course, Writing Your Debut Novel. They recognized a major flaw in the story and pointed me in the right direction.

Much thanks go to Ghislain Viau of Creative Book Design for his development of the cover and interior book design.

Amy Sheree Adams, my assistant in all things at the office, was able to keep me on track and the technology demystified for me.

The most thanks go to Judy, my wife, muse, motivator, and best critic. Little did I know forty-plus years ago my best decision in life would be convincing her to go through life with me.

www.ingramcontent.com/pod-product-compliance
Lightning Source LLC
Chambersburg PA
CBHW070205120726